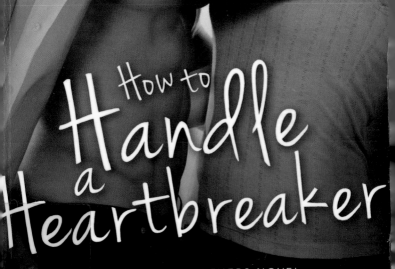

How to
Handle
a
Heartbreaker

A McCAULEY BROTHERS NOVEL

USA TODAY BESTSELLING AUTHOR

MARIE HARTE

THE STEAMY NEW SERIES FROM *USA TODAY* BESTSELLING AUTHOR MARIE HARTE.

Praise for *The Troublemaker Next Door*:
A *Publishers Weekly* Top 10 Romance for Spring 2014

"Filled with strong-willed characters and a reluctant
love affair. The love scenes…will make readers sweat.
Readers will get caught up in this story."
—*RT Book Reviews* Top Pick! Gold ★★★★✦

"The first in Harte's McCauley Brothers series…[is] a winner.
The story is fast-paced, with countless spicy scenes that will
make readers hungry for the next installment."
—*Booklist*

Praise for
The Troublemaker Next Door

A *Publishers Weekly* Top 10 Romance
for Spring 2014

"An amazing storyline filled with strong-willed characters and a reluctant love affair. The love scenes… will make readers sweat. Readers will get caught up in this story and feel like they have a front-row seat to all the antics."

—*RT Rook Reviews*, 4.5 stars, Top Pick! Gold

Praise for Marie Harte

"Harte has a gift for writing hot sex scenes that are emotional and specific to her characters."

—*RT Book Reviews*

"Hot and spicy… The author takes you through a range of emotions."

—*Night Owl Romance*,
Reviewer Top Pick

"Off the charts scorching hot. Ms. Harte wows with sex scenes that will make your heart pump."

—*Long and Short Reviews*

"Ms. Harte is an awesome writer. Her comedic timing is perfect. She creates endearing characters."

—*Romance Reviews*

How to Handle a Heartbreaker

MARIE HARTE

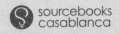

sourcebooks
casablanca

To my fellow Bend writers: Karen, Diana, Ruth, Mary, Paty, and Julie. Your friendship means a lot. Here's to future get-togethers that spur more ideas, as well as more goodies! And R&D, I love you.

Chapter 1

THEY STARED AT EACH OTHER, LIKE DUELING gunslingers waiting to see who would draw first. She'd be damned if she'd blink before he did. Despite his sheer size, drool-worthy body, and oh-my-God sex appeal, Abigail Dunn refused to budge on this issue. Her roommates might think she was one big pushover, but she knew better. It was time *he* did too.

After several tense moments in silence, Brody Singer rolled his eyes, then pinched the bridge of his nose and sighed in defeat. "Okay. Jesus. You're such a hard-ass. It's not his fault, you know."

"No. It's *yours*." She crossed her arms over her chest, doing her best not to turn pink when his gaze immediately followed the movement. And stayed there. After a moment, she cleared her throat. "My eyes are up here, Brody." She pointed to her face.

He slowly lifted his gaze to her face but didn't stop leering. Instead, the charming idiot wiggled his brows. "Beautiful. So...big. And so...brown."

She wore a brown sweater today, so she couldn't be sure if he referred to her breasts or her eyes. By the expression on his face, she was betting on the former. Anyone else talking to her like that would have received a kick in the teeth. But from Brody, she felt simultaneously irked and turned on. *So* not good.

"You know, you're really very good-looking."

He looked puzzled that she'd compliment him, but as he started to smile, she added, "Too bad you ruin it the moment you open your mouth."

He had the gall to laugh. "And the guys think you're shy."

Now she flushed. Dear Lord, did Mike and the others talk about her? Her neighbor, Mike McCauley, was the oldest of the four McCauley brothers, by which Brody had been unofficially adopted at a young age. She'd been dying to get the scoop on the whys and hows of his life, but asking would make it seem as if she wanted to know. And heaven help her if her roommates started on the sparks flaring between her and Brody again. Her head hurt just thinking about it.

Realizing he continued to stare in a way that made her all too aware of her now tingly girlie parts, she blurted, "I *am* shy."

"Not with me you're not." And that pleased him for some stupid reason, because his grin grew wider.

Abby planted her hands on her hips and counted to ten in her head. In a calmer voice, she explained, "I don't have time for this. I have to make my deadline by Halloween—in *five more days*. Get that mongrel out of our yard or else."

"You won't call the pound." He didn't seem to be taking her threat seriously.

Abby turned and stared out the back door of her kitchen, not surprised to see dog slobber and a furry face against the door pane. The smashed nose and tongue occasionally gave way to a gaping mouth of sharp teeth as Cujo tried to get more oxygen into his freakishly large body. "Pound? I was thinking the National Guard. That thing is nearly as tall as I am."

"But you're short."

"Petite."

"Not with that rack," he muttered.

"*What?*"

"Nothing." He swallowed hard but to his credit kept his gaze above her neckline this time. "Look, I'm sorry. He *likes* you, Abby. Mutt just wanted to give you a token of his affection."

"You mean the bone he buried in our backyard last week? *That* token?" She fumed, remembering the broken flower pots and her mauled garden beds. "I don't know why I bother. This isn't even my house. You want to piss off Beth and James, feel free. But when we move out, I'm getting my rent deposit back. If not from them, from you."

He frowned. "You're leaving? You guys just moved in eight months ago."

She hadn't realized he knew that. But considering their many connections, it shouldn't have surprised her. "You're spending too much time with Flynn and Maddie." Maddie, her roommate and best friend, had found a real treasure in Flynn McCauley. Great for Maddie, not so great for Abby.

Flynn and Brody were best friends and business partners. Mike was her neighbor. And Abby, Maddie, and Vanessa—her other roommate—had been pseudo-adopted by the entire McCauley clan. Which meant she saw Brody on a regular basis. She could handle his aggravating attempts at charm, but her libido was making it really hard to remember all the reasons why she should give this man a wide berth.

Like now, when he wouldn't stop staring at her.

"Cut it out."

"What?"

Did he just step closer? She backed up and found herself against the door. Behind her, that mammoth of a dog whined.

"See? We like you, Abby." Brody smiled, his amber eyes bright, like his golden hair, shining through the gloom of yet another bleak Seattle day.

She held up a hand and met his chest, doing her utmost to ignore the firm muscle under her palm. "Stay." To her bemusement, he did. She did her best not to laugh hysterically at the comparison of man to dog. "I think I made myself clear. Your dog needs to stay at *your* place. He keeps getting out of Mike's yard, and he's already torn up my garden."

"Garden?" Brody looked over her head through the door window. "You mean that dirt in a box? Anything out there was already dead, honey."

"It was dormant and would have been perfect for springtime next year, *honey*, but Fenris out there already dug up my bulbs."

"Hmm. Fenris."

"Yeah, Fenris. Loki's son? A demon dog that ends the world?"

He seemed to consider the name. "Catchy, but no. Doesn't fit him. Guess we'll stick with Mutt for now."

She gritted her teeth. "I don't care what you name your dog. Just get him *out*. Of. My. Yard!"

She stormed past him in a whirl of anger, frustrated lust, and hopelessness that she'd be able to concentrate on writing her story now that Mr. Wrong had shown his pretty face to distract her again. Bad enough she saw him in her dreams or when he tagged along with Flynn. But now he invaded her working hours.

"Oh you stupid muse." The damn thing needed to get laid. Then maybe it would stop painting her hero with Brody's face and smile. *Riiight. It's your muse that's been celibate for a year. Not you, oh she of the wide ass, freakish desires, and air of desperation...* Kevin's words were never far from her mind, and at that moment, she hated him and Brody equally. Kevin had been a jerk, but Brody made her wish for things she'd never have. She paused in the hallway at the doorway to her office.

The front door opened, and Maddie entered with Flynn on her heels. "Hey, Abby, what—"

Abby pointed at Flynn. "This is your fault. Take care of *that*," she thumbed at the noise behind her, "or I will." She seethed as she closed herself in her study— what she used to think of as her sanctuary—and did her best to ignore Brody's low voice and the happy barking no doubt forecasting a mess in the kitchen.

At the thought that Vanessa would soon be returning, Abby smiled with evil glee. The blond dictator would take care of it. She'd take care of *everything*. "Now if only she could type..."

———⁓———

Brody knew he shouldn't have opened the door. Now the damn dog was inside and making a friggin' mess. He fought to hold on to Mutt while he watched Abby's finer-than-fine ass disappear into her office. A glance around him showed a beautiful home with a woman's touch. From the kitchen he could see clear to the front door, through the spacious hallway that led to a set of stairs to the left of the front door. The living room off to the right was delineated by a large archway, no door, making the downstairs seem like one big living space with the exception of the powder room and the double doors to the closed office. Where Abby sat fuming at him.

Abby. He sighed. She belonged here, in a place she loved. Unlike him, his hellhound, and his twin who wasn't his twin, currently walking down the hall. Flynn entered the kitchen and stood staring at him with a look of displeasure.

Brody grunted while he tried to restrain an over-enthusiastic mix of Irish Wolfhound, Great Dane, and wolf. Or was that Yeti? Hell, the dog weighed over a hundred and twenty pounds and was strong as a bull. And he had a thing for women. Abby was hands down Mutt's favorite, but the leggy redhead making a face at him was the dog's second choice.

"Really, Brody." Maddie pursed her lips. "In the house?"

Flynn swore. "Better get him out of here before Vanessa gets back."

Vanessa, the other roommate. What did Maddie call her? *Hitler with a mop.* What were the odds three hot single women would move next door to Mike, of all people? The guy lived like a monk. Granted, he had a kid, but they all helped with Colin.

In a perfect world, the girls would have moved next to Brody. He'd have made a move on them way before now. Had a nice threesome or foursome, watched them wrestle each other in bikinis slathered with oil, then cornered Abby as his own after the others begged him not to take a favorite. He smirked at Maddie, who glared back at him.

At least Flynn was no idiot. He'd set his sights on Maddie and made it stick. They were a perfect couple, and she was just girlie enough not to want to interrupt his buddy's bro time while still thinking Flynn walked on water. Just what Brody had always wanted for the man he considered his un-identical twin.

If Flynn could nab a babe like Maddie, Brody could get Abby. Hadn't he always done one better than Flynn when it came to the ladies?

Now how to get Abby to stop running away long enough to get his hands on *her*. He'd start by investigating that soft brown sweater that hugged her curves. Then move down her legs to that round—"*Shit*." Mutt lunged out of Brody's hands and dove for Maddie.

She screamed. The woman had a mouth on her that made even the dog flinch. Still, it didn't stop him from a fly tackle.

Only Flynn's timely intervention saved Maddie's pretty dress from big-ass paw prints covered in muck. The dog and mud had a love-love relationship.

"Swear to God, one of these days I'm going to bury you where no one can find you, Brody." Flynn glared at him as he and Mutt danced. The dog had his paws on Flynn's shoulders and was trying to lick him to death while Maddie erupted into gales of laughter. Flynn frowned over his shoulder at her. "Yeah, it's funny now. But you were screaming two seconds ago."

From down the hallway, he heard a door open and his heart raced. Abby returned wearing sexy reading glasses, and she'd put her hair up in a loose knot. That, along with her soft sweater and leg-hugging denim, caused every nerve in Brody's body to stand on end. Thank God for tight jeans.

He glanced away from Abby to the dog and swallowed hard, avoiding the knowing smirk Flynn shot him. They'd talked about Brody's penchant for the prim and proper type, and for Abby in particular. For his last birthday, the guys had taken him to a gentleman's club, where a woman dressed like a librarian had stripped down to pasties and a G-string while grinding all over him.

And she had *nothing* on Abby Dunn.

"You are so pathetic," Flynn muttered and shoved the dog off him.

"What the hell is all this racket?" Abby yelled. "I'm *trying* to work." Her gaze zeroed in on Mutt. Before the dog could attack, she commanded, "*Sit*."

To Brody's astonishment, Mutt sat and wagged his tail like crazy, his gaze glued to Abby. *Can't fault him for that.*

Brody wanted to wag at her too. The woman was his every dream come to life. Curvy in all the right places with dark hair, rich brown eyes, full lips, and a smile that lit her from the inside out. When she used it. Unlike now, as she glared from the dog to him.

He coughed to clear his throat. "He looked so sad by himself, so I let him in just for a minute. I swear. I was trying to take him back outside when Maddie distracted me—"

"Please. I walked down my own hallway to my own kitchen."

"—and Flynn tried playing hero instead of letting me

take my unloved dog back out into the cold. Away from all this animal bigotry. The hatred. The lies. You poor, misunderstood thing," he crooned and gained Mutt's attention again. The dog walked back to him and stood quivering under his hand, no doubt dying to run back to Abby.

He wondered what she'd do if he imitated his dog, just jumped her and slobbered all over her. The idea had real merit, especially since she stood there looking like a centerfold, her sweater cupping her beautiful curves, her lips parted as she readied to blast him all over again.

She must have changed her mind, because she groaned. "For the love of God, just *please*, take him outside. Or—"

Just then, the front door opened and the clicking of heels drew closer. Heels. *Shit*. Vanessa had returned.

"Full house, I see…" She paused at the entrance to the kitchen, not a hair out of place, her pristine pantsuit unwrinkled, her subtle makeup unblemished. A professional to the nth degree. "What is *this*?" the blond bombshell shrieked as she stared at the mud all over the place.

Abby smirked at him before disappearing down the hallway once more. Flynn and Maddie shook their heads, then quickly skirted around the infuriated clean freak staring a hole through his head.

"Oh, ah, hey, Vanessa." He tried to appear smaller as he and the dog cowered together.

"What the fuck is all over the kitchen?"

Before he could blink, she had him by the collar. Not the dog. *Him*. Despite looking down at her, he felt a bit on edge when confronted with such unbridled fury. He wouldn't put it past her to kick his dog. Or him.

An hour and a half later in his upstairs bathroom, he glared at Mutt after finishing the messiest dog bath known to man. The dog sulked as Brody finished drying him off. "No more. I'm on thin ice with Abby as it is. Come on, Mutt. Help me out, man."

The dog sneered at him before loping off into the room he'd claimed as his own. Brody's bedroom.

With a sigh, Brody stared around the mess of his bathroom and left it. Wet dog smell, slimy mud, fur, and all.

Exhausted after the day from hell, he settled into the comfortable couch in the living room. Rain continued to pour outside and the sky had gone from cloudy to gunmetal gray. The chill outside emphasized the heating problems in the place, which reminded him of his neighbor in the duplex next door. Brody could handle the cold. His neighbor, not so much.

Brody reluctantly rose and called to the dog, "I'll be right back."

He didn't expect an answer, but he thought it pretty damn pathetic that while Flynn was no doubt getting felt up by his redhead, Brody had a pissy dog for company. "Blood brother, my ass. Where is he when I'm drowning in misery?" he mumbled as he left the warmth of his home and stood shivering on Seth's porch next door.

The old man answered on the fifth knock. "What?" he snapped.

"Is it me, or is everyone on the planet in a mood today?" Brody sighed. "You going to let me in or what?"

Seth mumbled under his breath but opened the door.

Brody entered and hid a grimace, not wanting to offend. But damn, what were Seth's kids thinking to let the old man live by himself? He could have starred in his own episode of *Hoarders*. Newspaper stacks lined the hallway, and though clutter filled every available bookcase, bureau, and table, a clear path remained throughout the living room into the dining room and kitchen.

Remembering the gasket he'd forgotten the last time he'd been over, Brody reached into his pocket and gripped it. "I'll be in the kitchen."

"Sure, make yourself at home," Seth called after him with no small amount of sarcasm.

Brody returned from the kitchen moments later. "Kitchen sink's good as new."

"Thanks." Seth stared at him, then frowned. "It's Friday night. Why are you here?"

"Huh?"

"Shouldn't you be with your brothers?"

Normally, Brody spent his Friday evenings playing cards at Mike's. But Cameron, the youngest McCauley, was out of town. And no way was Flynn's girlfriend taking his place. If you didn't have a Y chromosome, you didn't rate an invite to poker night. Three guys wouldn't cut it… Then again, Colin was almost six. The kid could palm a card and knew how to stack a deck, thanks to Brody's clever teaching.

"You know, you make a good point." Brody quickly double-checked the thermostat and the plumbing in the downstairs bathroom. All good. Seth wouldn't freeze to death. "You got food?"

"You are one nosy neighbor," Seth half frowned, trying unsuccessfully to hide a grin. "Yeah, yeah, I have food. Damn, son. I'm supposed to feed you now too? Invite yourself over for dinner, why don't you?"

Brody ignored him, as he normally did. He and the old man had an unspoken agreement. They liked the hell out of each other but refused to admit it. Before Brody had bought his half of the large building from Seth, he'd been the ideal tenant. Nothing had changed since he'd purchased the place. He still fixed both sides of the house, and Seth continued to treat Brody like an unwelcome relation. That, and the guy was always giving him stuff. Ancient record albums, figurines, things Brody didn't feel right taking—the old man's treasures. Brody had protested that he'd fix the house for free, but Seth wouldn't hear it. Proud old bastard. He totally reminded Brody of a crotchety James McCauley.

"And you know, it wouldn't hurt you to get a love life. Ain't seen a woman around in a while. You gone gay, boy?"

Brody blinked. "Ah, no. Not yet."

Seth shrugged. "Boy or girl, at least you wouldn't be moping around on a Friday night."

"Who's moping? I'm relaxing after a hard day's work."

Seth raised a brow.

"We had to fix a leak then relocate a water line in a new construction complex in Tacoma. And the traffic was nuts."

"Always is."

Brody nodded. "Okay then."

"Okay." Seth just stared at him.

Feeling foolish, Brody glared, warned the crankpot not to screw with the dog by pounding on the walls, and left. He returned to his bedroom and thought about just staying in for the night, but he wanted some company.

Being around Abby frazzled him. Brody had been

scoring with girls since the seventh grade when he'd grown out of his awkward stage and into his voice. Maturing early had its perks, and girls noticing him was a win-win, any way he looked at it. Hanging with the tough McCauleys had helped too. No one screwed with Mike's younger brothers. Though Brody's blond hair and obviously different last name said otherwise, the McCauleys had always treated him like a sibling. One that annoyed Mike, bossed Cam, and got into mischief with Flynn on a daily basis.

But now that Flynn had Maddie, it kind of left Brody at loose ends. Then there was that fascination with Abby that wouldn't quit.

"I am so screwed." He sighed. He wanted Abby like crazy. But there seemed to be no end to the obstacles standing in his way.

As he undressed and then scraped away the fur from the tub the dog had just used, he considered his myriad problems. Brody turned on the shower and waited with bated breath. After a minute or two, he stepped under the spray of hot water. No problem with the water heater tonight, thank God.

He watched rivulets of water race down the tile, just as fast as Abby ran from him time and time again. Granted, he hadn't exactly made his intentions clear. He flirted, leered, and teased. But he hadn't asked her out yet. Because she'd deny him.

And there was that weird resemblance she had to Lea, Mike's dead wife.

Brody groaned. How to make a move on the woman he couldn't get out of his mind without offending Mike? And if he did get a date, how not to mess things up with Abby so badly that he wrecked Flynn's relationship with Maddie? Because Maddie and Abby were tight, and Flynn had no intention of dropping his new squeeze. It was like geometry all over again. The transcendental proof, cause and effect—and now he had a massive headache.

Nothing a good beer and a beat-down over Mike couldn't cure. He just had to make sure he partnered with Colin, because lately Flynn was next to useless in a game. His head in the clouds, dreaming about Maddie. But the kid had potential.

Brody finished washing himself and continued to think of a way around Abby's wariness. Charm and flirting hadn't worked. The dog obviously wasn't getting him closer. So how to work an angle under her shields and into her pants, but far enough away from her heart so that when they ended, she and his brothers wouldn't be gunning for him?

Abby stared longingly at the wet windowpane, wishing she could rewind the clock.

"Missing your honey man?" Vanessa drawled. "Why don't you just put the guy out of his misery and sleep with him?"

"As much as I appreciate your honesty—"

Vanessa snorted.

"—I don't need comments from the peanut gallery. I'm not missing anyone."

"Uh-huh. That's why you keep looking at Mike's house through the window."

Abby turned to glare at her roommate. Vanessa was

Maddie's cousin, yet the two couldn't have been more different. Maddie had a vibrant joy, dramatic flair, and warm beauty. She glowed with her love for Flynn. Abby's creative mind likened Vanessa more to an icy Valkyrie. A warrior in business, logical, and eminently better suited to dealing with stress, Vanessa never panicked or didn't know what to do. She was like perfection on two long legs that ended in a gorgeous brain that never quit. Currently single due to her own desire for solitude, not because men didn't want her.

Abby should have hated her for that alone. So much confidence, and the woman deserved every bit of it. Yet she remained loyal to friends and family. And as much as Abby sometimes wished Vanessa would ease up, the woman regarded her as part of her family unit.

After drawing in a deep breath, Abby let it out and explained to Vanessa, *once again*, what the neighbor really meant to her. "I write, Vanessa. You know this. You also know I use the guys next door as reference material."

"Blah blah blah. Yeah. You want to make your male characters real, so you eavesdrop on the guys talking smack over cards on Fridays. I know. But that doesn't explain why you're always looking at Brody's ass. Mind you, it's a fine ass. But your interest seems much more prurient than scholarly."

Vanessa's blue eyes sparkled, her joy in the verbal battle clear.

Catching the spirit, Abby shot back, "Well, at least I have plans for the weekend."

Vanessa raised a blond brow and crossed her arms over her chest. "So do I."

Abby looked her over. From Vanessa's size eleven

running shoes to the running shorts and T-shirt sporting a *Go Vegan or Go Home* slogan. "Some Friday. You're going to drive to the gym to work out after putting in a full day." Abby huffed. "At least I have a good excuse for no social prospects. My deadline is looming."

"True." Vanessa shrugged. "But I use exercise to relieve stress. You say you want to listen to the guys for research, but in this weather, you can't hear a blasted thing anyone is saying with their windows closed. So I ask again, why are you staring at Mike's house? I'll tell you why. Because you and that blond doofus can't get enough of each other."

"He is that," Abby agreed. A great big galoot who'd rescued a monstrous stray dog from euthanasia at the pound, who taught his nephew how to cheat at cards and cry on command, and who'd been protective of his best friend when Flynn and Maddie had been on the rocks a month ago. Then what else Vanessa said penetrated. "Wait. What?" *Get enough of each other?*

"It's so obvious. Just sleep with him. Get it out of your system. Then use it to write those smut scenes you're always going on about in your books. And presto. Deadline problem solved."

The familiar argument made her see red. "*Smut?* I write erotic romance. Not porn. Not smut. Not raunchy—"

"Right. Raunchy." Vanessa snapped her fingers. "That's the word I wanted when I was telling Francie about your book the other day."

More comfortable arguing about her profession than about the crazy feelings for Brody she had no business even thinking about, Abby lit into her roommate

with gusto. It took everything inside her not to follow the flashing headlights when a truck pulled into
Mike's drive.

Chapter 2

BRODY STARED AT HIS CARDS, GLANCED AT COLIN, who had an eye on his father's hand, then folded at a subtle headshake from the boy.

Mike grinned as he won the meager five-dollar pot.

Next to him, Flynn muttered at his cards and slapped them down. "How are you winning? You suck at poker."

"I do not," Mike sounded affronted. He possessed the arrogant chin, stubborn nose, and bright blue eyes most of the McCauleys had. Only Flynn had green eyes, like his mother. Brody considered himself the blond beauty of the bunch and never hesitated to share his high opinion of his superior looks with the others.

"You do suck, Dad. But I still love you."

"Don't say *suck*," Mike corrected his son.

As Colin smiled back at his father, the nearly six-year-old palmed three cards under the table and turned them up for Brody to see. A glance showed two twos and an ace.

Brody smothered a smirk. But as he turned he saw Flynn's eyes narrow. Their gazes met, and Brody warned him without speaking not to say a thing. Their years together enabled them to often communicate with a look, and Flynn rolled his eyes and sighed but said nothing.

Good man.

"Let's play again, kid." Mike grinned at Colin. "This time, if I win, I get a free week of chores from you. You win, you get ten bucks and an extra hour before bed tomorrow night."

"All right." Colin held out a hand. "Shake."

While his father shook his hand, the kid slid another card off the table into his lap. Mike again didn't catch it, though Flynn chuckled under his breath.

Brody puffed up with pride. He'd taught the boy that move just a few months ago. Colin had real talent that Brody could see. Sure, Abby claimed Brody was setting the kid up for a stint in juvie, but what did she know? Knowing how to cheat meant you could *spot* a cheat. And Brody had grown up knowing who to trust and who not to, thanks to the nightmare he could claim as his biological family.

Quickly shaking free of the thought, he dealt the cards and played two rounds, then watched Colin scam Mike and Flynn into upping their bets. Brody remained in, and while Colin leaned over, he took the kid's high cards, the ones Colin had intentionally left on his lap for Brody to take. Not just one, but two aces. Nice. Considering he held one of his own, as well as two kings, he decided to win the pot.

"Tell you what. Let's make this super interesting," he said to the table and winked at Colin.

Mike scowled. "Now what? Whenever you say 'interesting,' that usually means trouble."

"If Flynn or I win, you still honor Colin as winner. We lose, we'll do his chores for the week with him."

Flynn frowned. "What's all this *we* nonsense? I can't dirty my hands with chores. My woman likes me pretty."

Colin gagged. "Girls are so gross." He blinked up at Flynn, his eyes as clear and blue as Mike's. At times like these, Brody saw very little of Lea in the boy. And then Colin would tilt his head or change the inflection in his voice and remind Brody of Lea all over again. "Why do you want to play with her when you can play with me? You missed tucking me in the other night."

Flynn lowered his hand, and as he did, his cards angled out so Brody could see them. Pair of fours, tops. Sucker. "Dude, I love you," Flynn was explaining. "But Maddie smells nice." He wiggled his brows. "She lets me kiss her."

"You can kiss me." Colin's lower lip quivered.

Flynn opened his mouth to respond, then closed it and narrowed his gaze. He instinctively pulled his cards to his chest and shot a glance at Brody, who looked innocently at his own hand, one that now held *three* aces and two kings—thanks to Colin's distraction. His discarded cards sat under his left thigh.

"You pulling one over on me, kid?" Flynn glared.

Colin sniffed. "N-no."

Brody nudged the faker with his foot.

The boy let out a forced giggle. "Uh, yeah. I was. Good, huh?"

Brody grinned and glanced up only to see Mike glaring at *him*. "What did *I* do?"

"You taught my kid to lie."

"Please. He's been lying since he left the womb. He's a McCauley."

Flynn covered his heart with one hand. "I'm so proud."

Colin snickered, but Mike continued to stare at Brody.

"Okay. Fine." Brody turned to the boy. So damn

cute. He'd be a real heartbreaker when he grew up. Flynn liked to think the boy took after him, while Cam credited Colin's intelligence courtesy of his own tutoring. And Mike, of course, claimed his own genetics had everything to do with Colin's lovability. But Brody knew the kid had the natural charisma of a born scammer—and *that* he got from Brody. Nurture over nature every time.

Brody cleared his throat. "Colin, it's not right to lie or cheat or steal. Thou shalt never offend thy father. Honor thy uncles. And the most important rule, according to your dad—always let your father win…because he's a bully."

"Brody," Mike growled.

Flynn laughed loudly while Colin frowned. "Really?"

"No," Mike interrupted. "Ignore Ubie. Play the cards, son."

Ubie, short for Uncle Brody. Brody loved the name, just as much as he loved being a part of the group. He never took for granted that they treated him like family. At the thought of his own again, he frowned. Normally he put them out of his mind. But he'd received a message a few days ago he dreaded returning.

"I call. Three twos." Colin laid down his cards.

Mike shook his head. "Straight beats three of a kind. Sorry." Mike, the big lug, didn't look sorry. Like the rest of them, he wanted to win. He'd raised Colin to accept losing, even if Mike himself didn't like it.

"Shoot." Colin's mouth thinned.

"Damn—er, darn," Flynn corrected when Mike shot him a look. "Sorry. Pair of fours."

They all looked to Brody. With a flourish, he laid out

his cards. "Full house, guys. Read 'em and weep. Aces over kings."

"Oh?" Mike sounded skeptical.

Flynn didn't bother arguing. "Just let it go, Mike. You'll never be able to prove a thing."

"I know. Next time, you don't deal," Mike warned him, then sighed. "But a bet's a bet. Colin, you get an extra hour tomorrow before bedtime. Now thank Ubie for his 'win'—and I use that term loosely. Then get to bed, you little monster."

Colin grinned, showing a missing front tooth, and jumped into Brody's lap. He hugged Brody so tightly around the neck Brody almost choked. The kid scooped the cards out from under Brody's leg as he did so. But Mike had been watching. He raised a brow at Brody but said nothing when his son let go and jumped to the floor.

"Off to bed."

"Yes, Dad." Colin rounded the kitchen table to give Flynn a kiss on the cheek. "G'night, Uncle Flynn. Suckers." Then he laughed and skipped down the hallway to the bathroom.

They all waited until a faucet went on.

Flynn stretched and cracked his knuckles. "Nice work, Brody. In no time, I'm sure Colin will be winning regular hands at King County. They have a juvenile detention facility, right?"

"He's smooth, I'll give him that." Mike chuckled. "The little weasel. I'd call him on it, but he's been good this week. Halloween is so close, and he's dying for a bow and arrow set to go with his costume. That ten bucks he 'won' out of me should cover it." Mike shook his head. "You're not as smooth as you think you are, Brody. I saw Colin take those two cards."

Brody didn't bother enlightening him that Colin had taken both the twos *and* the aces and given away the better cards to the man he knew would win him the game. "Touché, Mr. Mom."

"Asshole. But at least you're smart enough not to get caught." Mike glanced at Flynn. "Unlike some."

Flynn sneered. "Oh yeah, pick on me because I'm not a good liar. At least I'm *normal*."

Brody peered into the mouth of his bottle and didn't bother to hide a smile. "So you consider being so whipped by your girlfriend you can't concentrate on cards anymore normal?"

"Shut up, cheater." Flynn sniffed and took another sip. "You're all just jealous."

Mike and Brody grinned at him before Mike ordered Flynn to get everyone another round from the fridge.

"How come you never boss Brody around?" Flynn whined as he rose to grab their beers.

"Don't throw me under the bus just because you're too scared of musclehead to say no." When Mike turned that mean look on Brody, Brody shrugged. "Hey, I admit I'm scared. He's the one trying to act all brave."

Mike grunted. Flynn tossed their drinks to them and then sat down while they enjoyed the deep flavor of malted barley and hops.

"You know, I love when Cam's around. But have you ever noticed that in his absence, we get back to manly beer?" Brody said after downing a large quantity of his second and last beer of the night. He normally didn't do more than two beers at a time, and he had to drive home. He'd stay if he didn't have an annoyed canine waiting for him. Mutt didn't take kindly to being ignored.

"No shit." Mike groaned with pleasure as he guzzled his drink. "Little brother is all about the microbrewery. But his faves are so damn prissy."

"Truly. The last six-pack he brought had roses on the labels." Flynn shuddered and in the next breath said, "So Brody has a thing for Abby but he's afraid to tell you about it."

Brody choked on the beer he'd been drinking. It took him a full minute to catch his breath. He wiped his watering eyes and saw both Flynn and Mike watching him. "You are such a fuckhead," he said through gritted teeth to Flynn. In a louder voice to Mike, he explained, "I think Abby is attractive. I'm not afraid to say it or anything."

"Attractive? More like your personal wet dream," Flynn felt the need to add.

Brody punched Flynn in the arm. "Shut up." God, he could feel his cheeks heating. It didn't help that Mike had yet to take his gaze from Brody's face. "Abby's pretty. It's um, it's weird she looks like Lea." Just saying Lea's name seemed wrong, somehow.

Mike blew out a breath. "I can't catch a break with you people. For the *last time*, Abby is not Lea. I'm not crushing on my neighbor. I think we all know they're two different people." He stood up, hulking over the table at a solid six foot four. The guy was huge and had a fist that made a man want to be anywhere but on the other end of it. He smacked Brody in the side of the head.

"Damn it." Brody rubbed his temple and scowled at his assailant. He'd been right before. Mike was a bully.

"I'm not blind. Anyone with a pair of eyes can see the way you drool over Abby."

"I don't *drool*." Offended, Brody frowned—he never acted stupid over women. "She's hot. So what?"

"So the fact that she looks like Lea has me thinking maybe you used to lust after my wife."

Everyone stopped moving, and Brody stopped breathing. "It wasn't like that," he said in a garbled voice, because it very much was like that. He'd never acted on his feelings, but that he'd had them at all made him feel like a first-class heel.

"Brody, I know you loved Lea. Like a sister," Mike said kindly, and that made Brody feel even worse. "She loved you too. Hell, she loved all you morons. She was a peach." His fond smile seemed free of sadness, and Brody wondered how Mike didn't still hurt at the thought of his soul mate now dead and gone. Apparently he really had made peace with her passing.

"It's been almost six years. Colin's birthday is in little more than a week." Mike shook his head. "The past is the past. Yeah, Abby looks like Lea. It was weird at first, but now, when I see her, I see Abby. Not my wife."

This was the most Mike had discussed Lea in years. Brody looked at Flynn, only to see him equally fascinated with the conversation.

"So you're saying it's okay if Brody and Abby go at it like dogs in heat?" Flynn asked.

"Jesus, Flynn. Watch your mouth." Mike scowled. "Colin has big ears."

Brody took exception to the remark as well and yanked Flynn's hair.

"Ow, damn it. Pulling my hair like a girl? Please."

"Don't talk about her like that. She's your girlfriend's best friend, you idiot."

"I know that." Flynn glared back. "Doesn't change the fact you want her but you won't make a move. The woman is as slow as molasses when it comes to dating. And to my shock, suddenly so are you. Make a move, son. You're almost forty."

"In *nine more years*, asshole. We're the same age."

"Yeah, well, I'm not afraid of intimacy. I'm dating the love of my life. By Christmas we'll be engaged. It's all about commitment."

"Intimacy? Commitment? *You* need to be committed, Dr. Laura." Brody laughed. "God, it's like all you need is a pint of ice cream and a DVD of *Beaches* and you'll be on your way."

Mike agreed. "Brody called it. What's up with the inner feelings, princess?"

"Who's a princess, Dad?" Colin asked, looking minty fresh and sparkling clean. His hair stuck up in front, matted with soap he hadn't quite rinsed out.

"Your aunt Flynn," Brody answered for him.

Colin thought that hilarious. "Aunt Flynn." He clutched his belly laughing. "You're such a girl, *Aunt Flynn*."

"Come on. Let's go over how to wash your face again," Mike said as he rose to escort Colin back down the hall. "Aunt Flynn." Mike shook his head and chuckled on his way to the bathroom.

Alone with Flynn, Brody punched him in the arm.

"Damn it. Cut it out." Flynn punched him back.

"Good to know you just *sound* like a pussy." Brody rubbed his sore arm. "Why the fuck did you say that to Mike?"

"Because you're dragging your feet with Abby. Man up, bro." Flynn cocked his head, studying him. "Gary and Rick have been talking about her. Whenever I see them, they ask about her." Their friends Gary and Rick were a pair of electricians they often worked with on new housing projects with certain developers. All of them had gone out with the girls months ago. Clubbing at a spot downtown, and the guys had been coming on to clueless Abby like it was hunting season.

Brody hadn't liked it then. He liked it even less now. "What do they want?"

Flynn just looked at him.

Brody swore. "Dumb question. I know. It's just… Whenever I talk to her, I wonder what Mike will think."

"And now you don't have to worry. He's over Lea. Done. Finito. And he has no designs on Abby. You heard him."

Yeah, he had. One part of Brody breathed a sigh of relief, while the other part of him struggled to accept that his only roadblock now was the stubborn woman. Nothing to stop him from pursuing her but her objections…and the possibility of making a mess for Flynn with Maddie if he screwed things up.

On a personal note, Brody was killer good in bed and had a great reputation. Looks, charm, money. What could Abby possibly find at fault with him? "Great. Now Mike's not an issue. I get it." Brody hated to say it, but the truth wanted out. "Problem is, I get the feeling she doesn't trust me. Or like me." He shrugged. "I don't get it. I'm hot, built, and financially set. What's not to like?"

"Besides your ego? Heck if I know." Flynn considered him for a moment, then leaned in and lowered his voice. "Look, you don't know this. Maddie told me, and I'm sworn to secrecy." But Brody was his brother. Flynn *had* to tell. It was the guy code. "Abby had a hot and heavy thing with some asshole over a year ago. He messed with her head, has her thinking she's fat and unattractive."

Brody could kind of see the plump reference. No way Abby was fat, but she had curves. Not a stick-thin twig, but a real woman with a body made for loving. The word *lush* came to mind. Brody had had more fantasies about her curvy body than he'd had about any woman. Ever. He might have worried that her resemblance to Lea had carried over into an unhealthy fixation, except he genuinely liked Abby as a person.

He figured after they had sex a few times, the newness would rub off. He and she could chalk up the experiences to pleasure, remain friends, and move on to bigger and better things. And maybe he'd stop thinking about her all the time.

"I know she has issues."

"No, man. You're not hearing me. She's a *sexy* woman with issues, so she's vulnerable to any guy who'll treat her right. Who the hell wouldn't want her? She's smart, sweet, and really, really built." Flynn swallowed hard. "Hey, I'm with Maddie, but I'm not dead."

"So glad you noticed." And there, Brody didn't like that Flynn had taken an extra look at the woman. Since when had he ever been so possessive before? He dated casually and parted as friends. He wasn't an asshole, just a guy with a healthy sex drive who liked variety. He shouldn't care that Flynn thought her sexy. But he did.

"She knows Gary and Rick," Flynn continued. "They're decent guys, and she likes them. You know damn well they like her. How long before one of them has the balls to ask her out?"

That didn't work for Brody on any level. "Great. So what do I do? She's sarcastic or snaps at me whenever I try to be nice."

Flynn gave him a baleful glare. "This afternoon you brought your monster dog into her house after it dug up her garden. Not smart."

"I can't help it. Mutt likes her. He's always trying to get closer." *Like I want to.*

"Do something to fix this or she's going to be out of your reach." Flynn paused. "I love you, man, like Maddie loves Abby. You can't mess this up."

Brody groaned. "You think I don't know that? Trust me. If I could ignore my dick, I would. But any time she's near me, I can't think about anything but her." *Even when she's not near me, I think about her.* "It's like, I don't know. I *like* her, you get me?"

"Yeah, I do." Flynn cleared his throat. "So step carefully with Abby. Just don't let Mike—"

"Hear that you broke her heart," Mike said from the hallway as he entered. "Or I'll smash your face in."

"What if she breaks my heart?" Brody asked in jest, though inside he meant every word.

"That's what beer is for. Right, Flynn?" Mike taunted.

Flynn scowled. "You ever going to let that go?" When Maddie and he had gone through a rough patch,

Flynn had tried to drown his sorrows in cheap beer. Not a pretty sight.

"Well," Brody drawled. "Maybe if you hadn't gotten sloppy drunk on *light beer*, we'd be willing to overlook your girlishness. But seriously. Bud Light?"

Flynn called him a horse's ass. Then Mike insulted Flynn's sudden intake of estrogen, and the fight really got started when Brody happened to remind the pair that they'd agreed to watch Mutt for him in another week when he ran to Anacortes on a job—one he planned to bust his ass to finish because he needed to hurry home before he lost Abby to someone else.

He took another drag of beer while Mike put Flynn into a headlock and thought again about how best to use his resources to nail a stubborn woman he desired more than his next breath.

Five days later, Abby glanced at her clock and smiled. "With eight hours to spare." She hit *send* on her computer and shot her completed manuscript to her agent. On time and within word count. *I am awesome*.

This rounded out her four-book series, giving her a bit of latitude before she started her next project. She wanted to sing with pleasure, the heavy weight of her deadline sloughing off her like yesterday's troubles.

"Time to celebrate." Maddie pranced into the office she and Abby shared, waving a box of chocolates. She wore a skin-hugging black catsuit, complete with a tail and a headpiece with ears. Painted-on whiskers over her cheeks and a black nose gave her some *cute* to go with the *sexy*.

"What the slutty cat said," Vanessa chimed in from the doorway. She had a bottle of champagne in hand and still wore her work clothes. "Let's share some chocolate and booze and get ready for the Halloween party."

Startled to see Vanessa in a good mood about a party, Abby stared.

"What?" Vanessa set down her stash and uncorked the bottle. Then she poured into the coffee mugs in Abby's coffee area. "Unconventional, but it works." She handed one to Abby, then another to Maddie. After pouring herself a glass, she lifted the mug in a toast. "To our erotic romance writer. Wishing you many sales."

Abby and Maddie exchanged a glance. "Um, thanks?" Abby waited for Vanessa to add a snarky comment about raunchy books or smut, but her roommate tipped back her mug and drank.

Maddie shrugged and took a sip as well. "Don't question good fortune, Abby. Run with it."

Needing the drink, Abby took a sip. The bubbles tickled her nose. "Thanks, Vanessa." She paused. "I can't help it. I have to know. Not that I don't appreciate this, but the last time I finished a book, you patted me on the back, then sneered."

"You sneer a lot, but I do remember that particular expression on your face. Not pretty, Vanessa." Maddie grimaced.

Abby agreed. "Then, after sneering, you told me you thought I could probably sell more if I named my next characters Dick Cocksalot and Lady Legsopen and made it a historical romance. Which you thought was just hilarious."

As expected, Vanessa broke into a grin. "Oh come on. That's funny...Dame Fellatio."

"You're horrible." Abby had to laugh. "Don't give up your day job." Which was crunching numbers for a big-name corporate accounting firm.

Maddie laughed. "Legsopen. Classic." She pointed a warning finger at her cousin. "And don't even think of applying that name to me, Big Foot."

"Seriously, Vanessa. I didn't know they made heels in size gargantuan." Abby took another swallow of champagne.

"It's ten and a half," Vanessa snapped. "See what happens when I try to be nice? It never works." Vanessa finished her champagne and poured some more. "I made Joshua Taggert cry today."

They stared at her.

"The new guy?" Abby asked. "The one who just graduated from college?"

"Yep. That's the one. It was just...pathetic. Sure he's the boss's nephew, but he screwed up a major account. The only reason our client didn't end up paying penalties through the nose was because I checked and rechecked him." She took another drink. "Though in my defense, I wouldn't have called him an incompetent twit if I'd known Mr. Peterman had already read him the riot act."

"Interesting. I didn't know *twit* was considered an insult past the fifth grade," Abby said.

"Shut up." Vanessa laughed. "Oh my God. It was just... Why am I always the mean one for saying the truth? How come I'm always the one with the biggest balls wherever I happen to be? And believe it or not, I really am a woman." Vanessa looked strained.

Abby took note. "Um, I don't think we've ever questioned your femininity."

"Yeah, well, apparently if you're assertive, you're a bitch."

"This isn't news." Maddie finished her mug of champagne and opened the chocolates she'd supposedly brought for Abby. "It's still an all-boys club out there. Remember little old me? Sexually harassed by my boss? I quit because I knew I couldn't win against him. Mr. Moneybags and his—"

"Small penis." Abby had heard the story more times than she cared to remember.

"Yep. Small penis." Maddie nodded. "Versus me—beautiful but poor designer."

"Not so poor anymore," Vanessa added.

Maddie beamed. "Nope. Business is getting better every day. Maybe that's what you should do. Leave your firm and open up your own company."

Vanessa shrugged. "Maybe. I'm happy at work, actually. I just wish everyone would perform at my level, instead of me always having to yank them up to swim next to me."

"Swim?" Abby snorted. "More like your peers are treading water next to Ms. Corporate Shark."

Vanessa smiled through her teeth. "Ha ha. And on that note, I'm going upstairs to put on my costume. Try not to embarrass us, would you, Abby? You are *not* wearing that bozo costume. Maddie, take care of it."

Maddie mock saluted her. "Yes, *mein führer*." She laughed again. "Bossy, but you have a point." They both turned to Abby.

"What?"

"Tonight, you celebrate," Maddie answered. "Men will be at the party—eligible bachelors. Remember the hot electricians who ask Flynn about you almost all the time? When's the last time you had a man, anyway?"

She blushed. "It's been awhile. I'm fine about it."

"No, you're not." Maddie looked her over critically. "But we're not ruining tonight by mentioning asswipe again."

Kevin. He haunted her with bad memories. What hurt was that she'd really loved him. Unfortunately, he hadn't loved her.

"Nope. Get that miserable look off your face. I have this, Vanessa."

"Good. If I can be a bitch and be okay with it, you can be a freak and run with it," she said to Abby before turning on her big heel and leaving.

"Vanessa!" Maddie tried hard not to laugh. "Oh man, Abby. You are so red right now."

"She's such a jerk." Abby should never have confided in her friends about her breakup with Kevin. Even her family thought they'd mutually gone their separate ways. Not that he'd dumped her because…because she wanted to explore certain *needs*.

"Yep, and that's why we love her. Now…" Maddie circled around her, studying her like an ant under a microscope. "What to do with you. Something exotic, sexy. And no flats or moccasins tonight."

"Oh well. I don't have anything else to wear." She hated heels. Comfort all the way for mundane Abby Dunn.

"Good thing I was planning on tonight for you." Maddie smiled, her expression unnerving. The woman looked way too pleased with herself. She dragged Abby with her upstairs and into her bedroom.

Abby's hand still curled around her mug of champagne, and she took a drink for courage. "I don't know why you bother keeping a room here. You're always with Flynn."

"Yes, but this is my home. I don't know that I'm ready to cohabitate yet. Besides, he needs a bigger closet."

"No doubt you measured."

"Yeah, and it's more than six inches." Maddie pinched her finger and thumb together.

They both laughed.

"You're such a dork."

"Correction. I'm a *sexy* dork." Maddie's grin turned sly. "And speaking of sexy... Rick and Gary won't be the only hotties in attendance. The McCauleys will be there tonight too."

Abby found it hard to breathe. *Brody*. "So." She coughed to clear her throat. "Why not my hobo outfit? It's cute and comfy."

"It completely covers you from head to toe, not to mention it makes you look like a sack of potatoes. And that stick with the red bag on it? Get over it."

Maddie pushed some clothing aside in her closet and pulled out a very short, very sheer Grecian-styled robe. "Ah. There we go. I bought this for you last month because I knew you'd try to wimp out at the last minute. And here we have Aphrodite. Goddess of love. You write romance. See? It fits."

"I doubt it's going to," Abby whispered, stunned at how much she wanted to be a goddess for once in her life. To dress without care for how others saw her, but to be sexy in her own skin.

"That's the point. It's short, but so are you."

"Not short. Petite."

Maddie talked over her. "So it will look just shy of slutty on you. The ivory color goes well with your darker hair and fair complexion. And the deep V will show off your curves. I know you think those are your best features, but I like your eyes. I'm torn."

"Gee, thanks. Too bad you and I aren't dating."

"Isn't it though? Well? Let's go. And no flats. You're going in my golden heels, and that's final."

"Greeks didn't wear heels."

"Goddesses do. Come on, Abby. Treat yourself. You earned it."

Something in Abby clicked. Halloween, her favorite holiday. A time when she could pretend to be someone else for a night and enjoy herself. She took another sip of the champagne Vanessa had thoughtfully brought. "Why the heck not?"

Chapter 3

THE PARTY WAS IN FULL SWING WHEN THEY ARRIVED. A conglomerate of businesses sponsored the event every year at Muriel V's—a popular banquet hall—and put on a real bash. There must have been a few hundred people at least, laughing and dancing.

Abby stood with Vanessa just inside the doorway, out of the way of incoming guests. Dry ice fogged the floor in spurts. Strobe and disco lights lit the expansive room. Two large bars had been set up on either side of the hall, and in the middle was a huge dance floor. Rhythmic techno pumped through the place, a deep throbbing bass that echoed within her.

In front of them, Maddie and Flynn stood arm in arm. The kitten and the cowboy. Flynn wore chaps over jeans, a half-buttoned shirt, and a tan cowboy hat. Maddie had barely looked away from him since he'd arrived at the house to take them to the party. Abby couldn't blame her. Flynn made an amazing cowboy.

"How big is this thing?" she asked Vanessa, whose company was one of the contributors to the festivities. Vanessa wore a sexy nurse's uniform and white stockings held up by clearly visible white garters. And Vanessa being Vanessa, she sported a nametag which read Nurse Ratched and carried a huge toy hypodermic needle filled with fake blood. "By the way," Abby added, "your nametag suits you."

"Well, I am surrounded by crazy people." She pointedly stared at Abby tottering in Maddie's too-high heels.

Normally five-four—okay, five-three and a third—she now stood at an impressive five-seven. Unfortunately, they both knew she'd fall if she didn't continue to cling to Vanessa like a vine.

She held tight to Vanessa's arm and shook her head, feeling the wisps escaping her upheld hair tickling her neck. "I'm in costume, peasant girl. Watch your tone. I'm a goddess."

"You look good." A huge compliment coming from Vanessa. "Really pretty in that excuse for a dress. But you should have eased back on the champagne at the house." She stared at Abby's hand wrapped around her wrist at the same time Abby stumbled.

"It's not the booze. It's these stupid heels." Abby lifted her foot.

Maddie spotted her teetering on one foot and hurried back to her. "What the heck, Abby? Are you trying to flash the crowd already? Let's warm them up, then make your move." She glanced at a small group of men smiling widely nearby who toasted Abby with plastic cups of beer.

"Oh." Instead of blushing, Abby smiled back. So maybe she had imbibed more than she normally would have. But damn it, she'd finished her book. She was entitled to celebrate, both her victory over her deadlines and her new status as a goddess free from mortal worry. "I am Venus, hear me roar."

Vanessa fiddled with her stocking. "I thought you were Greek. Venus was Roman. Aphrodite was Greek."

"Don't rain on my parade, Ratched." She glared at Vanessa, who laughed at her.

"You really are cute when you're mad. Oh, wait, there's Lissa. I didn't know she was coming." A genuine smile lit Vanessa's face.

"Oh, right. Lissa, your buddy from work."

"I'm going to go say hi. Stay here with Maddie and Flynn."

Vanessa darted away before Abby could protest. Not that she minded Vanessa leaving, but she needed someone to hold on to for fear she'd fall flat on her face and moon the party. Since Maddie had convinced her to wear the stupid thong Abby had been saving for Mr. Right, if she did indeed fall, it wouldn't help cover anything, let alone her wounded pride.

Flynn joined them a heartbeat later and gripped Abby's arm to steady her. The hunky cowboy. But instead of a gun in his holster, she saw a tool.

"Have wrench, will travel?"

"Yes, darlin'. That's the plumber in me."

She laughed at his pitiful accent.

"Stop flirting with the goddess or I'll scratch your eyes out. *Reowr.*" Maddie curled her hand in the air, and Abby saw she'd gotten a manicure.

"Shouldn't those nails be white to be in character?" she asked, surprised to find herself having fun. The mood around her was contagious. Happiness reigned as the beat shifted, and she found herself tapping a dangerously clad foot in time with the music.

"Red is the color of passion," Flynn commented. "I like 'em."

"And the color of blood," Maddie replied. "So stay

close to me or I'll be forced to carve up the non-felines in the crowd looking to rope a cowboy."

He grinned widely. "Yeah? Because I saw some chick checking me out. Why don't you take me into that closet over there and—"

"God. You two need a room, and I need a drink." Abby yanked her arm from Flynn. "I'm not tipsy. Honestly." She felt a little flushed but otherwise sober. Kind of. "It's these heels. I'll be at the bar. When you're done doing…whatever it is you two do when you disappear…come find me." She nodded at the bar at the far end of the room.

More crowd-goers occupied the dance floor than clustered around the bars. Yet there were plenty of partiers on either side of the massive dance area as well. She figured she wouldn't have too much of a problem finding a seat or a drink. Not with all the guys eyeing her getup. Show a little cleavage or leg and they went crazy.

Go figure.

Abby kept her pace slow and constant and found the bar without incident. With so much other exposed female flesh on display, her allure faded as she blended with the crowd. She liked knowing that if she fell on her ass, only a few would see her embarrass herself.

"Whoa. You have got to be the prettiest thing I've seen all night." The bartender whistled as she sat on a stool. "I'm hooked. What'll you have?"

Her dress grew exponentially shorter as it hiked up her legs when she sat. Damn. The whole of her thigh showed. Then again, the lighting wasn't that great. Who was looking? "Hmm. How about a Long Island Iced Tea?" It tasted like tea instead of alcohol, and she could get a nice buzz going on without losing her mind. She'd nurse the drink all night and enjoy herself.

"You got it." He winked. "And in that dress, consider it on the house. I wouldn't want to piss off the gods or anything." He paused to find her a napkin to go along with the drink. As she looked around her, she spotted a few familiar faces. People from the neighborhood, her favorite barista, and a few of her library buddies, women she often saw when she made her rounds. "There you go, lovely."

She smiled at him. "Thanks." Not a bad-looking guy. He had a nice smile.

He nodded down at the drink. "Anything you need, *at all*, you just call. Name's Phil." Someone distracted him away with another order.

She looked down at her drink and saw a number on the napkin. What the…? Abby peered closer, wishing she had her reading glasses.

Holy crap. He'd left his phone number. Phil J. had left her his phone number.

Her self-confidence shot up several notches. *Maybe I should wear cleavage-baring silk every day.* She sipped the drink and felt eyes on her. Thinking it was Phil J., she turned only to see Rick Jackson, a guy she'd once partied with and one of Flynn's favorite electricians, staring her up and down with a huge grin on his face. He left the guy he'd been talking to and joined her at the bar, taking a seat beside her.

"Well, well. Abby Dunn. Fancy meeting you here."

Rick had kind eyes and a wicked sense of humor. She liked him a lot. By the expression on his face, he liked her costume.

"You going to arrest me, officer?" she asked.

He flashed an obviously fake badge and tipped back his uniform hat. "No, ma'am. Not if you'll finish that drink and join me on the dance floor."

Abby sighed. Her luck. "I would, but I'd kill myself in these heels." She sipped her drink and looked down. They sure looked glamorous, but what idiots put themselves through such torture on a daily basis to look good?

Maddie.

"Wow. That is a lot of leg for someone I hadn't thought was that tall." Rick held up his hands at her glare. "No, no. Not saying you're short. Just that…" He swallowed. "In that costume, you have really, *really* long legs. Pretty legs." He blew out a breath. "Oh yeah."

She laughed, amused by his attention. Normally she didn't garner more than a hello or a smile. But he and Gary had supposedly asked Flynn about her. That meant they were interested, right? "Is the goddess of love knocking you off your feet?"

Rick put his hand between the buttons of his jacket and thumped his heart. "Honey, I'm done for."

She turned to better face him, and someone bumped into her from behind. She braced her hand on his knee just as Rick caught her shoulders, his hands warm against her bare arms. Though she'd demanded to wear a jacket in the car, Maddie had made her leave it behind, claiming Aphrodite didn't wear wool in the winter. Now that Rick had his hands on her, Abby silently agreed.

Yet… Some part of her wanted another man's hands instead of Rick's. A taller, fairer, more obnoxious male whom she could cut down to size, and who should be made to worship at her feet. A man not worthy of her affections, she told herself and smiled back at Rick.

Then realizing her hand remained on his knee, she tried to pull it back.

"*Don't*. I mean, it's okay. You need to keep your balance." He took a long drag of his beer. "Damn. It's getting hotter in here by the second." He lifted his hand and ran a finger down her neck. A forward move.

She…liked it. She felt sexy in her costume, and Rick's admiration boosted her ego. "I put my hair up for tonight. Maddie insisted it's more authentic."

"It's gorgeous. I love your hair." Rick smiled, and she liked that the warmth in his expression reached his eyes. "So tell me about your day, Aphrodite."

"Nice. You got it right. I'm the goddess of love."

Rick nodded. "I was a big fan of mythology as a kid."

"No kidding?" Enthused, Abby sipped at her drink while she and Rick engaged in a discussion about the Greeks versus the Romans. As they talked, she didn't have to fight her inclination to look for a familiar blond head in the crowd. The drink relaxed her. In good company and trusting her friend not to molest her, she forgot her cares and her stupid crush and enjoyed a man's company.

⌇⌇⌇

Brody wanted to smash Rick's head in. He felt Flynn mosey next to him. "How the hell did you let her cozy up with him? The one guy, besides Gary, she might hang with?"

"Sorry, man. Abby took off. I was going after her

when we saw Phil tending bar. He's a good guy. And then Maddie, uh, well, she kind of distracted me."

Brody turned to note Flynn's bottom two shirt buttons gone and a few red marks on his neck. "You and your thing for public places."

"Shut up, Brody. Maddie's kind of shy about things. Keep it under wraps, man."

Like Brody didn't know everything about Flynn. The two had shared their quirks, faults, and wants for far too long to be embarrassed about them now. He understood his buddy not wanting to embarrass Maddie. Still, Flynn owed him.

"Either you get her away from Rick or I will. She's been sitting with him for over half an hour. And look." Brody curled his fingers into a fist. "Her hand's on his knee again." He took an unconscious step forward, unable to think past the need to get Abby away from a potential rival.

"Stop. I swear, that costume is going to your head. You're not some badass in the Wild West." Flynn eyed him up and down, a wary look on his face. "Just wait here and go with whatever I tell her. Okay?"

"Fine. Lie, cheat, steal, but if that woman isn't right here in the next two minutes, I'm taking matters into my own hands."

"Thought you'd been doing that anyway." Flynn gave him a pitying glance.

Brody shot him the finger, not pleased when his friend laughed at him.

He watched as Flynn approached the bar. Flynn shook Rick's hand while Brody turned to look as if he was perusing the crowd, trying not to seem as if he'd been shooting invisible daggers into his soon to be *ex*-friend, Rick. Flynn said something, and Abby laughed. A deep-throated chuckle that had more than one male head turning to watch her.

Jesus, she killed him with that dress. What had Maddie been thinking to pour Abby into it? According to Flynn, Maddie had thought to help Abby through a dry spell. Hello? Why had no one called *him* in to help? At least Flynn knew better than to keep him in the dark.

Abby wanted to celebrate? He'd help her party all night long. But a glance at her empty cup and the knowledge she'd already had a bit to drink gave him second thoughts. Brody and alcohol didn't mix well, and he'd never, *ever* take a woman not sure of her sobriety. He might be a Singer in name, but never by actions. His father and brother were sure as shit going to hell. Not him.

He had no problem drinking because he had limits he never breached. Abby had already rounded the happy bus and was sliding perilously toward sloppy drunk. She could barely walk next to Flynn as they joined him.

"Hey, Abby." He couldn't help his husky voice. Aroused and relieved she was away from a scowling Rick, he tipped his hat at Rick and watched with good cheer as the guy stomped away.

"Where is she?" Abby asked.

"She?" Poor woman. Drunk off her ass.

She teetered again, then slapped at Flynn when he reached for her. "I'm not drunk, I keep telling you. It's these stupid heels."

Not drunk? The possibility of a different ending for the night immediately translated to the needy part between Brody's legs. Oh boy. Good thing he'd fore-gone the chaps and wore plain denim to match his black shirt and hat.

Abby steadied herself by grabbing onto his arm and slid her feet out of her shoes. "Oh, that is *so* much better. So where's this woman you supposedly need saving from?" Then she glanced up at Brody and blinked. "Black Bart?"

Flynn guffawed. "Told you she'd know your costume. The outlaw thing suits your personality."

"Black is a good look on me." He tried keeping the smile from his face. Now several inches smaller without her shoes, Abby was holding onto him, and her small hand felt soft and warm over his forearm. Even through the material of his shirt, he could tell they'd combust if they ever had any skin-on-skin action.

"And…my work here is done." Flynn left after nodding at him to look after Abby.

He nodded back before giving her his undivided attention. "You look good enough to eat."

She frowned. "Haven't you used that line on me before? Did it work?"

"Dear goddess." He spread his hand wide, overly dramatic. "I cannot know what is in your mind. I can only offer you my willing sacrifice. Sex to ease the plight of my sick people." He waved around him for dramatic effect, pleased to see her lips curling into a smile. "You see how they seize and convulse with an unspoken malady. I fear only a sexual sacrifice will cure them. And it must be me, for I am the last virgin in our village of Seattle."

Abby took a good, hard look at him and burst out laughing.

Maybe she was a little more than buzzy after all.

But before he could ask her if she was okay, she tripped over a heel and fell into him.

He grabbed her without thinking and swore when her rockin' curves hit him in all the right places. She fit snugly between his legs, his cock rubbing against her belly. Her breasts smashed against his lower chest, while her head rested against his pecs. His nipples had never been so sensitive before, but he swore he could feel her breath against his skin as she blew out a laugh.

"See? Those heels are *cursed*."

Cursed, blessed. Whatever caused her to rub against him without backing away, he was all for it. Conscious of her bare feet, he knelt to scoop up the shoes, then swept her into his arms.

She let out a small shriek. "What are you doing?"

"Taking you someplace where we can talk. The noise is getting worse. Too much bass."

"Not enough, I'd say," she argued, likely just to be contrary. She held onto his neck and didn't protest his hold. "There's a table over there." She nodded to the far corner, a spot partially blocked from view by the large potted ferns providing a bit of atmosphere. The spooky corner seemed too far away to be a part of things, probably why it remained empty.

Perfect for them.

Brody walked with her to the spot, nodding at his friends as he passed. Flynn gave him a thumbs up and swept Maddie around, so the woman didn't see him carrying the tiny goddess away. Tipsy or not, Abby was going straight to his head. He'd had one beer and one beer only; his every intent was to get drunk on Abby tonight.

Not only did she look good and feel good, but she smelled like heaven. Some sultry perfume he'd never scented on her before. Then he looked down and saw her breasts pressed together, that gorgeous cleavage all but begging him to get closer and nuzzle. She toyed with the hair at his nape, and his arousal skyrocketed.

He set her down at the table quickly before taking the seat next to her.

"Hey, I can't see the dancing." She tried to lean around the trees.

"You're not supposed to." He scooted closer and turned her chair, forcing her to face him.

"Is this a kidnapping? You going to tie me to train tracks any time soon?" she asked with a grin in her voice. Definitely punchy, but not quite drunk.

"Maybe." He wouldn't mind taking her back to his place and tying her up in his bed. But that would have to wait, unfortunately, until she could walk a straight line.

"Yeah, right." She tapped her fingers on the table and studied him. "You do look good in black."

"Thank you kindly." He moved his chair closer, spreading his legs to accommodate hers between his knees. He put his hands on her thighs, which were bared nearly to her crotch. God, talk about heaven and hell in the same instance. Abby had creamy thighs, not as toned or muscular as her roommates', but with shape. That word *lush* came to mind again. He wanted nothing more than to spread her legs and shove his face into the sweet spot just—

"Yeah, black. All dark and gloomy. Goes well with your hellhound. Where is he, by the way?"

Was she wearing a thong? Maybe nothing at all? It

suddenly felt unbearably restrictive in his jeans. Way too tight. Before he gave in to his inner urgings, he shifted his itchy hands away from her dress toward her knees, where he held on for dear life.

"Brody? Or should I call you Black Bart?"

"What?" He pulled himself from his fantasies and concentrated on what she'd said. "Oh, Mutt? He's back at my place sulking. He really likes you, you know."

She bit her lower lip, and he wanted to smooth the sting with his mouth. Lick her all better.

"Was I too mean last week, do you think?"

"To him or me?"

She put a hand on his chest and spread her fingers. Her gaze moved from his eyes to his mouth, and to his extreme satisfaction, her breathing increased. Good thing they remained in public. If he'd been at home with her, he might have said screw morality. Hell, it was all he could do to keep his hands frozen on her legs. Her warm, silky legs.

"I, um, to him." She swallowed loudly and seemed to lean closer. "Oh shoot. Why not?"

He hadn't been prepared for her to take charge, so he nearly lost his balance when she yanked his mouth to hers. Instinctively, he clutched her thighs to steady himself.

And then her mouth was over his, and he forgot about the party, the costumes, his name. Soft lips tasting faintly of liquor caressed him and turned him into a man with no other purpose than to claim what he needed. And to hell with everything else.

Which he would have done, if the woman in his arms weren't Abby. He let go of her to grip the bottom of his seat, determined to do the right thing, even if it killed him.

She pulled back, and he saw the heat he knew raged within his own eyes.

In a gruff voice, he said, "You're drunk. But I'm not sorry about the kiss. I've been waiting for that."

"Not drunk enough, because I felt that to my toes," she rasped.

He clutched the bottom of the chair so hard his fingers hurt. "You're killing me, baby. We should probably get back to the others and—" He sucked in a breath. "What *the fuck* are you doing?"

Her fingers worked at his waistband. The snap of his jeans came undone, and then the slow slide of his zipper followed. Though the table blocked the view of their lower bodies, and the trees kept them nearly shadowed from the others, Brody had no intention of going too far with Abby in public. He wanted to take it slow, so as not to spook her. They had to do this right. No recriminations, no upset when it ended. But she—

"Abby, wait… You…" His eyes rolled back in his head.

He couldn't think as her hands delved beneath his underwear to stroke him. The tight fit of his clothes, hampered by the jeans, didn't seem to dissuade her. If anything, she seemed to be having a good time. Her grin wide, her eyes narrowed and concentrated on his face.

"You're big. I knew it. Big hands, big feet." She leaned closer and nipped his earlobe. "Big cock," she whispered.

Shocked, aroused, and unbelievably confused about what to do, Brody couldn't logically process while his body answered for him. He arched into her hot hands while trying not to look as if he was getting jerked off by his ideal wet dream come to life. Never in a million years would he have expected this scene from quiet, quirky *Abby*.

"I'm in charge tonight. I can do whatever I want. See the dress? I'm the goddess of looovvee." She giggled.

Abby didn't giggle.

He exhaled on a moan and cursed his bad luck under his breath. "Abby, honey, please. You need to stop. You're drunk."

Her grip tightened, and then she started pumping him.

Groaning, he released the chair with one hand and put it over hers. To stop her, had been his intent. But her rhythm grew faster. He was already hard enough to split wood, and every time she stroked him she jerked so that her breasts rose and fell, promising a peek at her nipples if she'd shift just so. What made it even worse, her perfume made him as lightheaded as her grip around his cock did. She smelled freakin' amazing.

"Abby, stop. I'm gonna come," he warned in a gravelly voice.

"Oh, Black Bart is threatening *me*—a goddess." She leaned even closer, her lips a breath from his, and stared into his eyes. "You'll come because I want you to. All over my hand. I'm in charge, Bart. My great big Adonis." She licked her lips and dragged her hand over his tip, sliding through the fluid gathering there.

He blinked, still shocked to find this really happening. A hand job from Abby Dunn at a public party, when he could normally barely get her to look at him without scowling. "Abby, I'm not kidding." He tightened his hand over hers and urged her to move faster. *No, stop. Get her to stop.* But his body refused to listen to his conscience. "I'm so close."

"Yeah. I want you to come hard all over my hand. Come now, Brody. Let me see it happen." The minx continued to watch him, appearing fascinated more with watching his expression than his dick.

He panted, moaned, and squeezed her hand over him. "Oh Abby. God, yeah. I'm coming, baby. *Oh shit*." He spilled into her palm and closed his eyes, completely done in.

The pleasure overwhelmed him while she whispered what a good job he'd done, continuing to rub him until he stopped her when the sensitivity became too much to bear.

Abby released him, and his hand over hers fell away, limp, like his now-flagging erection.

She wiped her hand under his shirt, over his belly. Then pretty as you please, she slid her chair back, put her shoes back on, and stood. He just sat there, the head of his dick poking out from his boxer briefs, a mess on the bottom of his shirt and belly, and stared at her.

"That was fun, hmm?" She giggled again and slapped a hand over her mouth. Then she got the oddest look on her face. "My hand was just on your cock."

"Stop saying cock." His shaft jumped at the thought of another go-round, though he'd definitely need time to recuperate. He tucked himself back into his pants, grimacing at the stickiness he'd have to live with.

"I say it all the time in my books."

He stood, the pressure against his fly no longer a concern. Instead, he wanted to find some place to lie down and take a nap with Abby cuddled up next to him. "Books?"

"The books I write."

He stared at her. "But you told me you only write content for websites. You're a web designer, right?" Yet another layer of Abby Dunn peeled away to reveal more than a shy yet sexy woman hurting over an ex-boyfriend. He found her absolutely fascinating. She wrote books? What kind of books?

"Ohhhh," she dragged into four syllables. "Right. I'm a web designer." Her overdone wink nearly knocked her over, because she stumbled again. "Shoot. These shoes are killing me." She blinked. "I wonder where Rick went?"

"Don't worry about him," he growled. "Worry about me instead."

She laughed. "You? You're all bark and no bite. Like your dog." She waved her hand in the air.

Only Flynn's timely interruption saved him from tossing her over his shoulder and showing her just how sharp his teeth could really be.

He stayed by her and his friends for the rest of the night, puzzled as to how to handle Abby now. She didn't flirt with him or act as if anything had happened, and if he hadn't felt the sticky discomfort against his belly, he'd swear she'd hadn't jerked him off at all.

But she had. Now what to do about it, and how to make sure that fuckhead Rick kept his distance?

In the end, he hung with Flynn, Maddie, Vanessa, and Abby, watched her dance with Rick, Gary, and a bunch of others, then joined the girls when they left to go back to their house for the night.

He followed them in his truck, all the while trying to figure out how to handle this sexier side of Abby he'd never known existed. And how to bring it out again when she no longer had the taint of alcohol clouding her decisions…

Chapter 4

ABBY HAD A THROBBING HEADACHE WHEN SHE WOKE the next morning. Her feet lay on a pillow and her head dangled perilously close to falling off another pillow at the edge of her bed. She cautiously glanced around and saw someone else covered by her grandmother's handcrafted quilt.

Big bare feet sat next to her head. What the…?

"Finally. She wakes."

"Brody?" she squeaked, then moaned when tiny men with hammers struck her temples.

"And this is why you should stick to coffee," he grumbled. He sat partially propped up by her headboard with his feet by her face and stared at her like a science experiment gone horribly wrong.

She pushed his sasquatch feet away and ran a hand through her snarled hair. Her loose bun must have unraveled during sleep. Brody continued to watch her, his expression flat, not telling her a damn thing.

He'd been awake and watching her. Had she drooled? Did she have bedhead? Bad breath? Wait. "Brody?"

"Yeah. Remember last night?"

"I, um. Well, sure." She cautiously peeked under the blanket and sat up, more than relieved to see her costume still in place. "Why are you in my bedroom?"

"What exactly do you remember from last night?" He crossed his arms over his chest. His *bare* chest. How in blazes had she missed that? A glance at his ankles showed denim, so he wore pants, at least.

Bummer. She felt her cheeks heat. "I never drink. I mean, like maybe twice a year. I'm a lightweight."

A slow grin started at the corner of his mouth and took over his entire face. When happy, Brody lit up like the sun, showering all those within view with equal joy. Abby wanted to sigh and stare at him all day. That face, that body…

But she needed to fill in a few gaps in her memory. How embarrassing to be so out of control, and around Brody of all people. And speaking of which, how had her roommates not thrown a hissy with the blond trickster in her room? In *their house*?

"So you're a lightweight…?" Brody paused, waiting for her to continue.

"Seriously. I don't drink. But yesterday I finished my, ah…"

"Your project?"

"Right. My project." Abby didn't advertise that she wrote erotic romance. People tended to get the wrong idea—men especially—that she went out and researched everything she wrote. Instead, she directed attention to her other job as a web designer—what her parents still thought she did for a living.

"How much did you have to drink last night?"

She worried her lower lip, unable to stop the bad habit of nibbling when she grew nervous. "Vanessa brought home some champagne. I had a cup or two, which is about all I can handle. But then at the party, I think I had two Long Island Iced Teas." She frowned, recalling her conversation with Rick. Him buying her another drink, a big one. The cute bartender smiling at her and telling her he'd made it extra strong. A phone number on a napkin? Whose?

"Yeah?"

"Yeah." She swallowed. "I remember talking to Rick, then Flynn came over and said some woman was bothering you. Or maybe he wanted me to meet your friend? Either way, we said good-bye to Rick. Then, um. You and I, we..." They what? "We talked and stuff, and here we are. So that's fuzzy for me, how we got here. How exactly did you get invited into my room?"

He looked as if he was biting back a smile.

"Am I missing something?"

"I guess not." His shit-eating grin grew, and she had a bad feeling. But for the life of her, she couldn't remember anything but a few sexy dreams of doing him at the party. In public. Like Abby would ever do something that crazy. Plus, if she had, no way would Brody not have said something already.

"Anyway," Brody continued, "we had a fun night. Vanessa spent time hanging out with her work friends and asked me to see you got home okay."

She frowned.

"Maddie and Flynn were wrapped up in each other, and you needed help with those shoes."

She followed his glance to the corner, where those heels from hell sat smirking at her.

"I was ready to leave when the others were," Brody said. "So I followed you guys back. By that time, I was beat, so I asked for a place to sleep. I was happy with the couch, but you insisted I stay with you."

"I did not." She sat up straight, no longer clutching the quilt to her chest.

Brody's gaze centered on her breasts before raising slowly to her face again. He tried to look innocent but failed miserably. "Yep, you did." Then he did something really strange. He looked past her at her bookcases crammed with her favorite books. Namely romances involving kinky couples, with a row dedicated to her own authored novels. She blinked at a space where a book was missing on her lower shelf.

"Something wrong?" he asked.

"N-no. Nothing." She'd wondered before if Brody somehow knew she wrote erotic stories for a living. But he'd never mentioned it. And he was the type that would take full advantage of any situation. He obviously wanted to get in her pants, but Abby didn't want to take a chance on either disappointing him or freaking him out with her needs. So she continued to keep her distance. Or she had, until last night, apparently.

Brody yawned and stretched, and she stared, caught in helpless fascination with so much sculpted muscle. He had a light dusting of blond chest hair that trailed down his belly. But not enough to impede her view of his corded abs. And he had those killer lines, the ones that narrowed over his hips and showcased a slender body filled with muscle. He had tone that Abby would never, ever have.

No six-pack for her. Just a soft tummy with a rounded bump she'd never been able to flatten, no matter how many sit-ups she did.

"Abby?"

Oh crap. Brody had caught her ogling. His obnoxious

grin both made her feel better and worse. They seemed to be on even footing again, except for the feeling that somehow he'd gotten one up on her. She didn't like it.

"What?" She made a big production of getting out of bed, then realized she should have stayed covered up when his eyes widened. She glanced down to see the edge of her minidress tucked into the tiny side band of her thong. Quickly righting her clothes, she missed him leaving her bed.

Then he stood right in front of her. So close she could feel his heat.

"Wh-where's your shirt?"

He laughed. "I got something on it. It's in your washer downstairs."

"Oh." That should be funny?

"Yeah. Made a mess of myself," he added in a husky voice.

An image of her gripping him came to mind. At the party, in public? *No.* No way in hell.

"You should be more careful," she said tentatively.

That big-ass grin stretched impossibly wide. "Oh, I will be. I figure next time I'm in that situation, I'll use protection." He leaned down and stared into her eyes. So much taller, he loomed over her, all muscle and strength.

She worked to suppress a sexual shiver. "Protection from what?"

"I—"

At that moment, a knock sounded on her bedroom door. Vanessa didn't wait before opening it. "What is with all the testosterone in this place?" She eyeballed Brody, then Abby, and frowned. "Seriously? You two fooled around in costume? Kinky."

"Vanessa." Abby knew her cheeks had turned scarlet.

Brody shook his head. "Dirty mind."

Vanessa snorted. "Me? I'm a peasant. The queen of dirty minds is right in your hot little hands. Or should I say *big* hands?" She chuckled. "So Abby, is it true what they say about a man's shoe size?"

Abby forced herself to ignore Brody's and Vanessa's snickers and tried to look down at him, which wasn't easy when she had to tilt her chin *up* to see him. "I guess. Brody, you wear what, a size five?"

He snorted. "Yeah, right. Try a twelve." Then he kissed her on top of the head—the head?—and walked past her and Vanessa out the door.

Abby and Vanessa stared at each other, then hustled out of the room and down the stairs to follow him.

"Tell me what happened," Vanessa whispered as they rushed into the kitchen to watch Brody take a shirt from the dryer, located in what used to be a butler's pantry. "I'm dying to know."

"So am I," Abby said under her breath. To Brody, she raised her voice. "I thought you said you washed the shirt. You dried it too? Make yourself at home, why don't you."

Vanessa stared at Brody as he buttoned up and hid all that golden skin. "Actually, I threw it in the dryer last night. Thought it was Flynn's. His car is outside."

Abby would have chastised her for staring, but she had a hard time looking away herself.

Vanessa continued, "I should have known the good cowboy would be too busy handling the pussy upstairs to do laundry."

Brody stared at her openmouthed, and Abby turned

to regard her roommate with shock. Even for Vanessa, that sounded crass.

To her surprise, Vanessa colored. "Stop it. I meant *pussy*—as in pussy*cat*. You remember Maddie's costume? Geez, guys. Grow up." She stomped away, but not before Brody exchanged a comical look with Abby.

"I don't think I can suffer too many more shocks to my system." Brody finished buttoning his shirt and shut the dryer door. Then, as if he lived there, he walked back into the kitchen, opened the refrigerator, and pulled out a carton of orange juice. He searched for a glass, found it, and poured himself a tall drink.

He took half and offered the rest to Abby.

Offended at his familiarity, she grabbed it and downed *her* juice while he put the carton away. "Mine."

"Hey, baby, anything you want is okay with me. You're in charge." He winked, and she had a bad feeling she was missing out on the joke.

"Ah, okay." She finished the juice and felt a bit better, even if she had consumed citric acid on top of the pool of alcohol still in her stomach.

"Well, I'd stay for breakfast—"

"That wasn't offered."

"—but Mutt's probably missing me. Seth feeds him and lets him out if I need him to, but the dog loves me best. And you, of course."

She frowned. "You rescued him and decided to keep him. Why not give him a real name?"

He shrugged, his shoulders broad and imposing, especially clad in black. "When I hear it, I'll know. But keep trying. Your suggestions are far better than anyone else's."

"Oh yeah?"

"Yeah. Mike calls him 'Get Off.' Colin wants to give him these long, descriptive names. Like 'Killer of Squirrels' and 'Alien Dog from the Deep.' Not sure where he got that one."

"Probably from the Godzilla movie on the other night. I heard your brother blasting Flynn for letting Colin watch it when he should have been in bed."

"Flynn is so weak. He always gets caught."

She laughed, unable to help it. "You're bad."

"But smart. You never see Mike slamming me for anything."

She nodded and realized she'd called Mike his brother, and Brody hadn't flinched. She wanted so badly to know how they worked as a unit. Her writer's mind started a new series of books right then and there, all centered around a golden-haired hottie who had women flocking to him, while he secretly nursed a wounded heart. What wounds and why, though?

"Why are you looking at me like that?" He sounded curious.

She blew out a breath. "I need food."

"So you want to eat me?"

She wanted to answer the smart remark in the tone it had been given, but Flynn and Maddie arrived just in time to misconstrue Brody's comment.

Flynn glanced from Abby to Brody. "Oh wow. High five, bro." He held his hand up to Brody, who slapped it back.

"Really, Abby? You went from virginal goddess last night to a rumpled walk-of-shame girl? And propositioning Brody, of all people, in our kitchen?" Maddie sounded pretty damn haughty for a woman who'd tied up and screwed her boyfriend in the room right next door to Abby's not so long ago.

"I said I need food," she snapped. "Not him."

"Oh, my bad." Brody danced out of the kitchen before she could smack him. "I'll talk to you later, guys. See you soon, Abby."

She followed him to the front door. "What does that mean?" And why did she keep feeling the heat of him in her hands? Smell the musky cologne of sex, citrus, and man whenever she thought of him?

"It means you have a website to design. Mine and Flynn's, remember?"

"Oh, right." She had forgotten. "But I can work with Flynn on it."

"Sorry, Abby. You can't." Flynn shrugged. "I promised Mike I'd help watch Colin while he and Dad work on some new project they contracted." Mike worked construction with his father, and he often used his family to help care for his son.

"So we'll talk next door. I'm flexible."

Brody nodded and said, "Good to know," in a suggestive voice that raced over her last nerve.

"Shut up."

Flynn laughed then quickly covered his mirth when she scowled at him. "Ahem. Right. Well, Colin is playing indoor soccer, so I'm having to run him across the city at odd hours to practice. But Brody's available, and he knows better what we want anyway."

"Oh yeah. I know exactly what I want."

That innuendo again. Brody's deep voice put her entire body on alert.

Behind her, Maddie said, "I don't see the problem, Abby. Besides, it'll really help business."

"True. Who the heck owns a business and doesn't have a website in this day and age?" She chewed her lip, then stopped when Brody homed in on the action. "Fine. But no more staring at my breasts while we talk."

"Brody." Maddie laughed. "Don't be such a guy."

"Yeah," Flynn agreed.

So nice to have them on her side for a change.

"Stare at her ass instead," Flynn suggested. "So when she's turned away, she won't know."

"Good advice." Brody gave him a thumbs-up, then winked at Abby before he left. "I'll call you," he said over his shoulder.

She slammed the door and turned to face her friends. "Flynn, if you even think of playing matchmaker, don't. You and Maddie have a great thing going. Throwing me and Brody together is a mistake."

"Don't worry. I have no intention of putting you two together." Flynn shook his head. "Not a good combination."

"Oh?" Maddie crossed her arms. "Why? Is she not good enough for your idiot bestie?"

He flinched. "First of all, he's not my 'bestie.' We aren't girls braiding each other's hair. Second, he's not an idiot." At their stares, he amended, "Well, not all the time. And third, *she's* probably too good for *him*. He's not a player. He's honest with women, but Brody just isn't ready to settle down yet. Not like me, Maddie."

Maddie dragged him into her arms and plastered a kiss on his mouth.

"Suck-up," Abby said with disgust.

He winked at her, and she turned to forage in the

kitchen for some toast. A banana, maybe. Something to settle her queasy stomach.

Two hours later, after eating, showering, and cleaning up her room, she frowned at her bookcase.

"Maddie?" she called as her friend walked by.

"What?" Dressed for the day in jeans and a pretty but practical sweater, Maddie looked ready for a day of staging houses. Her new profession.

"Did you borrow one of my books?"

"Nope. I'm not that crazy. I refuse to pledge my first-born to borrow from your personal library. You probably misplaced it." Maddie walked past her and downstairs.

"Maybe." Abby continued to look at the empty spot on her shelf, then finally trooped downstairs with her roommate and returned to work. The books certainly wouldn't write themselves, and it seemed she had a new client to work with. McSons Plumbing. Brody and Flynn's business needed help. Time to organize and get busy with scheduling through the holidays.

Yet the loss of her book irked her throughout the day.

———

"I refuse to continue with this farce! You said cards, chips, and dip! But this is ridiculous. I'm wearing my suit pants!"

Brody glared at the youngest McCauley brother, recently returned from a trip out East, and cinched down the bolts of his new water heater. "Cam, just hold the freaking tank. I'm almost done."

"You should have gotten a freestanding tank. What the hell, man? At least tell me you installed a recirc line," Flynn muttered.

"Dude, I know how to do my job."

"Jesus, this is heavy," Cam whined while Flynn said something Brody couldn't catch, something no doubt insulting that made Cam laugh. "Too true, Flynn."

"You can let go now." Brody tightened the bolts into the backboard he'd previously installed to hold the tank to the wall, now wondering if he should have gone with the freestanding water heater, despite the deal he'd gotten on this new model.

"The two-by-fours are solidly connected to the joist, right? Because if not, this tank will be on the floor before I've had my third beer tonight."

"Yes, yes. I did my due diligence. Flynn, so help me, if you don't stop telling me what to do, I'll tell Mike you gave Colin a shitload of soda and candy last time you babysat."

"Not nice." Flynn glared.

"But no doubt true." Cam shook his head. "Really, Flynn. Colin could do with less sugar and more discipline."

"And this is why I'm his favorite uncle."

"Hey, girlfriends, can the chatter so I can quit this," Brody said as he finished tightening the lines. In about an hour, he'd have a much more efficient water heating system, not to mention hot water again. "I swear, I would have had more luck recruiting Girl Scouts to help me. Or Seth."

"I heard that." Seth glared at him next to Mutt, who stood with his leash in his mouth. Seth held the flashlight while Brody, Flynn, and Cam replaced his new water heater in the basement. Unfortunately, he'd had a short in the basement while working on the replacement. Typical. His bad luck usually ran in threes. He hadn't talked to Abby in two days, it had rained on him at the jobsite this morning, and he had a bad feeling he was coming down with a nasty cold. Like postnasal drip would flash "Do me" signs at the woman currently avoiding him.

"This is just pathetic," Cam continued to complain. "It's Friday night, my calendar is finally free, and I'm helping numbnuts put a water heater in his house? A place that would be better off condemned?"

"Hey." Seth glared.

"Not *your* half of the building, Mr. Forelli," Cam recovered quickly. "From what I hear, your duplex is actually decent. It's no wonder you sold this half to Brody."

Decent? A lie, but Cam was a McCauley after all. The brothers had been finessing their way out of trouble since birth. Brody normally referred to Seth's place as a hoarder's paradise, and Cam knew it.

Seth gave a harrumph. Then the lights came back on. "I'm going back home. I'm missing my shows."

"He's big on the Game Show Network," Brody explained to the guys. He caught the flashlight Seth lobbed at him and watched the old man shuffle back up the stairs. Seth's crankiness only endeared the old bastard to him more. "Thanks, Seth."

"Yeah, yeah."

Mutt turned to watch him. Once Seth left the stairwell, the dumb dog dove off the stairs and knocked Flynn on his ass.

"Damn it." Flynn had to work to fend off that slobbery tongue.

Cam laughed. "Aw, he likes you, bro."

Flynn flipped him the finger while shoving at Mutt.

"Awesome." Brody wiped his hands and stared at his new water heater with satisfaction. "Now I'll have hot water again. I can stop showering at Mike's." Brody frowned. "Where is he, anyway?"

"He said he'd be a few minutes late," Cam offered. "Had to drop Colin off at Mom and Dad's before heading over."

"They live like four blocks over from his house."

Flynn shoved the dog off him and grinned. "Yeah, but Mom had a friend she invited over. A young, *single lady* friend, if you catch my drift."

"Damn. He's gonna be mad when he gets here."

"Truly." Cam dusted off his prissy pants and glared at the dog when Mutt would have made his love known. "Down. Back. Off."

Brody sighed and grabbed his dog by the leash trailing after him. "Come on, Mutt. Let's go get you a treat."

At the word *treat*, the dog darted to the stairs, ripped the leash from Brody's fingers, and bounded up in two big leaps.

"Gee, he seems to know *that* word." Flynn stood and scowled at Brody. "I'd think *down* and *off* would take priority over *treat*."

"Hey. He's new. Give him some slack."

"You suck at dog training," Flynn said. "That beast is totally ruling you."

"He is not." The dog barked, urging him to hurry. "That's his excited bark."

Cam snorted. "Yeah, right. Whatever. Just don't let the thing try to jump Mike when he gets here or big bro might break your dog in half."

"Good point." Brody had only seen Mike truly angry a few times in his life. Enough to know he never wanted Mike to be that angry with him. Ever.

The three of them trudged upstairs. After Brody tinkered with the faucets a bit and cleaned up, he rejoined his brothers in the kitchen, the only room in the house that surprisingly didn't need to be completely overhauled.

"This is a big space," Cam admitted as he leaned against a counter. "I still don't understand why you thought you needed to buy it when you were renting, but whatever. You should have Maddie help you design it. I bet she'd give you a discount since Flynn is pleasing her on a regular basis."

"Yes, I am." Flynn's goofy grin made Brody laugh. "When I'm ready to decorate, I'll call her."

"Really? 'Cause I'm thinking you want another woman to help you pick curtains," Flynn teased.

Brody wished Flynn would shut up. He'd been needling Brody nonstop since the party. Brody grabbed a soda from the fridge and opened it.

"Oh? You mean Abby, of course," Cam answered. "Don't look so surprised, Brody. I keep on top of things." Cam traveled for business. Of all the McCauleys, Brody included, he fit in the least. Unlike his blue-collar siblings, Cam worked as an investment specialist and had a head for numbers. The guy was a lot like Vanessa, but pleasant to be around. Normally.

Brody gave him a dubious once-over. "Uh-huh. So they sell men's clothes where you bought that getup?"

"It's called a suit, dumbass." Cam sniffed and glared at the beer in his hand. "You knew I was coming. Was it too hard to get what I like instead of this piss?"

Flynn laughed.

Brody blew out a breath. "Look, your highness, at my place, you get what you get. How is that different from Mike's?"

"Um, he has decent beer, food, and a nice kitchen?" Flynn offered.

"Don't help."

"Truth hurts." Cam and Flynn shook their heads in commiseration. "But back to Abby," Cam pushed.

Brody groaned and Flynn chuckled.

"What's the deal? Flynn said Mike isn't hot for her. You have a green light. And supposedly you and she did something at the Halloween party. Man, I wanted to be here for that. Too bad my new client insisted on me tailing it out to Maryland last week."

Brody turned to Flynn. "You tell him everything? I thought we enjoyed keeping secrets from the others."

"Normally we do."

"What?" Cam frowned.

Flynn continued. "But this is too good. Brody Singer, frustrated, with his dick in a knot over our own Abby Dunn."

"Our own? Since when does she belong to you?"

"He's balling the roommate," Cam explained. "Transitive property."

"Stop talking math. Please. I like to put those horrifying days of homework behind me." Flynn grimaced. "Drink beer, scratch your balls. Burp, damn it. Be a slob. It's Friday."

Mike strode through the front door at that moment and made a beeline for the kitchen.

"Take Mike." Flynn pointed at his brother. "See

that manly frown? Those ragged jeans and that holey T-shirt? How about those funky boots? And there, those monstrous fists ready to beat on some hapless—Hey!" He darted around the kitchen island, keeping it between him and Mike, who looked ready to break something—*someone*—in half.

Mutt whined from the bedroom, where Brody had earlier contained him.

"Did you put Mom up to this?" Mike growled.

Brody and Cam exchanged a grin they quickly erased when Mike included them in his glare.

"Flynn," they said as one. "*He* did it," Brody added for emphasis, not wanting to be confused with the guy ready to lose his pretty face.

"Dickheads," Flynn snarled. "I did not," he said to Mike and danced around the island again when Mike lunged for him. "You know Mom is getting all weird about grandkids. She's on me and Maddie to have them, for God's sake. And we're not engaged yet."

"I know." Mike huffed and seemed to settle down. "She keeps strangling Colin with cuddling and Grandma-time. Dad saved him tonight. Poor kid begged me not to leave him with 'the baby-lady.' His words, not mine."

"Poor guy." Brody shook his head. "It's just Bitsy excited about her sons hooking up again. Hey, it's a good sign, right? She wants you to be happy." Bitsy and Pop, what he called Beth and James McCauley.

Mike studied him with narrowed eyes.

"What?"

"So how come she isn't all gaga over you and Abby hooking up?"

Brody looked at Flynn. "Really? You told Mike too? Nice, Chatty Cathy."

Flynn had the grace to flush. "We all like the thought of you and Abby together. So I told them you kind of fooled around on Wednesday."

Thank God Brody hadn't told Flynn about what Abby had really done. Only that he'd kissed her and they'd spent a platonic night in her bed, head to foot.

"Yeah. Now that I think about it, Mom should know that *you're* her next project, not me. I made a kid. I'm done." Mike crossed his monstrous arms over his chest and smiled. A mean grin that didn't meet his eyes.

"Now hold on. This thing with Abby is casual. I'm not ready for a relationship."

"Uh-huh." Flynn tossed Mike a beer. "If that's the case, tell me. When was the last time you got laid?"

"I don't kiss and tell." Unfortunately, the guys didn't buy that one. They all laughed in his face. "Belinda."

"Yeah, six months ago. Try again, girlfriend."

"Shut up. You get laid and all of a sudden you're an expert on relationships?" Brody couldn't have said why, but all this talk of him and Abby and the R word made him itchy. "I thought we were here to play cards, or would you rather talk about the fact that you had a wine and cheese party with your new girlfriend the other week?"

Mike blinked. "Are you serious?"

"Too bad I wasn't invited." Cam frowned. "Was I out of town?"

Brody and Mike rolled their eyes. Cam *would* want to be included on something that lame. Mike, Brody, and Flynn would rather have had their teeth pulled. "Yeah, Mr. Fancy Pants. How do you like your chardonnay?"

They ribbed Flynn and left Brody alone, thank God. He went to let Mutt out of the back room, warned him to behave, and eased the dog into the group. Mutt took a look at Mike, slunk under the table and gnawed on a bone, and the poker game started in earnest. Everyone forgot about women issues as they discussed the Seahawks' season and Bitsy and Pop's recent sniping with each other. No one liked dissention in the ranks, especially not Brody.

An hour later, his cell phone vibrated against his ass, and he called a halt for a bathroom break, praying against all odds Abby suddenly needed help with a clogged bathtub during her bath and had called him for assistance. In his room for privacy, he answered without looking at the number, wanting to be pleasantly surprised.

"Hello?"

"Well, boy. It's about time." Alan Singer's slurred voice came over the line in a connection too crisp for comfort.

Brody went stone cold. "Alan."

"I'm your father, you little shit. Call me Dad." Alan laughed, and Brody thought he heard his brother Jeremy in the background.

"I'm busy." Brody wanted badly to disconnect, but curiosity forced his hand. "What do you want? Money? Forget it." He'd paid the old man his last dime ten years ago, back when he could ill afford to spend anything not on himself. Still, Alan contented himself to call every few years when he needed something.

"No. It's Jeremy. He needs a job."

Brody couldn't believe the balls on the prick. "Yeah? Put him on."

He heard the phone drop and unconsciously found himself rubbing his elbow, where a scar remained. He could still remember the pain of that broken bone. And who had caused it.

"Brody?" A voice much like Alan's but not as deep.

"Jeremy?"

"Hey, little brother. I've missed—"

"Fuck off." Brody disconnected and forced himself to let go of the tension invading his body. He closed his eyes and breathed deeply, in and out. After composing himself, he left the phone on his bed and deliberately turned his back on it. He returned to his *real family* in the kitchen and grinned. "So inquiring minds want to know, Mike. How hot was this chick your mom wanted to set you up with?"

The guys laughed, except for Mike. But then he too cracked a smile and filled them in on his mother's boring idea of the perfect Mrs. Mike McCauley. And all was right with the world again.

For now.

Chapter 5

ABBY FINISHED HER OUTLINE AND SIGHED. SHE SAVED her file, then took off her glasses and massaged the back of her neck. Flynn and Maddie had planned to spend the weekend together, and she didn't expect them back before tomorrow evening. Vanessa had surprised her by leaving for a weekend trip to Whidbey Island. So Abby had the whole house to herself.

What did she do? She spent her Saturday reorganizing her room…and turned the entire house upside down trying to find her missing book. When she'd driven herself crazy, she decided she might as well get some writing done.

A glance at the clock showed it had neared eight and she hadn't eaten yet. She was all alone, single, and had a free weekend in a bustling city full of things to do. Yet she had nothing better to do than type and hope she hadn't missed the latest *Dog Savant* rerun on TV. Considering she had no dog to speak of and no inclination to get one anytime soon, she knew her choice of programming was questionable.

"It's just you and me, Savvy. Now let's see you discipline the unruly." At the thought, Mutt came to mind. "What kind of a name is Mutt? Anything would be better than that." Truth be told, she had a secret soft spot for the rescued animal. Huge but not graceful, not cute in the slightest, Mutt had warm eyes. A sorry canine full of love and affection he wanted to dole on anyone not lucky enough to get out of his way.

A lot like his owner.

The warm and fuzzy thoughts continued to haunt her as she checked her bare kitchen cupboards for something to eat. She hadn't seen Brody since the morning after the party, and she still couldn't stop thinking about him. Nothing unusual about that. She'd developed a minor crush the day they'd met. But her imagination had never been so incredibly detailed before.

She'd swear she'd given him an honest-to-God hand job at the party, except he hadn't acted smug about it or made any rude comments. It wasn't like Brody not to say what he thought. Had she pleased him to that end, she had no doubt he'd have said something before now. Though relieved she simply had a dirty imagination, part of her wished she'd been bold enough for once in her life to take that step and demand what she wanted.

The one time she'd tried, timidly, to get Kevin to see her as a woman with unique desires and needs, he'd stomped all over her heart. Abby had learned a valuable lesson—trust had to be more than earned. Thoughts of that jerk put her in a mood, and she glared at the empty spot on the shelf where the bread should be.

It was Maddie's turn to buy, but she'd been distracted lately by her new boyfriend. Envy reared its ugly head, and Abby groaned, chastising herself for unkind thoughts. She genuinely liked Flynn, and she thought he and Maddie were perfect for each other. She just wished *she* could have that same kind of luck, to find a man to fit her needs.

She trudged back to the living room and readied to

veg out to stressed dogs and their idiot handlers when the doorbell rang. A glance through the sidelight made her heart rate leap.

Forcing herself to keep calm, she walked slowly to the door and opened it. "Speaking of idiotic handlers... Hey, Brody. To what do I owe the honor?"

He held out a large cardboard box and opened it, and the decadent scent of cheese, garlic, and basil caused her to groan.

"Let me in and I'll share." He wiggled his brows. Wearing simple jeans and a plain blue sweatshirt, he still managed to be the best-looking man she'd ever seen. Whereas she probably resembled a hag, wearing leggings and a tank under an old heavy flannel work shirt that hung to her knees. Her father's castoff that she'd happily kept for years.

"What's with the bribe?" she asked, still not letting him in despite the saliva pooling in her mouth.

"I'm bored. There's no one to play with."

She chuckled. "And?"

"Flynn's with Maddie. Cam is relaxing after being gone for so long, and Mike's still pissed that his mother tried to set him up with some single mom."

Oh, fodder to add to her mental McCauley gossip file. "Really?"

"Yeah. If you want details, you have to let me in." He peered over her shoulder and scowled. "You're not busy, are you?"

Startled at his abrupt change in mood, she asked, "Who crapped in your cornflakes?"

"What did you say?"

"Never mind." Her mother's favorite saying, one

that often had people giving Abby second looks. "It's just me and Savvy. Come on in."

He pushed past her and looked around. "Savvy?"

"Yeah, from that show, *Dog Savant*." She shut the door and turned to nod at the television. "Considering your lack of control over Mutt, I suggest you watch. Savvy can teach you things."

Brody raised a brow. "Oh?"

"Give me the pizza." She took the box from him and set it down on the coffee table. Then she gathered two bottles of root beer and some paper plates and napkins from the kitchen before returning to join him on the couch. She made sure to leave a respectable amount of space between them and tried her best to stop doing a mental victory dance because he'd come to her.

The man wanted company. Simple. She shouldn't be flattered or excited that he hadn't called one of his myriad women for a hookup.

Abby fixed herself a slice and sat back to eat. She'd taken a few bites before she realized he stared at her. "Problem?" she said around a mouthful of cheese. "Oh my God, this is good."

"Yeah. From my favorite place." He cleared his throat. "You look nice."

She glared at him. Once she finished chewing and swallowing, she asked in an overly polite voice, "Is that a joke?"

"No." He grabbed a piece of pizza for himself. "Just saying you look relaxed. Cute."

Frumpy. She sighed. "I was working, okay? I like to be comfortable when I wr—ah, work on the computer." His smirk warned her that her suspicions about her book were on the money. "You took it, didn't you?"

"I don't know what you mean." He bit into his pizza and turned to the television. "Oh, you know, that might work with Mutt."

On the TV, Miles "Savvy" Savant maneuvered another stubborn canine into obeying.

Abby wanted to put the two-finger move on Brody until he showed her his belly and submitted. Too bad it only worked on dogs. "Hey, I'm talking to you. You stole my book."

"Did I, *Ms. Abigail D. Chatterly?*"

She groaned.

"Damn, Abby. *Fireman's Kiss* was hot—no pun intended. So much for the shy little bookworm you pretend to be."

She leaned over to punch him in the arm when he leered at her. "And this is why I say nothing about what I do. People like you don't respect the work. You make it all so dirty."

"Hell no. I think it's great."

She opened her mouth to blast into him and checked herself. "You do?"

He nodded. "Damn straight. A woman not afraid of sex? Embrace it, I say."

"Ah, okay." Totally not how she'd ever thought she'd talk about her alter ego. "How did you know?"

"You kind of mentioned it at the party."

She'd recalled doing so, right before she'd taken him in hand… Purely fantasy. Or was it? "I, um, I didn't say or do anything weird, did I?" She scrutinized him for a telling reaction. He only shook his head and focused on the TV again.

"Nope. I love the extra cheese. Not a fan of meat on a pizza, I confess. Drives the guys nuts."

"Me too. About the cheese, I mean." She nibbled her pizza, thoroughly baffled by Brody. She'd fully expected some immature and snide remarks about her career. "Why are you not acting to type?"

He shrugged. "I am. Maybe your perception of me is all wrong."

"So you don't want to bend me over the couch and do me?"

He choked on his pizza. His eyes watered and he had to hurry to gulp down some soda before he could catch his breath. "Christ, warn me next time." He laughed and faced her, his gaze warm and flattering as it roamed her from head to toe. "Of course I want to bend you over. I'm a man."

She snorted.

"But I'm also a gentleman."

She took a sip of her drink.

"Case in point, I didn't tell anyone that you jerked me off at the party. Nor have I demanded you let me do the same to you."

She spit soda all over herself while he continued to speak calmly, as if talking about the weather.

"Instead, I saw you safely home, washed my cum-stained shirt in your washer, and slept head to toe with you, even leaving you in that sexy costume when by rights I should have been molesting you to at least a few orgasms."

She coughed, and he tapped her on the back until she glared at him to stop. "Y-you—that—no. No way."

"Yes way." His smile was too knowing to be anything but the truth.

She moaned. Her cheeks felt like they'd caught on fire. "Oh man."

"Yeah. You were so damn sexy in that getup. So pretty, even when you were flirting with Rick."

Eyes wide, she stared at him. "I didn't touch Rick, did I?"

"No. Not for his lack of trying." Brody huffed. "Bastard was all touchy-feely with you. I saved you."

"Oh?"

"Baby, I tried to get you not to touch me. But you had a tight grip." He squirmed on the couch, and she realized he sat a lot closer than she'd first thought. "And then I couldn't think when you started stroking me. I mean, you demanded I come over your hand. So bossy. It was really hot."

She couldn't help looking at his pants, stunned to see him fully aroused. And she knew what he felt like.

"I, I…" She didn't know what to say. Embarrassed yet turned on, she wanted to apologize. But she wasn't sorry. "You didn't tell anyone?"

"Nope. I wanted to talk to you about it."

She blinked at him. "Why?"

"Well damn, Abby. I want to do it again. But this time I get to do you first."

Brody watched her, thinking he'd never seen a woman do embarrassed with so much sweetness. The sexy woman next to him, the one who'd masturbated him, who wrote stories that had made his toes curl, seemed mortified that she'd given him pleasure.

"Look, if it makes you feel any better, I *wanted* to tell the guys. But I thought what we had was private. They're all over us to hook up. But you and I both know that if it goes to shit, where my relationships normally end up, then we make things awkward for everyone. Especially Maddie and Flynn."

She gaped at him.

"What?"

"You are being so incredibly mature about this."

"Thanks." He wryly admitted to himself he deserved her low opinion. Using humor and teasing as a shield to withstand her charms for so long had painted him in a less-than-flattering light.

"I just… You're always saying things and trying to hit on me. Like the way you do anything in a skirt—Flynn's words, not mine." She bit her lip, the tell that showed her discomfort. "I can't believe I did that to you."

"Believe it. I came so hard."

She refused to look at him, her gaze on the television.

"Abby, it's okay. I'm not mad you took advantage of me or anything."

She turned to him so fast she might have given herself whiplash. "*What?*"

"I mean, there I was at the party, trying to help Flynn out so he and Maddie could have fun. I was making sure no one messed with you."

"Great job." She wore sarcasm much better than embarrassment on her smart mouth.

"And then you unzipped me at the table. Granted, we were in private, but I was speechless."

"Yet I managed to get you off. Me and this little hand overpowered you."

The heat in her dark brown gaze had him unable to look away from her.

"Yeah." He cleared his throat. "You had a death grip

on my cock. And you were so incredibly hot in that dress. You called yourself a goddess."

"Apparently I had you under my spell."

"You did."

They stared at each other, and he would have given his left arm to know what she was thinking.

"So…what? You came by for round two?"

He bit back a grin. She sounded annoyed and turned on. He could see the bead of her nipple where the flannel parted to reveal her pink tank top. She had such wonderful curves. "Actually, I came bearing pizza so you would help me with our website."

She blinked. "Really?"

"Yeah, but since you brought up the party, I just wanted to clear the air."

"Clear the air."

"Yep. So can we get back to the show and the pizza? Because this dude is actually getting a Great Dane to behave. Wow." He deliberately turned away from her, determined to keep her on her toes. That way when he went in for the kiss, she'd be too off guard to deny him.

She made no more mention of the party, or that he still wanted her. After some silence, she made a few snide remarks about his weak handling with Mutt. When he answered by teasing her about handling her aggressive roommates, they settled into an easy banter. Abby slowly lost her wariness and relaxed into the couch.

He kept a healthy space between them while making sure he could reach out and touch her if he wanted. He stretched out his arm on the couch and ran his fingers through her soft hair. She wore it in a loose knot, much like the hairstyle she'd worn at the party.

"Hey. Hands off."

"What? My arms are long. I'm stretching out." He adjusted his legs too, watching her watch him out of the corner of his eye. He hid a grin, pleased she liked the look of him. He knew he had a great body and a face that kept the ladies interested. Unfortunately, he hadn't found a woman to retain his interest for more than a few romps in bed. Abby was…different.

He wanted to chalk up her attraction as forbidden fruit. His buddy's girlfriend's best friend. A mouthful, and a definite no-no when dipping his wick. Especially since she looked so much like Lea. Yet for all that he should have stayed far away from her, he couldn't deny she had a special spark that drew him. Funny, quiet, snarky, sexy. Her contrasts fascinated him, and their chemistry couldn't be denied. He'd never had that with anyone else, and it disturbed him that there were so many reasons not to even try with her. But he ignored them all.

"Did you hear what I said?" she asked, waspish and still so cute.

"What?"

"I said if you're firm with Mutt, he won't ignore you like he normally does."

"Firm, hmm?"

"Yes. Firm. Use discipline." She frowned. "You're totally thinking about something else right now, aren't you?"

"No." Damn straight. He was firm and wanted to show her some discipline. He swallowed. "So you watch a show about dog training yet have no dog. You want one?"

"Are you offering Mutt?"

He laughed at her horrified tone. "No. He's not bad once you look past the matted fur."

"And the big teeth, the poor manners, the smell…" Abby scrunched her nose. "So you're really keeping him?"

Brody shrugged. "Somebody needs to. I kept seeing him around the neighborhood. And then one day he was gone, and I heard someone had called animal control on him. So I went down there and found him. He looked so pathetic in that tiny cage."

"He might have been adopted."

Brody just remembered how sad and helpless the dog had seemed. Feelings he'd known all too well while growing up. Though he'd lived with the McCauleys, there had always been the possibility that Alan would yank his chain and keep him in that bleak world filled with hopeless unhappiness.

He shrugged, aware of Abby's keen gaze. "Yeah, well, about ten percent of the animals there don't get adopted out. I didn't want to take that chance."

She smiled. "You're a softie, aren't you? Big old brash Brody has a marshmallow for a heart."

"Yeah, whatever." He flushed, not liking that she saw him as weak. "So I took in a dog. Maybe I'm training him to fight."

"Yeah, right. The only thing that dog fights is the leash. Well, that and you." She nodded at the television. "If you paid attention to what this guy is saying, you could have Mutt trained in a few weeks, tops. You just need to be consistent."

"You know, that reminds me." The idea sprang on him suddenly, a way to be around Abby and integrate himself into her life a bit more. "I have to go to Anacortes to work on a custom house next week. I'll only be gone a few days, and—"

"No."

"And the guys are supposed to watch Mutt for me," he said over her protest. "But they don't love him like I do. They won't give him the attention or discipline he needs—what you said I should give him to train him. Why don't you do it for me? Prove me wrong."

She frowned. "I don't need to prove anything."

"You finished your last book, right?"

That wary expression crossed her face again. "How did you know that?"

"Baby—"

"Abby."

"—you were yelling at me just a few days ago. Remember? When Mutt got in the house? You said you only had five more days to meet your deadline. Halloween has come and gone. So are you working on something new?"

"Ah, yeah."

"But you're not in a rush, are you?"

"I'm trying to put together a proposal for my agent," she said slowly. "So not a rush. But I do have to work to earn a living."

"Right. Well, I do too. I have to go away for a few days on a job, and Flynn did say he'd watch Mutt. But if you'd watch him, I'd rather have you. I'll pay you."

"You already owe me for the website I'm designing for you," she just had to point out.

He thought for a moment. "Yeah, but how about I sweeten the pot?"

She turned to fully face him. "I'm listening."

"I pay you the standard fee for the website, not the family discount *I know* you were going to offer me and Flynn."

She snorted. "Great. What else?"

"I'll fix what Mutt messed up in the yard, plus I'll put in an irrigation system for you. Not something plumbers normally do. But for you, I'll pretend to be a landscaper."

"Hmm. But I'm renting this place. So technically you're really helping Beth and James. I can't take that landscaping when I leave."

He hated when she reminded him of how temporary her time here was. "So what do you want? Money? I could pay you to watch him."

"No." She clenched her hands on her leggings. "But..."

Curious, he dragged her hands into his, conscious of her much smaller size. Neanderthal that he was, he liked being stronger and bigger. And this close, touching her, his body reacted painfully. "But what?" he asked softly.

"Would you... Do you think you'd agree to answer some questions for me, for research?"

He paused, remembering the story he'd read. Her romance where her characters got up to all kinds of no good in the bedroom, the library, the park... He grinned. "Hell yeah. What do you want to know? Want to try out a few positions and see what clicks?"

She groaned. "This is why I never tell people what I write."

"Oh, come on. I'm only teasing. You know I want to 'bend you over the couch.' Ask me whatever you want. I'm an open book."

The intelligent gleam in her dark eyes only made her look sexier. "Really?"

"Sure."

"Because that's one of my problems, a lack of understanding when it comes to men."

He wanted badly to comment but kept his thoughts to himself. "Uh-huh."

"But I don't want you telling the others about this." She squirmed. "My writing is personal. Sure, it goes out to a mass audience, but when I'm writing, I'm close to the story. I don't want to be a punch line in one of your jokes. Especially since I like the McCauleys. I don't want you guys to think less of me if I ask certain things."

He didn't like the vulnerability he was seeing.

"Forget I asked." She shook her head. "It's stupid."

"No. Not at all." He tightened his hold over her hands. "You know, I read all of *Fireman's Kiss*."

"Oh boy."

"I liked it." A lot. He'd jerked off after reading it, imagining himself and Abby as the lead characters. "It was sexy and fun. The guy was a little douchie, but he got the girl, so I guess it was okay in the end."

"Douchie?" She didn't seem incensed, but interested. "How do you mean?"

"Well, most guys don't say *sweetheart* and *honeybear*."

"I was being facetious."

"Maybe." He shrugged. "I just thought he was bending over backward for her when a real dude would probably give her more crap about what she wanted. Flowers all the time? Candy? Talking all nice to her mom and pretty much bowing to her every whim? He was supposed to be this manly guy but he came across as a pussy. Just sayin'." Realizing he'd insulted her without meaning to, he tried to backpedal. "But I mean, it's just fiction. So it was good. I don't read that stuff, so what do I know?"

"No. I like that." She shifted closer, and he let her, wanting that intensity under him. "It's hard to get good feedback. I have a couple of beta readers who—"

"What?" The only beta he knew of was an aggressive fish.

"Test readers. They tell me what they think, but they always like everything I write. I need a broader perspective."

And he had his angle. "Well, I tell you what. You watch Mutt for me, and I'll not only help your garden, I'll fill you in on whatever questions you have. I'll give you a guy's perspective on life. Would that work?"

"That would be great." She lit up, her plump lips parted on a thanks.

"Well now, I'm not done." He pulled her into his lap and adjusted her legs around him. This close, she couldn't miss his arousal against the warmth between her legs.

"Brody," she breathed.

"I want you, and I think you want me." At her silence, he frowned. "I'm not imagining you like me, right?"

She blushed. "You're obnoxious, but handsome enough, I suppose. Happy now?"

"Not even close." He stroked her back. "I'll make you feel so good. This will stay between us, I swear. And hey, you can do anything you want with me and I'll just lie there and take it like a man."

She chuckled, losing that deer-in-the-headlights look.

"If you're concerned about being safe, I don't mess

around without protection. *Ever.* The guys think I'm a big player, but I'm not. Exactly. When I'm with a girl, I'm just with her. Period. And besides…" Was he really going to tell her? Looking into her big brown eyes, he had to. "You can't tell the guys this. But it's been six months since I've seen any action. I'm clean as a whistle."

She just stared at him. "Six months?"

He flushed. "You're distracting. Okay?"

When she just smiled but said nothing, he grew desperate.

"How about I show you how a guy acts when he's with a woman he wants? How he kisses her and touches her?" He stroked her back, petting away her tension.

"But—I—"

He kissed her and stunned her to silence. "Say yes, Abby. Let me thank you for the other night at the party. I came really hard. How about I show you what that felt like? Consider it research for your next book."

She bit her lip, and he felt a sinking sensation that rejection was sure to follow.

"Just between us," she said nervously.

"And no one else."

"And no one else," she whispered and kissed him.

Chapter 6

ABBY KNEW BETTER, BUT SHE WAS ONLY HUMAN. Having Brody so close had been playing havoc with her senses for the better part of the hour they'd been watching television. Or rather, he'd been watching TV, and she'd been watching him out of the corner of her eye.

The deal he'd offered was secondary to this—this passion between them. Knowing that she'd handled him so intimately at the party gave her a sense of weird pride. Abby Dunn had brought a man to orgasm. A sexy, powerful change of pace for a mousy woman more at home behind a computer than at a costume party.

And now, to have him under her, kissing him…

She controlled the pace, conscious of his large hands on her back, still stroking her while he moaned into her mouth. He tasted like root beer, and the sweetness encouraged her to sip deeper. She didn't feel caged or overwhelmed because his tender motions let her know in no uncertain terms that she could stop him at any time. And it made her like him that much more.

She shifted over him and he swore. "Shit. Easy. I don't want to go off in my jeans." He nuzzled her cheek. "So can I touch you? Kiss you all over?" He paused. "I have a condom in my pants."

"What if I say no?" She pulled back to stare into his light brown eyes.

"Then we stop." He sounded so firm. "You're in

charge, Abby. Of all of it. I think we both want to keep this uncomplicated. We have fun, we enjoy each other. No mess or fuss. And we agree to like each other after it's done. We're practically family as it is, with Maddie and Flynn in love."

"Agreed." Thank God he didn't want to complicate matters. No boyfriend-girlfriend talk. No need for a deeper meaning than that two people wanted to have sex. So different from her last mess of a relationship. This time, the pleasure came front and center. "So this is just sex."

"We'll call it research, hmm?"

She smiled, and he smiled back. So much delight and acceptance in his reaction. "Okay."

"For the record, I don't plan to kiss and tell. You can't either." He paused. "Unless you're telling your friends how big and manly I am."

She chuckled. "Well, now that I know it wasn't a dream, I can say with surety you're big."

"And manly. Don't forget the manly part. Because size doesn't matter if you don't know what you're doing."

Brody made their play both sensual and fun. Not dirty, but something to enjoy. "We'll see if you put your money where your mouth is."

He laughed. "Oh, I will." He leaned forward, then stopped. "Vanessa coming home anytime soon?"

"She's out of town until tomorrow night. It's just you and me."

He kissed her, and this time she felt the difference. He didn't hold back, and he'd taken control of the embrace. He pulled her closer as he kissed the breath from her. His tongue penetrated, and he was sweeping into her mouth with strokes she wanted to feel lower, where she ached between her legs.

He groaned and moved his hands, no longer holding her back. Instead he cupped her breasts.

"Oh yeah," she whispered and nibbled his jaw. "That feels good."

"I'm just gonna say it. I have a thing for your breasts. You're so full here." He held one and ran his thumb over the extended nipple. "Fuck. I need to kiss you." He took the flannel shirt off her and lifted the tank so that she wore only a serviceable cotton bra. No lace for boring Abby.

But he wouldn't let her be embarrassed. "Hell. I might come in my jeans after all." He put his mouth over her bra and teethed her nipple. The pleasure hit the core of her, and she rocked over his impressive erection, needing more.

Brody alternated his mouth over both breasts.

Abby wanted to feel him against her bare skin, so she reached behind her to remove her bra.

Brody latched on to her hands and held them pinned at the small of her back. "That's better."

Wow. Her lust skyrocketed. Being restrained was one of her hot buttons. And he did it so effortlessly. She whispered his name and kissed him again.

He only had to use one hand to keep her wrists in place. With the other, he unfastened her bra. And by the sound of his heavy breathing, he liked holding her as much as she liked being held.

"You're pretty good at that," Abby praised.

"I'm a plumber. We're good with our hands."

Her laugh turned into a moan when the bra fell from

her shoulders, exposing her. A moment of uncertainty struck. He said he liked her breasts, but were they too big? Did she look more like a cow than a woman? Would he—

His gaze darkened, and then he was kissing her, taking her nipple between his lips and sucking her close to orgasm.

She rocked over him, no longer able to worry about anything, lost in the moment. Half-naked on top of a sexy man she'd been lusting after for months. Before the party, she never would have imagined herself the type to take this kind of risk. Things with Brody could turn badly for her, but none of that mattered while he manipulated her into a sighing ball of *yes*.

"That's it. I want you to come for me," he whispered as he toyed with her other breast. He delved under the waistband of her leggings and between her legs. "You're so wet."

She gasped when he slid his finger inside her.

"Tight. Oh, baby, I need inside you," he crooned and laid her back on the couch, where he pulled the dangling bra off her.

Brody shrugged out of his sweatshirt and jeans while she watched. He took a condom out of his pocket and shoved down his boxer briefs to roll it over himself.

"See? I'm huge," he teased, but the hungry look in his eyes warned her he meant business. He might appear all fun and games, but Brody was all man. He removed the rest of his clothing.

She put her hands to her leggings, and he stopped her. "No. Let me."

She scooted up off her butt while he rolled the

leggings off her. Then he pulled down her panties. Plain white and without any holes, fortunately. Before she could protest that she wanted to see him again, to hold that cock in her hands, he shoved her legs wider and put his head between them.

"Brody...*oh*."

He put his entire mouth over her clit and sucked, and she swore she saw stars.

Abby keened as her world tilted on end and she came over his mouth. The rapture took her into another state, the climax sudden yet so fulfilling.

He continued to kiss her until she came down, and she realized her fingers were caught in his hair. Holding him to her without any chance he might escape.

She tried to move her hands, but he held her there, kissing her still. "That's it. You liked that, hmm?"

"Are you kidding me?" she managed in a croak.

He lifted his head and grinned. His lips shiny with her arousal, he licked them deliberately. "You taste so sweet." He slowly moved from between her legs and rose over her. "If I don't get inside you in like two seconds, I might die."

She found herself laughing.

"You okay with this?" he asked, and despite the levity between them, she knew he meant that she called the shots.

Warmth filled her. "Yeah. Let's see if you're good for more than just show."

He gave her a mean grin. "You up for a rough ride?"

"Are you?" she challenged back.

He lost his smile as he nudged her thighs wider and put the tip of himself at her entrance. Even though she had more than enough lubrication, the tight fit didn't surprise her. She'd gone a long time without a man, and lately her toys couldn't compare to the idea of fantasy Brody, so she'd gone without even touching herself.

He moaned her name and kissed her as he surged deeper.

She tasted herself on his lips, and she wanted more. She needed to see him come apart in her arms, to know *she* made him lose control. That a woman like Abby could bring Brody to climax. She wasn't freakish or clingy or bad at sex. *She* wasn't the one who'd had the issues—or so she desperately needed to confirm.

Lost in Brody's touch before, she hadn't thought about her pleasure. She'd experienced it. But now, with him inside her, he'd learn the truth about her. She was slutty and fat and bad at sex with a partner.

Except he didn't seem repulsed or turned off.

"God, don't hate me if I don't last." He started moving, faster, deeper, and she loved it.

"That feels good. You're so big," she gasped then groaned when he hit a spot inside her that flipped the switch on her excitement all over again.

"Yeah. That's it. Hold me tight. Fuck, I wish I was coming inside you. No stupid condom."

The raw words pushed her into a frenzy, especially when he added more graphic detail about what he wanted to do to her. She nipped his shoulder and scored his back with her nails. "Harder, Brody," she encouraged as he rammed with more force. "I want to feel you so deep."

He kissed her as he speared her with that impossibly large shaft, again and again, until she lost herself in him once more. He pulled back to watch her as he continued to thrust. "So sexy. God, come around me. Let me see you."

She cried out as she came and clenched her heels into his ass.

"*Abby*." Brody slammed one final time and stopped, shuddering while he spilled inside her.

After a moment, the realization of what they'd done hit her, and she stared up at him to see him watching her. It had been amazing. And he'd come, but had the intensity been all in her mind?

"Well?" he asked.

"What?"

He blew out a breath. "Hello. I want some compliments. Tell me how good I am. How big. Remember? Manly. I like hearing that." When she said nothing, he cringed. "You're starting to give me a complex."

To her amazement, he still felt hard inside her. "You're still hard?"

"I can't help it. Give me a few minutes and I'll go again. I swear."

She grinned, feeling better than she had in a long, long time. "You were very manly, Brody. Hard, thick, and *manly*. Okay now?"

He nodded and fixated on her breasts. "I'm not dreaming, right?" He leaned down and sucked a nipple into his mouth, then let it go with a small tickle from his tongue. "Totally not dreaming. Man."

"I came twice."

He met her gaze with a satisfied one of his own. "Now you *have* to tell me I'm the man."

She snorted. "You're the man inside me, that's for sure."

"Technically, I'm winning. I made you come twice.

You only made me come once. And no, Halloween doesn't count. Different night."

She'd never had so much fun teasing before, and not while naked. "Yes, but that's because I have staying power. You're a guy. One shot, you're done."

"Says who?" He rotated his pelvis and nudged her again.

"Really?" Interesting. She hadn't realized a guy could go again without waiting at least half an hour to get hard once more.

"See, this is where your research is shoddy." Brody started sliding in and out of her again.

"What about the condom?" she asked.

"I, ah, might have another in my jeans."

"Well? Go get it on."

He blinked at her, then grinned. Before she knew it, he'd left and returned wearing new protection. "See? Sometimes being quick isn't so bad. You can write that down later." He gently tugged her from the couch onto the floor. "Now we have more room. How do you feel about an encore?"

Abby spent all of Sunday in a daze. Brody had made love to her twice. She'd had three—*three*—orgasms in the span of one night. A new record. And then they'd spent another hour dithering back and forth on her arrangements to watch Mutt. He added a few conditions since he'd performed so well sexually. She'd been too satisfied to deny him.

What made the entire evening so surreal was that he'd looked at her tenderly and kissed her good-bye with a promise, once again, to keep their new "deal" between them.

She had exactly what she wanted. No-strings sex. Validation that she did not in fact suck—only in a good way—in bed. Brody hadn't been demeaning or cruel, the opposite actually. A man she trusted, who turned her on, had wanted her. She felt gooey and warm inside.

And then the stupid emotional basket case inside her wondered *why* he hadn't asked for more. Why didn't he want to turn their agreed-upon casual sex into a relationship? Maybe if she'd been better or more exciting he—*Stop it, Abby!*

She hated overthinking things. One of her biggest flaws. She'd had incredible sex with a guy she liked. No need to turn herself into Mrs. Abby Singer. Especially since she still didn't know all that much about Brody, truth to tell. Then again, considering he'd wheedled her into agreeing to spend the next week at his place to better care for Mutt, she might be able to learn more about the tricky con man.

After making sure she'd picked up and cleaned the place to Vanessa's satisfaction, she made herself a salad and sat down to dinner. On cue, Vanessa arrived at six and gave Abby a thumbs-up on the housekeeping.

"Ah. It is so nice to come home to a clean, organized house. I love Jeanine, but she's a slob."

"So the trip to Whidbey went well?"

"I needed it." Vanessa let out a breath. "Lately work has been a bitch. I'm always playing the bad guy and I'm tired of it. Jeanine lives in Langley, where the pace is so much slower. Plus, I got to ride the ferry, which I love."

A relaxed Vanessa meant a relaxed household. Just one more plus to add to Abby's stellar weekend.

Vanessa stole a carrot off Abby's plate. "Anyway, I lazed around."

"Meaning you ran five miles each day and only did a few hundred and not a thousand crunches."

Vanessa grinned and swallowed her food. "Pretty much." She tugged her ponytail. "I also read a book and watched the ocean. Saw some orcas on my way to the island. So cool."

"I'm glad you had a good time. I had fun too." *Did I.* "I organized my room and watched my favorite shows without bossy people telling me to turn the channel."

Vanessa snorted. "That dog show, right? Seriously? When you get that training to work on people, then I'll be interested."

"Positive reward for good behavior. It's basic behavior modification." She paused. "I'll be using it next week when I take care of Brody's dog."

"You're bringing that creature *here* after what he did to the kitchen?"

Vanessa had a serious grudge against dirt.

"Not exactly. I'm going to spend next week at Brody's place while he's in Anacortes on a job. I'll get to keep Mutt in his own environment, train him, and have extra alone time to write."

Vanessa just stared at her.

"What?"

"What's he paying you to do this? Sexual favors?"

"Get your head out of the gutter." She did her best to not blush. Because if sexual favor was the currency, he'd already given her a rather sizable down payment. "Actually, he's going to pay me more than agreed upon for the web design I'm already doing, plus he's adding an irrigation system to the backyard."

"Hmm. Garden favors." Vanessa nodded. "Not bad.

But I'm disappointed you didn't hold out for sex. From what I hear, he's quite the stud." Vanessa snickered. "And man, he does look good without a shirt. I'm not into blonds, but even I have to admit that seeing him half naked after you two slept together—"

"We didn't sleep together. I mean, technically, we did, but—"

"—was hot. The man has muscle. If you think about it, after Mike, he's probably right up there with Cameron."

"Cam?"

Vanessa shrugged. Too casually. "He doesn't always show it, but he works out."

"And how would you know?" Fascinating.

"I've seen him at the gym a few times. At first, he annoyed the crap out of me. He thinks he's always right."

"Wow. Who does that sound like?"

Vanessa ignored her. "But he's a smart guy who happens to be pretty good-looking. He comes from a great family and makes a lucrative living."

"Sounds right up your alley."

To Abby's astonishment, Vanessa turned pink. "Yeah, whatever. He's seeing some woman out East. I'm not interested in dating anyway."

"Uh-huh."

Vanessa glared. "I'm not. I'm too busy making men cry, haven't you heard?"

Abby grinned. "You make men cry, I'm about to make a dog cry. No wonder we get along so well."

"Funny girl. So where's my cousin? Still out doing the plumber?"

"Where else would she be?"

"You know, at first I wasn't sure about Flynn. But I really like him for Maddie."

Abby nodded. "She's a lot more stable, and he's great with her."

"As high strung as that side of the family is, that's saying something."

Abby studied her. "You never talk much about your parents." What Vanessa had said couldn't be considered good. "Is it true they're emotionless geniuses, a step away from the walking dead in that they don't eat brains, they just use them?"

"Yep. Maddie got that one right."

"Actually, *you* said that after the last time you talked to them. An off-the-cuff comment."

"Big ears."

"I see and hear all." She nodded. "So have you talked to them lately? Are you going to be here for Thanksgiving or not?"

"I'm staying here. Aunt Michelle is coming for the holiday. And to check out Flynn, but don't tell Maddie I said that."

Abby nodded. "Good. I'd planned to stick around but Teresa wants me to meet her new husband."

"Your sister... Teresa's the oldest, right? Four kids, husband number three?"

"Not to be confused with Meg, the middle girl, and the one none of us actually like. She even annoys my mom, though my mom will never admit it." She sighed, imagining having to deal with Meg *and* her annoying husband at Thanksgiving. "Two kids, still with husband number one, thinks the sun rises and sets on her. None of us are sure how it happened, but she's truly a brat. I can't stand her."

"Oh, right. But hey, at least you like the rest of them. My parents are like automatons." Which explained why Vanessa was the way she was. "Good grades and proper behavior gets you a pat on the head and money for college. Then you get the hell out. No more, no less. I swear, it's like they're not human. I might love them, but I don't like them."

"I love my folks."

"Yeah. So do they know that you write dirty books for a living?"

"Not dirty." Abby scowled. "Erotic romance."

"Call it *Dunn's Guide to Foreplay*. My point is you might love them, but you don't trust them enough to tell them the truth."

"I hate your honesty."

"The bane of my existence. I tell the truth and I'm hated for it." Vanessa let out a put-upon sigh.

"Yet how often do you tell *yourself* the truth?" Abby asked and smacked Vanessa's hand when she tried to steal another carrot. "Because you say you don't want a boyfriend, but lately I'm getting the impression you do."

Vanessa blinked. "I, well... Maybe I am feeling a little lonely. Maddie has Flynn. You have Mutt."

"I'm not dating a dog." She crossed her arms over her chest, miffed.

"Francie and Jeanine at work are all cozied up with guys. And Robin and Kim are so gooey in love it's gross." Robin and Kim were Maddie's designer friends who fit each other like a lock and key. Both women who liked to laugh and worked well with Maddie.

"Yeah, but they're so cute. And they seem so happy together. I want that kind of love."

"I have a bad feeling that stuff only exists in your books. Our friends are the exception." Vanessa sounded down and out of sorts.

"Are you okay?" Come to think of it, Vanessa's enthusiasm when Abby had finished her book, and now this talk about relationships and love, were out of character for the straight-shooting, confident woman.

"I'm fine. Just growing maudlin." Vanessa cracked a true smile. "Do you like that? Maudlin? I picked that up from your last porn book."

Abby groaned. "Would you stop that?" She couldn't help a laugh when Vanessa sang *boom chicka bow bow*. "You're such a pain."

"And that's why you love me."

"I guess." Abby made a face. "Because it sure isn't your love affair with fitness. So in advance, *no* to running with you this week. I'll be at Brody's watching his hellhound."

"Fine. Deny your body's need to ward off excess caffeine and the donuts you don't think we know about."

"How did you find those?"

"I know everything about this house." Vanessa grinned, the spark of joy back in her blue eyes. "While you're watching after Mutt, try to come up with a better name for him, would you? Now let's go to Maddie's room and find that stupid frog of hers. I've been dressing him in her underwear. It's a hoot." The little googly eyed frog had been one of the first gifts Flynn had bought her, and Maddie kept it on her bed as a reminder of her man.

"I *knew* that was you. She keeps blaming Flynn for it."

"I know. That's why I'm going to find it, then dress the thing in Flynn's socks. She won't know he didn't mess with the frog before they left."

"Nice. How'd you get his socks?"

"He left them in the dryer last time. That'll teach him."

Abby grinned, pleased to join in the conspiracy. If it helped Vanessa cope with her surprising loneliness, Abby would even dress the thing in her own bra.

After they'd disgraced the plush frog, Abby said, "You know, I might get lonely next week all by myself. And if his place stinks of man funk, I'll probably bring Mutt back here."

Vanessa shrugged. "Fine. But he's your responsibility. Mutt's dog piles will be handled by you and you alone."

Abby nodded, but she had every intention of forcing her roommate to help walk the monstrous canine. Abby might be little, but she was devious. And Vanessa had made one crack too many about her books, anyway.

Later that night, before she turned in, her cell phone rang.

"Hello?" She didn't recognize the number.

"Abby? Brody here." Pause. "What are you wearing?"

"Really?"

He laughed. "Just kidding. I told Mutt and Seth, my neighbor, that you're coming."

"I hope Mutt was okay with it," she teased.

Brody answered in a serious voice, "He'll be fine. He likes you, remember."

"I was kid—never mind. The food and instructions are all laid out?"

"Yep. I even made my bed for you. The place, well, it's a work in progress. But I just put in a new water heater and my bedroom is pretty nice. You, um, might have to sleep with Mutt. He likes the bed."

Share the bed with a dog? No. "I'll handle it."

"Right."

Silence settled between them.

"So, Abby."

"Yes?"

"I was thinking that you probably need to do more research. I mean, you're working on a book right now. Your proposal, you called it."

"The better question is, when am I *not* working on a book?"

"Right." He sounded relieved. Odd. "So I was thinking, maybe you need more information than I gave you last night. You know, there's a lot we didn't get to. Just not enough time in one night to hit all the high points."

She couldn't contain the excitement that threatened to spill free, so she gave herself a moment. "Well, I guess not. But I could always ask someone else if you feel obligated—"

"*No*. No, not at all. I mean, we're friends. You can trust me. Hell, you can ask me to do anything and I'll be all for it. Tie me up, tie *you* up, toys, videos. You name it, I'm your guy. Not *Rick*."

"Who said anything about Rick?" He seemed to have some kind of fixation on his friend.

"No one. Forget I mentioned him. So can we get together again when I'm back, maybe?"

After last night when he'd played her like an instrument, she had no qualms about admitting to herself she wanted another go at him. And he'd been the one to suggest alternative fun. So if she agreed, she wouldn't sound like a freak. *"You are one strange, perverted woman. I expected better from you."* She could hear Kevin's disgust clearly.

"Abby?"

"What? Oh, yes. Definitely. I was thinking of a new angle for my next book." She swallowed. "Kind of a kink thing. Like, D/s stuff."

"What?"

Her cheeks felt hot. "You know. Domination and submission."

The pregnant pause was nearly her undoing. She wanted to immediately retract her words. She'd gone too far, taken for granted that when he said *anything*, he meant it.

His low chuckle relieved her. "Oh yeah. That I can definitely help you with. Sorry. Before I thought you said C-S. And I had no idea what that meant. But the D/s stuff? I'm your man."

"Ha ha."

"I might put in some overtime so I can get back sooner. That kind of research is going to take some thorough work, you know?"

"Brody."

"Abby." He laughed. "Sleep in my bed while I'm gone and think about what we'll be doing when I get back."

"You're such a guy."

"That's me. A guy. And I know just what to do with a sweet thing like you."

Before he could hang up, she had to know one thing. "Brody? There's something I wanted to say."

"Yeah?"

"Well, if we're going to do this—you know, have fun together…"

"Have *fun*. That's one way of putting it."

"Then I have to know I can trust you. It's just you and me. No one else. I don't mean forever," she said quickly. "Nothing permanent or anything. But I mean, while we're hanging out, I—"

"I know exactly what you mean. And I agree. It's just you and me. Same goes. I'm the only one in your bed. For now," he tacked on.

But the message was clear. "Good."

"Not yet, but it's gonna be. I've been thinking about it. We should definitely keep this between us. The guys have a way of putting their noses where they don't belong."

"You have met Maddie and Vanessa, right?" At his laugh, she added, "No argument from me on being quiet."

"Perfect. Now be nice to my dog, or I'll know."

She snorted. "Get lost, Singer. Go play with your pipes."

"I'll be doing just that until I come back, day *and* night. Man, if you knew half of what I plan on doing to you… I'm gonna—"

She disconnected before he could say anymore. But she fell asleep with a big grin on her face. The week couldn't go by quickly enough.

Chapter 7

ABBY HADN'T THOUGHT TIME COULD STAND STILL, but just two days into her indentured servitude to a dog had her rethinking her agreement. She glared at Demon Dog, who stood in the kitchen with bits of paper in his mouth while he whined.

Next to her, newly six-year-old Colin McCauley stared wide-eyed at the scene of the crime. Her new magazine, her beloved *Entertainment Weekly*, lay in shreds on the floor. The culprit kept backing up, pretending not to be at fault.

She had twenty minutes to get Colin to soccer practice. A favor for Flynn she now regretted, because she had to rush into the ungodly traffic. It seemed like every time she turned around, they closed another street for repair.

"I think he ate the magazine." Colin, a miniature version of Mike, just stared at Mutt.

"I know." Concerned at the way he was looking at Mutt, she added, "But he'd never hurt you, sweetie. You don't need to be scared—"

"That's *awesome*!" Colin grinned, and she saw the gap in his front teeth. "I wonder if the paper will be in his poop. Will he poop it out, Abby?"

"I guess." *Brody, you owe me big for this.* "Come on. We need to go or you're going to be really late." She turned back to Mutt. "And *you*… Stay here. You're in big trouble when I get back, buddy."

He stared at her with sad eyes under bushy brows. Yeah right. Like she believed the dog possessed an ounce of remorse in his goliath body. She knew she couldn't discipline him later because too much time would have passed. With any luck, he'd destroy something else before she got back.

Colin grabbed his soccer ball and water and they left in her car. For once, the weather had been a mild cold and dry. Still, Seattle commuters might have been driving in snow for all their craziness. She turned down several side streets to avoid the busier roads and made a wrong turn.

At the rate she was going, it should have come as no surprise when she drove over something bumpy in the road and her car responded by lurching, then limping along. The tires didn't seem right. "Oh, hell."

"You said *hell*," Colin helpfully pointed out from the backseat.

"Heck. I meant heck." She swore to herself as she pulled to the side of the road and managed to turn off onto another street. The car made terrible noises and she knew she had at least one flat. *Damn it*.

She had no idea where she'd turned off because she hadn't been paying attention, and she needed help. Abby didn't do cars. She made a mental run-down. Flynn was busy with a project for his parents. Maddie would be useless with a tire. Mike was at work, hence the need for someone else to watch Colin, and Brody continued to work an hour and a half away. Vanessa, she had no doubt, could change it for her, but Vanessa had been working her tail off lately, and Abby didn't want to interrupt and add to her stress.

She sat there and gripped the steering wheel, not happy at all.

"Are we here?" Colin asked with cheer.

The sky remained light enough that they had some time before it turned dark and spooky and made it that much harder to fix the tire.

Abby sighed. "Not yet. Just sit tight, okay?"

"Sure."

She mentally thanked Mike for having such an easy-going kid. Abby left the car, grateful to see that the road they sat on didn't look too busy or rundown. She thought she recognized one side street's name from the online map she'd pulled up before leaving. By her calculations, she couldn't be too far from soccer practice.

She rounded the car and took a hard look at her tires. The back two looked fine, as did the front driver-side tire. But the front passenger one had issues. She could see a metallic spike sticking out of it. Not good.

"Shoot." She retrieved the phone from her pocket and peered down at it, wondering who to call. She'd canceled her auto service months ago, trying to whittle down her bills to the bare necessities. Cable—yes. Auto assistance—no. She could almost hear her car laughing at her. *Well who's laughing now, Abby?* Stupid Harry the Hyundai. It just figured the vehicle would be problematic…and male.

As she dithered about what to do, a sleek black muscle car purred to a stop behind her. Immediately envisioning a gang, a serial killer, or a pack of rapists bent on taking her down and selling Colin into slavery, she stepped back and tried to puff up her five foot three frame. She typed into her cell phone 9-1- and paused.

The car looked shiny and clean, but she couldn't make out much through the dark windshield.

"Who's that, Abby?" Colin yelled through the car window and turned in his seat.

"Just wait," she said back.

The car door opened and out walked a…woman.

Immediately, everything in Abby relaxed. Yet as the woman drew closer, Abby tensed again, not sure if she should be more scared now than before. The woman bearing down on her had to be six feet tall, because she dwarfed Abby. Long, ash-blond hair pulled back in a ponytail showed off angular features that couldn't be called pretty. Interesting, but not classically beautiful. The woman had cold gray eyes, an eyebrow ring, and a nose piercing, and she wore a white sleeveless tank in the cold weather that exposed sleeves of tattoos.

Colorful ink covered her arms from shoulders to forearms. Her tank top put Abby in mind of the old-fashioned, non-PC wifebeaters. Dark coverall pants, black combat boots, and rough-looking hands ending in short, ragged nails completed the stranger's ensemble.

The woman glared at her.

Holy Moses. She's going to kick my ass, rip off my arms, and use them for batting practice. Must save the boy before she ties him to her bumper and drives away.

"You need help?" the woman asked in a smooth, husky voice, which contrasted with her rough and tough appearance. Abby also caught a peek at white, even teeth.

Anyone who used a toothbrush regularly couldn't be all bad, could she? Abby nodded, unable to speak.

The woman walked around the car, assessing it. She glanced at Colin waving madly in the backseat, then looked back at Abby and offered a surprisingly non-threatening grin. "Cute kid."

"He's not mine. I'm babysitting and we're late to soccer practice." *Ramble much?* Abby took a deep breath and let it out slowly. "Sorry. I'm freaked because my tire is blown and I'm not good at mechanics."

"Lucky for you I was heading back from our parts dealer." Body parts? The woman put a hand in her back pocket and retrieved *a knife—*

Abby shook off her delirium and accepted a *business card* with a picture of a car on it.

"Name's Del. My dad and I run an automotive place together. It's down off Rainier Avenue."

Abby thanked her good fortune. "You're a mechanic?"

"Yep." Del moved around Abby and crouched to stare at her tire. "I think you're going to have to replace it. A patch won't cover that damage."

"Right." What were the odds she'd have a problem and a mechanic would zoom in to save the day? A female one at that? It was like her muse had decided to give her an early Christmas.

"You have a spare?"

"Oh, yes." Abby moved to the back of the car and released the trunk. Fascinated, she watched Del grab her jack and spare and return to the flat. Then Del walked over to her own car, retrieved a weird-looking wrench, for the lug nuts, Abby supposed, and returned.

"Can you get the kid out? Have him stand with you."

Colin got out and stood with Abby, his gaze fixed on Del. "Oh wow. Her arms are all colored!"

"Colin, this is Del. She's a mechanic, and she's been nice enough to help us with the tire."

"Hi." Colin held out his hand.

Nonplussed, the woman looked from him to Abby and slowly rose from her crouch by the tire to take it. "Hi. I'm Del."

"Del what?"

Del continued to shake his hand, the big intimidating woman and the small smiling child. They made quite a picture. "My name is Del Webster."

"I'm Colin McCauley. I just turned six, and I lost a tooth before Brian Daugherty did." He beamed.

Del laughed and gently disengaged her hand. "Nice. When I was four, I accidently broke my brother's front tooth with a wrench. I got in big trouble for that. My brother wasn't happy at all."

Colin nodded, his eyes wide. "Wow."

"Yeah. My dad was so mad, he took away my play tool set. I cried for a week."

"Always knew you wanted to be a mechanic, huh?" Abby asked.

Del's eyes lost some of their warmth when she looked back at Abby, even as she answered, "Yeah. Anything to be with my dad."

"Me too." Colin moved closer when Del looked into the car at the dash.

"It's in park," Abby said, realizing why she checked. A safety-conscious woman. Good.

"Just checking. Don't want to run anything over if we can help it."

"Yep. I'm just like my dad too," Colin was saying as Del jacked up the car. "I'm going to build stuff. I have my own hammer. And maybe I'll make a lot of money, like Uncle Cam. And I'll know how to fix pipes too, like Uncle Flynn and Ubie. And I'll—"

"Hold on, Colin. Let's not distract Del while she's working." Abby prayed the poor woman wouldn't up and leave. Colin had cuteness down to a science, but he also had a tendency to run at the mouth. That could be especially wearing after a full day's work.

"I don't mind," Del said as she started on the lug nuts. She muscled them off with an easy show of strength.

"Wow. She's strong. But her muscles aren't as big as Daddy's."

"Heck, Colin. Charles Atlas isn't as big as your daddy," Abby murmured.

"Who?"

Del grunted. "You should see my dad and brother. Huge guys. I'm considered the little one."

"They must be giants."

"They are." Del grinned at Colin over her shoulder before removing the tire, replacing it with the spare, and putting the lug nuts back on.

"I hope you know I'm watching everything you're doing," Abby said. "So next time I'll be able to change it myself."

"That's good, but those nuts were on tight. Not saying you couldn't handle it, but well…"

Abby sighed. "I know. I'm not an imposing figure. Short and mealy."

"Mealy? Like a meal? Because I'm hungry." Colin rubbed his belly. "Uncle Flynn forgot to give me a snack."

"Why didn't you tell me that at the house?" Abby asked.

"Because Mutt was eating the magazine and I forgot."

He turned his attention back to Del. "Mutt is Ubie's dog, and he's big. He eats everything. Even squirrels. And he's gonna poop out paper. Isn't that awesome?"

Squirrels? Brody hadn't mentioned that.

"Cool dog." Del lowered the car to the ground and removed the jack. She tightened the lug nuts, showing the power apparent in her toned arms.

"Oh wow. Is that a dragon?" Colin asked and moved forward. He touched Del's forearm before Abby could stop him.

"Colin."

"He's okay," Del said with a softness Abby wouldn't have credited her. "Yeah. I got this when I turned twenty-two." In a lower voice, she confessed, "My brother did it for me. He's an artist. You should see his arms."

"Oh, can I?" Then he turned to Abby. "Can I get a tattoo? Please?"

"Ah, well…"

Del flicked him on the nose. "No can do, sport. You have to be at least eighteen to get tats. And only if your mom and dad say it's okay."

"My mom's in heaven."

Del blinked at him and glanced at Abby, who nodded. "Oh, well. Mine too. Maybe they're playing together right now."

Colin's sweet smile gave Abby butterflies. When she spent time with him, she imagined what it must be like to have a child. To her bemusement, she found the thought didn't freak her out the way it had when she'd been with Kevin. An uninvited image of Brody came to mind, with his sly grin and bright gold eyes. She wondered if he ever thought about kids, because he loved Colin like crazy.

"Yeah. They could play rummy." Colin nodded. "My dad said Mommy liked that a lot."

Del grinned and held up a hand. "High five?"

Colin slapped it hard, and Del pretended it hurt. "You're a pretty strong guy yourself."

"Oh, did I hurt you?" Typical Colin. He sounded proud, not sorry, to show off his power. Then he blinked. "I didn't really, did I?" He leaned closer to look at her palm.

"Nah, just kidding you." Del mussed his hair as she stood. "Guess you need to get to soccer, huh?"

Distracted, Abby had forgotten all about soccer. "Oh, crap."

"You said *crap*," Colin pointed out.

"Crap isn't a bad word," she said absently. "Thank Del and get in the car, you monster."

"Thanks, Del." Colin tugged Del by the arm, and she lowered to hear him better. Then he shocked her by planting a kiss on her cheek. "Bye." He darted into the car.

Del rubbed her cheek. "Bye."

Abby smiled. "He's a McCauley. They're all like that."

"Damn."

"Don't let him hear you. That's a 'bad word.'" They shared a smile. "Seriously though, can I pay you something for your time? You really helped us out."

"No, no. Just doing my civic duty. You ever need auto help, give us a buzz." Del turned to her car, but before she got in, she snickered. "Gotta say it. You looked pretty damn pathetic just staring at your tire. Glad I could help."

"Well, thanks again." Abby waved. She entered the car, started it up, and managed to drive Colin to practice. Del must have been going the same way, because she followed, and then, in a burst of speed, passed them when they turned into the complex.

What an astonishing woman. In some ways she reminded Abby of Vanessa. That air of competence and disregard for how the world would see her. But what gave a woman so many rough edges? What pushed her to get so many tattoos and piercings, or to work in a male-dominated environment? Del had a hardness to her at odds with that softness she'd shown when talking to Colin. Depth of character. The perfect foil for Abby's newly imagined hardheaded hero.

She mused on story ideas while Colin played indoor soccer for half an hour. Flynn showed up at the end of practice in his work clothes.

"Hey, Abby."

"Flynn. You didn't have to come out here. I could have taken Colin home."

"No problem. I really appreciated you helping me out. First Brody, now me…" he trailed off, his gaze focused on Colin. "So how's it going with Mutt?"

She snorted. "About how you'd think. That dog is stubborn. He thinks he owns Brody's house."

"House? You're being nicer than I thought you would."

"House, pit, scrap heap, haunted horror. Take your pick."

"Yeah. All that."

They laughed.

"Actually, his bedroom is nice."

Flynn turned to her and wiggled his brows, and she made sure to keep to the script. No one but her and Brody needed to know they'd been intimate.

"Stop. You know what I mean. Brody and I are just friends. That's it."

"Uh-huh." His knowing grin aggravated her.

"Vanessa's right. You are annoying."

"Consider the source."

She swallowed a laugh. "So anyway, I've been thinking about your website and I—"

He held up a hand. "Stop. I am not dealing with your freaky technological issues. You want me to unclog your sink or install new fixtures? Call me. The computer shit is Brody's bag."

"It's not shit. It's my job."

"Oh really? Because Maddie told me you're an amazing *writer*." He gave her a superior grin.

"She has a big mouth."

"That she does."

Abby sighed. "You're not telling people about me, are you?"

"Nah. That might imply I read, and I like to be underwhelming. I'm all like I don't know what books are, focused on nothing more than being beautiful on the job. Takes women off their guard."

She huffed. "So you're keeping the field open while you play with my best friend's heart?"

"What?" He blinked. "Hell no. Where do you get your ideas?"

"Creative license. Writer." She pointed to herself.

"Ah. Yeah, well. I was talking about our female clients." He grinned, oozing charisma. "The prettier I am, the more business I bring McSons."

"It's like I want to kick you in the knee, but then you start smiling and I forget myself."

"Right. See? A gift."

She laughed at him. "Stop being a ho and collect your nephew. And by the way, he told me you forgot to feed him."

"Shit."

"That's a bad word," Colin said from behind him.

"Damn."

"So's that."

Abby refused to help him out. "He's right. Colin, I think you should tell your dad about Uncle Flynn's bad words. Maybe he needs a time-out."

Colin cocked his head, that devious gleam in his eyes all Brody.

Apparently Flynn thought the same, because he groaned. "You look exactly like Ubie when he's trying to con me into doing favors for him."

"Learn anything new, Colin?" she asked.

"Not since Ubie left. When's he coming back? I want him to come to my party."

"Wasn't your birthday on Monday?" Flynn asked. "Didn't you have cake at Grandma's?"

"Yeah, but I want a sleepover too. Brian is going to come over for a sleepover and bring me a present. Dad said so." Colin turned when another boy called his name, and he left them to kick the ball again.

Flynn shook his head. "Mike is such a pushover."

"Like his brothers."

He grinned. "You know, it's not too late. Mike is still single. You obviously like Colin. And Mike, though no Flynn McCauley, has his fair share of charm."

"Yeah, about that..." She liked the flummoxed expression that crossed Flynn's face. "No, you goof.

I don't think about Mike like that." *Not like I think about Brody.* "I heard your mom had a single woman waiting for him the other night. What happened? Come on, dish."

Flynn sighed. "I knew Maddie wouldn't keep quiet about it."

"Brody told me."

"Another big mouth. Well, if you must know…" He didn't look upset but amused at sharing the information. "My mother is on a grandbaby rampage. She's head over heels for Colin, of course."

"Who isn't?"

Flynn grinned. "Right. Takes after me, you know."

She rolled her eyes. "Yeah, yeah. All your charm. Anyway…?"

"Anyway, she's over the moon about me and Maddie. But I told her flat out we're waiting to have kids. I don't want to rush or pressure Maddie, you know?"

He was such a great guy for her best friend. "I know." Abby squeezed his arm, then let go.

"Mom's been leaving me alone lately. Thank God," he said fervently. "But she's stuck on Mike for some reason. She's not so worried about Brody or Cam. Brody because he's so fun loving. And Cam is smart enough to stay away for long periods. None of us knows what's going on with his chick out East, although I think it might be over. But Mike is so antisocial when it comes to women."

She felt a moment's discomfort. "Be honest. Do you think my resemblance to Lea bothers him?"

Flynn squeezed her shoulder. "No. Not at all. I was teasing before. I don't see any kind of spark between

you and big brother. Though I might wish otherwise."
A compliment.

She flushed. "Thanks."

"Although I don't mind telling you I'm happy
enough to see you with Brody. The way you two look
at each—"

"*What?*"

"Come on, Abby. It's obvious. The guy can't take his
eyes off you whenever you're around. And you try so
hard not to look at him it's funny. Well, not funny. More
like sad, pathetic, and more than a little stalkerish."

"*Stalkerish?*"

"But maybe it's his good looks that have you freaked
out. Being around us hot McCauleys has rubbed off on
him. He might seem like he plays around, but he's a
one-woman guy. He dates a good bit, but he's not a
cheat. Women love him. He—"

"Shut up already. Gah. Go grab your nephew and
go home. Quit pimping out your best friend. It's 'sad,
pathetic, and more than a little stalkerish,'" she sneered
and turned to leave.

"But he's good in bed," Flynn called in a voice just
a little too loud. "Seriously. Ask around. Not that he's
been dating for months. He's more than that crappy
house and dog. Really. Call him."

She hurried away, wondering why he thought his
best friend's promiscuity and mention of Mutt would
be selling points. Then again, she could attest to the
man's skills in bed. Holy Hannah, but Brody could
work magic with that tongue.

And Mutt…she was coming to seriously like. She'd
given him a thorough scrub-down, and he didn't smell

anymore. Plus she'd taken to brushing his coarse fur nightly, a treat he seemed to love.

She drove home and entered the dark house, calling out for the great beast. "Killer?"

Nothing.

"Rambo?"

Still nothing. So far, no good on the names.

"Mutt?"

She heard a thump from upstairs. Must have interrupted his nap. Then the pounding of big feet on the steps. Brody had a two-story with a basement. A creepy basement she had no intention of entering without Mutt by her side. There was something to be said for having one's own personal demon close.

Before Mutt could attack her with joy, she held a hand up. "No." Firm, decisive.

The dog still quivered, but he stopped from jumping on her.

"Sit. Stay." Waiting until he obeyed, she left him there and deliberately went to the kitchen for a treat for him. She stood in the kitchen holding it. "Mutt, come." That name really had to go.

He streaked into the kitchen and stopped.

"Sit."

He sat hard, his tail wagging.

She made a noise until he stopped fixating on the treat. When he glanced down again, she called him to her. "Come."

He slowly walked to her and waited. He must have had training before Brody found him, because he followed her commands easily after steady reinforcement the past two days. She fed him the snack, and once he finished, she stroked his head and praised him for his behavior. Too bad men weren't this easy to handle. With a sigh, she grabbed the leash and several doggie bags.

"Time to see about collecting my magazine back." She attached the leash and took him for an evening stroll.

They returned to see Seth Forelli, Brody's neighbor, sitting out on his porch wearing a heavy jacket. He smoked a pipe, and darned if he didn't remind her of a curmudgeonly old sailor in his peacoat. For two days she'd respectfully called him Mr. Forelli until he'd griped at her to "stop with the formality and just call me Seth, damn it."

"Hi, Seth." They walked up his front porch instead of Brody's, so she didn't have to yell while speaking.

"Abby." He nodded at the dog, who made no attempt to attack him with kisses. Finally. "Doin' fine work on the dog. How about his owner?"

"Brody?"

"You visiting for good? Or has he really gone gay? Not that I mind. But some people can be funny about coming out."

She just stared at him. "You think Brody's gay?"

"Never had a woman over before you. In the past six months, nothing but men. Of course, most of those were his brothers. I like the youngest, Cameron. Mike, I don't mind neither. But Flynn's got a smart mouth on him." He frowned. "A lot like Brody."

She grinned. "True. Flynn's dating my roommate. He's a smart aleck, but she knows just how to handle him. It's like a match made in heaven. She's perfect for him."

"And you're perfect for Mutt."

"You know, I really detest that name."

"Why? It suits him. Look at him. He's huge, hairy, big fangs. Some kind of hunting dog. Looks like he could tear a body in half and not miss a step. Not a bad dog to have by your side in the dark though." He nodded. "Had a husky, myself. Back in '84, had to put him down. Best damn dog I ever had."

Surprised to see tears in his eyes, Abby pretended she didn't notice when he hurriedly blinked them back. "Anyway, tell the boy when he comes back that I need him to find me someone to look at my sink again. Thing's clogging."

"I will." She'd call Flynn tonight and ask him to swing by tomorrow. Brody had left her instructions to look after Seth as well as the dog. The old man had grown children who never came to visit, and Brody worried about his health. Just one more reason she found it so hard to relegate Brody to the loser column. He was handsome, a genius between the sheets, and cared about dogs and older people. She kept waiting to find something bad about him so she'd stop wanting more than they'd agreed upon sharing—a casual friendship with benefits. Nothing long term, or so she kept telling herself.

"Oh, and one more thing. There's a fast-talking blond in the house. Said her name was Vanessa and you were expecting her."

"My other roommate."

"A little scary."

"I know. I live with her."

He cackled and slapped his leg. "Best of luck. You need anything, let me know." He shuffled back inside. Once he'd gone in, she took Mutt with her to greet

Vanessa, not surprised to find her neat freak of a room-mate sweeping up the mess in the kitchen.

"This just reinforces what I said—keep him *here*." Vanessa pointed the broom at Mutt, and he hightailed it upstairs to the bedroom. "Great. Now I'm scaring dogs too." She finished sweeping. "I'm also bored out of my mind. Anything amusing you'd care to share about your day?"

Abby stifled a laugh. "Well, I lost a tire and got scared by a woman earlier. Oh, and Mike's mom is try-ing to set him up with single women, or so I hear."

"This sounds interesting. Good thing I brought pop-corn." She held up a bag of healthy, air-popped organic corn. "And drinks." Hurray. Earth-responsible tea made from fair-trade farms. It might not taste good, but it would have little in the way of calories.

"Why not?"

Abby sat with Vanessa at the scarred kitchen table and talked about the McCauleys, Del—her new inspira-tion for her next novel—and Colin. As they sat together, Abby felt a sense of belonging she'd never felt with her family. She wondered why, with Vanessa of all people, she should feel free to be herself. When for twenty-six years she'd been showered with love and affection, but had always been in hiding.

Chapter 8

FRIDAY NIGHT, STANDING IN FLYNN'S KITCHEN while he shared the job's details, Brody felt as if he couldn't wait a moment longer. It killed him to pretend he wasn't in a rush to get back to Abby as he gave Flynn the invoices and filled him in on the work he'd done for Polvon Custom Homes, as well as some additional work they'd have coming in the future. For five long days he'd thought of little else but his pushy little goddess. The break in Anacortes to work on a job for contractor buddies brought in some nice cash, but the timing absolutely sucked. As did the fact that he'd had more work than he'd thought, so cutting out early hadn't happened.

He'd never been so consumed with a woman before. To his amazement, he kept wondering if she'd changed her mind and chalked him up to a one-night stand. It wasn't as if he and she had committed to anything more than another go in bed. He wasn't a threat and had given her orgasms. He still recalled those moments with pride, and that mind-blowing night freaked him out a little. He'd wanted immediately to do it again, but he hadn't wanted to rush or pressure her, concerned that he might give the wrong impression.

And what is that? He didn't do commitment. Even the thought of it gave him hives. Brody knew better than most what the wrong parents could do to a kid.

It didn't help that Alan had called him several times during the week. Never a good sign when the Singers made their presence known.

He'd done his best to ignore each and every call, but the constant anxiety of seeing his relatives refused to fade.

"Yo, bro, you good? You're ignoring me."

Brody realized he was staring sightlessly at his buddy's head. "Oh, ah, yeah. I'm good." He looked around. "Where's Maddie?" Friday evening and no hint of the redhead?

"We're not tied at the hip."

"Uh-huh." He waited.

"Up yours. She'd have been here sooner, but she's been with Vanessa and Abby taking care of *your* damn dog," Flynn complained. "Happy now? From what I hear, he eats magazines, paper, and underwear. Dog has a thing for silk." He snorted. "Colin is uber impressed while Abby's totally grossed out."

"Oh boy." He'd hoped Mutt might soften her toward him. He'd rescued a dog, for God's sake. That was right up there with handling babies and walking grannies across the street.

"Don't worry. According to Maddie, Abby's half in love with the dog."

"Oh?" His heart raced. That was good. A step closer to the woman without having to commit himself. Again, he asked himself what he wanted, and again, he had no answer. He just knew he wanted Abby to himself for the near future. The far future would have to work itself out.

"Yeah. I saw Abby the other day. She took Colin to practice for me." Flynn wiped up his counter and tossed the towel on the sink. "So how long have you two been shacking up?"

Brody didn't react, knowing Flynn to be fishing. No way in hell Abby would confess to Flynn that she'd banged Brody. "What's that?" He blinked, adding a bit of confusion to the innocent expression he'd spent years perfecting.

"Come on, man. It's me. Your best friend. The left half of your brain." They looked nothing alike yet had more in common than anyone else. And they'd always joked that they shared the same mind. "Tell me true. You're sleeping with her, right?"

It hurt him to lie, especially to Flynn. But they didn't share *every* secret. Some things Flynn had never known, shit Brody didn't need or want his best friend to know. He added Abby to that short list. "Sorry, Flynn. I'd love to say yes and look as accomplished as I actually am"— Flynn snorted—"but the truth is, she and I are friends. Now I *want* to get in her pants, hell yeah, but I don't want to rain on your parade with Maddie, you get me?" Which was why he rationalized it okay to fib to the man.

Flynn sighed. "I do. I was so sure… Look, I appreciate you taking it easy with her. But you like her, bro. I know you. You're fixated on her. You always look for her at get-togethers. And not to be all Cam-like about feelings and shit, but I think we both know you *like* her. I mean, she's not just a piece of ass."

The front door rattled. "Speaking of a piece of ass…"

"Brody," Flynn growled. "We'll talk about this later."

"Yeah, sure. Time for me to relieve Abby of dog duty." At Flynn's stupid grin, he warned, "D-U-T-Y, you moron."

"I just spent last night with a six-year-old fascinated by dog crap. Cut me some slack."

Brody shook his head and made his way to the door, spotting Maddie. Thank God. Now he had an excuse to hightail it back to his place.

"Hey, Brody. Welcome back." Maddie gave him a big grin as she shut the door behind her.

After a smirk over his shoulder at Flynn, Brody held out his arms for Maddie. "Give us a hug, gorgeous."

"Brody," Flynn growled again.

Maddie laughed and accepted his embrace, as well as his smacking kiss on the lips.

"*Hey.*" Nope. Flynn definitely didn't like that.

"Gotta go." He flipped Flynn the bird behind his back, then left before his best friend could school him on how *not* to deal with Flynn's girlfriend.

Girlfriend... Not for long. Brody knew Flynn planned on proposing over Christmas. And what that might mean to the dynamics of everything gave Brody more cause to panic about the state of his future.

Brody could do change. He'd always been pretty adaptable. But he'd counted on Flynn and the others as his family for so long. Though he loved Maddie and knew Flynn would one day marry and procreate—all the McCauleys had that intrinsic need to make babies that Bitsy and Pop had passed down to them—he still wasn't prepared for everyone to grow up and leave him behind.

Mike had been *the* older brother forever. It made sense for him to have a kid and make Brody an uncle. Add to that how much Brody had adored Lea, and he'd always be there for Colin. No matter what. But Flynn and Cam were different. And then there was Abby...

He drove himself home, still mulling over his weird emotions. He'd been so excited to get back to Abby, but now he didn't know how to feel. He kept trying to pin her down as just a sexual attraction, to ignore those other feelings he kept having.

He continued to try to talk himself out of his enthusiasm for close contact with the woman, even as he parked in his driveway. He walked around the side of the house to the front porch, determined to fix the garage door—so that it would finally *open*—before winter hit. But as he moved step by step closer to home, his heart raced with the knowledge that Abby waited for him.

He started to knock on the front door and stopped. "It's your house, asshole." Shaking his head, he unlocked and opened the door and braced himself, ready for Mutt's welcome. When nothing happened, he took a cautious step inside and closed and locked the door behind him.

"Hello?"

"In here," Abby called out.

Relieved she was indeed in his home, he took off his boots in the foyer and turned into the living room. To his bemusement, nothing seemed changed, yet the place looked different. Same knotty pine built-ins around the fireplace. Same ugly plaid couches and scarred wooden flooring. But it smelled faintly like…lemons?

"Abby?"

"Right here. And don't move." She stood by the back window in the shadows, so she must have seen him park the truck. By her stood Mutt, his tongue hanging out, his tail thumping on the floor so hard

Brody cringed to think he might break something. Not his tail, but the floor.

"Ah, everything okay?"

"Yes, fine. I'm training your dog. He's going to wait until you say it's okay to greet him. Go walk around. Don't make eye contact. Get comfortable on the couch or something."

He dropped his duffel bag on the floor and did his best not to look at the dog. But he couldn't help watching Abby out of the corner of his eye. She wore a pair of jeans and a clingy sweater that made it hard to swallow. Or breathe.

"So, ah, Vanessa here?"

"No. She left with Maddie. Mutt, *stay*." She kept her hand on the dog's back, and to Brody's amusement, she didn't have to reach down to touch him. Mutt's head came to the middle of her belly.

"How'd you know she was here?" Abby asked.

"I stopped by Flynn's on the way over. Had to give him the rundown on the job and drop off a few invoices."

"Oh." She cleared her throat. "Thanks for texting me about your return. I had a few men sniffing around me but decided you probably wouldn't want me doing them in your bed or anything. So you coming back today was a good thing."

He froze and stared at her, wide-eyed. "*What?*" Abby never talked to him like that. She had snappy comebacks and an obnoxious banter down pat, but she seemed to steer clear of anything sexual. Or at least, she had.

She chuckled, and the tension left him. "Oh wow. If you could see your face."

"Ha ha. Not funny. I've been looking forward to

tonight all week." It didn't make him a pussy to admit he wanted her, right?

"I bet you missed your bed. The rest of the house might need work—and that's putting it mildly."

"Gee, don't hold back."

"But your bed is super comfy. It might be better than mine."

"Yeah." He sighed. "I love my comforter." And it would look perfect pooled around her naked waist while she rode him hard. He'd cup her breasts and watch her take him, see her sigh as she came around him and moaned his name…

He sat on the couch and crossed a leg over his knee, hoping it hid his erection. He might not mind admitting to wanting her, but he didn't want to appear overeager. Amazing how just moments ago he'd been confused and in a bad mood because of it. But none of that mattered right now, looking at her.

She had her hair pulled back in a clip that let strands lick her neck, framing her face along with those sexy glasses. The erotic librarian. The sweater clung to her curves but couldn't be called anything but decent. No plunging neckline or sleek design, just a soft weave that hugged the form of a woman very well put together.

"Why are you looking at me like that?" she asked with suspicion.

"Like what?"

"Be nice or I'll sic your dog on you."

"I'm not sure who that is, but that can't be my dog." Mutt's fur looked well groomed. Not a waft of doggie smell hit Brody's nose. Not even from the afghan Bitsy had made him that sat over the back of the couch. "Okay, I've gotta know. Why does my house smell so…"

"Clean? Vanessa stopped by a few times. You can eat off your kitchen floor, it's so sparkly."

"Really?" He grinned.

"Well, I wouldn't. Your dog may look clean, but trust me, he isn't." She stroked Mutt's head, and he blinked with satisfaction. "Okay. He's going to come to you. If he even tries to jump on you, you have to tell him no and push him down. Be the alpha, for God's sake. I'm tired of doing it."

"Yes, ma'am."

She glared at him, then released the hound.

Mutt barked and raced to him, but before the dog could jump on him, Brody gave him the death glare. "*No*. Sit."

Mutt paused, glanced at him in question, and Brody thought he'd finally gotten the hang of owning a— "*Damn it*." Mutt launched himself into Brody's lap and landed on exactly the wrong spot.

Seeing stars and trying to catch his breath, he wasn't aware of much until Abby put her hand on his shoulder. "Are you okay?"

He wheezed and tried to glare at her through the pain. "That…would sound…so much…more sincere…if you weren't…laughing."

She broke out into more gales and patted him on the shoulder, as if he was the dog. "There there. You'll be okay. I hope. He didn't break anything, did he?" She paused to wipe her eyes, then collapsed by his side into more laughter. "I don't know why, but a guy getting hit in the groin is just hilarious."

"Yeah, just." He slowly straightened until he could breathe normally again and leaned his head back against the couch. "Did you train him to do that?"

"Oh no. Not at all. He's been really good all week. Didn't once try to jump on Vanessa or Seth. There's something about you."

He looked at her, not pleased to see her still grinning. "It's not funny," he snapped and glanced around. "Where is that creature from hell, anyway?"

"While you were seeing stars, I put him in the back room so he wouldn't do any more damage." She bit her lower lip. "I'd offer to kiss your hurt and make it all better, but I wouldn't want you to accuse me of jumping on you too."

He blew out a breath and yanked her closer when she tried to inch away. "Uh-uh. You stay."

"Please. That only works on dogs and men."

"What's that?"

She looked like she was ready to laugh again. "Nothing."

"You think you're a comedian tonight, eh? Good. Laugh it up. Because you can be damn sure I'm going to make you kiss it all better in about ten minutes. Maybe. If I can walk again."

She exploded into loud guffaws, and he used the distraction to pull her into his arms.

"Hey." She tried to move away, so he tightened his grip.

"Reparations. Sue me."

She settled into him and snickered. "Okay, okay. I really am sorry he jumped you like that. Honestly, he's been so good. I just think he's not sure who to obey. You or me. And you don't cut it yet."

"Great. My dog thinks *you're* in charge." He positioned her to straddle his lap, facing him because he wanted to drink her in. She really did have the most beautiful eyes. So deep brown, like melting chocolate. Right now, she had that gooey sweet expression in them he wanted to label as affection, or something more, but didn't dare. *Friends. Just friends who have sensational sex. That's all she wants, dumbass. Don't blow this. Play things right, and you can* blow her.

"How was Anacortes?"

"Cold." He pushed a strand of her hair behind her ear, hiding a smile when she clenched her fingers on her thighs. "Boring. Too many guys in one place. It was great to see old friends, but doing a job is doing a job. Not a lot of time for shooting the shit while I busted my hump to rough out the house in five days."

"Yeah. I thought you'd be home Wednesday, but your message said Saturday. So I guess you could say you're early."

"Uh-huh. Tell me about you. How's the writing going?"

She gave him a look.

"What?"

"Is this where you offer to tie me up so I can finish chapter three?"

"Wow. They hit that at chapter three, huh?" He laughed when she smacked his chest. "I'm kidding. I'm sincerely curious about your week. You know what I was doing. Roughing in a custom home with eight fixtures. And Jesus, were the homeowners a pain."

"They were there?" She dragged a hand from her thigh to his chest and spread her palm.

He felt the heat smack him upside the head, and it

started the healing between his legs on the spot. "Yeah. Had to deal with the framers, who were done and leaving, because I had to fix the pipe line. Not pretty when I told them they had to move a few things to get the piping right. And it got worse when Harry Homemaker started adding his two cents, and he knew jack shit about shit."

"Nice mouth."

"Sorry. A week without civilization. I think I regressed." She grinned.

"But I want to know. What did you do except train my dog to sic balls?"

She coughed to cover yet another laugh, and he found her joy infectious. He had to touch her, so he rubbed her legs while she talked, aware of how her breath hitched at odd times.

"Yeah, well. I was working on my latest proposal when I met the most fascinating woman." She described Del, then went on to talk about a new idea. "So I'm thinking of making my next heroine a tough cookie. Rough on the outside, a softie on the inside."

"Like this Del?" Chicks covered in tats had never appealed to him, not that he faulted them for getting what they wanted. Brody liked a softer, stereotypically feminine woman. A woman like Abby.

"I don't know what she's really about, though she seemed to like Colin well enough."

"Everyone likes that little dork."

She smiled. "Yeah, he grows on you."

"Like a fungus."

"Brody, that's not nice."

"But true. In that regard he takes after Flynn."

She laughed.

"So what else did you do?"

"I spent most of my time here. When not training Nanook, I wrote or spent time with Seth and Vanessa."

"Together?"

"No way. I'm not a glutton for punishment," she said drily. "Seth is a funny guy. Flynn fixed his sink for him, by the way. No biggie, just a stuck clog, or so Flynn said."

"Yeah, Flynn mentioned that when I saw him."

"Oh, and Seth's still not sure if you're 'going gay' or not, but like he said, no need to cover things up. I told him I wasn't your beard, but I don't know that he believed me."

He felt his cheeks heat.

"Apparently you don't bring women over. Ever. So you're either very private, Seth is mistaken, or you really have gone to the other side." Her smirk made him eager to wipe it away.

"Shut up. This place is a mess. I didn't want you here either, but I didn't think you guys would be okay with Mutt at your place."

"You got that right. That's why Vanessa cleaned your house from top to bottom. She was bored and OCDing. Be grateful."

"I am. Trust me." He settled his hands over her hips and brought her closer to the hungry part of him, now ready to make his dreams a reality. "So you were productive, you handled Seth, Vanessa, and Mutt. You definitely deserve a reward."

She squirmed over him. "Obviously Mutt didn't do any lasting damage."

"Nope. I'm a fast healer. But I'm still aching."

"I bet."

He watched her while he slowly slid his hands underneath her sweater and up. "You have soft skin. Like silk."

Her breathing grew faster as she stared at him. "Your hands are rough. I like it."

"Good." He reached to unfasten her bra, and she let him. "I take it you saved all the parts of your stories needing research for me?" To his bemusement, he couldn't find the hooks on the back of her bra.

"It connects in the front." She watched him from behind those glasses, so sexy, yet a touch reserved.

"The front. You're torturing me, right? First the dog, now this?" He quickly moved his hands to her front, molding to the large globes encased in satiny cups. *Fuck. If I last more than a minute, I'll be lucky.* He took a breath and let it out, forcing himself to go easy. He wanted this to last all night. And into tomorrow. And maybe the next day.

"So what do you have planned for this weekend?" she rasped, as if reading his mind.

"Nothing but relaxing and helping a friend of mine."

"Oh." So cute. She sounded disappointed.

"Yeah. She's this smokin' hot chick who writes for a living, and she needs my skills to help her with research. I'm all about research."

Abby's slow smile melted that core of detachment he normally held when dealing with a woman. God, he couldn't understand how just seeing her eyes gleam or her soft lips curl could make his heart hammer so fast.

"You know, Brody." She leaned into his hands, and he had to swallow a groan of his own. "I feel really bad

about Mutt, the way he hurt you." With quick movements she withdrew her arms into her top, pushed his
hands aside, and then shifted around inside the sweater.
He watched in awe as her bra dropped to his lap and she
put her hands through her sleeves again in less than a
minute. She removed her glasses and put them on the
table next to the couch, giving him clearer access to the
emotions shining in her eyes.

"That's impressive." He put his hands over her
breasts again, now naked under the sweater. Her tits
were full, her nipples hard, and she rocked over him
when he kneaded her.

"Yes," she hissed. "That feels so good."

"It does," he responded in a gritty voice.

"I was on the field hockey team in high school. We
used to have to change shirts on the bus. You know,
home team/away team colors."

"What's that?" He wanted to see her, to take her
nipples between his lips and suck.

"My ability to remove my bra under my shirt," she
explained. "You're totally not listening to me, are you?"

"God no."

She gasped on a laugh.

"Take off that sweater. I need to see you." He stared
at her, seeing the same desire he felt. While she took off
her sweater, he did the same with his sweatshirt.

Bare chest to bare chest, but hers was so much more
enticing. He didn't wait and took her nipple into his
mouth while he plumped and played with her. Brody
loved a woman's body, but he was partial to breasts.
Abby had the nicest set he'd ever seen in his life—and
he'd seen more than his fair share.

He continued to tease her, sucking, nipping, and licking while she clutched his head.

"Yes. Oh, more. Brody, *please*."

He loved that she forgot herself to beg. The feminine moans and pleas for what he could give her, what he *would* give her, only enhanced his pleasure. Because in making her happy, he pleased himself. His orgasm could wait. His own needs mattered little compared to making sure Abby got off.

Determined to thank her in the best way he knew how, he decided to show her a few tricks he hadn't gotten to the last time they'd played together. And then he had to find a way to figure out just where the hell this thing with her was going. Because it felt anything but casual.

Chapter 9

ABBY COULDN'T THINK. FOR AN ENTIRE WEEK SHE'D spent her days and nights surrounded by Brody's things, Brody's dog, Brody's neighbor. Sleeping in his bed had been a torture all its own, because Abby had a terrific imagination. She too easily envisioned what they might have been doing if he'd been back.

But this… The man would not be a onetime wonder. She couldn't believe the way he touched her. With a gentleness and an intensity so mired in the man she couldn't tell if he was always like this or just with her. He didn't rush, didn't seem hurried to make love to her. Not Brody. He petted and teased, drawing out the pleasure. Just touching her breasts, and she was ready to come.

She squirmed over him again, aware of the hard cock prodding her center. She remembered exactly how big he was and wanted him inside her. Like yesterday.

"Come inside me," she whispered as he continued to suck her breasts. He squeezed a nipple with more pressure and made her gasp, then soothed the sting by taking attention away from her other breast to suck it better. "Oh, yes."

Yes, please. Moaning and groaning. Pathetic that the man reduced her to a clichéd lover, but God in heaven, he had magic hands. And that mouth… She'd had dreams about that mouth that left her waking all wet between her legs. Tingly and frustrated, because the man she desired had been too far away.

She'd done her best not to touch herself, but one night she'd been desperate. She'd almost called him for phone sex. Had wanted to. But Abby Dunn didn't do things like that. This liaison was as close as she'd ever come to being so naughty, and she still worried about freaking him out if she pushed too hard too fast. Then he might tell the guys, and everyone would know she was a freak in bed. Just like Kevin had not so long ago, and she'd never felt such passion for him. Not like she experienced with Brody.

"Hey, where did you go?" he asked softly and let go of her breasts to cup her face. "You got tense on me, baby. You okay?"

She felt three shades of stupid. "Yeah. Just... I hope this—us like this—is okay."

He blinked at her. "Sorry?"

She felt worse than stupid. Pathetic. Moronic. Slutty, sitting half naked on top of him in his living room with the lights on, showing all her flaws. *Oh man.*

"Hold on. You want to stop, we'll stop. But Abby..." He looked so dejected. "I might die of blue balls. Men do, you know."

She couldn't help a snort of amusement.

"There we go. That's what I want to see. Besides your beautiful breasts, I mean."

"Brody." Her cheeks felt hot.

"Yeah. That smile. You get me so hard." He rocked her over him again. "I want to come inside you so bad it's not funny. Yeah, I know. Condoms, a must. But... This is more than okay. You can't honestly believe I don't want you?" He paused. "Or is this too fast? I mean, last week was incredible, but maybe you have second thoughts?"

To her amazement, *he* now appeared uncomfortable. Vulnerable even, which she never would have pegged for Brody "Stud for Hire" Singer.

"It's okay if you want to stop," he said in a low voice and grimaced when she shifted over the bar in his pants. "But I—"

Annoyed with herself for almost ending something special, especially because it was more than apparent he wanted to continue but thought she didn't want him, she ignored her inner doubt and kissed him. With tongue. And lips. And more tongue.

He froze for a moment, and then he kissed her back. Demanding, insisting on taking charge.

She sighed into his mouth, loving his dominant side. Normally easygoing, Brody turned into someone else when he kissed her. And damn, he got her so hot.

"Tell me what you want," he whispered into her ear when he broke the kiss. "In detail. The dirtier the better."

She couldn't help grinding over him, wanting him in the worst way.

"Come on, Abby. Tell me." He paused and nipped her earlobe, which made her jolt. "Or I'll have to spank you."

She moaned, and when he cupped her breasts again, she told him. In detail. "I want you to suck my clit into that amazing mouth. Eat me out, Brody. Make me come. Then let me suck you down. Sixty-nine. I want to kiss you and make you all better. You're so big and thick. And I bet you'll be nice and sweet when you come down my throat."

He shuddered under her, and she took advantage of the heavy silence to scrape her nails over his nipples.

"*Fuck*." He hurried and moved her to the side. "Strip. Now." They raced to tear off their clothes. He took a condom out of his jeans pocket but didn't bother donning it. "If we're using mouths... I want you to take me raw, baby. Just you and me. No barriers. I'm clean. That's something I won't lie about."

She believed him. One thing Brody wouldn't do was put her in any kind of jeopardy. She still got goose bumps knowing he'd been celibate for so long because of her. "Me too."

He smiled, and the warmth in that grin turned her heart inside out. "I know." His smile turned mean. "Now do what I tell you. Turn around and put that pussy over my lips. Then take my fat cock in your mouth and suck me dry."

She'd always been a sucker for dirty talk, and Brody could have made a career out of his own 1-900 number. "I'm really wet."

"Don't brag. Just get over here," he barked and lay down on the couch.

Though ugly as sin, the couch was surprisingly comfortable and extra wide, a throwback to the eighties or nineties with a plaid pattern from hell. But she'd never been so grateful for the extra space. Abby joined him as instructed and stared down at his thick shaft, moist at the tip.

She shivered to realize she'd made him this way, that his desire was real. For *her*.

Then she stopped thinking, because he drew her down to his mouth and started to feast.

"Brody," she moaned and took his shaft in hand. He jerked but continued to lick her, sucking in intervals that told her if she didn't hurry, she'd come without him.

She licked the tip of him before sliding her mouth over his crown. He moaned and arched up, and intensified his suction over her clit. He didn't give her warning before he thrust a finger inside her. Then another. Thrusting deep while he worked her taut nub.

Losing her mind, she sucked harder and cupped his balls. Rubbing the soft yet firm sac while she grazed the inside of his strong thighs with her nails.

Brody went crazy. So she did it again. She couldn't get all of him inside her mouth, but she did her best, sucking at least half of him with long, deep draws.

He pulled his mouth away and warned in a low rasp, "I'm gonna come, Abby. Down your throat, baby. Swallow me down and come with me. All over my mouth," he moaned and returned to her flesh.

She gave him the same intensity, caught in the maelstrom of sensation and feeling. Her heart beat not just for the physical release, but for the emotional catharsis of desire and need long denied.

Brody Singer writhed for her. She had power, as much as he did as he consumed her. And then he removed his fingers and gripped her ass with both hands, pulling her cheeks wider as he ground his lips and teeth against her clit, sucking impossibly deep.

She drew down and nearly gagged herself on him, bobbing in time with his rhythm. He groaned and released into her mouth at the same time she climaxed, the rush of desire overwhelming.

She continued to swallow him until he gave no more, and she took her mouth away, dimly realizing he'd pushed her up. She should have been embarrassed at the thought of nearly smothering him. And for a half second she was, but then he pulled her around and hugged her to him.

"Jesus Christ, Abby. I go away for a few days and you nearly kill me with that mouth. Go easy or I might die from the orgasms." He chuckled weakly. "Oh man, I don't think I can move. You literally blew my mind. Holy shit."

He swore a few more times, and she felt like a queen.

"You okay?" he asked after a few moments of peaceful silence.

"Mmm." To her astonishment, he still seemed half hard. "Brody?"

"You taste good."

"Ah, okay."

"What do I taste like?"

She pushed up on her elbows and stared down at him, loving that sleepy, satisfied look she'd put there. "Are we really having this conversation?"

"Yeah. I mean, some women don't like to give blow jobs because they say guys are funky. And I know women are the same way. You're not funky. At all. You're so fucking sweet. I could eat you for hours."

"Good to know," she ended in a squeak.

"Oh my God. You're blushing? After you sucked me like a Hoover?"

She groaned and dropped her forehead to his chest.

His rumble of laughter made their joining all the better. *Imagine having sex and liking the afterplay.*

Brody didn't make her feel dirty. He encouraged the
sexual talk, the non-missionary position. And wonder
of wonders, he seemed to be gearing up for more than
one shot.

"Well?" he asked.

"Well what?"

He blew out a breath. "It's a good thing you're amazing in bed, because you can't hold a thought. What do
I taste like?"

"You taste good, okay? Geez, I can't believe we're
talking about this."

"What? None of your exes ever asked? Or are you a
virgin? Was I your first? Abby, I'm so thrilled."

She lifted her head and tugged on one of his chest hairs.
"Ow."

"No, I never discussed the taste of a man's sperm
with him. For your information, there haven't been that
many guys. But the ones there were, well, I just did it.
They didn't want a blow by blow afterward."

He looked at her. "So how many blows we talkin'?
By my count, that's like three you just mentioned." He
grinned at her, his expression almost boyish. "You are
so red right now."

She leaned down and bit his nipple. But instead of
groaning in pain, he reached for her shoulders and demanded she do it again.

"Really?" She kissed him, wanting to lick the
sting away.

"Oh yeah. I like that. My nipples are sensitive. Like
my cock." He wiggled his brows. "So feel free to 'blow
by blow me' again."

She chuckled. "You're fun. I hadn't expected that."

He linked his hands behind his head and stared up at her. "What did you think sex with me would be like? Because you know you've been thinking about it since we first met."

"Your ego has no limits, does it?"

"Nope." He grinned again, and she caught a slight dimple.

"I bet you were a handful when you were a kid."

His smile faltered for a second before his grin grew broader. "You have no idea."

She wanted to know why a reference to his childhood would make him pause, how a six-year-old boy with the last name of Singer could suddenly be living with the McCauleys. Had his parents passed away? Why then had the McCauleys not adopted him? They loved him and treated him like one of their own.

But the caution in his gaze warned her now was not the time.

"Well…to answer your question, I thought sex with you would be intense. You'd come, I'd come, then you'd light out of bed so fast my head would spin. But you're, I don't know, fun."

"So are you."

She shook her head. "I'm neurotic most of the time. We have some incredible chemistry, otherwise you'd probably be running for the door." She tried to come across as joking, but it must have fallen flat because his grin faded.

"Why do you do that?"

"What?"

"Put yourself down. I've heard you before with your friends. You're smart, sexy, funny, and God, you rocked my world three times now. Why the hell would you ever think you're not good enough?"

She just stared at him, not sure what to say. "Um, well, I was joking."

He looked down his nose at her. "Uh-huh."

"Hey, I gave you a hand job at a party. I'm sure of myself."

"You were drunk. Look. You have no reason not to talk to me. We both agreed to keep everything that happens between us between us." He paused. "Flynn tried forcing the truth out of me earlier."

"Oh? Did he use pliers and threats of violence?"

"He tried tricking me, but that boy needs to get up pretty early to get one over on Brody Singer."

"And then he refers to himself in the third person. Classic narcissist."

He laughed.

Despite not wanting to talk about her insecurities, she liked knowing she'd brought him amusement. She hadn't liked that vulnerability in his gaze before.

"You're funny, too. Did I tell you that?" he asked. "Gimme a kiss."

"Only if you stop trying to psychoanalyze me."

"Fine. Just tell me if your poor self-image is because of that dickhead Kevin."

She froze. How—?

"Didn't think I knew about him, huh? Well, you're not the only one who can eavesdrop on your neighbors."

The blood drained from her face. "Wh-what do you mean?"

He smiled like the Cheshire cat. "I knew you used to listen to us on card night. The little voyeur next door with the hot bod. No, I never told the guys. Instead, I used Mike's open window policy to listen in on you, girlie."

"*What?*"

"Yeah. That's right. I know that Kevin was an asshole who treated you like shit. Vanessa's words, not mine. And that he was never good enough for you. I also know you like looking at my ass."

She sputtered. Trust Brody to have only half of it right. "For your information, Vanessa doesn't know everything."

"Not according to her."

She snorted. "And according to her, you're a doofus who has eyes for me. So is she wrong?"

"Nope."

She hadn't expected that. "Huh?"

"Look. I'll say it straight out. You're hot. Just my type."

"I'm not hot."

"Yes, you are. You have huge tits."

"Breasts."

"A tiny waist, long dark hair that hits you nearly to your waist. And that mouth. I have wet dreams about that mouth."

Talk about a boost to the ego. And he wasn't done.

He focused on her lips. "I used to beat off to that mouth. You and your smart-alecky responses. I'd imagine you saying something obnoxious, and then I'd make you apologize. On your knees. I'd hold my cock to your lips and you'd lick me, then suck me like you did tonight."

She bit her lip, and he groaned and dragged his hands out from behind his head to hold her waist, grinding up into her.

"Yeah, that. When you bite your lower lip. That is so sexy." He rocked into her, and she leaned down to kiss the impossible man who seemed to like everything about her. He knew she wrote books about love and sex and didn't mind. And he liked a little kink. Oh man, she could totally, *absolutely,* fall for Brody if she wasn't careful.

He stabbed his tongue into her mouth and licked her, retreating and pushing forward in a rhythm he soon echoed with the rest of his body. When he angled against her and the head of him slipped inside, she knew she should stop him, should demand he put on a condom. And then his kiss deepened and he slid inside her fully. Skin to skin, no protection.

He gripped her hips and dragged her up and down over him, his movements spiraling out of control. He pulled back from the kiss. "You feel so good. So damn good, Abby." He nipped her throat and sucked hard, moving her with greater ferocity as he plunged into her again and again.

And he did feel amazing. So big, filling her up. She didn't want to put a halt to anything but her next orgasm. But the thought of a little Brody reared its head. She wanted someday to be a mother, but not yet.

Before she could remind him to use a condom, he swore and moved her completely off him. Then he brought her back down, so that she rested against the base of his cock. He groaned, and she looked between them to see him spill all over his belly in one sexy hot mess.

"Oh shit. *Abby.*" He continued to pulse and moan her name until there was nothing left. He blinked up at her and flushed. "Damn. I didn't mean to… I mean, being inside you like that. I just… I lost it. I'm so sorry."

She studied him, seeing the remorse and knowing how serious things might have been had he not had the presence of mind to withdraw. She sighed and stared down at him. "I could have stopped you. If I'd said no at any point, you wouldn't have continued."

He exhaled heavily. "Yeah, but I never should have put you in that position. Fuck, I'm sorry." Then he blinked up at her. "You didn't come, did you?"

"I… Well, no."

"We need to fix that." Before she could shriek her shock at his manhandling, he had her on her back on the couch as he hunkered over her belly and pushed her thighs wider. He leaned down to grab his sweatshirt and wiped his belly clean, then he returned to her. "Now where were we?"

Concerned that the moment was lost and she'd take forever to come, as normally happened with a man after he'd had his fill, she tried to shrug Brody off. "It's okay. You don't have to—*oh*."

He loved her body as if worshipping at a temple. Kisses and strokes, fingers in places she never would have imagined could be erogenous zones. He managed to trigger her hot spots and took his time about it. A kiss to the back of her knee, running his hands up and down her ribs, tugging at her nipples while he sucked her clit into a hard little bead.

And then he pinched her nipple and nipped her clit, and she fell headlong into ecstasy.

She cried out as she came, and he lapped her up like a great big cat. His tongue must have been tired, but

Brody continued to caress her until she calmed down. Then he gave her a final kiss and cuddled with her on the couch.

She sighed, worn out. "This would be better on a bed."

"Yeah. Next time. And I promise, condoms all the way. Unless you're loving my giant manliness with your mouth."

She giggled, which told her how tired she was. She only gave that high-pitched laugh when drunk or exhausted. "Next time, huh?"

"Abby, please. I'm all about literary development. We haven't been anywhere near that D/s kink you mentioned. Honey, I would be a complete louse if I didn't at least offer my services."

"God. I don't think I can move, and I need to get home. And then you're tempting me with more sex. Can I survive you?" she teased, but inside, she meant that question on a deeper level.

Unlike Kevin, Brody was well liked by her friends. Even Vanessa tolerated him, and she hadn't liked Kevin at all. Not even from the beginning. Brody could be so sweet, telling Abby how great she was, not to be so down on herself. And he seemed to respect her work. The sex… *My God, the sex.* He wanted more, and so did she. But she feared she would confuse love with lust. With Brody, it would be way too easy. She had a bad feeling she'd already started the trip downhill.

"Abby, I'm totally survivable. I'm easy."

"So it says on the bathroom walls."

"Hey." He tickled her, and she retaliated by tickling him. Then they were laughing and teasing while trying to come up with excuses for her to stay the night.

In the end, she knew her roommates would see right through her. And she needed some distance from a man she had no business falling for. Though Brody might not realize it, he was way out of her league.

"Oh, come on." He whined as he remained naked and watched her dress. "You really packed your stuff?" Her bags sat in the corner near the front door.

"Yes, I really did. I've done my part with the dog. I'm working on your website, and you've already agreed to help me 'research.'"

"The website." He pounced. "We need to work on that. I'm losing clients without a web presence."

"And who's been telling you that for months?" she asked waspishly. "Now I have to go. My car is in front of the house. I'm ready to face my nosy roommates if they're still up." She groaned at the clock. "It's nearly midnight. They'll want to know what I was up to."

"So tell them you sucked the most amazing cock you've ever handled in your life. They'll understand."

She snickered. "You're so bad."

"And yet so good." He walked up to her, his big naked self, and hugged her tight. "You smell so good all the time. Even after sweaty sex, you smell like flowers."

She hugged him back. Why did he have to keep saying such wonderful things? "Hey. I have to go. But I tell you what. I'll see you…Sunday?"

He let her go when she wriggled, his expression one she couldn't read. No wonder he often won at cards. Between his cheating ways, his poker face, and his sheer luck with anything involving money—according to Flynn—the man was a triple threat.

"Okay?" she asked, her voice soft.

"Sunday's good." He gave her a sly grin. "I'll have some toys for you to play with."

"I was thinking we could talk about your website." She smacked at a wandering hand too close to her boob. "Brody."

"Abby," he mimicked. "Fine." He sighed. "Sunday. But I want to have some fun. And if it's not gonna be in bed, then it's bowling."

She frowned. "Bowling?"

"Yeah. I'll text you directions. Let's say, three?"

"I guess that'll work."

He nodded.

Her gaze strayed to his chest and continued down the fine line of blond hair to his amazing lower body, and in particular, his cock. Even flaccid the thing was huge.

"Hello? Abby? My eyes are up here," he said with mock indignation and pointed at his face.

"Ack. I'm leaving."

"Sure you don't want stick around for the second half?"

"I don't think I have the energy."

"Lightweight. Don't worry. I know you're just scared."

She had reached down to grab her bags and stopped. "Scared?" She straightened and faced him with a frown.

"Of falling for me." He brushed off the idea like it was a done deal, which annoyed her, because it kind of was.

"Please."

He shook his head. "Yep. There it is. Starts with the begging."

"Don't be an ass."

"And there. Your inability to stop fixating on my body parts. In particular, my ass."

"God. Stop."

"Prayers, begging. Abby, honey. Make it easy on yourself. Meet me Sunday and I'll help you handle your growing love for my amazingness."

Now amused as much as annoyed, she stepped into his personal space. Looking up at him—and my, how that grated—she poked him in the chest. "I don't think so. See, if I'm so perfect, then you'll be falling for *me*. My amazing breasts, my firm ass." Saggy, but who was she to point out that flaw? "My fuckable mouth." Oh yeah, he stared at her lips and swallowed hard on that one. "Like you said. I'm smart, funny, and sexy. I can have any man I want wrapped around my finger. Better be careful I don't set my sights on you."

He gave a harsh laugh. "Abby, sweetie, don't beat yourself up for falling for the old Brody charm. If anyone's gonna fall, it's you."

"Oh? Bring it, Jethro."

"Fine. Consider it brought."

They stared at each other in silence. Then she stood on tiptoe and dragged his mouth to hers. She kissed him until his thick erection told her he'd had enough. Before he could yank her back into sex land—and yeah, her panties would *totally* need a good cleaning—she pulled away. "See you Sunday, Slick."

"Fine." He licked his lips. "Pleasant dreams."

"Back at you." She turned on a shaky heel, shrugged into her coat, grabbed her stuff, and left the house. She hurried through the cold bite of midnight and shoved her things into her car. Once in the driver's seat, she saw him at the window, peering out his front curtain, only his face in view. He continued to watch her until she drove away.

During her trip home, she wondered what she'd just done and why. *Did I really bet I could make him fall for me? To protect* myself? *Great move, Abby. You are such a fool.* She groaned and kept talking herself out of feeling any excitement for their stupid challenge, a contest she'd make sure to end on Sunday. When they met to bowl and talk about his website. At a public place, where nothing sexual could happen. No dark corners or tables there. Just bowling balls, pins, weird shoes, and open lanes.

No challenge. No more attachment. She needed to put a stop to her growing feelings. In the past, avoidance had been the key. Time to reinforce her shields, because tonight had been much, *much* scarier than she'd anticipated. She'd started to step off that cliff, and if she fell this time, she didn't think she'd recover.

Chapter 10

CAMERON MCCAULEY STOOD OVER THE LUMP THAT was his burden for the day. Brody—Flynn's twin. Twin idiots, more like. The dog glanced up at him before settling back down across Brody's feet. How the guy could sleep with half a ton over his lower legs was anyone's guess.

"Hey. Brody."

Nothing, just some soft breathing. Brody never snored, never drank to excess, and never had a problem with women. Sometimes it was hard to like the guy.

He stared at the dog, who let out a loud sigh. *I know, buddy. Sorry it has to be this way.*

It was past noon, and Brody had agreed to lunch with the family. Everyone at Mom and Dad's to celebrate Colin's birthday. So what that the scamp had already had a party last week? He'd insisted on his uncles and grandparents celebrating again now that Ubie was home.

Instead of settling back into his condo after a few hellacious months spent out East, Cam had been bullied into taking on the responsibility for seeing that Brody arrived on time. Mike was apparently too good to do it because he'd fathered the birthday boy. And Flynn was too busy getting laid or having a tea party with Maddie, some lame excuse to get out of handling the blond lunk refusing to move.

"Hey Princess, I know you worked hard. Like, maybe five whole days in a row, and need your beauty sleep. But Mom and Dad are expecting you for Colin's party. You know, the one I texted you about twice yesterday?"

Still nothing. The dog, however, raised his head and thumped his tail on the comforter.

Cam grimaced at the rundown house. He knew Brody had been slowly renovating. But from what Cam could see, the outdated wallpaper, stained wooden floors, and crappy-ass furniture screamed *condemned* each and every time he stepped into the place. But try telling that to Mr. Know It All. Brody was a McCauley in every sense of the word, and if it had been up to his parents, they would have adopted him into the clan years ago.

Cam loved the guy, but God forbid he admit having real emotions. Like the rest of the McCauley men, Brody would make fun of him for being overly sensitive. Cam's lot in life, apparently.

With a sigh, he nudged the dog off the bed. For all that Brody claimed the thing was untrainable, the dog seemed to listen to everyone *but* Brody and Flynn. So naturally Cam and the dog got along famously. The unappreciated younger brother and the unappreciated guard dog.

Then again, Mutt hadn't reacted when Cam had knocked, walked in after using Flynn's spare key, or after he'd closed the door behind him with a solid *thunk*. Must have been because Mutt had smelled Cam, his favorite McCauley.

Cam and the dog looked at each other, then Cam went into the attached bath. Ensuite? More like horror from hell. The bathroom had a nasty tub and shower that appeared to be clean, just old and ugly. The toilet and sink, brass-framed mirror, and broadway lights over said mirror put Cam in mind of a funhouse. But he didn't think Brody would appreciate the comparison.

After filling a paper cup with water, he returned to the big bed, the only decent piece of furniture in the entire house. Wishing he'd thought to bring his cell phone to record this instead of leaving it in the car, he pulled the covers down from Brody's head.

The big bastard still didn't move. Even though Cam had been hitting the gym regularly, he didn't have Brody's mass. Mike was a powerhouse—an inhuman freak who should have been a pro wrestler named Manic Mike. Big brother didn't like that name or the inference that only men on steroids grew that huge. Flynn and Brody had about the same build. Both were large and broad shouldered. Cam, for all that he tried, had a more slender build, but he could outrun any of the bozos in his family, as well as out-lift Flynn.

Ah well. Cam tried once more, just so he could say he'd given it his best shot. "Brody?"

Brody opened his eyes and swore at him.

Too late. Cam doused him with water straight to the face. "Oh, sorry. You're up?"

More swearing and sputtering. Of the four of them, Brody could be the most creative when assigning body parts to certain orifices.

"Oh man. Is that even possible?"

Another finger, a recommendation to kiss an ass or two, and some more talk about being a dickhead as Brody wiped the water from his eyes.

"So can we talk or do you need another liquid

wake-up? Hungover, big guy?" Cam had never, *ever*, seen Brody drunk. He didn't think the guy had ever been that out of control. Brody at most drank two or three beers before sobering up to drive. The proverbial designated driver, hence his status as Mr. Popular when it came to a night out on the town.

"I'm up, I'm up. And when I'm outta this bed, I'm going to kick your candy ass all over the place." Brody paused. "What did you do to my dog?"

Cam stood petting Mutt, who tilted his head and whined for more. "It's called affection. Try it sometime."

Brody scowled. "I give him affection and he decks me for it. Hit me right in the balls last night." He sat up in bed and pulled his blankets tighter around his waist.

"Good dog," Cam crooned.

"*Hey.*"

"What? He's obviously in charge. I'm just praising him for being a good boy."

Brody's jaw clenched, and Cam smirked. Brody always clenched his jaw when trying to remain patient. "Why the fuck are you here?"

"Concise, if not polite. Fine." He held up a hand to stop Brody's inevitable rant. "Today is the party. You know, Colin's sixth b-day?"

Brody shook his head. "He had a party the day I left. Mike told me. Colin and a few miscreants from around the neighborhood had cake and ice cream at Bitsy's."

"Nice. Can you spell *miscreants*?"

"Without a dictionary? Probably not."

"Too much to hope for. Anyway, this party is Colin's idea because he missed you at his other one."

"Did Flynn go? Did you?"

"No, but that's beside the point. The kid wants more presents. Obviously this is *your* influence over the poor boy rearing its ugly head. Not mine."

Brody puffed up with pride. "Kid's a genius. Takes after me."

"Let's hope not. You can't even control your own dog."

Brody glared at him and pushed the covers away.

"Ack. God. *Stop*. I don't want to see your hairy ass. I'll wait in what you call a living room. More like a dying room where taste has been long gone since the nineties. Although seeing that couch, make that the seventies."

"Scared of my big dick. I thought so. It's okay, Cam. Someday you'll hit puberty and might grow a pair. Gee, maybe your voice will drop too. One can only hope."

Cam shot him a dirty look, for which Brody, the *big dick*, sneered back.

As Brody rose from the bed, Cam darted out of the bedroom to the stairs. Seeing a naked brother did not a great Saturday make. "I'll be out here," he yelled. "Making coffee if I can wrestle the roaches for it."

"Hey, I heard that! I don't have bugs. Ask Abby. She can vouch for me. So can Vanessa!" Brody yelled from the bathroom.

Cam froze on the stairs. "Why was Vanessa here?"

But the shower had started, so Brody didn't hear him.

Fuming at the thought of Brody making a move on Mike's neighbors, he slammed cabinets and drawers while he searched for the coffee filters and coffee. He brewed a pot and then sipped from a cup, more alarmed to see the kitchen clean. Vanessa had indeed been by.

Brody tromped down the steps with Mutt by his side. The dog might not see Brody as his owner yet, but the dog loved him. They made a pair, those two. Both mongrels with blustery outsides and warm insides.

"Ah, good. Java." Brody inhaled and let out a pleased sigh. Then he poured himself a cup and added a liberal dose of creamer and sugar.

Cam asked Brody what he really wanted to know. "Why the hell is Vanessa cleaning your kitchen?" He couldn't see her and Brody together, no matter how much he tried. Vanessa wore class and decorum like a second skin. Unlike Brody, who considered fart jokes and tits-and-ass magazines fine art.

Brody smirked, and Cam fought the urge to put his fist in Brody's face.

"I'm waiting." Best to remain calm. His brothers loved nothing more than to pull his chain. Brody in particular had never felt a qualm about reducing Cam to near tears if he thought it amusing. Cam had grown up the "emotional McCauley," so he did his best to always school his expressions.

"Don't get your panties in a twist, Cam. After me and the girls had our threesome, Vanessa decided to clean my house in payment for my manly prowess."

Cam gritted his teeth but didn't otherwise react.

Brody burst out laughing. "You look annoyed. Why is that, I wonder?"

"Please. You salivate anytime Abby's anywhere near."

Brody shrugged. "She's sexy. Vanessa scares me."

The woman had it all going on. Looks, finances, esteem, smarts. It would take a very assured and collected man to handle her. Cam gave Brody a wide smile. "She scares everyone." But not him. "Seriously, what's with the nice smells and clean kitchen? If it wasn't for the Norman Bates décor, I might think I was somewhere else."

Brody flipped him off.

"That's all you've got?"

"You are so annoying. Still the little brother from hell." But Brody smiled while saying it, and Cam felt the affection his pseudo-sibling had for him. It was too bad Brody was just like Flynn, because he'd have been an ideal ally against the others. Between his lying, cheating ways and Cam's intelligence, they might have run rings around Mike and Flynn. Alas, Cam was left constantly defending himself for having feelings and not being afraid to show them. Thank God his mother saw his value to the family. His father and the others often looked at him like a three-headed PMSing goat.

Brody finished his coffee and slicked back his damp hair. "Since I know you won't let this go, Abby watched Mutt while I was in Anacortes on a job."

"Oh?"

Brody shrugged, but Cam saw a lot he didn't say. "Mike flat-out refused to watch the dog."

"He's afraid Mutt will eat Colin."

Mutt whined at his name, and Brody reached down to scratch him between his ears. "Not funny."

Cam smirked. "Why didn't Flynn want him?"

"He's afraid the dog will eat Maddie, okay?"

Cam laughed. "So you suckered poor Abby into it?"

"Nah. It's an exchange. She ah—" Brody abruptly cut off.

Cam leaned closer. "She what?"

Brody coughed and put his mug in the sink. When he started washing it, Cam knew the guy wanted desperately to change the subject. Brody never washed dishes until they practically crawled out of the sink themselves.

"Tell me, or I'll tell Flynn and Mike you're harassing poor little Abby." Cam noticed the glare Brody shot him, one filled not just with anger, but with worry too. "What's up, man?"

"Shit." Brody turned and wiped his wet hands on a dishtowel. He put it back on the counter, but as he spoke, Mutt put his big face close and dragged the cloth to the floor. Then he quietly moved under the table with his new prize.

Cam shook his head. "Well?"

"You can't tell anyone."

I knew it. They had sex. "I won't."

Brody sighed and sat with Cam at the table. "Abby's going to do the McSons website for her usual going rate."

"How's that a deal?"

"I'm helping her with some research for her book."

Cam frowned. "She writes steamy romance, right? How exactly are you helping with that? Telling her how you best like a blow job?"

"It's not like that." Brody seemed genuinely angry.

"Whoa. I'm just kidding. I like Abby."

"And how the hell do you know what she writes?"

Cam shook his head. "Bro, I know everything. I met Abby and the others months before you and Flynn knew their names. Abby's smart, but all those books on her shelves by the same author kind of gave it away."

"You've been in her bedroom?" Brody's eyes widened, then narrowed with rage.

"Jesus. Leap to a conclusion, why don't you. No, dumbass. She has a bunch of her titles in her office on the ground floor. Hello? We've all been in there at one time or another since they moved in." Cam paused. "Why would you ask me about her bedroom?"

"No reason."

"Oh, come on. I'm the smart McCauley, remember? You've obviously been in her bedroom. She's needing you for research? Yeah right. You're totally having sex with Abby Dunn, aren't you?"

"No."

Cam read the lie for what it was. He couldn't wait to talk to Flynn and Mike about Brody and Abby. But he'd let Brody off the hook for now. "Okay, then explain yourself." Brody opened his mouth, no doubt to protest, and Cam added, "Better me than Mike and Flynn. I mean, the old Flynn might have kept his mouth shut. But the new, Maddie-and-Flynn Flynn, who knows what secrets he shares in the heat of the night?"

Brody blinked at him, then laughed. "You're such an idiot. Heat of the night? Fine. You want to know, I'll tell you. Abby writes sexy books. Like, about sex and love and stuff."

"And stuff," Cam parroted, realizing how funny the situation was. The biggest liar of the bunch was doing a terrible job of hiding his feelings for Abby. Fascinating. "Go on."

"So she wanted some help from a guy's perspective. Not about sex, but how guys talk to each other and shit."

"And shit."

"Did I stutter? Why are you repeating me?" Brody scowled. "So anyway, I help her with research, she does our website and agreed to watch Mutt for me last week. Vanessa came over to hang with her, I guess. I mean, God forbid poor Mutt spend a second at their pristine house."

The dog heard his name and walked out from under the table, strings of the dishtowel hanging from his jowls.

How Cam kept a straight face he didn't know. "God forbid."

Brody looked at the dog, then put his head in his hands. "Fuck. I don't know how she did it, but Abby had him trained. He didn't jump on other people and listened to her. To me, he walks around like he's the man."

Cam chuckled. "You're too soft on him. And you know, we really need to get to Mom and Dad's. You can bring him. Dad said."

"Great. I'll grab his leash. Can you get some food for him from the pantry? If I don't bring it, we'll end up being there forever. If I do, we'll probably have a short party."

"For Colin? Are you kidding? The kid will milk today for as long as he can."

"Oh, right. Speaking of that, I guess we need to make a stop at a toy store on the way. Hey, don't give me that look. I just got home last night, and it was a bitch of a job."

After they wrangled the dog into Brody's truck, Brody drove Mutt to the toy store while Cam followed behind in his car. Brody scolded the dog to behave, and as usual, the great canine grinned at him as if to say,

"Behave? Make me, pretty boy." Or at least that's what Brody thought the dog would say if he could talk. He really needed Abby to help him with Mutt.

A legitimate excuse to spend more time with her. *Perfect*. He beamed at the dog before going into the store with Cam to buy Colin some Nerf guns. The war-like little monster would love 'em. "So you going to stick to me all the way to Bitsy and Pop's?"

"Those are my orders." Cam sighed.

Brody had to laugh. "Mike?"

"Colin."

Brody laughed again. "Well, come on. Let's not leave Napoleon hanging."

They made it to the house in half an hour, ten minutes before the festivities were due to start. Since the toy store had wrapped his gift, all Brody had to do was sign the card, which he did in the truck. He carried the present in one hand and Mutt's leash in the other.

Baffled that the dog never pulled or strained when leashed but acted like an angel, Brody knew he had to figure out how to train the creature before Mutt leaped on some kid without wearing said leash. He couldn't keep the dog on a tether all the time. Could he?

"Behave yourself," he said with a warning to the canine.

Mutt panted, his tongue hanging out, and licked Brody's hand.

"Talking to the dog or yourself?" Cam asked.

"I'm always on my best behavior." Brody nudged Cam from the door and rang the bell.

Bitsy answered in seconds, apparently waiting for them. "Oh, good. You're here." With her expertly cut dark bob that framed a stunning face and soft green eyes, she was the epitome of a warm welcome. She'd kept her figure as well, and Brody thought she and Pop made a convincing argument for marriage. They looked like the perfect couple, like the ones on TV that advertised for a happy, healthy life. The motherly but pretty woman and the manly guy with a touch of silver in his hair.

Then she turned a mean eye on the dog. "*He* goes in the backyard. And tie him up this time, Brody."

"Yes, ma'am." He handed her Colin's present and gave her a kiss on the cheek. "You look amazing. You losing weight again? You really shouldn't. You're too skinny as it is."

She blushed and pulled him inside.

"Thanks, Mom. I'm good," Cam shouted through the screen door that had closed in his face.

Brody chuckled and followed her inside. Someday he'd have a house that looked like this. A four-thousand-square-foot home with warm colors, lived-in furniture that actually looked as if someone had spent money on it, and knickknacks all over the place that spoke of a family's history and travels. She had prints on the walls she'd painted, as well as their artwork from the time they'd started school. He saw several pictures of himself and the guys as kids on the mantel, and he swelled with pleasure at the feeling of belonging.

Most of his trophies and odds and ends remained in a box in a spare room at home. He couldn't display them in his house as it was now. But someday he'd have a place this nice. He might have a steady girlfriend in ten or more years. Maybe even a wife. It could happen. Of course, she'd inevitably run out on him or tire of him before too long. But he'd have her for long enough to decorate his place.

"Brody?"

He blinked. Had he manifested Abby's voice out of his desire for a woman by his side? He turned and saw Abby, Vanessa, and Maddie walking out of the kitchen with Flynn on their heels.

"Hey now." He couldn't help the broad grin threatening to split his head wide open.

When Abby had mentioned getting together Sunday instead of today, all his plans of togetherness had gone out the window. So much for a weekend of nonstop sex. But bowling with her tomorrow would satisfy him as much, and that had annoyed him as well. Since when did he just want to spend time with a woman who got him hard on command?

Not that he disliked women or didn't want something steadier than one-night stands, but most of them bored him. He never let them get close, didn't want to share the intimate parts of himself that they all claimed to need. He didn't just fuck his dates, but he normally saved his favorite activities for his brothers. Cards, bowling, football. Guy stuff.

Movies, walks along the waterfront, romantic dinners—woman events.

But this woman he'd agreed to go bowling with. She wore a pair of jeans that flattered her sexy ass, and a goofy long-sleeved T-shirt with some grammatical saying on it. Something about *there* and *their* that completely bypassed him. She wore a smile on her face and had her hair down, that glorious mane that had only last night settled over his thighs while she wrapped her full lips around his cock. Man, he needed to stop thinking about crap like that with everyone watching them.

"Yeah, we were commanded by Herr Colin to be here. Or else," Vanessa was saying, so he hastily ripped his gaze from Abby, hoping he hadn't looked overly horny or desperate to be with her again. Because he wasn't. At all. He just wanted to be neighborly. Friendly. To offer a hand—or a cock—as needed.

He glanced to Flynn and saw Cam whispering something to him, something that had both brothers grinning at him. *Shit*.

"Nice to see you again, Brody. You clean up nice," Maddie teased. "I saw him last night at Flynn's, and he looked pretty tired," she said to Bitsy. She stopped speaking and took a healthy step back, and he realized Mutt was straining at his leash. He wanted to jump Maddie.

"Geez, Brody. Have you learned nothing?" Abby rolled her eyes, crossed the room, and took the leash from his hand. She smelled like lilacs or lavender, some floral scent that encouraged him to follow her wherever she went.

Instead, he stood in place and watched as she tugged Mutt to a sitting position and ordered him in a hard voice to stay.

"Pussy," Mike muttered by his side. "That little woman gets that huge beast to obey, and he leads you around by the nose."

Colin raced to Mutt and hugged him, both of them nearly at eye level. The dog's tail wagged and he licked Colin's face clean of whatever had been on his mouth. Knowing only half of what Mutt had eaten that morning, Brody cringed.

"Ech." Bitsy took Colin by the arm and dragged him away. "Time to wash your face, mister."

"But Grandma, he's kissing me!"

"I know. That's nice." Bitsy wasn't hearing it. "And Brody, the dog? *Outside*."

From behind him, he heard Pop add, "The boy comes home and not a hello? Rude." He slapped Brody upside the head before grabbing him in a bear hug from behind and lifting him.

"Easy, James!"

"Jesus, woman. I'm not an old geezer yet," he snapped. The same size as Mike, James McCauley looked only a decade or so older than his firstborn and had the strength of a man in his prime.

"Sorry for caring," Bitsy muttered and dragged Colin with her down the hall.

Brody looked at his brothers, concerned to see them frowning at the interplay. The last few times he'd visited, he'd sensed something amiss between the two, but he chalked it up to one of those dips in marital harmony he often heard about. The ups and downs. Bitsy and Pop had to be in a down. No biggie. They'd weathered plenty before and had come out on top. Not many could say that, especially in this day and age.

"Hey, Pop." He turned around and smiled at the man he wished could have been his biological father, but had given him everything he'd needed and more anyway. He gave Pop a mock frown. "Hmm. You putting on weight? You seem bigger somehow."

"Smartass." Pop chuckled. "We missed you, boy. So Flynn tells me you did a bang-up job at the site. And Abby says you're ready for me to build you something."

"I thought I was going to do it?" Mike frowned.

"Fellas, please. There's plenty of me to go around." Brody grinned then winked at Abby. "You sweet thing, you didn't need to bring in the big guns to clean up my place. Just swing Vanessa around again when she's in a mood. Eventually the cleanliness will make the house shine."

"I'd suggest burning it for the insurance money," Vanessa offered. "But I don't want to have to go to court and testify to the fact. Why don't you go burn some candles at home, Brody?" she suggested. "Then leave them alone…"

Cam snickered, as did the others. "And while you're at it, call in an exorcist."

Mike cracked up. "Hell, yeah. Isn't pea green the same color as the tub in your bathroom?"

"You guys are hilarious." Brody refused to smile.

Abby smirked.

"Not you too. I let you stay with my precious dog as a show of faith. Don't go ruining my trust by making fun of my castle."

"Castle? Try dungeon."

James crossed to Abby and hugged her until she squeaked. "She's a quick one. Even helped with our website, didn't you?"

"You helped him before us?" Flynn protested.

"Hey, he asked first. And he paid me."

"We're going to pay you."

"I'm not talking about Monopoly money, Flynn." Abby frowned at him.

"Oh please. If it's good enough for the monocle man, I don't know why it's not good enough for you."

"Yeah, Abby. Just think. You buy Park Place or the Boardwalk and you're set for life," Vanessa snarked.

Cam grinned and said something that probably made sense to a person who knew finance, because Vanessa laughed out loud. The woman's eyes were sparkling, and the way she and Cam leaned in to each other told Brody he wasn't the only one wanting one of Mike's neighbors.

"Well, well." Brody stared at Cam until he looked up at him.

Cam made some excuse to help his mother—the coward—and darted down the hall toward Colin.

Abby took Mutt outside while the others fetched drinks and snacks from the expansive feast laid out on the dining room table. A bit formal for Brody's taste, but the room suited Bitsy to a T.

"Dig in folks," Pop boomed. "It's not every day my grandson turns six."

"Not to be a stickler, but isn't this his second party?" Vanessa chimed in. Pop glared at her, and she held up her hands. "What did I say but the truth?"

"He missed Ubie," Mike said as he loaded his plate with wings, fritters, poppers, and other food any health-conscious person would avoid like the plague. Vanessa and Maddie steered clear of the fried stuff, while Flynn, Mike, and Brody hogged the goodies.

Abby returned from the kitchen, where she'd gone with Mutt to access the back porch. "Well, he's not happy, but he's not destructive either. I tied him off where he can't get to anything. Brody, you want to put a bowl of water out there for him?"

"Yeah. Here." He handed her a plate filled with food her roommates wouldn't touch with a ten-foot pole.

When Abby frowned at the plate, he growled, "Eat it. You know you want some. Don't be a sissy like your roommates. Your ass is just fine the way it is."

"And mine isn't?" Maddie said in a near shout.

Flynn swore at Brody and tried to calm his girlfriend.

Brody left before he could pat Abby's sexy rear and give himself away, and tended to his dog. The poor thing looked miserable, despite the sunny though chilly weather. With that thick coat, Mutt wouldn't freeze. But with the fun inside, he was clearly missing out.

"Don't worry, buddy. I'll bring you something before we leave. Maybe a nice meatball or some paper napkins to chew on."

Mutt slapped his tail and licked Brody's fingers. Then he rolled onto his back and demanded a belly scratch. "Starved for affection, eh?" *Might as well be talking to myself.* He felt stupid for wanting to spend every available waking moment with Abby, more so now after having had sex with her. The notion to bed and forget her didn't appear, and he didn't like this obsession for the woman. She'd even affected his appetite. She made him nervous, and he had to force himself to eat when around her.

He left Mutt and returned to see Colin laughing at Abby, his enjoyment clear. For a moment, with her head turned, Brody had the uneasy sensation of seeing Lea sitting with her son. But the moment Abby turned, he saw *her*, any hint of Mike's wife and Colin's mom nonexistent. He knew, then and there, that this thing he had for Abby had *nothing* to do with Lea, and *everything* to do with falling for Abigail Dunn.

Not good.

At least if he'd transferred his affection from Lea to

Abby, his deepening feelings for the stubborn woman would make sense. But that he might actually be falling for her all on her own unnerved him. He'd pretty much dared her not to love him at their last meeting. And she'd all but told him she'd have him at her feet begging for more before she was through.

Damn if she hadn't nailed it, because he wanted to roll over on his back and have her scratch his belly. He wanted her to laugh at his jokes, to hold his hand and invite him back to her place for multi-orgasmic sex.

Instead, he watched her shyly respond to something Pop said. That dichotomy of this Abby—the quiet one with the big smile to the mouthy vixen who liked to give him shit on a daily basis—captivated him.

"You might want to blink, Brody." Mike punched him in the arm.

"Ow. I was just making sure she didn't toss the plate I gave her. It totally goes against the grain to give up Bitsy's wings."

Mike snorted and in a lower voice said, "Yeah, that's why you keep looking at her breasts."

"I'm just trying to read the caption on her T-shirt. What does it say?" He forced a squint, and Mike shook his head and stepped away.

Brody made himself a plate and sat in the living room next to Flynn. They shared obnoxious commentary as Colin opened his second round of presents.

"Wow. This is just like déjà vu," Flynn said, sounding shocked. "I could have sworn I already got this little snot something."

"No, Uncle Flynn," Colin said in his best little-boy voice. "That must have been some other boy."

"Nice one, kid. You know you got a stuffed dog and video game last week." Maddie snorted.

"Ohhh, yeah. That." He grinned at them, the little mini-Mike with his big dimples. "Thanks."

The others laughed.

When Colin got to Cam's present, he frowned. "An envelope?"

"It's a savings bond, dork. So when you're bigger, you'll be rich."

Colin didn't seem convinced, until his father cleared his throat. Then Colin smiled widely and said, "Uh, yeah. Thanks *so* much, Uncle Cam."

The fake cheer made Brody cringe.

Colin opened Abby's gift. "What's this?"

"A story about a boy who's a dark elf. He helps his friends defeat the return of the gods. It's like *Lord of the Rings* but for kids and not so bloody."

Colin's eyes grew wide. He'd just started to read and had an amazing capacity for retention—according to Momma Mike. "Wait, not bloody? That's no good."

Abby laughed. "Your dad can read it to you before bed."

"Or you could, Abby." Colin layered his smile with what Brody liked to call the kid's super charm. "You know, if you and Maddie help babysit me."

"For God's sake," Mike muttered. "Colin, we're not inviting the entire neighborhood to watch you at night. Just sometimes your uncles and grandparents help out. I'll read to you."

"Or I can," Maddie chimed in.

"Me too, honey." Bitsy scowled at Mike. "Honestly, son, he wants to read. Encourage him."

"I'm not…" Mike trailed off as everyone watched him. "Oh fine, you little con man. Everyone can read to you."

"Not me," Brody said proudly.

"You have something against books?" Abby asked.

She was so cute when annoyed. "Nope. But when I come over, we'll *play* with my present."

Colin scrambled to open Brody's gift next, and his eyes grew huge when he saw the guns Mike had forbidden him to have after the last Nerf incident.

"Brody," Mike growled.

Pop and Flynn grinned, because Mike had expressly forbidden the three of them from purchasing them. But since when did Mike tell him what to do?

"You're not the boss of me," Brody said in a sing-song voice.

Abby chuckled, and he winked at her. Even better, she winked back.

The others laughed at his antics, and then Colin was loading his gun and shooting everyone and everything in sight with those sucker darts that shouldn't hurt but did when hit between the eyes.

"Ow." Brody rubbed his forehead.

Mike glared. "And this is why I said no."

"Spoilsport." Vanessa shocked all of them by grabbing the second gun and charging after Colin.

Colin cried for help from the hallway. "Uncle Cam! Save me from—"

"Darth Vanessa," Vanessa yelled with an evil laugh.

"No, seriously. She makes us call her that at home," Abby said.

Maddie nodded, and laughter filled the house.

Brody's heart felt so full he feared it would burst.

It felt odd that Abby should fit so seamlessly within his family. So demure until she looked at him with challenge in her eyes. She turned to Bitsy and smiled, talking about some show on television about landscaping that had Maddie chiming in. Flynn sat with his arm around Maddie's shoulders and argued with Cam, Mike, and Pop about the Seahawks' chances of taking this year's NFC West championship.

"Yeah. That'll happen." He had to give his two cents. "Just as soon as they name me Pope Brody the XVI."

Mike grinned. "Sad to say, but yeah. What he said."

They continued to argue, and Brody was glad he'd come home a day early so he could be with his family. When his cell phone vibrated and rang from his back pocket, he pulled it out and checked the number. Not about to let anything ruin his day, he turned off the phone and tucked it away.

"Anything important?" Mike asked.

"Nah. Nothing that can't keep." Until hell froze over.

Chapter 11

ABBY GRABBED HER COAT AND PUT IT ON, READY TO leave after watching Flynn and Brody consistently beat everyone at a *friendly* game of Uno. And not to be considerate of Colin's feelings, whenever they won, they rubbed the six-year-old's nose in his defeat. To be fair, they did that to everyone until the women had finally quit in disgust.

"What?" Flynn said in response to Maddie's frown.

"You're impossible."

"He started it with that lame victory dance." Flynn glared when Colin stuck out his tongue.

Maddie sighed. "He's only six, Flynn."

"Oh, and that makes him too young to learn that only the fittest survive?"

Vanessa frowned. "We are talking about Uno, right?"

Abby swallowed a laugh and turned to Beth. "Thanks so much for inviting us."

"That was all Colin." Beth walked her to the door a little bit away from the others. "Would you mind giving me a minute when the others leave, Abby?"

"Not at all. I'll wait with Mutt."

Beth snorted. "That dog needs a better name. Nothing yet?"

"Not that his lord and master will okay." She glanced at Brody, still arguing about some stupid championship with Mike. The only reason she watched football was to get a look at men in tight pants. "I've tried Cujo, Killer, Nanook, Fenris, and a bunch of others. No luck so far."

Beth shook her head. "I don't know what that boy was thinking to adopt a dog. But he's always gone his own way. What can you do?"

Beth left her in the kitchen and went to say good-bye to the others, who made noise about leaving.

Maddie entered the kitchen holding Flynn's hand and asked Abby, "What are you up to today?"

"Thought I'd take a break and hit the bookstore. You two?"

Flynn hugged Maddie from behind. "New chick flick at the movies. I agreed to see it, and Maddie has to let me watch football tomorrow with the guys without complaining."

Maddie sighed. "What I do for love."

"And hot sex," Flynn added and rubbed his girl-friend's belly.

Abby threw up her hands. "Ew. Stop. Why do you people constantly find it okay to over-share?"

Maddie blew her a kiss. "Love you too, Abby. See you tomorrow."

The pair left through the back door. Then Vanessa tromped through with Cam on her heels, arguing about something. Abby caught the words *percentage*, *yield*, and *investment opportunity*. When she heard *workout* and *gym* as they left, she tuned the rest out. What normal people willingly sweated for fun?

Outside, Mutt barked and whined when they walked past him and through the gate to the alley behind the house.

"I know, buddy. Just a few more minutes and I'll get

you since your 'master' is busy playing," Abby murmured, feeling sorry for the big guy. How pathetic was she that she was starting to find him cute?

"Oh, there you are." Beth entered the kitchen and looked over her shoulder. She pulled Abby with her to the table and sat. "James and the others are working on something with Colin in the back. I think Mike and Brody are trying to help him build that new model James got him. But this is good, because it gives us a chance to talk privately."

Abby had no idea what Beth wanted to discuss. Then she remembered what Brody had mentioned about Mike, and she prayed she wouldn't have to talk her way out of an arranged date with him. Awkward.

"I hope you don't mind, but I've become a bit concerned about Colin."

Abby stared. "Colin?"

Beth frowned. Even the worried expression didn't detract from her attractiveness. Beth had a wholesome, loving vibe going for her, a terrific husband, and a smile that could light up a room. *I so want to be her someday.*

"He keeps talking about this Del person. But honestly, Abby. From what he's described, I'm not sure I want Del around my grandson. Can you shed some light on this? The woman didn't really have tattoos all over, did she? Muscles larger than Flynn's? Really? Because she made a huge impression on Colin. She's all he's been talking about lately."

Breathing a sigh of relief that the conversation had nothing to do with Mike, Abby explained exactly what Del had done for them. "To be fair, Del didn't have to help. But she did. And let me tell you, I was not looking forward to changing that tire myself."

"Honey, you should have called James or Mike for help." Beth put a hand over Abby's on the table, reminding Abby of her own mother.

"I was okay. I would have figured it out. Fortunately, I didn't have to. I even offered to pay her, but she said not to. It's funny, because she looked and acted tough, but she was really sweet with Colin. He kept chattering the whole time she worked on that tire, and she answered him with patience and humor. I liked her." Why she felt like she had to defend Del, she had no idea. But it didn't sit right that Beth should think less of the woman for a few tattoos when Del had done Abby and Colin such a huge favor.

"Well, okay then. I trust your judgment."

"Thanks." Abby smiled. "I guess I'll head back home and—"

"Just one more thing."

"Sure, Beth."

"It's complicated." She stood, glanced over her shoulder again, and urged Abby to head outside.

In the cold. Abby had a jacket on, but Beth didn't. "Hold on." She left Beth to unleash the dog, then returned to the older woman. Mutt danced around, running out some nervous energy, then walked up and sat by her side, calm as you please.

Beth didn't seem to feel the chilly weather. "Well look at that. What a gentleman." Beth petted him, and he sat with restraint.

It was like he was a completely different dog without Brody. Abby wondered what that said about the blond Adonis.

"You really need to help Brody," Beth said as if reading her mind. "He's terrible with discipline. Always has been." She smiled, clearly fond of him. "Anyhow, that's not what I wanted to talk to you about. It's about Lea."

Abby stilled, and by her, Mutt tensed as well. She tried to relax and pet him, but she couldn't make herself more comfortable. *Don't say it, Beth. Please…*

"You look so much like her, and I think that's kept you from being friends with Mike."

Friends? Or more than friends? Gah. "Oh no," Abby hastened to reassure her. "I like Mike a lot. He's a terrific neighbor. A great guy. And I love Colin. Trust me. We're all over the weird look-alike thing. Mike told me so." Had she been glad about that. She had no wish to be a dead woman's stand-in, or to make Mike, such a terrific guy, uneasy.

"That's good to know." Beth sounded relieved. "Because I really like you, dear. You're great with Colin, so smart, and you've helped so much with that web business. Mike and James think the world of you." Her large smile put Abby in mind of a predator about to pounce.

"Well then. That's great." Abby swallowed her nerves.

"I just think that maybe you haven't looked at Mike as a potential date, for a relationship. That resemblance to Lea threw you. I understand. However, I think if you—"

"Beth, let me stop you right there. I love your family. Heck, I want to *be* a McCauley." Beth laughed with her. Good, this might not turn out as discomfiting as it felt. "But I have absolutely no interest in Mike that way. He's handsome, yes. A great dad, a great guy. But there's no spark. You know what I'm talking about. You have that with James."

"Hmm. Sometimes a spark isn't all it's cracked up to be."

Abby frowned. "Are you okay?"

Beth's lips trembled. "Oh, just me being silly, I guess. I'm sorry if I put you on the spot."

"No, no. I'm flattered you'd think I'm good enough for Mike."

"Oh hush. You're wonderful. You and the girls are so helpful. I couldn't be more pleased you three decided to move next door to him. You're a breath of fresh air compared to the last tenants." Beth rubbed her arms. "Time to head back in, I think."

Abby followed her back inside, only to see James and Colin scowling at Beth.

Abby bumped into the back of her. "Oomph. Sorry."

"Grandma, I was calling for you a lot."

"What were you doing out there, Beth?" James frowned. "The boy could use your help while his father and uncle are arguing like cats and dogs. Stupid football."

"Stupid football," Colin repeated.

Abby smothered a grin and stepped beside Beth. When she glanced at the older woman, expecting to see the same amusement, she saw anger instead.

"I was talking to Abby," Beth said stiffly.

"About what?"

"None of your business. You don't own me, you know. If I want to talk to her, I will. *Oh*. I'm going for a walk." With that, Beth stormed out of the kitchen into the living room and out of sight. The front door opened and slammed shut, while the three of them—Abby, James, and Colin—stared at one another, nonplussed.

"Grandma's mad." Colin's eyes grew huge.

"What else is new?" James sighed. "I bet the woman didn't think to take her coat," he muttered under his breath and went after her.

Abby tried to shrug it off, but it seemed to her that James and Beth were having some real problems.

"Come on, Colin. Let's go see who's winning the argument in the back." She heard Mike's voice grow louder, then Brody's as he laughed at the idea of the Eagles getting into the playoffs. The boy grinned and grabbed her hand, tugging her with him, and that dimple just killed her. She leaned down to kiss his adorable cheek. So cute...and such *a thief*. "Hey, give me back that soda!"

He ran with it toward the loud voices, and she followed with a groan when Mike bellowed, "Who gave you soda? You know you're not allowed to have that."

"Abby did, Dad."

"I did not." She had just joined them in time to ward off Mike's accusation. "The sneak stole it. Brody, your dog is loose. And Mike, you might want to give your parents some space. They seemed a bit, ah," she paused, glancing down at Colin.

"Grandma yelled at Grandpa and slammed out the door. Then he ran after her." Colin didn't look happy anymore. "I think they're fighting. They fight a lot."

Mike put his arm around Colin. "Don't worry, buddy. That's what grown-ups do sometimes."

Colin blinked up at his dad. "Did you and Mommy fight?"

Abby saw what looked like pain cross Mike's face before he smiled. "Sure did."

"About what?" Colin persisted.

When Mike floundered, Brody answered.

"I remember one big fight they had. Yeah, your mom wanted to call you Lancelot, and your dad wanted to call you Fish Face."

Colin gaped. "Fish Face, Dad? That would have been *awesome*."

"Well, I did suggest Buttwipe and Bigfoot, but then your mother starting throwing Arthur and Galahad around. So we settled on Colin."

"Yeah." Brody grinned. "'Cause you get beat up less if you're not one of the Round Table."

"Huh?"

"Ask your cousins Theodore, Gavin, and Landon how names can hurt you." Brody snickered. "Your dad and the rest of us used to bail them out of trouble on a regular basis. I mean really. *Landon*?"

Mike chuckled.

Abby shook her head. "Oh brother. I can feel the testosterone from here. And don't ask, Colin. Yes, you have it too. Well, I'm heading out. The others left, and I want to be gone before Beth and James get back. Give them some privacy to talk, you know?"

Brody jumped on the idea. "Yeah, what she said. Come on, Abby. I'll give you a lift. You walked over, right?"

"Hold on." Mike frowned. "Where's your dog?"

"Let's go, Abby." Brody walked her faster.

"But Dad, Ubie's letting us watch him tonight, for my birthday."

"Oh he is, is he?" Mike asked, his voice a little too soft for Abby's comfort.

Brody dragged her with him in a hurry for the front door. He yanked his coat from the closet and put it on while Mike joined them, followed closely by Colin. "Don't worry, Mike. I brought plenty of food for him. I'll get him in the morning. Trust me. I love my dog. I hate to leave him. But I love Colin too. And he'll be heartbroken if I take Mutt with me after promising he could dog sit."

"He can't possibly be buying this," she whispered as she saw Colin nodding enthusiastically behind his father and winking at Brody. "You're corrupting a minor."

"No way, he's corrupting me," he whispered back. In a louder voice, he said to Mike, "So we're gone. See you tomorrow. You know, when I come to get my dog at your place."

Mike scratched his head, his biceps bunching, and she stared at the sheer strength in the man. "I don't know…"

Brody didn't give him time to say no. He yanked Abby out the front door and hurried to the truck. "Get in, get in."

The moment she entered and closed the passenger door, he screeched in reverse and drove away like a bat out of hell. She struggled to belt herself in. "What the heck, Brody?"

"Colin's been nagging Mike about a dog for months. Now I'm giving him a chance to prove he can take care of one. Trust me. Colin and I have been planning this for a while."

"You're always up to something." Instead of being suspicious, she admired his persistence. "Drop me off at home, and thanks."

"Really? You're going home?"

"It's kind of ugly out." Another gray November day. "I'm actually going to the bookstore later." Not what she should have said if she'd wanted the day to herself, because Brody turned away from the direction of her house toward the bookstore. As they drove, he continued to amuse her with anecdotes from Colin's party.

Twenty minutes later, he parked in front of her second favorite place to go, the first being the library.

Brody turned off the engine and sighed. "They do have coffee, right?"

"Why, so you'll have something to do?"

"Yes. I'm so glad you understand." He left the truck after she did and walked beside her. Not touching, not holding hands, but so close he might as well have marked a *mine* stamp on her forehead.

"God forbid you read," she muttered. "Plebian."

"I hate when you highfalutin folk use big words." He crossed his eyes at her, and she laughed. "You want to hit me where it hurts, call me a dick. A Republican." He leaned close and whispered, "An Eagles fan."

She shook her head as they entered the store. "I'm not talking politics or football with you. Frankly, both give me a headache."

"Welcome to my world with books."

Offended, she flounced away from him.

"Not *your* books," he said too loudly, and several customers looked in their direction.

When he caught up with her, she whispered, "Shh. Not so loud."

"Come on, Abby. Let's see if your books are here."

The reason she'd wanted to come to the store in the first place.

He walked in the wrong direction, and she sighed. "No, this way." She led him to the romance section and frowned at the selection. "Man. You get one week, maybe two, before they shuffle you around."

He ignored her, perusing the titles and getting in the way of several annoyed women trying to browse. "Aha! Here it is. *Fireman's Kiss*, by Abigail D. Chatterly. That's the one I read." He pulled out the book and waved it at her.

She flushed. God. Why had she let him come with her?

One woman behind him cleared her throat. "I've been looking for that."

"Oh? Because *she* wrote it." Brody smiled and pointed at Abby. "That's the author."

The woman's eyes grew wide. "You're Abigail Chatterly?"

Brody nodded. "Yep. That's her."

"Um, yeah." Abby hated this. She refused to do book signings for the same reason, embarrassed at being the center of attention.

A few more women drew closer.

"Oh my God! I love your stories." The lady wanting the book snagged it from Brody's hand. "This is your newest, right?"

The other women crowded closer. "I liked your last series," one of them said. "Which one is this?"

The lady holding the book answered. Then the ones at her back asked Abby questions about the series she'd been talking about on her website, the one that now sat with her agent.

Before she knew it, she'd entered into an engaging discussion about the genre and her books and had promised to attend a book club the following week, where they'd be discussing *her* novels.

As the women left her, she felt on cloud nine. People actually liked her work. It always astounded her that the same fiction she wrote to entertain herself could appeal to others.

"That was very, very cool," Brody said, and she realized she'd completely forgotten he was there.

She found him down the aisle watching her. "Sorry."

"No. That was awesome." His grin took her aback. He seemed...*proud*. "Man. You have fans. Besides me, I mean." He winked at her. "*Fireman's Kiss* was hawt," he teased.

She flushed. "Shut up."

"But I really think you should write about sexy plumbers."

"Plumbers aren't sexy."

He frowned.

"Well, except for you and Flynn. Most women envision a plumber and think 'big man bending over showing butt crack.' Not appealing."

"Oh, come on. What if I bent over?"

"Now I'd read that book," a white-haired woman said from behind him. She laughed when Brody wiggled his brows at her.

"See, Abby?" Brody grinned. "You're limiting your audience. Readers want plumbers."

To the lady, Abby said, "Don't encourage him."

"Honey, if I were your age, I'd be doing nothing *but* encouraging him. Now where are those Chatterly books I heard the others talking about?"

Brody led her to the spot while Abby watched. He flirted and charmed and managed to sell six more copies to strangers passing by. She had to leave or she didn't think she'd survive the heat burning her cheeks.

He met her at the coffee counter in the back. "I want a commission."

She took her cup from the guy delivering it and walked quickly to a seat. Brody followed her holding a tangerine soda.

"I am never coming to the bookstore with you again." Over his shoulder, one of the readers who'd bought her book prodded her friend in the arm and pointed at Abby.

The pair grinned and waved at her, and she weakly waved back. "Never," she emphasized.

"Why not? Those ladies liked your books. That's terrific."

"It's embarrassing," she answered in a low voice.

"Why? Because you write about sex?" he answered *loudly*.

At that, more than one person clued in to their conversation.

She wanted to bury her head under the table, but then she'd no doubt give everyone the impression that she didn't just write about blow jobs, she gave them in public too. "Stop, please."

He chuckled. "You're so cute when you turn red like that. So what else are we doing today?"

"*We* are not doing anything. *I* am going to browse a little, then go back home and relax."

"Relax how?"

She didn't like how he was making her feel. That pride he'd shown in her meant something. He'd given her a sense of accomplishment just because he seemed to believe in her. And he'd bragged to those people about the same books Kevin had sneered at and called trash. Brody, that sneak, was making her fall for him hard without even trying. At this rate, she really would be lost in love with the big jerk in no time at all. She needed distance, and she needed it fast.

"Brody, are you getting clingy?" she taunted. "Because that would mean I'm winning, and that you're falling for me already. Wow. Who knew you were that easy?"

His face darkened. "Please. If anything, you're running scared. I'm a prize. A total catch." He lowered his voice. "I'm great in bed and out. I'm fun, I'm hot—"

"Arrogant, much?"

"—and I'm available. The big three, yeah, I hit 'em all. Besides that, you know I love your body, and I think you writing romance is terrific. So you're thinking, what's not to like about this man?" He continued in falsetto, "I'm so over the moon for him. In fact, I think I might just write about sexy plumbers, because he's all I can think about." He paused to guzzle more sugar water. "So, princess, I'm thinking you're working hard *not* to fall for me. Hence your need for space."

That he'd read her perfectly both annoyed and alarmed her. So she scoffed. "Dream on. It must grate your ego to know that a bubble bath and the television are right up there with Brody time."

"Bubble bath?"

She tried not to but couldn't help laughing. "I *do not* need you to scrub my back. Believe it or not, I like myself. I like being alone." Well, she liked being alone—sometimes. Though she didn't exactly love everything about herself. Like the size of her ass. Or her average features. Or the fact that she was addicted to Brody.

"Sure, cat lady. You keep thinking that."

She glared at him.

"Yeah, yeah. Fine. I'll take you back home so you can be a hermit. But you're going to hate knowing you blew time to spend with me, because I have to take a rain check on bowling. I've been guilted into football tomorrow with the guys. We're watching at Mike's place. No girls allowed."

She swallowed her disappointment. "I heard Maddie and Flynn talking about that." She forced a casual shrug. "So we bowl another time."

"Yeah, Tuesday at six. I called. They don't have league until Wednesday. Besides, Tuesday is wing night. I love wings." He drank another sip and eyed her chest. "But I'm a breast man at heart." He snickered at the subtle finger she shot him. "You wish, sweetheart. But I'm content to wait until you're begging for it again."

Begging? "You're so full of it."

After they disposed of their trash and she took another few moments to browse the store, she followed him out to the truck. She snapped at his gibes and gave back as good as she got during the ride home. He dropped her off with a reminder about Tuesday.

"Oh, I'll be there Mr. Big Shot. Just wait until I out-bowl your ass."

Brody grinned. "Always thinking about my ass. Just proves my point. Until Tuesday, sweet cheeks."

She slammed the door, and he drove off, leaving her sputtering to herself as she marched inside.

To her great regret, she missed the big oaf not two seconds after she shut the door behind her. The wait until Tuesday would stretch interminably long. She just knew it.

Chapter 12

AT JAMESON'S GYM, VANESSA FINISHED RUNNING ON the treadmill and did her best to ignore the fact that Cameron stood talking to some bimbo in tights by the water fountain.

That she and he worked out at the same gym was no coincidence. They both liked being in shape and had an aversion to wasting money on trendy places calling themselves fitness centers. Vanessa worked out to keep fit, as did Cameron. Unlike the rest of the thugs he was related to—including the blond doofus—Cameron had a brain in his head and an uncanny sense of value.

The many investments he and she had discussed on the drive over showed him to be quite intelligent. She admired that in a man.

She also admired a tight ass, wide shoulders, and runner's legs. Man, he had nice legs.

She finished her workout and while catching her breath, wiped down the equipment.

"Hey, I can finish that." A good-looking guy about her age smiled and held his hand out for the rag. She hadn't seen him before, but the gym was always getting new members.

"Oh. Okay." She handed him the rag, then tried to move around him, so as not to waste his time on the treadmill. There was a waiting list to use it.

"No problem." He didn't move. "So, you work out here a lot. I've seen you."

"Yes."

He nodded. "That's cool."

He still didn't move.

"Ah, you're in my way."

"Oh, sorry." He moved aside, but instead of getting on the treadmill to maximize his time, he turned and continued talking. "So are you seeing anyone?"

Not beating around the bush, this guy. She could appreciate that. "I'm seeing you right now." She decided to cut him a break because he had nice calves. "But if you're asking if I'm currently dating anyone, then no."

"Now that's a surprise." Instead of a lingering once-over that would have turned her right off, this guy smiled at her. "My name's John." He held out a hand.

She took it, not thrilled with the wimpy handshake, but at least his palm wasn't clammy. "Vanessa."

"Would you like to grab a drink sometime?"

Would she? A glance out of the corner of her eye showed Cam still laughing at Breasty McGee. "Sure, why not?" Then she tacked on a smile, lest he think she was being too *meh* about her agreement. Honestly, she hadn't been looking for a hookup, but it might take her mind off her stresses at work…and the way Cameron kept chatting up that fat-assed woman leaning way too close to him.

The guy—*John*, she reminded herself—tore a small piece of paper from the sign-up sheet. He used the pencil attached to scribble something down and handed it to her. "Here's my number. I was thinking maybe next weekend? Call me and we'll set it up."

"Sounds good. Talk to you later." She walked away and tucked the paper into her inner shorts pocket, where she normally kept her keys.

Feeling better about herself since for once she hadn't alienated a man or made him cry, she wandered into the free weights room and lifted some smaller dumbbells to tone her arms.

"Made a friend, eh?" Cameron said directly into her ear, startling her.

She nearly dropped the weights. "Don't *do* that."

He chuckled, but when she looked at him, he didn't seem all that pleased.

"You okay?"

"What? Yeah, sure."

"You look upset. Problems with your *friend*?" She nodded in the direction Bimbette the Great had been working out.

"Huh? Oh, you mean Karen? She's a client's wife. Nice lady. A little clingy, but…" He shrugged. "Sometimes you have to be diplomatic about *no*."

Vanessa nodded, feeling better about the way her afternoon was progressing. "True."

"So." Cam picked up a set of forty-pound hand weights next to her and started doing bicep curls.

She struggled not to stare, but she hadn't expected him to be so strong. She normally saw him running at the gym, not lifting. The man moved like a gazelle. Cameron had a lean build. Whereas Mike looked like a linebacker, Cameron reminded her more of a soccer player, muscular yet streamlined. With killer thighs.

"So?" she asked, since he hadn't followed up his one-word sentence with anything.

He did another few reps and asked, "What did your new friend want?"

She put her weights down and wiped her forehead with her sleeve. What a great sweat today. "Ah, something about going for drinks. He gave me his number."

"Nice." Cameron said nothing more and finished out a set while she drank from her water bottle and used her towel to mop up the rest of her face and neck.

She finished and decided to ask what had been on her mind lately. "Can I ask you something?"

He put the weights down and nodded to the exercise mats. Needing to do her crunches, she followed him down.

"What's up?"

"Brody and Abby. What's going on there, do you think?"

He paused on the floor, his hands behind his head, and she zeroed in on his broad chest. It should be illegal that the McCauleys should have three amazing-looking sons. Four if you counted Brody.

"What do *you* think is going on with them?"

She blew out a breath. "Honestly? He's balling her. I can tell. And she likes it. Likes him."

Cameron blinked at her. His lips curled, and she had a weird urge to lean down and kiss him, just to see what he might do. "Yeah? Well, he's hooked. I can tell. Brody doesn't do relationships. He's normally bored by date number three. But he barely blinks when Abby's in the room."

She nodded. "I know. Earlier at the party, he was staring so hard I thought he might have a medical condition. When I kindly suggested eye drops to help, he glared at me and stomped off."

Cameron snickered. "Yeah? Well, your girl has a thing for his ass."

"I know, right?" She laughed and lay down to do sit-ups next to him. "I told her she's too obvious, and then she tried to lie about it. Do they really think they're fooling anyone with that 'We're just friends' crap?"

"I don't know. But it's pretty damn interesting that for once Brody is doing his best not to reveal that he's in a relationship when the rest of us aren't. And I don't mean Flynn, because he and Maddie are like one person."

"I know." She fake gagged. "They're so happy it's cloying." She paused, then asked as casually as possible, "I thought you were dating someone."

"Nah. The distance didn't work. She was out East, and I'm a West Coast kind of guy. Know what I mean?"

"Totally. My family lives in central PA, but you couldn't pay me to leave Seattle. I love it here."

They did sit-ups together, and when they finished, Cameron suggested they stop by a frozen yogurt shop on the way home. "We deserve it for having the discipline—unlike some other losers I won't name—to work out on a Saturday. Plus we can gossip about Brody and Abby some more."

She laughed, not feeling tired at all from her workout the way she normally did. Just the opposite. Vanessa felt ready to run a marathon. "Sounds great. I love fro-yo. Let's go."

Life suddenly seemed very, very sweet.

Sunday afternoon, Brody sat with the others, nursing a water and pretending fun he wasn't really having. He couldn't stop thinking about how eager Abby had been to ditch him. Son of a bitch, but the woman *was* winning their little game of *who's falling for whom*, because he never stopped thinking about her.

"You going to eat those?" Cam asked, pointing to the meatballs on his plate.

"Nah, go ahead."

Flynn gave a mock gasp. "That's it. Feel his forehead. Touch his nose. Is it hot or cold?" The bastard had the nerve to smirk at him. "Feeling blue, buddy? Missing sexy Abby, are we?"

Brody flushed. "Fuck off."

"It's a good thing Colin's at Mom and Dad's," Mike griped. "You three don't seem to know any words besides *fuck off*, *shit*, and *hell no, they did not just score*."

"Please." Cam snorted. "You sent the boy away because you can't keep your big mouth shut when it comes to your precious Packers. Wuss."

"I love it when Cam talks like a guy, don't you?" Brody drawled.

Cam glared. "Fine. You want to go there? Let's talk about you and the woman you're trying to pretend you aren't tapping but we all know you are." Silence descended. Cam, that little snot, raised a brow. "Well?"

Brody shrugged. "Hey, I'm grown enough that I don't kiss and tell. Abby's a great girl, and she's helping me and Flynn out on our website." *Shit*. They weren't buying his nonsense at all. "But there is something we *should* be talking about." He leaned over the coffee table and put his water down. A great diversion, but he was serious about the topic. "What's going on with Bitsy and Pop?"

At that, the others faced him with serious expressions.

Mike muted the game. "That's a damn good question. I don't know. Before we left yesterday, Mom wasn't talking to Dad, and he looked mighty damn pissed."

Cam frowned. "Something's definitely going on because I saw her crying last week. I asked her about it, and she told me she'd been watching a sad movie. You know how she gets about her Lifetime." They nodded, and he continued, "But there's been something so sad about her eyes for a while. She laughs, but when you look closely…"

If anyone could pick up on that stuff, it would be Cam. He was more attuned to emotions and all that sensitive crap than the rest of them.

Brody didn't like the idea of Bitsy and Pop arguing. None of them did. To him, they'd always served as an example of what a true marriage and love should be. If they couldn't make it work, what chance in hell did he have?

Flynn blew out a breath. "I didn't want to say anything, but…"

"What?" Mike snapped. "Spit it out, boy."

Flynn scowled at him. "Don't get testy. Something Maddie said the other day. She said it was funny how Mom had suddenly latched on to your private life. Like maybe she was feeling unfulfilled at home or something, so she was all over you. I laughed it off, but now…maybe she's right."

Mike nodded. "Makes sense. But what's wrong with them? I mean, they're always so happy."

"Yeah?" Brody asked, thinking about the pair. "When's the last time they went out together? Like, on a date? Something that didn't involve one of us or the kid?" Meaning Colin. "Do Pop and Bitsy ever do anything together, just them?" He remembered when they used to go out. Years ago, they'd go dancing or to the movies, always holding hands, making eyes at each other. The guys made fun of them, but Brody secretly loved their open shows of affection.

Mike's eyes narrowed. "They *never* go out anymore. And come to think of it, Dad's been more than happy to put in overtime at work. I didn't think anything of it. But it seems like maybe he's spending more time with a hammer than with Mom."

Flynn urged, "Talk to him, Mike. You guys are close. He'll listen to you."

"Yeah, play the good son card," Brody suggested. "Cam can do his emotional weepy-guy thing with Bitsy."

"Asshole," Cam growled.

"Oh, come on. We all know how tight you and Mom are. You girls bond over all sorts of shit," Flynn added.

Cam glared. Then he threw a corn chip at Flynn.

Flynn threw it back.

"Whoa. Hold on, guys." Mike's eyes widened in alarm. God forbid anyone get a crumb on his ugly carpet. Since having a kid, all his sloppy behaviors had transformed the former bum into the king of OCD cleanliness. Well, next to Vanessa, anyway.

So Brody picked up a chip and threw it at Mike.

The scowl he received more than made up for the beating he was sure to get. And this way they kept their attention off him and Abby and centered it on aggravating Mike.

He, Cam, and Flynn looked at one another, then grabbed handfuls of tortilla chips.

"You fuckers are going to pay if you—*No*."

They launched the chips. Flynn turned the volume on the game back up, and Mike flew into a panic scooping up snack food as Cam laughed hysterically. Brody joined him. Unfortunately, he didn't avoid Mike's tackle. And when the other two idiots piled on and shouted victory to the Packers, he swore he cracked a rib as he wheezed and laughed and defended his suckass team.

———

Abby was having a terrific Sunday. For the first time in forever, all three of them were at home enjoying the day together. She'd missed her girls' weekends with Vanessa and Maddie. And with Robin and Kim over, they enjoyed their marathon B-movie day while indulging in chocolates, popcorn, sodas, and all things bad for one's figure, making the day complete.

As a couple, Robin was more butch, Kim more girlie, but they suited each other perfectly. Whereas Robin had a head of short, dark spikes, wore boots and a shapeless sweater with jeans, Kim looked like a supermodel with her long blond waves, designer dress, and hooker heels.

"Don't say it," Kim warned when she saw Abby staring at her shoes. They had the same conversation every time Kim came over, because the woman was addicted to height.

Robin frowned at Abby, then leaned back so Kim couldn't see her and mouthed, *"Say it."*

"I saw that," Kim said without turning around.

"So…do you get paid by the hour or what?" Abby had to ask.

The others laughed.

Kim sighed. "They're not that bad."

"I'm surprised you don't get a nosebleed while walking." Vanessa snorted. "Jesus, Kim. They're like five inches tall."

"Four," Robin corrected. "I measured. Hey, my woman wants to look hot, let her. And if she breaks a pretty ankle, then... Well, that will be a huge pain in the ass at work." The pair owned an interior design company, like Maddie. Lately the three of them had been working together on different projects. "But we can always plug Maddie in for a while if you become useless to me."

"You'd replace me? You *bitch*," Kim huffed, then laughed and hugged and kissed Robin. "I know, I know. The shoes are a walking nightmare. But they're so shiny. And pink." She turned to Vanessa and added, "It's too bad they don't make them in size thirteen, honey. But I have a friend with connections who—"

"Ten and a half," Vanessa said loudly. "I wear *ten and a half* size shoes."

Abby smiled kindly. "If you say so, dear."

The others laughed again, and Maddie snickered at the finger Vanessa gave them. "Oh, good one, cuz. So original."

"Shut up, she who constantly gets laid. That's why you three are always in a good mood." Vanessa slowly turned to Abby. "Or should I say...four?"

Everyone focused on her, and Abby could feel herself blushing. "I don't know what you mean."

Maddie pointed and screeched, "Liar! That's your lying face. I knew it!" She turned to Robin. "You totally owe me ten bucks."

Robin grumbled while pulling out her wallet. Money

changed hands, and Abby didn't know whether to laugh or hide her head in shame.

"Hey."

"Please. You and Brody have been going at it since before the dog-sitting," Vanessa huffed. "Why else would you bother to watch Mutt?"

"Aw. I love that cutesy-wootsie dog," Kim cooed.

"You would," Robin muttered.

"I know you don't want me making any comparisons to those I love, now, do you?" Kim asked archly. "Because you're much cuter than Mutt. But he's nicer."

Maddie laughed and explained to Abby, "They met Mutt when Brody and Flynn stopped by their shop. Brody had Mutt with him. He's a great big galoot, but he's well-mannered."

"Brody?" Robin asked.

"No. And neither is Mutt," Vanessa chimed in.

"Ha ha. Very funny." Abby didn't like them dissing the dog *or* the man. "For the record, Mutt is a wonderful dog with a crappy name. I blame Brody for that."

"We all do." Maddie shuddered. "But I wouldn't call Mutt well-mannered. That dog is always trying to attack me."

"He likes you. Don't be so dense." Abby started to grow impatient with them. "And Brody's a really nice guy." She told them about yesterday in the bookstore and how he'd helped sell her books.

The gang stared at her in awe. Or at least, she thought it was awe until Vanessa whistled.

"Yep. She's totally banging him. And probably giving head too, if he's admitting he reads her books."

Abby lost it. "What *the hell* is wrong with my books?"

Robin, Kim, and Maddie sat watching in silence.

"Just that no man would admit to reading romance, and not smutty romance."

"You big-footed bitch! At least I'm having sex. The last time you lost your breath in orgasmic ecstasy was on a treadmill. The words *faster* and *harder* are good for more than running, Flo-Jo."

Robin cringed. "Ouch."

Vanessa actually grinned. "And doing sit-ups. Don't forget my crunches."

"Oh you…" Abby didn't know what to say.

"Relax, cupcake." Vanessa chuckled. "We're all happy you're finally getting laid. Brody's hot."

"Yeah." Kim nodded. "We might be gay. Doesn't mean we're blind. He's exceptionally good-looking."

"And he fixed our bathroom for free. Well, I paid for the parts, but he didn't charge us for the labor," Robin said. "I like him."

Abby had expected more resistance to hers and Brody's new sexual relationship. "So, what then?"

Maddie answered by shoving a chocolate covered strawberry at her. "So enjoy yourself. You and I both know he's not the committing type. But you and I *know* that. Just don't get your hopes up for anything more. Since you've mentioned — repeatedly — that you don't want a relationship anytime soon, enjoy him while you can. From what I'm hearing, he's totally into you."

Vanessa had to go and ruin it by adding, "Right now. Not for a relationship. Remember, you're just shagging."

"That's British for fucking, right?" Robin asked.

"Yeah. Watch *Austin Powers* sometime. You learn

things you can't find on the home shopping channel."
Vanessa smirked.

"The scary lady is being mean to me," Robin said to
Kim. "Make her stop."

They laughed and teased and eventually returned
to the movie. Abby went to the kitchen to grab more
sodas, and Maddie followed her.

"So. Brody."

"Yeah?"

Maddie looked over her shoulder, then turned back
to Abby. "Is he any good?"

Abby chuckled. "A lady shouldn't tell."

"Please. You're no lady. Well? Spill."

Seeing no one around, she confessed, "He's amazing.
I mean, as in *holy crap* I had multiple orgasms amazing."

"I knew it. He looks the type."

"Yeah, right. How can you tell if a guy's good in bed
by looking at him?"

Maddie shrugged. "I can just tell." She paused. "Be
careful, Abby. He's a terrific guy, but he has a history
of short-term dating."

"Hey, we're not even dating. Just *shagging*." She
laughed, but deep down she took the caution to heart.
She thought about him constantly, and she admitted to
herself that she wouldn't say no if he asked to deepen
the relationship. "Like you said, I don't want a boyfriend right now. But a sex buddy? No problem. He
doesn't want serious either. In fact, he and I have a
bet going on. He seems to think I'll fall for him. As if.
He'll be falling for me before that ever happens. He's
a breast man." They both looked at her boobs. "He's
going down. Right around my little finger."

"Oh honey, you've hit rock bottom if the man is going down and you're showing him your *finger*." Maddie shook her head.

Abby laughed. "You're such a goof. I can't believe you're the same woman who was freaking out a few months ago because Flynn wanted to call you his girlfriend."

"And you're not the same woman who hid in the shadows because her dickhead of an ex told her she was abnormal for wanting passion in her relationship." Maddie poked Abby in the chest. "There is nothing wrong with you. Play with Brody. Have fun with life. Just don't fall for him." Maddie glared at her. "I'm not kidding. He's not allowed to break your heart."

"What if I break his?"

Maddie shrugged. "That's okay. His heartache becomes Flynn's problem. But I can work around Flynn." In a lower voice, she confessed, "He's easy. Sex in a public place and he's like putty in my hands."

"You two." Abby shook her head but couldn't help laughing. Since no one had joined them yet, she confided, "Guess what else happened yesterday?"

"Oh, gossip. Tell me, tell me."

"Beth asked if I was interested in Mike. She wanted to set me up with him."

Maddie's eyes widened. "She did not."

"Did too." Abby nodded. "But it's more than Mike. I think there's something seriously wrong with her and James."

From the living room, Vanessa yelled, "Where's my pomegranate juice?"

Abby rolled her eyes. "She can't even binge

properly." In a louder voice she answered, "You're having root beer, Big Foot. Live a little. And hold on."

"We'll talk about Beth later," Maddie promised.

Abby nodded. She trudged back into the living room with drinks and tuned into the girls' commentary on *Evil Dead*. She made a mental note to ask Brody if he liked Bruce Campbell. Because if not, well, that might be a deal breaker.

Not really, but she'd make him work to prove it wasn't. At the thought, she smiled and ate another strawberry.

Chapter 13

ANOTHER LONG, SHITTY DAY AT WORK. WHY WAS IT lately that the poor weather turned their clients into raving loonies? First on Monday, the guy who'd scheduled them to upgrade his bathroom fixtures had kept them waiting while he took a last, long shower. Then he conveniently met them, still wet in only a towel, and managed to drop it right in front of Flynn. Okay, that had been pretty funny, and the guy's check more than made up for the hassle.

This morning a witchy mother with too many kids for her frayed patience blamed *Brody* when her kid cried—because Brody had taken away rubber ducky number three heading for a flush down the toilet. And this afternoon he'd had to go through another goddamn crawl space—the bane of every plumber's existence—to figure out how to rough in the lines.

But he put all that behind him as he readied for his bowling date with Abby. And it was a date. They were meeting for bowling and to talk. For fun.

His heart raced, as always, at the thought of her. Damn, the three long days without her had felt like an eternity. *I am so screwed.*

He had no idea how to handle his obsession with the woman. And far be it for her to feel the same for him. She hadn't once called or texted him. Instead, he'd had to text *her* to confirm the time of their date. He planned on calling it a date at least five times tonight to annoy the ever-living crap out of her. Or at least get her annoyed enough to transfer her raging energy into a few climaxes in bed. God the woman was hot.

He hummed to himself as he showered, dried off, and dressed in jeans and a casual sweater. "What do you think, Mutt?"

Even better, he and the dog had come to a new understanding. Mutt had accidentally jumped on his jewels one too many times, and Brody had had it. A newspaper against the dog's ass and some tough talk had convinced him Brody meant business. Now Mutt sat calmly, his tail wagging and his tongue hanging out, as he watched Brody get ready for his *date*.

The doorbell rang, and Mutt raced to answer it, barking.

Brody frowned. He could have sworn Abby had texted back saying she'd meet him at the bowling alley.

"Hold on," he yelled when the doorbell continued to ring. Not Abby. Seth, maybe?

He walked downstairs and ordered Mutt to sit. After waiting until the dog settled under *his* control, he opened the door.

And found his personal nightmare waiting for him.

Jeremy and Alan Singer, his brother and father, stood on his front porch.

They had decent-enough clothing, actually wearing jackets in the cold, which meant they weren't rolling on the floor high or drunk. They looked a lot alike, both blond but rundown, gaunt, and typically bleary-eyed. Except on Alan it was from the drink. On Jeremy it had normally been from whatever he'd been snorting that day.

Brody just stood there staring at them.

"Uh, hi. Can we come in?" Jeremy asked. To Brody's surprise, his brother's eyes looked clear. Alan's didn't. No surprise there.

Brody stepped outside to join them and shut the door behind him. "No."

"You're such a rude little shit," Alan sniped. "Ain't got time for your father or brother, huh? You too good for us?" he sneered.

"Yeah, I am." Brody kept his arms loosely at his sides, his adrenaline pumping. He wasn't a kid anymore, could match Jeremy in a fight if he had to. His older brother looked thinner than he had been in a while, and while Jeremy was a few inches taller, Brody now had more muscle.

Alan didn't count as a threat. The old man used words, not fists, to insult him and knock his self-esteem. *Been there, done that.* Jeremy, however, had real skill when it came to leaving bruises in places that wouldn't show.

Jeremy shook his head. "You know, Dad, maybe we should go. I'll come back another time, Brody."

Not sure what they were after, Brody didn't want to play any more games. He just wanted them gone. "Just say what you came to say and leave."

Alan scowled. "Boy, you forget your place. Tough guy with a fancy truck and a big job now. Can't spare two minutes for your old man?"

"Fine. You have two minutes."

Alan blinked, clearly not having expected that.

"Dad, maybe you should—" Jeremy started.

"Shut your fucking mouth." Alan slapped Jeremy

in the back of the head. "Quit sniveling. Be a man. Jesus, Jeremy, you're acting like a little bitch. If I'd-a known you'd be like this sober, I'd have bought you a hit months ago."

What was this about Jeremy being sober?

Jeremy pinched the bridge of his nose. "Dad, just stop. Or better yet, go wait in the car."

"Fuck that. Brody, we need a place to stay."

"No, we don't."

Brody looked back and forth at them, confused and curious. "What's going on? I haven't seen either one of you in two years, since the last time you tried to shake me down."

To his shock, Jeremy looked shamefaced.

Not so Alan. "If you were a real man instead of a pussy hiding behind a cell phone you never fucking answer, you might take pride in helping out your father. But you never could fight your own battles. Always had to suck up to them McCauleys for everything. Boy, they took you in 'cause they pitied you. Not 'cause you're one of them. You poor, dumb shit." Alan shook his head.

Brody refused to let old insecurities rise. "*And...* you're done." He turned to Jeremy, ignoring his swearing father. "And you? You here for a place to stay and money too?"

"No. I'm here to—"

"What the sensitive bastard is here to say is he's sorry. Ain't that right, you big pussy?" Alan teetered on his feet, and Brody saw he'd made a mistake. Alan was indeed drunk, just not wearing it. The man used to smell like a brewery, his stench enough to cause inebriation in anyone unfortunate enough to inhale him.

"Shit. I told you not to come with me. Go home."
Jeremy tried to nudge his father toward the porch
stairs, but Alan took a swing at him instead. Jeremy
ducked, and their father fell on his face on the porch.
He burst out laughing and swearing, and Seth's door
opened. *Terrific*.

"Brody, you okay, son?" Seth asked.

"*Son?* What?" his father slurred. "You sucker another poor family to take you in, boy? And you call
us losers."

"I'm fine, Seth," Brody said over Alan. "Just some
trash on my porch. Don't worry. I'll clean it up and get
rid of it."

"Okay." Instead of going inside, Seth sat on his
bench and smoked his pipe.

"Look, Brody," Jeremy was saying. "I'm sorry. I
didn't think Dad would follow me. He's high off his ass."

"That's new. The booze not cutting it anymore?"

Jeremy shook his head. "Guess not."

Odd, because Jeremy and their father used to be
drinking, thieving, and bullying buddies.

"I came here tonight to apologize. What he said
is true," Jeremy admitted. "I'm clean. Been that way
for ten months. I'm just now getting my shit together.
Taking responsibility to those I harmed and—"

"Save it. I don't want to hear it." His arm throbbed
as if the bone had broken yesterday.

"Brody, it was the drugs, the booze. Well, and Dad.
Not the best influence, you know?"

Older by ten years, Jeremy had always seemed larger
than life to Brody. A huge bully who had beaten the shit
out of him for as far back as he could remember. He'd

never thought about Jeremy without that niggle of fear. When his father got tired of the McCauleys paying for Brody's upkeep, he'd demand his son come home for a spell. And then he'd go off and get drunk and leave Brody to Jeremy's creative care. Jeremy had been smart. Except for that one time, he'd rarely left marks that scarred or could be seen. After the arm, Pop and Bitsy had put a stop to Brody's visits home for good.

But they never knew about the times his brother or father found him after school, when they'd shake him down for whatever he had on him for liquor or drugs. It hadn't paid to keep a job during high school, not with his family making weekly withdrawals.

"I have nothing to say to you." Brody clenched his fists by his sides. From inside the house he could hear Mutt whining. And the fact that Seth—a man he thought of as a cranky extension of his family—sat right next door and could hear everything, kept him from saying half of what he wanted to. God, he didn't want anyone to know about this side of him. Not even Flynn knew the truth about Jeremy and Alan. Just that his family had often missed him and wanted him to visit. A load of shit, but it was worlds better than telling the guys he'd been born a mistake, that his sole purpose in life was to take abuse when dished out and lie, cheat, and steal for his "real family."

"I was wrong." Jeremy wouldn't shut the fuck up. "I gave you a concussion. Black eyes, bruises. I broke your arm in two places, nearly killed you. And the tricks I used to play on you." He swallowed. "I think about that every day. How I hurt you."

"A few times," Alan added as he rose unsteadily

to his feet. "Not a big deal. It was all in fun, nothing serious. Remember that old handgun?" He guffawed and pointed at Brody. "Now that shit was funny. Boy, you pissed yourself you was so scared. And it wasn't even loaded."

Brody turned and reached for the door. "You aren't out of here in the next five seconds, I'm calling the cops."

A hand rested on his shoulder. "Wait. Don't—"

He turned and decked Jeremy, hit his jaw so hard his brother went down and didn't get up right away. Then he did the same to Alan when the bastard tried to smack him. His father didn't get up at all.

"You come here again, I'll fucking kill the both of you. *Get out! Get your motherfucking asses out of my life*," he roared, done with pretending he didn't hate the sight of them. Of how they reduced him to that scared, needy little kid just by breathing. He was sweating and shaking. And so damn angry he wanted blood.

Jeremy wobbled as he stood and fingered his jaw. "I'm sorry. So sorry, Brody. I was so wrong, such a shit to you and you never deserved it." The fucker had tears in his eyes. Well, too little, too late.

"Be sorry somewhere else. I hope you rot in hell," he seethed before letting himself inside and slamming the door behind him.

Mutt whined as Brody leaned his back against the door and slid to the floor, doing his best to even his breathing and calm down. But nothing worked. Memories hit him hard, the way Jeremy's large fists used to. He heard his father's high-pitched cackle. Felt the fear overtake him, reducing him to that sobbing mess of a terrified kid. The first year with the

McCauleys he'd slept on the floor under his bed, trying to keep out of sight. Until Flynn had started doing it too, so he wouldn't have to be so alone. So scared.

Still shaking, Brody texted Abby and apologized for canceling. He promised they'd meet another time.

Mutt lay next to him and rested his head in Brody's lap. And Brody did his best not to cry like the goddamn pussy they'd always accused him of being and clutched the dog tight.

A week later, Abby still hadn't met up with Brody. And it was killing her. He hadn't answered her calls but had at least texted her. Dealing with some personal issues, he'd said, and politely mentioned he'd call her soon. Not wanting to appear overeager or worried, she'd backed off. But seven days was seven too many. When she'd asked Maddie to question Flynn about Brody's distance, he'd only said Brody was going through some stuff and needed space.

"Stuff? What is stuff?" she asked Maddie as they prepared dinner. "I mean, it's one thing if he just doesn't want to hang out anymore. I'm a big girl. I can take it. Can't he just tell me in person?"

"I don't know. Something's off with him." Maddie chewed her lip as she rinsed the lettuce for salad. "Flynn's worried. Brody does his job. He smiles, makes jokes, but Flynn can tell there's something wrong." She paused. "I'm not supposed to say anything, so you didn't hear this from me. Swear."

"I swear." Abby tried not to feel hurt that she'd been kicked to the curb. If Brody was dealing with something emotional, she wanted to be supportive. "Come on. Tell me."

"Well, Flynn said Brody's been like this a few times in his life. I mean, he and Flynn are super tight. They've done everything together since they were in kindergarten. Brody grew up with the McCauleys."

"Why?"

"Flynn won't say much, but apparently Brody's biological family are lower than scum. Flynn and his brothers never knew much about the Singers growing up, only to avoid them if they spotted them. But Brody would visit his dad and brother—I think—every now and then over the years. And every time, he'd withdraw into himself after. So Flynn's betting that his family contacted him. But Brody won't say. Flynn said when Brody gets likes this, he normally gives him space, and in a few days Brody will snap out of it."

Abby didn't like the situation at all. She'd come to care for Brody—okay, she liked him more than was healthy, she admitted. She wanted to help. "I won't say a word. Thanks. I'll just give him space, like I've been doing. And hey, if he decides to blow off what we had going, no problem." She shrugged, doing her level best to convince Maddie she meant it.

She must have done a good job because Maddie blew out a breath of relief. "Oh, good. I was worried you might be falling for him. He's so charming, great in bed—your words, not mine—then add in he's funny and he likes you. The real you. That's a recipe for disaster."

You got that right. They ate dinner, and Vanessa joined them after coming back from her run. She spent the time bitching about her last date with some dullard named John, a guy who had bored her nearly to death while talking about himself for their entire night out.

"The nerve. He wants to go out again. I swear to you. I think I got in the words *Hello* and *thanks for dinner* the entire night. But I can tell you his golf score, his income, that he has three houses, and loves sampling wines." Vanessa scrunched her nose. "Ugh. Why me?"

"Why did you go out with him in the first place?" Maddie asked as they cleaned up.

"He had nice legs." Vanessa shrugged. "And I wanted to go out. The only saving grace of the night was that we ate at a nice restaurant and he paid."

"A free meal, but with a catch."

"Yeah. He's like a walking timeshare. Suckers you in and makes you suffer endlessly while trying to sell you something you don't want. Whatever. At least I haven't been slacking off on my exercise. I feel great."

The woman did have a sparkle in her eyes. "Hmm. You look energized, I'll give you that." But Vanessa also had a spring in her step and a joy that had been missing lately. "You look good."

"I always look good." No ego, just truth.

Abby rolled her eyes. "Vanity be thy name."

"Vanity. Vanessa. Both start with a *van*. Close enough," Maddie added.

"Your petty jealousies soothe my soul," Vanessa said with her mouth half full.

"God, Vanessa. Close your mouth when you chew." Abby grimaced.

"What, like this?" She opened her mouth wide, then finished her food and laughed.

Vanessa was still chuckling as she deposited her plate in the sink. She washed her dishes, dried them, and put them away. "I'm just in a good mood because I'm feeling healthy and energized."

"Oh?" Maddie winked at Abby. "Wouldn't have anything to do with your new running partner, now would it?"

"Who's that?" Abby saw the shutter close over Vanessa's eyes.

"Cameron McCauley seems to be hitting the gym pretty hard lately, according to Flynn."

"Oh wow. So you're into a McCauley too, huh?" Abby teased. "Just your type. He's a nut about numbers too."

"He's intelligent, yes. Attractive, athletic. And he's *a friend*." Vanessa crossed her arms over her chest.

Defensive much?

"Just a friend?" Maddie pressed.

Abby wanted to see Vanessa laughing again. "Leave her alone, Maddie. Cam's a good guy. And you can see why they'd buddy up." Personally, she thought Vanessa had a crush, but she didn't want to get in the way of Vanessa connecting with happiness. It was all too rare an occurrence. "They both like to exercise, and they both think they're way too smart for the rest of us."

Vanessa relaxed. "Exactly. Now, my minions, I'm off to shower and get a bit of midweek preparation in with work. Unless you're on fire, don't knock." Vanessa strode out of the kitchen with purpose.

Maddie and Abby turned to each other. "Do you think she likes Cam?"

Abby shrugged. "I don't know. But she's been down lately. If she does like him, let's be supportive, okay?"

Maddie narrowed her eyes. "You're kidding, right? Do you not remember how many times she's called me a drama queen? Told me to, and I quote, 'Suck it up, princess'? Or that she still calls me flighty and says my chances for failure at my new business are growing as fat as my ass?"

"That's so you'll exercise more." Abby tried not to laugh. "You have a tiny butt. You're good."

Maddie smacked her playfully. "You're no fun when I'm trying to dig on Van-zilla. Good one, by the way."

"I thought so." She sighed. "Well, I'm going to do a few more pages before I turn in for the night. I have a lot to do if I want to get ready for Thanksgiving. Two weeks is going to go by like that." She snapped her fingers.

She and Maddie parted to work, but as Abby typed, she couldn't help wondering about Brody. No matter what she'd said to Maddie, she planned to check up on him. Just as a friend. And what better way to show she cared than to see how he and Mutt were doing?

"Yeah, that will work." Not too obvious, but enough of an excuse to get a look at him and see for herself that he was okay. She nodded and threw herself back into her book, more than aware of how much she needed to change her new hero so that he stopped resembling Brody.

The next day, she took an early morning break and drove to Green Lake. She parked in front of Brody's house, hoping he'd be home. She'd checked with Maddie and, without asking directly, had weaseled the fact that the guys had no one scheduled until later that afternoon.

She walked up the sidewalk, but before she could reach the porch, Seth opened the door of his home and stepped out.

"Hey, Seth—" She stopped talking when he put a finger to his lips and frantically motioned her over to his place. Hurrying across the yard to his walk and up the stairs of his porch, she met him. "Are you okay?"

He didn't answer but hustled her inside his house and closed the door.

"Whoa." She gaped at the stacks of papers, collectibles, and, well, stuff all over the place. He had clear paths for walking, but criminy, the man had knick-knacks everywhere.

"Yeah, yeah. I collect a lot. Come here. We need to talk."

She followed his shuffle into the living room and sat in one of the two unoccupied chairs. For all that he hoarded, the room looked clean. No dust or cobwebs. Just tons of clutter. She sat and studied him. "What's wrong?"

"It's not me." He scowled. "It's Brody." He paused. "It's not my place to say, but I like the boy. Something happened last week, and he's been keeping to himself since. Not in a good way. I don't like it."

Abby liked Seth. She had from the day she'd met the cantankerous old man. And now, seeing his concern and knowing he cared about Brody, she liked him even more. "I haven't talked to him since last week," she admitted. "We were supposed to go bowling Tuesday, and then he canceled. He's texted a few times but hasn't responded to my calls since."

"Yeah, well, if you'd heard what I did, you'd understand." He exhaled heavily. "I ain't one for gossip, mind you. But I think he's hurting. That doesn't sit right by me. Not at all."

"I want to help him. I think his situation might have to do with…his family?" she prodded.

His eyes narrowed. "Yeah. Not that bunch he's always hanging around with. But two who looked a lot like him. A brother and father." He repeated to her, what sounded like word for word, all he'd heard, and her heart bled for Brody.

"That's awful."

"Yep. The brother seemed sincere to apologize, but what do I know? The father though. He was a real piece of shit, excuse my French."

She nodded, lost in thoughts about what Brody might be going through. She ached for the little boy who had been abused and scared. It didn't seem to fit with the man she knew at all. And yet some of it did. She couldn't explain it.

"I bet he'd like some company, especially if a pretty girl were to offer it," Seth nudged.

"He's home?"

"Yep. Haven't heard a peep outta him all morning. Not that I listen," he rushed to say. "But I normally hear that truck move. Not a thing today."

"Okay. Thanks, Seth. And I promise not to say anything. I'm worried about him too." She stood and Seth stood with her.

"Good girl. You let me know if I can help."

She leaned in and kissed him on his whiskered cheek before he could back away. "Thanks."

He flushed. "Oh, stop flirting with me, woman. Get yourself to the boy and get him out of that funk. And

if he wants to know why you were over here, tell him I
had an antique typewriter I thought you might be interested in, you being a writer and all."

Brody must have told him, because she hadn't mentioned it. "I will. Thanks again, Seth."

He nodded, and she saw herself out. She hurried to
Brody's house, hoping he hadn't noticed her talking
to Seth. Composing herself and going with the plan
to check on Mutt, she knocked on the door, then rang
the bell.

It took a few moments, but she heard Mutt bark.
Then footsteps. Good. Brody wouldn't pretend he
wasn't home. He opened the door, looking fresh, as if
he'd just showered. He wore jeans and a sweatshirt, but
he seemed as if he'd lost weight, and his eyes had lost
that sparkle he normally wore with her.

"Hi, Abby."

"Hey, Brody." She smiled. "I hate to bug you, but I
hadn't heard from you in a while." She glanced at Mutt,
who sat and wagged his tail. "I came to check on Mutt."

"He's good." Brody didn't move from the door.

Uh-oh. She thought fast, remembering the notebook
she always carried in her purse with her, and made a
new plan. "And I came to talk to you about that web
design." She needed to get inside and feel him out.

"Well, now's not the best time. I'm kind of busy—"

She shoved past him and entered. "Close the door,
would you? It's kind of cold out there."

"Come on in, why don't you?" He shook his head
and closed the door behind her.

"Thanks. I could use a cup of coffee if you have any."
She walked into the kitchen and settled at the island,

making herself at home. Then she turned and motioned to Mutt. "Come here, Mutt. How are you, boy?"

He barked once, his happy bark, and joined her in a shake. So wiggly, he danced under her hands and licked her face, happy to see her. Unlike his owner.

Brody stood there with his arms crossed, leaning against the counter. He stared with a brooding gaze, and that cautious mien made her want to hug him and tell him everything would be all right. She didn't feel a sexual pull, but an emotional one, and she knew then that no matter how much she'd been telling herself to keep her distance, Brody had won their contest. She was well and truly hooked. *Hell*.

Chapter 14

HE WASN'T READY TO DEAL WITH HER YET. BRODY watched Abby, seeing her innocent gaze and knowing she'd talked to Seth not five minutes ago. He loved the guy, but damn. Seth had probably blabbed about his shitty father and the abuse he hadn't wanted anyone to know about.

Fuck.

But Abby didn't look at him with pity. So maybe Seth had kept his big nose out of Brody's business after all. Flynn had been on his ass at the beginning of the week, urging Brody to tell him what was wrong, but Brody couldn't explain it to himself, let alone his best friend. Being around his father and brother turned him inside out, made him wonder again why any of the McCauleys had taken a chance on the little piece of shit with dirty hair and hands that took what didn't belong to him.

He'd never gotten caught, a lucky thing. Because Brody had been a bad, bad boy during his first few years with the McCauleys. And in high school, he'd done a lot of shit he wasn't proud of.

But none of that mattered with Abby standing so close. As much as he'd tried to stop thinking about her, about how he didn't deserve to come close to her, he'd dwell on images of her mouth, of how it curled when she smiled. How bright her eyes grew, or how her cheeks lit with red when excited or embarrassed, and how beautiful she was.

"Hello?" Abby clapped her hands in front of his face. When had she moved closer? "Coffee?" She held up a cup he'd had sitting on the table.

He let out an aggravated sigh and started a pot for her. "I'm really not in the mood to talk about the website."

"Too bad. Because I have clients other than you and Flynn. So get your skinny ass over here and tell me what you want." She pulled a notebook and pen out of her bag and waited.

You. I want you. To kiss you, touch you, come inside you, and forget about the shit in my life. God, he hated sounding pathetic. Like a victim. He'd taken his last beating from Jeremy at eleven. Twenty years ago. Would he ever get over the past?

He forced himself to deal with the present, to include the feisty sexpot sitting expectantly at his kitchen island while she petted his dog. Mutt looked like he'd died and gone to heaven as he sat calmly under her touch.

"The website. That's what you want?" He still didn't trust her reasons for coming, especially after that visit with Seth. "So, what did Seth want with you?" he decided to ask.

She glanced at the coffeepot, then to her cup, then back to the pot.

"Christ." He grabbed her cup and filled it, then brought her some cream and a bowl of sugar.

She smiled at him as she fixed it, and damn if he didn't feel better. "Thanks."

"Seth?"

"He had an old typewriter he wanted me to see.

Apparently *someone* told him I'm a writer." She frowned at him.

Relieved that Seth hadn't said anything about his embarrassing situation with his deadbeat family, Brody relaxed. "Not just a writer, a *great* writer. I said 'great.'"

"Big mouth," she grumbled and sipped her coffee with pleasure. "Oh, this is good."

"I can't cook, but I can do coffee." He grabbed a cup for himself and sat next to her. "Okay, so what do you need to know?"

An hour later, he surprised himself by having fleshed out a design for the site. With Abby's skilled help, at any rate. She was all business as she talked about design and spacing and metadata. He ignored her code talk though, and seeing that he had no interest in applets and JavaScript, she left well enough alone.

"Great, Brody. This is just what I needed to get you guys started."

"Yeah, well, we need that site. Not that business isn't still great, which in this economy is saying something. But every little bit helps."

"Yeah, it does." She fetched herself more coffee. "Now tell me something."

He tensed. *I knew it. She knows about Jeremy. And Alan. And—*

"How did you get Mutt to obey?"

"Who—what?"

"Mutt. He's been calm and totally terrific since I've been here." She looked around. "Although that does look like a brand-new dish towel. He still eating those?"

He relaxed. "Yeah. He and I finally had a

come-to-Jesus moment, and now he no longer jumps up on people. Or their crotches."

"Ouch."

"Tell me about it." He chuckled, the first time he'd genuinely done that in a week. "He's a good guy. But I don't think 'Mutt' is cutting it anymore. He deserves a better name."

"Thank God. Well? What have you decided to name him?"

"Me? You're the writer. Give me something good."

She shook her head. "I've tried. You vetoed all my good stuff."

"Yeah?"

"Yeah. You didn't like Killer or Death Dog. How about Marvin, Jethro, or Gomer?"

He shook his head. "Not feeling it."

"Vader? Shaggy? Wolfen?"

"Nah. Those don't work either.

She sighed. "I'm tapped. So when are we going bowling?"

"Oh, uh. I don't know."

"We don't have to. We could just have sex here instead."

He had the coffee cup to his lips and could only be thankful he hadn't taken a sip, or he'd have spit it all over himself. He carefully lowered the cup to the table. "Say that again?"

"Sex. Here. Now. Unless we're done with that." She sounded so damn casual about it. "That's no problem. I admit, you're really good at it, but I understand if you need something new to spice things up. No problem. And really, it's okay. No hard feelings." She smiled at him. "I was thinking about maybe dating again. I think it's time. But I need someone I can trust. You know people. Rick seems like a good guy. What do you think?"

What the ever-fucking hell was she talking about? He rose, dragged her off her stool, and tugged her with him.

"Wait. Brody? Are you okay?"

"Okay? *Okay?*" he yelled. "No. I am not okay. 'Unless we're done with that'? Are you fucking nuts? Yeah, there are gonna be hard feelings. Fuck bowling. Fuck everything. Right now, you and I need to have our own come-to-Jesus meeting." Over his shoulder, he growled, "Mutt, stay."

The dog whined but didn't continue up the stairs. Brody dragged her into the bedroom, closed the door, then pulled her into his arms. She felt right against him, fitting him perfectly and warming all his cold spots.

Then, before she could question why he'd gone all caveman on her, he did what he'd been missing for ten days. He kissed her and swallowed the little moan of pleasure that made him hunger for so much more than her body. He wanted all of Abby. Right here. Right now.

Brody kissed her like a starving man, and Abby met him halfway. God, he felt so good. She'd missed this, missed him. He'd somewhat returned to the old Brody in the kitchen. Shaking him up with a request for sex had been sneaky and totally spur of the moment. That it had worked soothed her wounded ego—and hurt feelings—that he might have tired of her so soon when she'd only gotten started on her need to be with him.

"Yeah. Kiss me. I missed you," he murmured against her mouth, and she sighed into him.

Like a woman who couldn't think straight, she let him move her and undress her without protest. When he had her completely naked, he looked down on her with fire in his eyes.

He backed her up until her knees hit the edge of the bed. "Lean back," he ordered in a guttural voice.

She quickly lay down and sat up on her elbows to watch him undress. He took off his sweatshirt but not his jeans. "Tease," she said, exhaling.

He didn't smile. He didn't laugh. Just stared at her until she thought she'd done something wrong. "You are so beautiful, you make me ache."

She blushed at the compliment. Because he'd said it with such intensity, she knew he believed it to be true. "Brody…"

He joined her on the bed. Leaning over her, he kissed her, brushing his bare chest against her breasts and stimulating her already sensitive nipples. He continued to rub against her while his tongue penetrated her mouth, and he began thrusting in a rhythm begging for sex. She clutched his shoulders, his arms, and reached around his back, urging him for more.

"Yes, please," she moaned when his lips trailed to her ear.

"You're so warm. God, I want to bury myself inside you." He nipped her lobe then thrust his tongue in her ear.

She jolted into him, her breasts plastered to his chest. She loved the way he kissed her, touched her. Like she was precious and desirable. Like she mattered.

He continued to kiss her neck, sucking just below her ear while one of his large, calloused hands cupped her breast.

"Yeah. Gonna fuck you so hard, Abby. All of me inside you." He trailed a blaze of kisses to the hand holding her breast, then took her nipple in his mouth and sucked.

"*Brody.*" She gasped, threading her hands through his soft hair. "Do that again. Yes. More." She couldn't stop herself from moaning and writhing under him. It had only been a little more than a week, but she'd felt so empty without him. Just seeing his smile or his golden eyes soothed her need for him. But this… Their intimacy involved more than bodies touching and seeking pleasure. This caressing, his taking his time. This wasn't fucking. She might not be as experienced as he was, but she could feel his care in every caress.

He sucked and kneaded her breast while fondling its twin. Then he turned his mouth to her other nipple and gave it the same petting and licking. She was so wet she feared she'd make a mess on his bed before he ever got inside her.

And speaking of that… "I'm—I'm protected. If you wanted to come in me," she whispered. After their last encounter, she'd made a hasty appointment with her doctor and done her research. Abby knew now to be a safe time for them to forego protection. She'd been all too aware of the fact on her way over this morning, though she'd told herself over and over she hadn't come for this, but to make sure Brody was okay.

He froze and leaned up from her. "So you're saying I can come inside you, and it's okay? No chance of you getting pregnant?"

"No." She stroked his hair, loving the burning desire in his eyes. "I'm on the pill, and even if I wasn't, it's the wrong time for me to be pregnant." She swallowed, seeing the intensity deepen. "I haven't been with anyone but you in a long time."

"Yeah." He sounded hoarse and caressed her breast, stroking and pinching her nipple while he watched her with an expression she couldn't read. "Me neither. Not in like six months."

He returned to her breast and bit her nipple lightly, enough to send a streak of erotic fire straight to her core. "God, you're too good for me."

She moaned and tugged him up to kiss her mouth again. "No, you're too good for me. Out of my league, but I'm batting anyway."

"Sex and baseball," he murmured around her mouth. "You are *perfect*." Then he stopped talking and kissed her until she couldn't breathe. His hands were everywhere, his knee riding against her clit, stirring her to near orgasm time and time again before he'd back off, then rub some more.

"Brody, please."

"Not yet. Not rushing this," he growled and moved slowly down her body, leaving kisses as he went. He spread her thighs wider and paused until she looked down at him. "I love sucking your tight clit. You taste so good. So sweet. And I love it when you come all over my mouth." Apparently seeing in her face something that satisfied him, he did his best to make her lose her mind.

He sucked her with delicate draws, fingering her folds before easing a finger, then two, inside her. He licked her and nibbled her clit while pumping those fingers into her, at first lightly, then with a more forceful pace until he hit that spot inside her that made her see stars.

"I'm going to come. Oh Brody."

"Yeah. Come for me, honey. Drench my tongue." He sucked again and shoved those fingers deep. Then one hand crept over her belly to cup her breast. He pinched her nipple at the same time he drew her clit into his mouth, and she cried out and came in a rush.

He continued to lick her, moaning with her as she released the tension and worry and surrendered to him on every level. After easing her through her climax, he pulled back and kissed his way up her belly to her mouth again.

"So good." He kissed her, and she tasted herself on his lips, an arousing pleasure to know he wanted her as much as she'd wanted him.

Her heart raced, unable to come down gradually off her endorphin high. "Brody, you're amazing."

"Not as much as you," he said, his kisses growing in intensity once more. "I need to come in you. You sure you're okay with that?"

"Yes. I want you in me. All of you."

"You're sure?"

It was as if he was asking something else, and she wanted to share with him the joy she'd just experienced. "Well, only if you let me kiss you."

He smiled and moved his head closer, but she put a hand over his lips. "Not there."

His breathing grew shallow. "Yeah? Where?"

"Take off your pants and I'll show you."

He moved off her and stripped in seconds.

She chuckled. "You sure can move when you want to."

He walked back to the bed, but before he could join her, she stopped him. "No, wait." She pulled herself to the edge and reached for his hips. Then, dragging him closer, she looked at the hard, insistent part of him. "You're pretty wet yourself." She licked his slit, taking the moisture into her mouth, loving the light taste of him. Brody smelled like soap and man, clean and fresh and sexual.

"Damn, woman. I nearly came eating you out. It was hard. And still is," he teased.

She felt her heart crumble before him, loving that he'd lost that tough shell with her, that he'd reverted to the caring lover, the charmer from before. The real Brody.

"I love this." She looked up at him while she licked him from tip to root. *I love you.*

He pushed her hair aside and kept his hand on her cheek. "Yeah." He sighed but didn't close his eyes. He watched her like a hawk as she licked and sucked the head of him. "All of it. Take me in your mouth, Abby. I want to fuck those lips."

She opened wider and let him pump in short thrusts into her mouth. Threading her hand between his legs, she cupped his balls and felt him jerk. A spurt of fluid hit her tongue, and she sucked him harder.

"Oh yeah. Wait. *Stop.* I want to come, but not in your mouth. Let me have that hot pussy."

Feeling naughty and loving every second of it, she pulled away from Brody and flipped onto her back, then stretched out on the bed and spread her thighs wider. "This pussy?"

She fingered herself, enthralled at the attention he gave her while he started jerking himself off.

"That's it. Touch yourself," he said in a gravelly voice. "Play with that plump little clit. Come again, but this time, while I'm in you."

"I don't know if I can," she said honestly, then bit her lip. "You'll have to make me."

He growled and pounced, and before she knew it, he had her hands pinned over her head to the bed and his thick thighs nudging her legs wider. "Wrap them around my waist. I'm coming in." He angled himself at her entrance and slid through her cream. So deep, so full.

Brody moaned her name as he took her with hard, punishing strokes that had her begging for more. No one had ever made her feel so good, and his possessive hold, the strength keeping her from moving, turned her on like crazy.

She cried out as he surged faster. "Harder. Yes, yes," she said on a moan as she—impossibly—came again, this time clenching him inside her. The pleasure was indescribable.

He shouted her name and thrust as deep as he could go. He shuddered as he came inside her, and the knowledge that they'd shared something as intimate as two people could meant so much she couldn't say. She hugged him tight, praising and whispering his name.

They kissed again, a gentle meeting of mouths that conveyed all the feeling she had balled inside. That passion and need for him, and only him.

He answered with tender nips and strokes, holding her tightly to him. "Oh, Abby." He kissed her again, and to her astonishment, began moving inside her.

"Brody?"

"Yes. Just…let me. I'm still half hard. Fuck, I need

you. Need to come again inside you. You're so good, so sweet." He murmured, to himself? To her? She didn't think he knew. But then his movements grew hurried, and it didn't take him long before he moaned and came once more.

Too tired to join him, she waited for him to finish, loving everything about this moment and committing it to memory. No matter what happened from this point on, she knew everything between them had fundamentally changed.

She wasn't sure whether to be happy or sad about the fact.

———⁓———

Brody finally withdrew from Abby's heavenly body and stood up, looking down at her. Christ, she was like one of those paintings come to life. Where the woman had glowing, golden skin, a ripe fullness to her, and pulled emotions from him he'd never thought possible.

"Be right back," he promised.

"Mm-hmm." She laid there with her arms over her head, looking like an invitation to a never-ending love-fest. If he hadn't been so bone-deep drained, he'd have gone back for more. But after an emotionally demanding week and their physically wearing lovemaking, he didn't have it in him.

He moved to the bathroom to clean up and returned with a warm cloth for Abby. After cleaning her up, he pulled her with him under the covers and into his arms, never having felt better in his entire life.

He just lay there with her, loving how she stroked his chest, his hair. Her body heat bleeding into his. The calm he'd been sorely needing, his center, returned to him, and his entire world made sense again. With a sigh, he hugged her even tighter, until she squeaked.

"Oh, sorry."

She gave a low laugh. "Honey, you can hug me as tight as you want after what you did for me. I swear, I don't have any bones left. I'm one big slug right now."

"A slug in my arms. Attractive image. I'm sorry, you say you're a writer?"

She laughed again and planted a kiss over his heart. *In* his heart. He didn't understand it, but the sex had gone beyond a physical release into something much more profound. And though scared like hell, he wanted to hold on to the feeling and treasure it. Treasure her.

"Funny guy. I missed you, Brody," she confessed in a small voice. "I hope that doesn't freak you out, because it freaked me out for a little. But I'm nothing if not honest with myself. And somehow, like that fungus you once compared Colin to, you're now etched into my proverbial walls."

"Not sure I followed all that. You called me a fungus, I'm on a proverbial wall—whatever that is—but you're hugging me, so that's a good sign, right?"

She bit his nipple, and he felt a sluggish sense of desire try to wake his cock. No going after two climaxes back-to-back. "Nice try, Abby. Maybe in another hour I'll be ready to go again. But not yet. You drained me."

"Hush." She snuggled against him, and he thought she'd gone to sleep when she said, "I don't know what made you so sad, Brody. But I'm here if you ever want to talk. No pressure, no big deal. I just want you to know I…care."

To his surprise, her announcement didn't give him the same anxiety he used to feel when Bitsy and Pop tried to get answers from him. His natural inclination was to fold in on himself, to bury his pain deep and deal with it by not dealing with it. But Abby gave him that option to unburden himself. And he knew, just by knowing *her*, she'd never judge him.

"Seth told you I had visitors, didn't he?"

"He did. But I already knew something wasn't right. You didn't take me bowling, and I know how much you were looking forward to losing to me."

He chuckled. "You do make me laugh." She hugged him tighter, and he basked in her affection. The moment felt right, and he decided to talk, because he needed to. It was time. And he wanted her to know.

Chapter 15

"MY FATHER AND MY BROTHER SHOWED UP LAST WEEK, Alan and Jeremy."

She didn't say anything, and Brody let the words pour from him, needing her to know the real him, for someone to know the truth.

"I went to live with Flynn when I was a kid. My family… They're not good people. My mom died when I was a baby. OD'd on heroin. Alan, my father, is a piece of trash, and Jeremy's not much better. Alan is trying to drink himself to death, and Jeremy is a druggie. Or *was*, because he showed up last week with some dicked-up version of an apology for all the wrongs he'd once done me." Brody snorted. "Like a big old 'my bad' could ever atone for the bastard making my life a living hell."

He felt her kiss on his skin, and it soothed that part of him still reeling from his family's unexpected visit. "I hate them. I feel bad, but I fucking hate them. I see them and I'm a scared little kid again, you know?"

"Oh, Brody."

"Alan wasn't physically abusive. Just used to tell me how worthless and useless I was. That my mother died rather than put up with me. I moved in with Bitsy and Pop when they found me just hanging around the play yard a few times too many. Alan didn't care. He didn't want to feed or support me anyway, and by that time Jeremy was a teenager. Old enough to take care of himself. So while they would be out getting drunk or high together, on one of their many cons, I got to live with a real family."

"Beth and James."

"Yeah. They were so good to me. Gave me a home, a place where I didn't have to worry about stuff. Flynn's always been my best friend. And that never changed." He paused. "The guys don't know a lot about this."

"Brody, I won't say anything. I'm just here to listen. That's all."

"Thanks." He blinked, surprised to find his eyes watery.

"Beth and James never called social services?"

"They didn't need to. Alan agreed to let me stay with them full time if they left it alone. Otherwise I'd have been shipped into foster care and had to deal with a lot of bullshit. Bitsy and Pop had him sign some guardianship papers and it was a done deal. Legally they could care for me. But every now and then, Alan and Jeremy would show up and I'd have to visit for a time."

He grew quiet, remembering the nightmare that had been his life.

"You okay?"

"Uh-huh." He blew out a breath. "Alan would have me steal. Jeremy... He was a sick little creep. Used to scare me all the time, torment me. If I took in a stray dog, he kicked it and let it loose. If I tried to make a friend, he'd spread lies about me. But mostly he liked to use me as a punching bag. He never hit me where it would show, but I hurt. And he'd terrorize me into keeping quiet, telling me he'd do something worse to Mike or Flynn or Cam if I ratted him out."

"So you didn't, because you loved your brothers."
She understood.

"Yeah. That went on for a long time, until one time
Bitsy and Pop got a call from the hospital. I'd broken
my arm and went into shock. Nearly died. Then I
stopped having visits." He remembered Jeremy holding
the gun to his head, pulling the trigger over and over.
Then forcing him to climb the tree to get some stupid
baggie one of Jeremy's buddies had hidden for him.
Jeremy kept screwing with him as he'd climbed. Even
at eleven, Brody had been an agile athlete. But when
Jeremy had hit him in the head with a rock, he'd lost his
balance and fallen a good fifteen feet.

"God, Brody. What happened?"

"Got bullied into climbing a tree. Fell and broke my
arm. Went into shock. Jeremy's fault," he answered in
a condensed version.

She rubbed both his arms, from his shoulders to his
wrists, and he melted under her touch. "Man, I want to
belt that guy."

He chuckled. "You and me both." He paused. "I hit
him. Hard. Knocked him down when he put a hand on
me last week."

She bolted up and stared wide-eyed. "Did he hurt
you? Did he try to hit you?" She studied his chest, pushing the blanket away, and he couldn't believe how good
her concern felt.

"No. He came here to apologize for being a grade-A
dick. I was going back inside, and I think he just wanted
my attention. But when he touched me, I snapped.
Abby, I hadn't seen either one of them in two years.
And before that, it had been a year or more. Every so

often they show up wanting money or a job or a place to live. And every time I ignore them. I just wish they'd go away."

"I do too." She bit her lower lip, and he hated the shine of tears in her eyes.

"Damn. Don't cry."

"I'm not. Just something in my eye. And stop looking at my breasts," she chastened even as she sniffed. She lay down and put her head on his chest again, just where she belonged.

"Yes, dear."

She pulled his chest hair.

"Ow."

"Focus. So you hit Jeremy."

"And Alan. But in my defense, he really did take a swing at me."

"The bastard."

"Yeah." He warmed up to the idea of having Abby at his back and taking his side. For so long he'd wanted to tell Flynn, but he hadn't wanted things to change between them. Flynn and the guys were his rock. They knew the Brody he wanted them to know. But Abby...she comforted just by being there. "I slammed back into the house and they left. Period. End of story."

"Except it's not the end, because you've been in a funk since they were here. Flynn's worried."

"I know."

"And you didn't hear this from me, but he had a feeling it was your *biological* family bothering you. Because they're not your family. Your *real* family is Beth and James, Flynn, Mike, and Cam."

"Not technically, but—"

"Yes, technically. They love you so much, Brody. I hear it whenever Beth brags about you or James grabs you in a bear hug. When Mike and Cam give you crap at parties, or Flynn laughs with you. You're the blond McCauley—but a McCauley. You're so lucky to have that."

He rubbed his cheek against her hair. She was so soft on the outside, yet so strong emotionally. "Yeah, I am lucky." *Lucky to have you here with me. And I don't want that luck to end.* "So can I ask you something?"

"Well, okay. But only because you gave me orgasms."

"Were you serious about going to Rick?"

She stilled, and he tensed with her. *Shit.* She hadn't been kidding. He'd known she was too special not to have men fighting over her. And after today, he planned to be one of those idiots bent on keeping her attention.

"Brody?" she whispered and rolled him to his back, then braced on her arms to look down at him. He could get lost in her dark eyes, that full mouth. Even her petite nose turned him on. God, the woman was so perfect for him. He felt for her, something real and sure. Something like…love.

"Yeah?" He cleared his throat, prepared to pretend to give in easily while he worked behind the scenes to push Rick and every other asshole from her life but him.

She leaned closer and whispered, "I win."

The look on his face was priceless. He just stared at her, the momentary anxiety clouding his gaze gone. She smiled wide. "Yeah, I'm so winning. You liiiikkkke me."

She hadn't wanted the tense conversation to drag

him down again. Hearing what his jerk of a father and sadist brother had once done chilled her. To imagine carefree Brody being abused like that...she couldn't understand it. She loved Beth and James so much for taking care of him.

But sensing his shame for the way they'd treated him hurt her inside. Brody was a man worthy of love. She wondered if he knew that. If maybe that's why his relationships never lasted. Or maybe, like her, he just wasn't that good at man-woman connections? Then again, she and he seemed to connect with ease.

"You little witch." He yanked her to him and rolled until he loomed over her. So much larger, he conquered her with ease. But when he started tickling her, she lost her empathy and started to get mad.

"Ack. I hate getting tickled. Hate, hate, *hate it!*" She tried to shove him off her but he grabbed her wrists with one hand and easily pinned her down. And like that, she started to grow aroused again. The covers slipped off them, and he laughed at her as he tickled her with his free hand.

"Stop, stop. Please," she begged, gasping for breath. She laughed when he grazed her ribs. "Uncle. *Uncle.*"

Brody grinned down at her, a sly expression of victory. "That's right. Who's your daddy?"

"Ew. Brody."

He laughed and then to her surprise, kept his hands firmly around her wrists while he nudged her legs wider and positioned his cock between her legs. Then he pushed inside her, moving easily, but he felt bigger because she wasn't as slick this time.

"That's it. Yeah, you cried uncle. Now you have to pay the price."

"Oh. Okay. Yes, whatever you want."

Brody nodded, no longer laughing, and leaned down to kiss her. He thrust his tongue and his cock in time with each other, and his movements grew frenzied. He left her lips and pulled back to watch her as he took her. "This time come with me. All around me while I fill you up."

She nodded, lost in the lust and love she felt as they watched each other taking fulfillment. When the end came, she cried out his name and clamped him tight within her. Never letting go.

"Okay, so why am I here?" Del asked Abby two days later. "It didn't make sense when you tried to explain it to me over the phone. And, well, in person it ain't making much sense either."

Friday night at the bowling alley, and Abby needed all the help she could get. "Look. I owe you."

"So you blackmailed me into bowling on a Friday night?" Del crossed her arms, now somewhat concealed in a long-sleeved black button-down shirt that actually gave her a sexy edge.

"Um, hello?" Del bent her head to peer at Abby. "Anyone home?"

"Oh, sorry. Yes, I wanted you to come meet my friends. You'll like them. And then I was thinking maybe you'd like to join a book club with a few friends of mine."

"A book club."

"Yeah. We read all kinds of things, not just romance. And uh, I was kind of hoping you'd talk to me."

"We're doing that right now." Del sounded amused, and her dry wit only made Abby like her more.

"I meant about research. I'm a writer, and I'd like to make my character a female mechanic. You're the expert there."

Del blinked. She'd let her hair down tonight, and the light strands curled around her shoulders. She was exotic, rough, sensual. Not fresh like Vanessa or gorgeous like Maddie. The eyebrow ring and nose piercing, a small stud just over her right nostril, added to her tough look. The visible parts of her tattoos between the edges of the sleeves at her forearms and her wrists painted her as a woman not to be bothered, but she had attracted more than her share of attention since showing up at the crowded bowling alley, though she seemed to ignore it.

"So tell me again why this is considered repayment for fixing your tire. Seems more like I'm doing you another favor."

Abby sighed. Like a dog with a bone. "Work with me here, Del. I'm offering friendship."

"So what's that in dollars?"

Ignoring Del's amusement, Abby huffed. "You can't put a price on friends." Or great research potential. "You seem to be a practical woman."

"Now you're trying to butter me up."

"Isn't any good business about networking? My roommates know people, and the opposite team we're playing knows people. Vanessa is a CPA. Maddie's an interior designer. Flynn and Brody are plumbers and seem to know everyone in Queen Anne. Cam is an investment guy, and Mike's a contractor. He's Colin's dad."

Del smiled, and in her pleasure Abby saw the real

woman behind the gruff exterior. "Oh yeah, the kid. How's he doing?"

"Good. He kicked butt at soccer. He's got a sleepover tonight, so Mike is joining us. See? Four guys, only three girls. We needed you."

"I feel so used."

Abby laughed. "Come on, stay. The beer and wings are on me."

"Well, if you're buying."

"And it's not like you had anything better to do tonight. Or at least, that's what some guy named J. T. said when I asked for you."

"Yeah. My brother." Del scowled. "Huge pain in my ass. He told me I had to come by tonight to satisfy an unhappy client. You're not even a paying customer."

"Nor am I unhappy. See? You're two for two. Come bowl with us. Make merry. Eat chicken. Drink the pig swill that passes for beer."

"Sounds appetizing." Del cracked her knuckles. "Okay, I'm in."

"We're on lanes three and four. Come over after you get your shoes."

She caught Del muttering about her being bossy as she left to join the others. Abby had warned Maddie and Vanessa what to expect, though she just knew Vanessa would stick her foot in her mouth at least once. She'd made Brody extract a promise from the guys to behave as well, but who knew how that would hold up?

Ever since she and Brody had become a kind-of couple, they'd spent the past two nights together since his admission about his family. She felt their closeness to her toes and wondered if he sensed her love at all.

She saw him standing with Flynn as they bragged to Maddie and Vanessa about how they planned to crush the competition.

She joined them. "Oh please. You and what army?"

Flynn snorted. "I hate to break it to you, but Maddie is afraid of chipping her nails. I doubt she'll be throwing down strikes."

"Oh?" Maddie glared at him. "Vanessa and I were all-state champs."

To Abby, Vanessa murmured, "Do they actually have all-state bowling champs?"

"No idea."

"And when you lose, you *lose*," Maddie said to him.

Flynn's brows rose. Apparently he and Maddie had made a prior bet. "It's on, baby."

"*Baby?* Oh, the love talk. I may swoon," Vanessa said dryly.

Del walked over to the group wearing her bowling shoes and holding her black biker boots.

"Our shoes are under there." Abby pointed to the spot under the table, then made introductions.

"Wow. Did that hurt?" Vanessa asked, looking at Del's forearms. Del had rolled up her sleeves to her elbows. "They say getting tattoos where it's not fleshy is painful. And you don't look all that fleshy to me."

"Thanks?" Del raised a pierced brow. "Yeah, it hurt. But not that much."

Flynn and Brody drew closer to look at her arms. "Nice artwork," Brody said. "Flynn thought about getting a Snoopy on his ass when we were back in high school, but as usual, he chickened out."

Flynn turned on him. "Oh? Because I never saw ink

on your body. Except for that time I wrote *idiot* on your forehead with that tanning gel."

"Which didn't come off for two weeks. Thanks for that." Brody glared at him.

Del chuckled. "You two must be brothers."

"Twins," they said at the same time.

Abby said to Del, "I'll just apologize for them ahead of time and save us all the trouble later on. Cam and Mike aren't here yet, but— Oh, there they are." She waved, and Cam waved back.

"Holy shit, is Cam actually wearing jeans?" Brody asked.

"Yeah, but they no doubt have a fancy label on them." Flynn shook his head. "I swear the guy won't buy anything under a hundred bucks—including underwear."

Abby smiled at the guys as they reached them. "Cam, Mike. Hey. This is Del." She thumbed in Del's direction. "Mike, this is Colin's friend with all the colors on her arms."

Del nodded. "Hi. Cute kid you got."

"Thanks." Mike grinned. "He'll be plenty impressed when he hears I met his favorite mechanic and beat the pants off her in bowling." He lifted his bowling bag.

"Are you kidding?" Vanessa huffed. "If I'd known we could bring our own equipment, I'd have brought my ball."

Abby looked at Maddie. Vanessa didn't have a ball. Maddie shrugged.

"So that's a handicap for you then." Vanessa lifted a notepad and wrote something down.

"Wait a minute." Cam frowned and looked down at what she wrote. "No way. That's cheating." He wrote something down, and they haggled like tradesmen at a bazaar.

"Ignore them. They're both OCD when it comes to numbers," Abby told Del.

Vanessa turned to scowl at her.

"I heard that," Cam said without looking at Abby.

"Try you *resemble* that," Mike muttered. Then he glanced at Del. "You're not going to cry when you lose miserably, are you? I mean, we already tolerate a lot from Maddie. But one sobber is about all I can handle."

"Hey." Maddie frowned.

Del laughed. "Hell no. I was hoping you guys were a little tougher than you look. Abby said losers pay for the game."

"I don't remember that."

"Deal." Brody rubbed his hands together. "This will be the easiest win I've ever earned."

Three games later, he stared at the back of Mike's head and willed the big bastard to bowl like he had more than just thumbs. Mike was sucking big time tonight. The guy normally rolled a one-sixty or better. But man, either he had the worst case of bowler's luck or the tattooed chick was scaring him.

Brody liked her. Del had a funny sense of humor, a lot like Cam's, actually. Dry, witty, and she didn't say much, but when she did, she hit her target right between the eyes. The woman had a heck of a body too, if one went for Amazons with piercing gray eyes and muscle. Fortunately for Abby's team, they had Del and Maddie—who'd turned out to be a pretty decent bowler—and his team had been handicapped with Mike.

"Nailed it," Mike said as he released the ball.

"You only knock so many pins down because you throw it so hard." Del shook her head. "But bowling is all about finesse. See?" She pointed to his ugly split.

"Shit."

"Nice mouth." Vanessa shook her head. "So that's where Colin gets it."

Mike turned to her. "What?"

"You mean you haven't heard the kid playing outside with his mutant turtle guys? This bastard, that asshole. Etcetera, etcetera."

Del raised a brow. "Really? He's what? Five?"

Mike flushed. "Six. That's a lie. Colin never swears. Well, not those particular words, anyway."

"Mike, you're up again," Abby said.

"Hold on." He turned to Vanessa, and Abby grinned at Brody over his shoulder.

Great. If Mike continued to bowl the way he'd been all night, it would be up to Brody to nail it.

Vanessa shrugged. "Sorry, Mike. Just saying what I've overheard."

Del glanced at Abby, who winked. Del smiled and turned back to Mike. "You know, *I* don't believe it. Kid was really nice when I met him. Polite too."

Mike stepped up to bowl again. "Damn straight." He readied to aim, to release, and drew back his hand.

"Yep. He was so cute. Said he wanted a tattoo like mine, but I told him he'd have to wait until he turned eighteen at least. Or course, the way he was eyeing my bitch'n ass, I—"

Mike sent the ball rushing right between both pins. He swung around. "*What?*"

She rolled her sleeve higher and showed him a dagger held in a dragon's claw. "I like to call this one my bitch'n ass, because when my brother did it, he told me to stop bitching, and I called him an ass while he tried to make me cry. *Tried.* Anyway, long story short, Colin liked the dragon a lot."

Mike glared down at her. Del didn't bat an eye.

"Well, fuck."

"Nope. I have no idea where the kid gets his language skills," Vanessa added.

Cam chuckled. "You got served, bro. Brody, save us from these evil women."

"As usual, it's up to the handsome blond to save your ugly asses." Brody let out a put-upon sigh. "The golden god of strikes and spares, pins and balls."

"Well, Mr. Balls," Abby said, and Vanessa snickered. "How about you put your money where your mouth is?"

Brody turned to her. "Oh? Gentlemen, I believe *my date* wants to place a bet."

"Seriously. This is no surprise, Brody," Cam explained. "We all know you two are…ah, going out."

"We call it shagging," Vanessa said.

"Vanessa. Geez." Abby blushed. She was so cute.

"Date, huh?" Maddie narrowed her gaze. "You two going steady? Gonna go necking when we're done too?"

Brody grinned. "Maybe. Don't be jealous, Maddie. I know Flynn was your second choice, but he tries."

"Ass." Flynn socked him in the arm.

"You guys really are funny." Del stood and stretched. "I'll be back. Another round of beer?"

"Yeah, sure." Cam shrugged. "But I'm not paying since it looks like we're going to be stuck with the tab tonight."

"Have faith, young one," Brody said, staring at Abby. She hadn't flinched when he'd called her his date in front of the others. Should he try for more? "In fact, my new girlfriend wants to place a bet."

"Could you stop with the theatrics and bowl already?" Vanessa complained.

"Hey, Mike, it's okay to blink now. She's gone." Cam nudged him.

Mike flushed and looked away from Del's retreating back. "Shut up. I wasn't staring. Okay, I was at first. But man, that woman has got some serious tattoos."

"Uh-huh. That's what you were looking at. On her *ass*."

Mike aimed for Cam, who dodged around him and hid behind Vanessa.

Brody would have laughed, but Abby's odd expression worried him. Had he pushed too hard with the girlfriend bit? He couldn't help it. He felt ready to take that step, because damn, but he wanted exclusivity.

"Hold on for a minute." He dragged Abby away from the others. "You okay?"

She cupped his cheek. "Your girlfriend?" she asked softly.

He swallowed hard. *Really, really falling at this woman's tiny feet*. "Um, yeah. I mean, I like you. You like me. I don't plan on seeing anyone else. And you aren't. Right? We like spending time together." He sure did. Had he misread the signals he thought she'd been sending?

"Brody, relax." She smiled and pulled him down to offer a kiss, one that went straight to his gut and sucker-punched him. "I like having a hot boyfriend."

He beamed. "I am hot, aren't I?"

She laughed. "I tell you what, Mr. Balls. You win, I'll let you tie me up in bed, any way you want. I win, I get to do the same."

"Awesome. Either way I'm tying you up."

She huffed. "No, nimrod. If I win, I get to tie *you* up and do wicked things to you."

"So it's like you want me to throw the game." He wiggled his brows. "Sorry, baby. No can do. If we lose, the Machos"—what they'd named their team—"will blame me, even though we all know if Mike had spent more time concentrating on the pins instead of Del, we might even now be winning."

She chuckled. "I thought I was the only one who'd noticed."

"Nah. Big brother is smitten. Isn't it cute?"

"Will you two stop flirting and come on?" Cam whined. "Vanessa just finished the Lady Brawlers' game with a strike. Brody, you're our last chance at a win."

"Help us Brodi-Wan Kenobi," Flynn sang. "You're our only hope."

The others laughed.

"Kiss for luck from my girlfriend?" he asked.

"Only for my boyfriend." She gave him a kiss that made his knees tremble. "I can't wait to tie you up later," she whispered. "And rub myself all over you." She walked away laughing.

Brody had to take a minute to collect himself. And will away one hell of a hard-on so he could bowl without hurting himself.

Chapter 16

ABBY HAD A HARD TIME BELIEVING HE'D PULLED IT off. Despite the catcalls and teasing, he'd managed two strikes in his tenth frame, putting the guys ahead and leaving the Lady Brawlers with quite a tab. Especially for her, since she'd picked up Del's portion despite the woman's protests.

"You sure you're okay with this?" Brody asked as he used fuzzy handcuffs to fasten her wrists to scarves tied to the bed posts. "I know we talked about it, and I'm dying to tie you up, but you don't have to do it to please me. We can make the bet something else."

Lying belly-down on his bed, Abby turned her head to watch him. He continued to restrain her, keeping her naked and spread-eagle on his bed. But she knew one word from her and he'd stop. "I want to do it to please *me*."

He glanced up from tightening her ankle and grinned. "And that's why you're so perfect for me. You like what I like—you naked and tied up."

Just one more thing she and her *boyfriend* had in common.

"Don't you look pretty," he murmured, standing behind her. He'd given her a good bit of slack by her wrists and feet, leading her to wonder what he intended. She turned her head and saw him naked and holding a bottle. "Time for your massage."

She wriggled. "But I'll get your bed all messy."

"Sheets wash." He shrugged. "Besides, you were a good sport about getting spanked at the alley. I figure I'll soften you up before I spank you here."

Her heart raced. Spanking. Rough sex. Being tied up. Her real turn-ons, and she'd gotten him to play with her without exposing herself. Not bad. She shifted on the bed, and he groaned.

"Man. I wish I had a camera right now. Your ass is perfection."

"Not too big?"

He snorted. "Are you kidding? Every time I look at it, I imagine bending you over and pushing inside you."

"In my *ass*?" One kink she'd never actually wanted to try.

He laughed. "No. Why? You want to try it?"

"*No*."

"Okay then. We can cross anal off your list."

"Brody."

"Hey, I'm doing this, not because I want to, but because my *girlfriend* writes sexy books and needs some help with research. I'm actually pretty selfless. If it were up to me, I'd be hanging with the guys and playing canasta."

"You're so full of it. Canasta? You know how to play that?"

"Well, no. But I like saying 'canasta.' I sound more sophisticated than a dude who just wants to fuck his lady until she can't walk, you know?"

She let out a breath and faced the bed, her head in the pillow. "I'm really getting turned on."

"I know." He chuckled low. "Now let's get you oiled up." He must have applied oil to his hands, because when he touched her, he slid right over her shoulders and upper back.

"Oh, wow. That feels so good."

"That's it. Relax. No more stress."

"Mmm."

A comfortable, sensual silence fell between them as he rubbed her all over, never coming close to her sex or the sides of her breasts. Just a smooth, gliding touch over her shoulders, arms, back, and legs. He sat over her, and she felt his erection on her skin, the spark of attraction between them always flaring hot.

"So you're really okay with us dating?" he asked after a while. "I kind of felt like I pushed you on that."

"Brody, it's fine." She moaned. "Better than fine. Now you belong to me." She tensed—she hadn't meant to admit how much she wanted to have him to herself. Would that freak him out?

"Nice." He chuckled. "Easy, baby. Don't tense up. Trust me, the feeling is more than mutual." He continued to rub away her knots. Then he scooted back on her legs and found her ass. He rubbed and pushed, smoothing out her muscles, turning her into a pile of goo.

After a while, he moved off her. "Brody?"

"Shh. This is all part of the massage." He manipulated her butt cheeks, pulling them wider each time, and she found the sensations arousing. That was before he put a finger there, sliding along the rim of her anus. Her arousal shot through the roof.

"God, what are you doing?" Hadn't she said no anal? Why then did she want him to do that again? But slide lower, toward her wet core?

"No talking back." He slapped her on the ass, and for a moment, she froze, shocked at the sting.

He rubbed it away, and a hand slid between her legs to cup her.

"*Brody.*"

"You begging me already?" he asked in a low voice, the one he used when he was aroused. "No staying power, Abby?"

He slapped her again, not hard, but enough to sting a bit. The fiery sensation went straight to her pussy, and she squirmed.

"Oh, that's it. You like that. I thought you might. Just like you like being tied up." He bent over her to whisper, "I like it too. A lot." He dragged his cock up her back, the thick shaft swollen with arousal. "Makes me want to fuck you hard." He slid against her, his body now pressed to hers, his front to her back. He sucked her neck, nipping hard before rubbing the ache away with his tongue. He slid his hands under her and cupped her, holding her tight. Moving to better fit against her, he shoved his cock between her legs, not penetrating, but just there, grazing her clit. He rubbed while he played with her breasts, his weight heavy, oppressive, and nearly bringing her to climax.

"Brody. Yes. More," she begged, lost to anything he wanted.

"You want it, don't you? My kinky little woman. So curvy, so feminine. And deep down, you're naughty." He nipped her ear. "Even…slutty. Aren't you?"

She moaned. "God, yes. Fuck me. Fuck me so hard."

He pushed inside her, still cupping her breasts and shoving her down into the bed with his bulk. "Christ, you're wet, and so hot," he rasped and moved.

Long, slow thrusts that did nothing but frustrate her. "Harder. Come on. I need you." She tried to gyrate under him, anything to increase his pace. Instead, he pinched her nipples.

She bucked up against him, ready to come.

"Yeah, there she is. My little slave. You like this? Tell me what you want. You want me slamming into that pretty pussy? Taking you hard? Can I pull your hair? Make it hurt?"

She sobbed, needing him desperately. "Yes, yes. Pull my hair. Put your hands around my throat and squeeze. God, I need to come. I need you to fuck me deep, Brody. Now," she moaned.

He let go of her breasts and surged deeper into her sex. Then he slowly rose to his knees, keeping himself inside her while he pulled her hips up to meet him. Now on her knees with her ass in the air, she was poised before him, submissive, lost to his hold. His control.

"I'm going to ride you hard. Come with me, baby. Come all over me." He gripped her hips with slippery hands but managed to hold on tight as he withdrew from her warmth, then slammed back inside her.

He touched the heart of her womb, was all she could think, because he'd hit the spot that sent her spiraling out of control and into orgasm. She cried out as he continued to hammer into her, her ecstasy one that continued to fog everything but the man owning her. Possessing her. Taking her.

"Yeah, squeeze me. That's it," he moaned as he pounded into her with a force that shook them both. "Take it. *All* of it." He slammed one final time before jerking inside her.

The force of the orgasm left her dizzy, and she knelt, quivering, as he released inside her. He continued to thrust in and out a few more times, and she felt a mess run down her legs, but he didn't stop coming.

Finally spent, he withdrew and pulled her down with him. He turned her onto her back and blanketed her with his body. "You okay?" he managed, still breathing hard. A lock of hair had fallen over his left eye, and she wanted badly to push it back. To touch him and thank him for finally breaking through the barriers that she'd been hiding behind for so long.

"That was amazing." She wanted to cry.

"Oh, yeah. God, Abby. Why have you been hiding your kinky side? I have so much more dirty talk to share. That was nothing."

She laughed, feeling amazing and loving the fact that she could lie there, tied up, slicked up, and not feel like a whore or a loser or a pervert because she'd liked him being rough.

"You called me a slut," she said after a few moments. "I liked it."

"Yeah?" He rolled to his side and rested on his elbow. He grinned and pushed her hair off her face. "'Cause I have to say, all that dirty talk really revs my engine. You little slut. You bad girl with that wet, wet pussy. I love shoving my cock into you."

"Stop it." Because he turned her on as well. "Am I weird for liking that?" She wanted to know.

His smile faded. "Why would you think that? Wait. Don't tell me. The ex."

She didn't want to talk about Kevin right now.

"Abby, stop. Look. I don't want you to ever think

things between us are wrong. I mean, it's consensual, right? Kink? Trying new things? I'm game."

She snorted. "Brody." Yet relief made tears slide down her cheeks. "Ignore me."

"Oh honey. He did a number on you, didn't he?" Brody released the fuzzy cuffs from both her ankles and wrists. Then he tugged her into his arms for a hug before pulling away to look at her again. "Tell me."

Considering he'd spilled his guts about his family, she knew he deserved the same trust. But still, it hurt to say it out loud. "Kevin and I met years ago. He lived near my family before moving away. I was roommates with Maddie in college. She was a business major at the time before she saw the light and found design."

"Relevance?"

"Just adding important details."

"You writers. Continue." He kissed her forehead, and she snuggled closer.

"Well, anyway, when Maddie got a job in Seattle, I decided to come with her. Later I found out Kevin had transferred out here for work. He and my parents keep in touch. I met up with him soon after and we started dating. It was hard for me, because I used to be pretty shy around guys. I hadn't even known he was interested until he flat-out told me. I was flattered. I'd been with a few other guys, but none as successful or handsome as Kevin. And he was someone I'd had a crush on when I was younger. We were together for close to a year and a half. I thought he loved me."

"But…?"

"But I freaked him out. Kevin was a nice guy, and he wanted a nice girlfriend. Someone thinner, less talkative, less funny, less brainy, hell, less everything. I was stupid and tried to change for him. He complained about our sex life too."

"He must have been out of his fucking mind."

She really, *really* loved Brody at that moment. "That hurt more than the other stuff, if you want the truth. I like sex. I admit it."

"Good. Me too."

She grinned before Kevin stole her joy once more. "Well, he never liked to have sex. And he didn't want to do anything…creative."

"No dirty talk?"

"No."

"No tying you up, no rough stuff?"

"I wish." She stopped talking, afraid she'd just committed a major foul by admitting the truth.

But Brody sighed and pushed back so he could look into her face—no longer buried in his chest. "What a loser. He missed out on some really exciting fun."

"Well, maybe he didn't. It's not exactly normal to want your boyfriend to choke you while having sex. Or to spank you or tie you up. Or—"

"Do any of the things we just did? 'Cause honey, in case you missed it, you came hard. Harder than you have since we've been doing it, anyway."

"Oh."

"Don't 'oh' me. So did I. I left a *huge* mess inside you." And didn't he sound satisfied at that.

She felt herself blushing. "Crude, but effective. Okay, I get it. You like kink."

"I like what *you* like. Getting you off gets me excited. That's what great sex is about. That and a connection."

He shrugged. "We have that. I…" He paused. "I really like you, Abby."

I love you, Brody. "I like you too." She cleared her throat. "But I need you to be honest with me. If I ever want something you don't, don't pretend, okay? Just tell me the truth."

"Okay."

A huge weight fell from her shoulders, and she finally realized what her friends had been telling her since she'd broken things with Kevin. There was nothing wrong with *her*. She simply needed to be with someone who could appreciate her. God, what a moron she'd been for letting Kevin get to her the way he had. Brody showed her she could be free to be herself, both in bed and out.

And then he let out a breath, and the other shoe fell. "In the spirit of honesty, I have to tell you something."

She didn't want to face him but knew she had to. She respected his willingness to be candid. "Yeah?"

"Well, it's something I read about in one of your books. I just don't think I can do it."

She tried to blink back tears. "Sure. I mean, wait. You said books. I thought you only read *Fireman's Kiss*?"

"I had a lot of time to think last week. I read a few others."

Oh boy. Hadn't she gone all out in the *Marines Do It Best* series? "So tell me."

"Fine. Here it is. Don't hate me for this…but no way am I ever up for sharing you with another dude. Uh-uh. No man is putting his junk in my woman. Or near me. I'm not homophobic. Ted is gay, and he's one of my tight buddies. But he knows better than to try shoving his tab B into my slot A, the one in back."

She relaxed, almost giddy. "Is that it?"

"No. I also refuse to call you *honeybunches* and *love bunny*. Really. Your heroes need to grow a pair."

She sputtered. "That was all said jokingly. My heroes are alpha types."

"You mean assholes. They're either dicking a woman over or crawling all over themselves to say they're sorry." He snorted. "What kind of a man covers a floor in rose petals, anyway?"

She sniffed. "A romantic man. So obviously I won't be getting rose petals from you anytime soon."

He blinked at her. "You want romance?"

"Not now. But yeah, sometimes romance is nice."

He frowned. "Like what? What's romantic to you?"

"I don't know. Hearing a man tell me he loves me." She flushed. "Not you. I mean, if I was in that kind of a deeper relationship."

"Right. What else?" He propped his chin in his hand and watched her. "Flowers? Chocolates?"

"Those are nice. But I guess it's being made to feel like I matter. That's romantic to me. Like if I'm working late and he makes me hot chocolate. Or if my feet hurt and he rubs them."

He gave her feet a disbelieving glance. "With those calluses? I don't think so. Not unless you grind down your heels first."

"Brody."

He laughed. "I'm just kidding. Tell me more."

Abby outlined her ideals of romance, of which, most of the things on her list didn't cost a dime. "It's about being thoughtful, not buying someone's love."

"Hmm. Good to know." He looked pretty attentive.

"What about you? What do you consider romance?"

"Me? Well, right now you're being pretty romantic, keeping that wet spot on the bed covered."

She grimaced as he laughed. "I know. It's gross, and it's all your fault."

"Hold on." He pulled her off the bed and nudged her into his bathroom.

To her shock, he'd remodeled it. "Oh my God. This is...*nice*."

The tub was no longer pea soup green, but an ivory color. He'd put in new towel bars, as well as a new *clean* shower curtain. The sink and toilet were brand new and high-end—and, to her surprise, stylish.

"It's pretty much a copy of what Cam has at his condo. Little shit is cocky but has good taste. You like it?"

"Wow." She stared in awe. "Last week you said the bathroom was broken. That the toilet didn't work and the shower was busted."

"I lied. Didn't want you to see it until it was finished."

"It's amazing."

He beamed. "Good. Now into the shower with you." He turned on the overhead rain shower head and got it hot, then nudged her inside. "My idea of romance is a woman loving her man."

"O-kay."

"And she shows him by soaping him up, maybe giving him a nice scalp massage with the shampoo." He waited patiently, glancing at the shampoo and soap until she smiled and took the hint.

After cleaning him up, he did the same for her.

"And then a terrifically romantic gesture to end all

gestures would be for her to thank him on her knees. You know, blow him until he forgets his own name."

"That's romantic?" She raised a brow and slicked her hair back.

His gaze rested on her mouth. "Uh, yeah. Especially when she looks like a mermaid in the water. You know, drops of water clinging to her nipples. Her belly slick with soap and water." He licked his lips. "She'd be so into him and want him so happy she'd sink down." His breath hitched when she moved to her knees. "And she'd lift his cock, massage his balls." He moved his feet apart and hissed when she followed his instruction. "Then she'd suck him dry," he rasped.

"And he'd watch the whole time, even as he came down her throat," she purred and wrapped her lips around him.

He gifted her with moans and thanks and an amazingly sensual climax. When she finished, she stood and let the water run down her back, feeling like the goddess she'd once pretended to be.

"You are the absolute best girlfriend, most romantic woman, *ever*." Brody nodded fervently. "And I do mean *ever*." He paused and met her gaze, his eyes full of emotion. "Move in with me."

Chapter 17

Stupid, stupid, stupid. He knew he'd rushed things, especially when his "romantic" girlfriend had stammered that she had to think about things and hightailed it out of the shower. They'd finished up the night goofing off, but he'd seen the panic she hadn't been able to hide.

"Brody, pass the rolls, honey."

He smiled back at Bitsy. Thanksgiving with his family. He wished Abby would have spent it with him, but she'd had plans to join her family that she'd made months ago. Hopefully she'd spend her days missing him, the way he was missing her. She'd only been gone two days, but it felt like forever without her near.

"Someone has it bad," Cam muttered and eyed him knowingly.

"Oh?" Bitsy heard everything.

"Yeah, Mom. Brody and Abby are a thing now."

Bitsy bobbled a roll. "What's that?"

"Yep." Mike nodded as he cut up Colin's turkey. Mike, Colin, Vanessa, Cam, Pop, Bitsy, and Brody. A McCauley family Thanksgiving minus Flynn and Maddie, who had plans to stop by tomorrow with Maddie's mom. With Vanessa keeping Cam and Mike in check when they grew too obnoxious, the holiday had turned out to be fun, if lonely. He couldn't understand how he could feel so deeply for a woman he'd barely committed to.

Barely? You asked her to move in, dumbass.

"I like Abby," Colin said around a mouthful of mashed potatoes.

"Son, don't talk with your mouth full."

"Yeah," Brody agreed as he stuffed an olive in his mouth and held it on his tongue before chewing extra loudly. "That's just gross."

Colin giggled while Vanessa and Bitsy sighed.

"Some boys never grow up," Bitsy teased.

"Oh relax." Pop slapped him on the back, and he nearly choked on the pimiento. "Boy's just having fun. Congrats on snagging Abby, son. She's a good girl."

"Not that good," Vanessa murmured and raised a brow at Brody.

"True. Where's the fun in that?" Cam said with a big smile.

"Cameron Thomas McCauley, watch your mouth," Bitsy warned him.

"Ooooo," Colin howled. "You're in trou-ble."

"Yep. Triple name is a sure sign of disgrace," Vanessa nodded. "But *you're* being so good, Colin. Maybe you can show your uncles how to properly behave at the table."

Bitsy beamed. "Yes, that's right. Good boy."

Mike grimaced. "He's not a dog, Ma."

"Michael, eat your beans."

He sighed. "Yes, Mom."

Brody laughed. "You know, it's like some things never change."

"You got that right," Pop muttered.

Brody shot him a sharp look, not happy to see the man's mouth in a grim line, his blue eyes fixed with frustration on his wife.

Bitsy ignored him and continued to talk to Vanessa, Cam, and Mike.

"You okay, Pop?" Brody asked quietly.

"Just fine. Been busy at work is all." Pop finished his plate and stood. "Man. I'm full. Tell you what. I'm going to go for a stroll. I'll be back in a bit. Think I'll head down to the coffee shop and on my way back, bring someone a treat." He winked at Colin.

Vanessa clapped her hands. "Oh goodie. What are you bringing me, James?"

Pop laughed. "You're a pip, Vanessa. Tell you what, we'll adopt you too. What the hell. We have the room." He grinned.

Brody glanced at Bitsy, not surprised to see her sober expression, her eyes on her husband.

What was going on with these two?

Then she blinked and smiled, erasing her tension. "I'll clear the table and set out the pie while you're gone. We'll be waiting on you for dessert."

"Right," Pop said with false cheer.

Brody met Cam's and Mike's gazes, all three of them knowing they needed to fix whatever had broken. If they could figure out where to start.

Brody finished his dinner and helped Bitsy clear the table while Mike and the others went out back to play with Mutt. Now behaving himself, he'd turned into everyone's favorite canine.

Walking into the kitchen, Brody saw Bitsy cleaning off plates in the sink to put into the dishwasher. Her shoulders were slumped, and he swore he could feel her sadness from where he stood. Wanting to liven her spirits, he made noise as he walked in and joined her at the sink. To his horror, he saw tears in her eyes.

"Bitsy?"

"Oh." She wiped her eyes with her shoulders. "Don't mind me. Just looking out the window at my grandson and realizing how much time has flown by." She smiled back at Brody. "I'm so proud of you, son."

"Me?" He scoffed. "I'm just lucky to be alive and out of jail."

She laughed, as he'd meant her to. "You sure were a slick one. But so cute." She lifted a soapy hand out of the water and put it in his hair. "And you still have that cowlick right...here."

"Man, I hate that. The wet smooth-down is right up there with mom spit when you try to wipe a smudge off my face."

She laughed again and eased into a comfortable tempo with him. She rinsed off the dishes and he stacked them in the dishwasher.

"I like Abby a lot." She handed him another dish. "I thought she'd be ideal for Mike."

He froze in the act of accepting another plate. "Mike?"

"Because of Abby's resemblance to Lea, I suppose." Bitsy sighed. "But that ship sailed long ago. And now that I think about it, you've had eyes for Abby since she moved in. At first I thought it was because of her uncanny resemblance to Lea." Bitsy grinned. "I think it's more than that though, hmm?"

"I guess." He shrugged. "She's a great person. Smart, funny, really sex—er, pretty."

Bitsy pursed her lips.

"I mean, she's so cute." He expelled a breath. "I really like her."

"Oh?"

He looked around, and seeing them alone, confided, "I think I made a mistake though. I asked her to move in with me a few days ago. Think I freaked her out."

Bitsy stared at him. "*Move in with you?* Why, for you, that's akin to marriage."

That the word *marriage* in conjunction with Abby didn't alarm him or make him want to run and keep on running worried him. This *like* he'd tried convincing himself he had for the woman was more like love. An emotion he'd never had for a woman who wasn't Bitsy. Even Lea had been no more than a crush based on attraction and her sweet disposition. Certainly he'd never felt love for the woman who'd given birth to him, the one who'd thrown him away, more concerned with getting high than caring for her son.

"Yeah, well. She's great. She makes me feel good."

"About yourself?"

"About everything. I'm kind of afraid I ruined it by pushing too hard."

"Brody, let me tell you something."

He groaned.

"No, no. You listen. You've always kept your cards close to your chest, afraid to tell anyone how you feel or what you're really thinking."

"That's not true. I—"

She poked him with a soapy finger. "Let me finish. You joke and you smile and you tease, but inside you're still that scared little boy afraid to open up and be loved."

"No. I know you love me."

"We all do. All of us, Brody. James, Mike, Cameron,

Flynn. Of course I do. You were my little blond prince."
She smiled and ruffled his hair.

"Ew. More soap." He grinned back at her, awash in
the comfort only Bitsy could give. *No, not only Bitsy.
Remember how Abby made you feel? How safe, how
loved?* His grin faded. "What if she goes home and re-
alizes she can do better? What if she doesn't want me
anymore?" he asked and was immediately ashamed for
expressing his darkest fear.

"Then she's not the smart girl I took her for." Bitsy
hugged him. "When a person can't see the truth of love
when it's hitting them in the face, they don't deserve the
good things that love can give them." She pulled back,
and he saw her tears again.

But this time he had a feeling they were as much for
herself as they were for him.

"Yeah, well, screw all of them who can't feel it," he
said in defiance. "I love you, Bitsy. You've been the
mother I always wanted, and the only one who matters.
I'll always be here for you. No matter what." Fierce
in his support and meaning every word of it, he pulled
her close for another hug and let her cry it out. "I love
you." *And you, Abigail Dunn. One way or the other,
we're gonna have our own hug-out when you get back.
So hurry home.*

Abby groaned as her young nephew eyed her purse. She
thought she'd hidden it better than that. After rescu-
ing it from Timmy's devious hands and placing it high
enough that he couldn't reach it again, she ignored the
toddler's cry and returned to her seat at the dining room

table, where the rest of the adults sat drinking coffee after enjoying their Thanksgiving. The entire family had gathered this year, and despite Meg being a major pain, it was nice to see both her sisters, their husbands and kids, and her parents in one place.

Meg, her older sister by two years, glared at her. "That wasn't nice."

So much for reveling in family togetherness. If only Meg and her annoying husband would leave early. Surely their church needed them to be superior to someone else pretty soon? From the time Meg could talk, she'd been telling everyone how important and special she was. Their mother claimed it was a sign of Meg's insecurities playing out. But Abby and her oldest sister Teresa agreed Meg had been born a bitch. Sad, but true.

"Tell you what, Meg. Let's give him *your* purse to pour his orange juice in. Where is it and I'll get it for him?"

"Oh, ah. Never mind."

"I thought so." Abby smirked. She'd missed her family like crazy and refused to let Meg's bossy attitude dissipate the holiday cheer.

Meg balanced Julia on her knee and fed her daughter warm rice cereal. "It's been too long since you've been back. Look. Julia's almost one. And such a good girl," she crooned as the baby gurgled and ate.

Next to her, her husband Tim looked on as a proud parent, while little Timmy wreaked more havoc in the living room. Granted, his cousins were supposed to be looking out for him, but putting a ten-year-old in charge of his three rambunctious siblings *and* his three-year-old cousin was a disaster waiting to happen.

Abby watched and waited, wondering if her sister or brother-in-law thought saving her mother's antique lamps worth getting up for. Since Abby had been the one trying to keep the peace for a while, she thought maybe they were waiting for her to step in. But she planned on drinking her coffee while it was still warm and eating her pie before someone else gobbled it up.

Something crashed, and Tim rose with a sigh. "I guess I'll check on them."

Abby smiled at him. *Idiot. He's* your *kid*. She heard a fight break out and sighed. She loved Teresa dearly, but the woman had no handle to speak of on disciplining her children. Abby knew she felt guilty about being on husband number three. But honestly, Jack, especially when compared to her previous husbands, shone like a star.

He chuckled. "Boys being boys."

Abby glanced around the partition behind her. "Yeah? Well, your boys are bullying their little sister."

Teresa rose to corral them. At least she hadn't waited for Abby to move. This time.

Her sisters seemed to think that when Abby came home for a visit, the kids' favorite aunt would assume all child-sitting duties, giving them time off to party. *Hell to the no*. Abby loved her nieces and nephews, but she'd long ago accepted the kids were monsters. They listened to her when she had them to herself, but not near their own parents. Surprisingly, the same training that had worked on Mutt worked wonders on them. Consistency, she thought, was the key.

Thinking about Mutt automatically turned her thoughts to Brody. Did he miss her? Had he rethought his spontaneous invitation for her to move in with him?

She still wasn't sure how she felt about that.

"Abby? More pie?"

She glanced down at her nearly empty plate while Teresa and Tim returned to the table. "It was great, Mom. But I'm stuffed."

Teresa studied her. "Are you losing weight?"

"I love you too." Abby blew her a kiss.

The others laughed. Then her mother exchanged an odd look with her father. They'd been doing that a lot since she'd been home. Looking at each other, and then looking at her.

"Okay, you two. What's up?"

The room fell silent. To her dismay, her sisters and their husbands appeared worried and refused to meet her gaze for more than a second or two.

Her mother finally answered. "It's about Kevin."

She'd been waiting for someone to mention him. Since she'd been prepared, Abby shrugged. "What about him?"

"Well, there's no other way to put this. He's engaged."

She let that sit in her mind and sorted through her feelings. The biggest one she felt turned out to be relief. "Good for him."

Her mother explained, "He keeps in touch. His aunt lives down the street, and the woman he's marrying lives next door. Lydia's girl. Miriam Wentworth."

Her father frowned. "We know how hard the breakup was for you, so we never mentioned that he's kept in touch. He was a nice boy. We liked him a lot. I'm just sorry it didn't work out for you two."

"Trust me, Dad, it was for the best." How terrific that she meant the words. Not long ago, she would have been hurt to think of Kevin moving on. Even though he'd been a complete dickhead there at the end, they'd had good times. And he had a nice, funny side to him that had been pleasing, until she'd realized his jokes weren't meant to be funny, but at her expense. Until he'd turned into Reverend Asshole.

Meg shook her head. "He seemed so perfect for you. Such a shame."

"Not really." Abby snorted. "Kevin was an asshole."

"Abby." Meg gaped. "The kids are in the other room."

"Please. They can't hear me over that noise." The television blared with cartoony music.

"Honey, I know this hurts, but—" her mother started.

"No, Mom. I never told you half of what he was really like. I knew you had a good opinion of him. But that man used to belittle everything about me." It felt good to get it off her chest. At the time of their breakup, she hadn't wanted to badmouth him in the event he told her parents about her books. But now, she didn't care. She planned on telling them herself.

"He did?" Her dad stared. "You never said anything."

"Because I didn't want you confronting him. He'd have told you what I really do for a living." There. Bag open, cat out.

The only thing to be heard in the dining room were Julia's lip smacking and gurgling and the drone of cartoons and kid chatter drifting in from the living room.

"You know, this is better than *Downton Abbey* for drama," Jack murmured.

"Shh." Teresa turned to her. "Well? Tell us. Are you stripping? Hooking? What?"

Meg gasped. "*Teresa.*"

"*Meg*." Teresa huffed. "Don't be such a prude. It must be something scary if she kept silent about the asshat."

Of her two older sisters, Teresa was her favorite; she'd made her share of mistakes and tried to laugh at them. Meg took herself far too seriously. To hear Meg tell it, she'd never done a thing wrong in her life, had married the perfect man, and had two adorable children. Abby thought it telling they couldn't find a more creative name for their firstborn than Tim. With any luck, the kid wouldn't grow up to be a dunce like his father, or a holier-than-thou know-it-all like his mother.

She winked at Teresa, then faced her parents. "Mom, Dad." *Just tell them. Let the truth set you free.* "I write books for a living."

Her mother gasped, "Why, Abby. That's *wonderful*. Why would you keep that a secret from us?"

Meg's eyes narrowed. "What kind of books?"

"Yeah, what kind?" Jack leaned forward. "This is getting really interesting."

Teresa smacked him but laughed.

"Well, they're romance books. They're kind of…steamy."

"Steamy?" her father asked with a frown.

"Yes, Dad. They have S-E-X in them."

Everyone gaped at her.

Meg's expression contorted to one of horror. "Oh my God. You're one of those women living in sin. You're writing porn?"

Teresa snorted. "Say it a little louder, Meg. I don't think New Jersey heard you."

Meg shook her head, looking on the verge of tears. "No. Please tell me my little sister is not writing trash."

Funny, but when Vanessa called it smutty or raunchy,

Abby knew she was playing. Sure, Vanessa liked to make fun of her, but God forbid anyone else mess with Abby. Vanessa would be the first to line up to defend her. Abby's sister saying the same thing made her career sound dirty, unworthy of respect.

And that hurt.

Abby clenched her jaw and did her best not to lash out at her ignorant, judgmental, overly dramatic sibling. "First of all, it's not *trash*. Romantic fiction is a billion-dollar industry."

"So is *porn*," Tim added in a quieter voice. "Tell me you use a pseudonym."

"I do, but that's not the point."

Meg breathed a sigh of relief. "Thank God. I can't imagine what I'd tell my friends at church."

"That your sister writes inspirational stories about God," Teresa said and turned to Abby with a wink. "Don't they usually finish up their business with 'Oh, God. Oh, God!'?"

Jack burst out laughing, and Teresa joined him.

But Abby didn't smile, because in addition to her disapproving sister and brother-in-law, her parents seemed less than pleased.

"Honey," her mother said slowly. "I thought you had that web design business."

"I do, Mom." *Be patient, Abby. They just need time to process.* "But my true love has always been writing. I worked at the tech firm while writing my first series. By the time my second series started, I was making enough from writing to support myself, so I branched off from the tech company and started my own web design firm." At about the time she'd started dating Kevin. "I did it so I could scale back my web clients and ramp up the writing."

Her father rubbed his forehead. "You like doing this?"

"It's not a bad thing, Dad. You look like you just swallowed a lemon." Abby frowned. "I'm happy and I'm successful." The first time she'd said that out loud. "I make a decent living. Do you know how hard it is to make a living writing? But I'm doing that and still running my own small web design company. In *Seattle*—maybe the most expensive city in the world," she exaggerated. Though for what she paid for a cup of coffee at home, she'd get a full pot in town here.

"Well, I'm a bit hazy on the whole steamy romance book thing. But if you're happy, I'm happy." Her father grinned.

One down. Teresa gave her a thumbs-up. Two. But her mother, Meg, and Tim continued to look at her as if she'd started worshipping Satan. Abby sighed. "You know what? I don't care whether you like it or not. I'm a writer." She forced herself to be proud and not ashamed for providing the stories she herself liked to read. "Maybe if society wasn't so prudish about physical intimacy, this wouldn't be an issue. My characters fall in love and in lust. Why is that a bad thing?"

"It's not, honey." Her mother seemed sincerely bothered. "It's just… What do I tell people?"

"Just tell them what we've always told them. That she works in web design." Meg shrugged. "That's what I plan to say if asked."

"You know what, Meg?" Abby said as she stood. "Maybe if you weren't such a tightass, you'd have fun with the fact that your sister is a writer."

Meg's face turned red. "Writer of *porn*? I don't think so."

Something crashed and the kids yelled.

"Wait. What's that? Your terror of a toddler is destroying something *else* in the living room, I'll bet." Abby gave Meg a wide smile. "Spend a little more time working on your own flaws and I guarantee you won't be spouting off about what you see as mine."

Tim gasped. "Did you just call our son a flaw?"

"No, Tim. I'm calling your wife a lousy mother."

Meg stood, pointed her finger, and started yelling insults. Tim joined her. Abby fired back, tired of being the family whipping girl. At some point, Meg said something so ridiculous Teresa burst out laughing and Jack hurried to grab the kids and take them all downstairs for games in the basement. Their father sat there watching the train wreck while their mother glanced back and forth between them, as if not sure what to say.

"So much for thinking my family might actually support me." Abby glared at Meg.

Her father frowned. "Hey."

"Not you, Dad."

"Or me. I think your job is terrific. What's your pen name?" Teresa asked.

Abby enunciated clearly. "Abigail D. Chatterly. And I'd like to say a few more things before I suggest we stop talking about this altogether." She didn't know if she liked the way Teresa stared at her. In shock or awe?

"Fine by me, *Abigail*," Meg said snidely.

Her mother had the nerve to scowl at Abby. "Some Thanksgiving this turned out to be."

"Oh my gosh. You think it's somehow odd that I'd be upset my family, minus Teresa—" Jack had returned and raised his hand to be noticed. "—Jack, and Dad, don't support me? Because I have to tell you, Mom. You disappoint me the most. You've always told us to reach for our dreams, to be independent and not stop until we reach our goals. I always wanted to write. Now I'm doing it, and people *pay me* to do it,

"If any of you would take the time to actually *read* one of my books, you'd be able to tell the difference. Which brings up the question of how you can even compare my work to porn, unless you've seen enough porn to know what you're talking about," she aimed at her sister, and Meg flushed bright red.

"Could we *please* stop with the P word?" her mother asked with desperation.

Teresa frowned. "But I thought P was for *pussy*. Am I wrong? Is it penis? Penetration?" Teresa's face cleared, as if she'd had a revelation. "Oh, right. *Porn*."

Their father burst out laughing. Tim looked as if he was about to suffer apoplexy, like Meg.

"Teresa, really." Margaret Dunn's face was beet red.

"Oh, come on, Mom." Abby huffed. "It's not like any of us were the result of a virgin birth."

"Definitely not Abby, the pornographer," Meg pointed out and Tim nodded.

"Oh my God. Tell me you and Mr. Monotone aren't judging. Because you go to church regularly you're better than us?" She turned to Tim. "And please tell me why your degree in biology makes you so overly qualified to manage a chicken plant that pays eight bucks an hour."

Tim literally raised his nose in the air. "I help raise healthy poultry that feeds half the state. My job is more than important."

"To Foghorn Leghorn, maybe," Abby muttered.

Teresa and Jack coughed to hide laughter.

Tim glared. "Meg, I'm getting the kids. We're leaving." He stood up, threw down his napkin, and stormed from the room.

"See, Teresa?" Jack said with a wide grin. Abby was liking him more and more. "That's where the P word comes into play. Tim is a being a…you can say it."

"Pussy."

"That's it. Pussy. Yep. Oh, and I'm sorry, Meg. But I never liked Tim either. He treats me and Teresa like shit because he disapproves of your sister's seventeen divorces."

"Two, you idiot. Maybe three if you don't watch it." Teresa narrowed her eyes but grinned at him anyway.

Their mother rose and left the table. Meg just stood there with her eyes wide open, gaping like a dying fish.

Abby would have followed her mother, unhappy to have made her upset, but her father stopped her. "No, let me. Honestly, she's more upset about you and Kevin not being an item than any of this. Though I must say you threw me for a loop with the fake writing name and the sex." He grimaced and rose from the table. "Let's just call it romance for adults. I am your father."

Abby hugged him. "Thanks, Dad." She let him go. "But I don't understand why Mom should care about Kevin. We've been broken up for more than a year. We're over."

"I know that and you know that. But she always

liked the boy. Wanted you two to marry and have kids to settle down close to home. She worries about you so far away from us. With him marrying Miriam, we'll be seeing a lot more of him. Rumor has it they're moving here."

"Good—for me, not you. He's a jerk. Told me I was too fat, too boring. Then too perverted for his tastes. As if wanting my boyfriend to kiss me in public and hold hands is asking too much." She didn't mention the bondage, toys, or edible body chocolate she'd wanted to try.

Jeffrey Dunn scowled. "You know, there's another P word you could you use in this situation. Kevin is a *prick*, with a capital P." He patted her shoulder. "I'll see to your mother. You and Meg fight it out." Under his breath, he added, "And thanks for getting rid of Tim. Another prick I have to tolerate at family gatherings." He left to find her mother.

Abby could only be glad she had an early flight out in the morning. Not stretching her time at home had been an extremely smart move on her part.

She turned to see Meg glaring at her. "What? Upset that your perfect family is now smudged by my bad name?"

"No one will know." Meg sneered. "You're going back to Seattle tomorrow. So it's no big deal. *You're* no big deal." Then she twisted the knife and added, "I was invited to Kevin and Miriam's wedding. I wasn't going to go, but now I plan to attend."

"Well, give him a big old congratulations from me. And while you're at it, express my condolences to Miriam."

"You're such a little bitch. You know what, Abby?

Don't call me. Don't write me. And please, *don't* come back." Meg turned and stalked to Tim and Timmy by the front door, Julia clutched tightly to her chest.

"Don't worry, I won't." When had she ever conversed with Meg willingly? The rare times Abby called to talk to a sister, she'd chatted with Teresa. Otherwise she stuck to talking to her mother and father, whom she truly cared for.

The sudden silence grew deafening. Abby turned to see Teresa and Jack staring at her. "What?" she snapped.

"So you're Abigail D. Chatterly?" Teresa asked.

"Yeah. So?" Though Teresa had been on her side earlier, she might have done it to snub Meg. Abby was ready for round two.

"So *Fireman's Kiss* is like my favorite book!" Teresa shouted and jumped up from her seat to hug Abby. "Oh my God. My friends are not going to believe this."

Abby blinked.

"I know. Shocking that she actually has friends," Jack teased. "Oh, and I have to thank you as well. Because after Teresa reads one of your books, we usually end up having a really, really good night."

"God. TMI, Jack." But Abby laughed, feeling good if not great about the way dinner had ended. She talked to her sister and new brother-in-law for a while. Eventually her father returned to the table with her mother, but Margaret Dunn insisted on pretending the earlier argument with Meg had never happened.

Resigned to making her mother happy with a charade of joyful content, Abby finished her evening at her parents' counting down the minutes until she returned to Seattle. To *home*.

The next evening, Vanessa met her at the SeaTac

airport. Abby had secretly hoped Brody would meet her at the airport and felt a little let down when she saw just Vanessa. But after she'd all but bolted after his suggestion to move in with him, she couldn't blame him.

"Hey, Big Foot. How was your Thanksgiving?" she asked Vanessa and grabbed her bag from the carousel.

"Oh, just great. I had to do the perfunctory call-home thing that I dread at holidays. My parents are pleasant, and they still try to be friendly, but it's rough. I'm not sure they're actually considered living anymore, since the robotic quality of my father's voice has only gotten worse."

Abby flinched. They walked out of the airport together and through to the parking garage. "Yeah? Well I finally came clean to my family about my books."

"And? Don't leave me hanging." They entered the car and drove out of the garage and finally toward home.

"Well, the big news is that Kevin is getting married to the lady next door."

Vanessa snuck a surprised glance at her. "No shit?"

"No shit. My mom is upset I'm not going to marry the missionary man and have his dreary little babies."

"Like there was ever a chance of that happening."

"I know. Then I told them I write steamy romance—and don't say it, because right now I can't handle dealing with more snide remarks."

"Ouch. That bad, eh?"

"Yeah. Meg and I got into it, that sanctimonious little witch. Wasn't happy when I called her husband a bore and her kid a monster."

"He the one that dumps crap in your purse when you visit?"

"Yep."

"What about Teresa? I like her, even if she is a mess. Husband number three working out?"

Teresa had visited a year ago, and she'd made a big impression crying and going on about her fear of committing to Jack.

"I like Jack a lot. He stood by me. So did Dad. And get this, Teresa's a fan. She's read all my books."

Vanessa held up a hand and they high-fived.

"My mother though, I think she and I are now on opposite playing fields. I'm the new black sheep."

"Welcome to my world." Vanessa snorted. "You think your Thanksgiving was rough, there's more you missed. On a good note, Brody seemed to me to be mooning over your absence."

"How nice." She smiled. Best piece of news she'd had in three days. "So where is he?"

"Out with the guys…and Maddie and Aunt Michelle. It's going great, by the way. Aunt Michelle's in love with the McCauleys."

"Dinner with Michelle should be fun for everyone. Maddie's mom is so sweet."

Which had Abby's thoughts returning to her own mother. "You know, it was really liberating to finally come clean to all of my family. Even when Meg called my work porn, it felt good to be honest."

"Porn? What a little bitch." Vanessa scowled.

"You call it porn."

"In fun. I also call it smut, whore-otica, raunchy rhetoric, and a bunch of other words your new boyfriend can't spell. Doesn't mean I don't respect the hell out of what you do." Vanessa shrugged. "I support you.

Don't tell the others, but I read your Marine trilogy. I especially liked the one about the military police guy." She cleared her throat. "Remember when I was dating Officer Schmidt a few months ago? You could say you inspired me. Sadly, he had no idea how to properly use his cuffs."

Abby stared at Vanessa, her mouth open, and then started laughing hysterically. "*You* read my books? Cuffs with a cop? Really?"

Vanessa grinned. "I wanted to try them. Turns out they hurt when they're too tight."

"Oh man. No lingering scars for you, I hope," Abby said when she could catch her breath.

"Who said I was the one wearing them?" Vanessa wiggled her brows suggestively, and Abby broke into gales of laughter once more.

Chapter 18

BRODY FELT LIKE MUTT. EAGER, EXCITED, AND ABOUT to come out of his skin. When familiar headlights pulled in front of his house, even though the hour had reached ten, he broke out into a wide grin.

He glanced at the dog. "She's back."

Mutt wagged his tail and looked out the front window, his nose glued to the glass. Brody watched her stride up the front walkway to the porch. He dropped the curtain he'd been holding back, which engulfed the dog and made him look like a pointy-eared ghost. While Mutt fought the drapes, Brody took a deep breath, let it out, and fought for calm. He wiped his sweating palms on his jeans and casually moved a step over to the door when she rang the bell.

He opened it and looked at her, thinking she'd grown even prettier than any woman had a right to be.

She smiled, her dark eyes full of happiness. "Hey, stranger." Mutt stepped out and rolled on the ground. She bent down to give the dog a long belly rub.

"Hey, back at you." He wanted to eat her up, slam her up against the wall, and fuck her until neither of them could move. Instead, he took a step back, waited for her and the dog to enter, and closed the door behind her, locking it with a soft *snick*. "So how was your holiday?" He shoved his hands in his pants so he wouldn't grab her. Appearing like a lovesick loser wouldn't earn him any points. After the last fiasco of moving too fast, he was determined to let her set the pace.

"My holiday was great. My parents were so happy to see me. I got to visit with my nephews and nieces. Saw my sisters." Her lips quivered, and her big eyes grew shiny.

"Abby?"

A sob escaped. "Oh, it was horrible." She threw herself into his arms, and he caught her, concerned.

"Damn. What happened?" She cried harder, and he cupped her head to his chest, hurting inside for her. "Shh. It's okay." He guided her to the couch, where he sat and took her in his lap. She sounded so pitiful, so unlike his strong, sarcastic Abby. After a few moments, she sniffed and wiped her eyes.

"God, I feel so silly. I'm sorry for getting all weepy on you. I'm just tired. It was a long trip."

"Tell me what happened."

She did in detail. But it was her mother whom Abby continued to talk about.

"I mean, I was gearing up to tell them all about you, but my mom told me about Kevin, and then I—"

The ex. "What about him?"

She wiped her nose on her shirt. His kind of gal. "Oh, him? He got engaged."

He stilled. "Is that why you're so upset?"

She snorted. "Are you kidding? That loser is welcome to date whoever he wants. Marry, divorce, remarry. Whatever. I'm just happy to be free of him."

"Oh. Okay." Good. She was over the bastard.

"But my mom has always been there for me." More tears trailed down her cheeks. "I can't believe she'd be so stupid about some romance books. They're just stories."

"Sexy, hot, well-written stories. With great plots."

"And asshole heroes, right?"

"Well, yeah. But we're working on that."

"*We* are?"

"I'm trying to show you what a real man is like. Like me. He has a great job, a big dick, and he's amazing in bed. That, and he never calls you snickerdoodle."

She laughed. "You make me feel better."

"I'm sorry they were mean to you. But hey, at least your dad and your sister liked your stories. And she's a fan, huh?" He wanted to meet Teresa. Hell, he surprised himself by wanting to meet all of Abby's family, even the unworthy ones. He wanted them to know what he was to her, and she to him. Even if he still wasn't sure himself.

"So you didn't tell them about your studly new boyfriend."

"No. My mom went off about Kevin. I said good riddance, then confessed I'm actually not just a web designer, but a writer. I'd never told them before because the stuff I was writing was pretty niche. Erotic romance wasn't as accepted back when I started as it is today. And then I was dating Kevin, and he made me so ashamed of what I did. It took me a long time to let Kevin know, and you see how that turned out. Well, I finally got the nerve to tell them the truth.

"Meg I understand being mean. But Mom has always been my rock." She drew in a deep breath and exhaled slowly, holding back more tears, it seemed.

"You can let it out, Abby. Cry if you want to."

"No. I'm an ugly crier."

"Nah. I think it's cute you keep rubbing your snot all over your arm."

She cringed, tucked her head against his chest, and laughed.

He rubbed her back. "Did Vanessa fill you in on our holiday?"

"Yeah. It's like everyone is falling apart all of a sudden. Be careful. That kind of stuff happens in threes."

He felt a distinct chill in the air, the thought of losing Abby unimaginable. "Well, we'll make sure that doesn't happen with us."

She pushed back and put her hands on his shoulders. "How will we do that?"

By loving each other. He wanted so badly to give her the words, but he'd never said them to a woman before—well, not counting Bitsy—and it scared him to think of putting himself in someone else's hands like that.

So he'd show her how he felt instead. Cupping her face in his hands, and seeing her watery eyes, wet cheeks, and red nose, he kissed her.

So soft, so gentle, expressing the love he felt that had yet to fade. She kissed him back, melting into him. He felt her slight resistance crumble, and the passion under the surface paled next to the warmth of emotion enveloping them both. He cradled her in his arms, and she sighed his name against his lips.

"Brody, I missed you," she whispered.

"Mmm. Me too." So much. Three days had felt like an eternity. While he'd called himself every kind of fool in the book, he'd still been beside himself counting down the minutes to see her again. Now he clung to her like a second skin and the comfort turned carnal in a heartbeat. She ground against him, no longer sitting in his lap but straddling him. And then she was pushing her pants down and kicking off her shoes. Her panties followed while they continued to kiss.

He reached between them to unbutton his jeans, and then her hand was there, wrapped around him. She pulled him out and sank over him before he could catch his breath.

"Oh yeah. I missed you, Brody. So much." Her breath ghosted over his lips while she rode him, slowly at first, then faster.

They watched each other as their climaxes neared too fast, too soon. But Brody didn't want to wait. And neither, it appeared, did Abby.

Her panting and soft gasps of pleasure did him in, and Brody plastered his mouth to her at the same time she groaned and trembled, coming around him. Her body gripped him in a vise, and he emptied on a swallowed groan, the release cathartic in more ways than one. As he pulsed inside her, she drew her head back to stare at him.

"Damn, Abby," he managed. "You're so… I…"

"Yeah." She sighed and kissed him tenderly. "Me too."

They snuggled together, until Mutt joined them and placed his head near Brody's thigh.

"Uh-oh. He's too young to be seeing this." Abby flushed.

"He's a dog, Abby. They hump for fun. To make puppies. For dominance. Hell, just because. I think his canine sensibilities can withstand seeing me buried to the hilt inside you." Brody grinned. "Besides, he's still waiting on you to find a new name I'll accept."

She grinned. "Well, Snickerdoodle isn't going to work for me. I'll keep thinking."

"You do that." He hugged her. "So what do you say, to celebrate you being back, we just sit like this for a while."

"Or forever, because I think my legs are numb."

"Great minds think alike." He kissed her again.

―᪥―

They spent the next week enjoying each other's company. Abby invited Seth over a few times to play board games, and he seemed to get a kick out of baiting Brody. Flynn and the guys came by for Friday night poker, while she, Vanessa, and Maddie watched Colin for Mike at Mike's place. To Abby's amusement, she'd also been tasked with dog-sitting. While at Mike's, Colin chattered about all things dog and all things Del. He'd apparently taken to drawing on his arms and coloring them in with marker, making his own tattoos. Which Mike frowned upon.

After reaffirming to her roommates that she'd survived her family's poor treatment, they *allowed her*— Vanessa's exact words—to spend more time with the "doofus," because he made her happy. She didn't know whether to feel glad or alarmed that everyone seemed to be taking her relationship with Brody in stride.

For her part, she hadn't forgotten his invitation to move in. Part of her wanted to live with him, to love him up close instead of leaving every evening. They spent their free time together as it was. He'd been honest when he said he couldn't cook, but the man did have a sweet tooth he liked to indulge, so she'd been baking like crazy. What made him even more special, he constantly tried to get *her* to eat. He complimented her figure. Instead of telling her to watch her portions and nix the cake and ice cream, as Kevin always had, Brody stared at her ass longingly and pushed leftover pumpkin pie her way. She felt less self-conscious around him, and more like a sensual woman in charge of her life, her sexuality.

Friday arrived, and she'd made plans for a cozy stay-in—watching movies with her man. Deciding to live in the moment and not worry about tomorrow, she let Brody pick her up at home and drove with him back to his place, where poor Mutt moped, waiting for her to come back. She wondered if Brody would object to her taste in film, which leaned toward gratuitous sex and violence. She snorted. Yeah, right.

"What are you doing that makes Mutt like you so much?" Brody asked, looking suspicious. "Because I swear, he whines more when *you* leave than when *I* do."

"How would you know?"

"Seth tells me."

"Speaking of Seth... How do I give him back his things without offending him?"

Brody laughed. "What's wrong? That harlequin mask he gave you not fitting in with your décor?"

"It creeps me out." The porcelain mask meant to be hung on a wall sat in her chest at home, buried under blankets. "I didn't want anything from him when I gave him those cookies. I just wanted to be nice."

"That's his way of saying thank you. The man needs to give as well as take. Let him. It's a pride thing."

She saw a lot of Brody in the old man but didn't say so.

"You know, Abby, you had me with those large

breasts and curvy ass. You reeled me in with the hot sex, but knowing you're the queen of cookies... I'm having a hard time not falling at your feet and begging you never to leave again."

Which was exactly what she wanted. "As long as I'm barefoot in your kitchen, right?"

"Hey, works for me."

Unfortunately, it worked for her as well. Though she mentally added *pregnant* to barefoot and in the kitchen. Brody would make such a great dad...if she'd been in the market to be a mother. Which she wasn't, or so she kept telling herself. Going home to Pennsylvania usually scared her straight when it came to thoughts of procreating. Some day she wanted to have little ones, but not yet. And not with the wrong man. Problem was, she had a bad feeling Brody was the *right* man for her.

She couldn't deny to herself how much she loved him, and it scared her, because as much as he liked spending time with her and being together, even without the sex, part of him seemed reserved. Losing Brody would put a hole in her heart she didn't think she'd recover from. Just the idea of it made her blink back tears. *Happy thoughts, Abby. Remember, you're on a fun date. Quit with the melodrama of forever.* "Gee, Brody, you always know just what to say."

He chuckled. "Long as it's about sex and food, I'm all poetry, baby."

They parked in front of his house, got out of the truck, then started up his sidewalk. Someone waited for them on the porch.

Brody immediately placed himself between her and

the stranger, and she heard Mutt barking from inside. "Go wait in the truck, Abby."

"Brody?" the man on the porch called. He stepped from the shadows, moving down the porch stairs, and stopped, his hands in his pockets.

The resemblance to Brody was unmistakable. Handsome but worn down, this man had short blond hair, brown eyes, and a lined face. From what Brody had said, his brother was ten years his senior. This man looked even older, worn down by years of drugs and abusive behavior.

"Dad's not here," the man said quickly. "Look, I know nothing I say can ever make up for the past, but can I just have a few minutes of your time? I swear, I won't take long. Just let me say it and I'll go."

The hopeful look on his face tore at her. On the one hand, she wanted to crush him for having hurt Brody as a boy. But on the other, after some careful thinking about all Brody had told her about his childhood, she understood how a young man, with only Alan Singer as a role model, could develop into what Jeremy had.

"Talk to him, Brody," she said before she could stop herself. "Get some closure, at least."

Jeremy studied her but said nothing.

Brody didn't seem to want to go toward him, but he hesitated long enough that she knew he needed to, even if he didn't think he wanted to.

"I'll go take care of Mutt. You talk to Jeremy. Then we'll give Seth the cookies I made for him, which I forgot in the truck, by the way."

He nodded but didn't smile. "Fine." He walked her to the door, putting himself between her and Jeremy. Once inside, she took Mutt out back for a break.

—⁓—

"What the fuck do you want now?" Brody didn't want to hear what Jeremy had to say, but to get him to leave, he'd do just about anything. Having this scum near Abby felt wrong. But he'd been unable to dismiss him. *I'm a dumbass, no question.*

Jeremy hunched in his jacket. "Well, first, I'm sorry about last time. I hadn't meant for Dad to follow me here. I should have left as soon as I saw him."

"No shit."

Jeremy frowned. "And I should have taken your feelings into account more. I'm not here to make your life even more miserable than I made it back then. I want to atone, not cause more hurt."

"Step nine?" He'd read about it, drawn to the potential recuperative powers of AA. Back when he'd had a shred of hope his father and brother might be saved.

"Yeah." Jeremy gave him a withered smile. "I won't bother you anymore. I won't bother anyone, not your friends or family. I just wanted to explain something, to help you understand."

Brody's rage surged to the surface. Help him understand? "What? How my own flesh and blood could scare the piss out of me every time I was forced to come home to visit? How you could use me to steal to help your dirty habit? I was in elementary school, for Christ's sake. Or how about how you could almost kill me and not care?"

"Shit. I cared, okay?" Jeremy's voice rose. "Not a day goes by I don't think of how I hurt you. But you had the McCauleys to help you. Brody, if it hadn't been for them, you might have been me."

Brody blinked. On his worst day he wouldn't have been Jeremy. "I don't think so."

"Really? Because you thought Dad was bad, but Mom was worse. Yeah, she was awful, so unhappy with life, with him, even before you were born. Always bitching about everything. She was sober too, which made it worse, because she knew what she said and did was wrong. She didn't even have the drugs as an excuse for being an absolute bitch. She only started those after she had you. You know she used to tell me she wished she'd aborted me? That I was a curse on her and Dad?

"To this day I still don't know what turned her and Dad so bitter and hateful toward each other, toward us… I don't know. But man, growing up with Mom always on my ass, Dad constantly trying to be my drinking buddy. I'd had my first drink when I was seven. Drunk and stoned by the time I was ten."

Brody frowned, not wanting to feel for his sibling, but unable to resist the lick of compassion stealing into him. "No one you could talk to?"

"No. No McCauleys for me. Man, you have no idea how I used to envy you. You were the cute kid everyone liked and wanted. A family took you in. Gave you food and a place to sleep. They acted like they loved you, like you were one of them."

"I am," he said softly, never taking that gift for granted. Even though that secret, shameful part of him questioned his belonging.

Jeremy's smile shocked him. "Good. I'm glad you got what you deserved, what you never got from us. I'm sorry I ever made you think I'd hurt them if you didn't do what I said. I was hateful and jealous, and let's face it, high more often than not.

"I came here to tell you not to let hate rule your life, but I didn't need to. You have a family and friends who love you. And your girlfriend about glared a hole through my head before." He chuckled. "Lucky bastard."

To Brody's shock, he didn't sense any malice or bitterness in Jeremy's tone. "What do you really want, Jeremy?"

Jeremy sighed. "Nothing, Brody. Just to say I'm sorry. I won't bug you again." He reached into his pocket and withdrew a card. "I don't want a thing from you. But if you ever want to talk, or, you know, whatever, you can reach me here."

Brody took the card, not sure why, and saw the name of a halfway house across town, a number scrawled underneath it.

Jeremy shoved his hand back in his pockets. "So, well. I know we'll never be close, but we don't have to be enemies."

Brody shrugged. "I guess." He wanted to feel more, which surprised him. But any affection he might have felt for Jeremy had died a long time ago.

Jeremy nodded and walked away.

Brody stood there, watching him, until he disappeared from sight. Not sure how to feel, because the anger and numbness he normally experienced when dealing with Jeremy started to hurt, he tucked the discomfort away and walked back to the truck to grab Seth's cookies. Then he fetched Abby and Mutt and walked next door.

"You okay?" she asked.

"Yeah." He handed her the plate. "I guess."

"If it makes you feel better, it was killing me not to come outside or eavesdrop at the window."

He grinned. "Actually, that does make me feel better." He knocked on the door.

They waited, but Seth didn't answer. He knocked again.

"Seth?" Abby called.

Mutt, however, had a strange posture, one he'd never used before. He sniffed a few times, cocked his head, and scratched at the door.

Brody had a bad feeling. He pulled out the spare key Seth had given him and unlocked the door. "Seth? We brought cookies."

Mutt darted past him.

"Mutt, come back here," Abby yelled.

Brody followed him, worried about what the dog might find. In the kitchen, Seth sat at his cramped kitchen table, slumped in his seat. In front of him lay the daily paper. But Seth's eyes were closed, his body unmoving. Mutt nudged the man's elbow and whined, and Seth didn't respond.

"Shit. Seth?" Brody hurried to his side and felt for a pulse while Abby put down the cookies and grabbed her cell phone from her pocket. He heard her dial 9-1-1. The thready race of blood through Seth's veins was so faint Brody could barely feel it. But it was there, thank God.

"Brody?" the old man mumbled, still not moving.

"Seth." He gripped Seth's hands. "You hang in there. We've got help coming."

"Waited for you," Seth whispered. "Don't..." He blinked his eyes open and saw Abby. With a smile, he closed his eyes, "Be good, boy. I'll miss you." Then he blew out a final breath. Brody couldn't describe it, but he felt Seth slip away.

"*No.*" He pulled Seth to the floor and attempted CPR while Abby continued to talk on the phone, but after minutes of compressions and breaths, nothing seemed to work.

"Brody, he's gone." Abby sidled next to Brody as he rose from his knees. She hugged him and let out a sad sigh. "Oh, Seth."

Tension, grief, anger. A crux of emotions pulled him taut and made it hard for him to breathe. He pulled away from her to pace, in what small space there was in the cramped kitchen. "If I hadn't been dicking around with Jeremy, I might have been able to help him."

"This had nothing to do with Jeremy—"

"He fucked me over, once again." Knowing she'd pushed him to do it had him glaring at her.

She blinked. "Are you upset with *me*?"

He wanted to punch Jeremy for delaying him, Seth for dying, the wall for fucking being in his way. Never Abby, but he couldn't help his sorrow and frustration. Seth had always treated him like a man, a worthy friend and neighbor.

"Brody?"

"Not now, Abby." He shook his head. "Can you wait for the medical people outside with Mutt? I don't want him near Seth when he's... I just don't want anything to touch him right now," he ended in a cracked voice.

"Sure," she said softly. "We'll be right out there when you need us."

He paid no attention, lost in another irreparable loss, and a change that turned everything upside-down. He didn't need her. He didn't need anyone. The walls that had protected him throughout his life came back up to shut out the pain, allowing him to breathe and not cry like a baby.

Chapter 19

ABBY DIDN'T KNOW WHAT TO THINK. SHE'D TRIED BUT hadn't talked to Brody in five days. Not since Seth had died. She'd seen him at the service, at least, but he'd done little more than thank her and her roommates for coming before leaving her to talk to Flynn. Apparently Seth hadn't had any family, though he'd pretended not to be so alone. He'd only had Brody, and he'd left behind wishes that Brody take everything, assuming control of his estate.

She only knew that much from Maddie, who'd heard it from Flynn. Once again, Brody had pulled away. She had no idea what she'd done wrong, but he'd ignored her multiple calls. And the two times she'd tried to talk to him at his house, Brody had refused to see her. *Refused to see her.*

She sat at her kitchen table that night, staring at her coffee cup, when Flynn walked in to join Maddie, also sitting with her.

"Hey, guys." He leaned over to kiss Maddie. "How you holding up, Abby?"

"Not well." She frowned, lost in thought. Why was Brody punishing her? "What's going on with your best friend? Because I can't keep up. Hot and cold. He's mad, he's sad. We're dating, I don't exist. Tell me, Flynn. How do you put up with his moods?"

Flynn shrugged, looking uncomfortable. "I know it's hard, but that's just what he does—"

"So you tolerate him treating you like crap when he's upset? That's crazy."

"No. We hash things out. We fight, trust me. But when he gets hurt, like, emotionally weird, he just needs space. It's a guy thing."

"It's stupid," Maddie said bluntly. "Brody can't just walk away when things get hard, then come back when he feels like it. That's no way to have a relationship."

"Maybe you see why he's been single 'til now," Flynn pointed out. "Abby, the guy is gaga for you. I mean it. Don't give up on him. Just give him time."

"Why? To reinforce that what he's doing is okay? That every time he has a hissy he can go off to his man cave and sulk?" She loved the wounded jerk, but that love didn't temper her anger. "I can't live like that. And neither can he. You all might enable him to be that way. I'm not going to."

"Good for you." Maddie nodded. To Flynn she said, "I told her she should stop his nonsense days ago. But she's tried to be fair."

"Yeah, because Seth dying isn't exactly a hissy," Flynn growled. "My boy's hurting. Leave him be."

"No, you leave *them* be," Maddie corrected. She kissed Flynn's cheek. "She's good for him. They're good for each other. And you told me yourself you hate when he pulls this crap."

He flushed. "Maddie. That was private."

"You love him. You want what's best for him. Right?"

"Yeah."

"Well, that's Abby. Let her try to straighten things out with the silent one."

Abby didn't hear any more. She had the key Maddie

had stolen for her off Flynn's key ring earlier in the day. She'd been trying to be patient, more than sympathetic to Brody's pain. But if he thought running away whenever life got messy would work for *them*, he had to know he was wrong.

She drove over to his place, sad for him and angry on her own behalf. For days she'd done nothing but try to understand Brody and put herself in his place. Seeing Jeremy would have put Brody into a bad tailspin, and then to have Seth pass...

She pulled in front of Brody's home and hurried to the front door. She knocked and rang the doorbell. "Brody?" Inside, Mutt barked. Then she heard footsteps, but the door remained closed.

A minute passed. Then two.

Scowling, she used Flynn's key and entered. She found Brody lying on the couch dressed in grungy clothes. According to Flynn, Brody had refused to take any time off until Flynn had insisted. Tonight, Brody listlessly lounged in ratty jeans and a sweatshirt that had seen better days.

"Surprise." She pocketed the key.

"What are you doing in here?" He frowned up at her.

Mutt hurried to her for some petting. *At least someone likes me.* "Brody, what's going on? Why won't you talk to me? You're avoiding me. Again."

"Seth is dead, Abby. This isn't like before. We could reschedule bowling. We can't reschedule Seth," he muttered. She heard so much anger in his voice.

"I know that," she said softly. "I'm so sorry. He was a funny man with a big heart, but it was his time."

"I could have been there, could have seen he was

having trouble if I hadn't talked to Jeremy." He put his arm over his face, hiding his expression.

He was blaming Jeremy for Seth's passing? Would he try to blame her too, because she'd nudged him to deal with his brother?

Trying to balance her need to help him with his odd mood, she calmly said, "Jeremy isn't the issue, Brody. You had a much-needed conversation with your brother, which had nothing to do with Seth."

"The dick." Brody rolled to his feet and swore again. Between them, Mutt slunk down to lie on his belly and hung his head. "Should have kicked his ass out. Never talking to him again."

"Regardless," she continued. "Seth died because *it was his time*. That's no one's fault. It just is." She did her best to remember he was grieving, that he needed support, not family counseling right now. "Look, I'm not here to argue. I'm here to help."

"So leave. I need to be alone. That helps."

She shook her head. "How? So you can mull in your misery for days, weeks? Everyone tiptoes around you because they're afraid of hurting you more. You have people who love you," *I love you*, "who care that you're okay."

"God, Abby. Don't get all clingy now."

"You asshole." She glared at him, wanting to smack the numbness trying to steal the anger from his gaze. "I care about you. I want to help you."

"How? By fucking my brains out again?" He snorted and looked her over from head to toe. How he could see seduction in her yoga pants and sweatshirt, she had no idea. "Fine. But I'm probably only good for one round tonight. It's late, and I'm tired."

She stepped close and slapped him.

They both froze.

Horrified by her loss of control, she stepped back. "I'm sorry. For the slap. But I'm not a whore to spread my legs on command. I love you." She laid it right on the line, tired of fighting herself. And him. "Partners— lovers *in love*—work together on problems. Everyone needs their own private time and space, but not like this. Not when I can see the wounds you refuse to let anyone help you heal."

"Whatever."

"Not whatever. Brody, I want to know you're okay, to be able to talk to you. I spilled my guts and shared my hurt, but you can't come to me for a hug?"

"I told you about my family," he said angrily. "And you used it to guilt me into listening to that shit-for-brains when I should have been next door with Seth."

"You're not making any sense. But then, you don't want to. You just want me and everyone else in your life to butt out. Yeah, Brody. You had a shitty childhood. I feel sorry for that little boy."

His eyes flashed with fury.

Not so numb now, are you? "But I don't feel anything but pity for you—the man—who can't share his life with anyone. You only give the bits and pieces you're comfortable with. Why can't you share all of yourself? Why can't you trust me?" She paused. "Talk to me, Brody."

He just stared at her, and she thought she'd finally gotten through to him.

Then he snorted and said, "So we fuck, and you all of a sudden think you have the right to dictate how I grieve and how I act? Seth *died*. Jeremy—"

"Had nothing to do with this," she interrupted, feeling his pain as if it were her own.

"What do you know about any of it?" he yelled, and for a second she felt a frisson of fear. Brody was a big man, and he was starting to lose that handle on his control. But he needed to, because no one else in his life had seen past the scared little boy. They'd let him push everyone out when he needed them most.

In a soft voice, she answered him. "I know I love you."

He seemed to almost curl in on himself. "No, you don't." *You can't* hung unspoken between them.

"I know that you're angry and hurt. You don't want to forgive Jeremy, but you know you have to in order to get on with your life. You don't want to love me, or for me to love you, because you don't want to be hurt again."

"Thanks for the lecture." He sneered, regrouping. "I admit the sex was amazing. But the psychobabble is wearing thin. The next time you force yourself into my place, don't be wearing anything. You'll get a much better response than *get out and leave me the hell alone*, which is what I'm telling you right now." The anger was there, a bite in his tone as well as his words. But so was the panic. That she might leave? That she might stay?

She realized nothing she could say would get through to him. Not now. And maybe not ever. *"I love you."* *"No, you don't."* How could she possibly convince him she loved him when he didn't consider himself worthy of that love? She could cuddle him and convince him until she was blue in the face, but the person he needed to have his own "come-to-Jesus meeting" with was himself.

"Brody, don't be like this." *Don't keep shutting me out.*

"Be like what? This is who I am."

So sad, because he seemed to believe he had nothing of value. Brody could be fun and sweet, and he had the potential for so much more. But he had to help himself before she or anyone else could help him.

She stepped closer, braving his wrath, and put her hand to his cheek, aware of his flinch. "If this is really what you want, I'll go. But you're making a mistake thinking you don't deserve happiness. Seth would want you to have that." She pulled her hand away and stepped back.

He snarled at her, "You don't know what Seth would want. He—" His voice broke. He turned around, breathing heavily. Then he cleared this throat. "Abby, just go. None of this makes any sense. You least of all."

She nodded, her heart breaking for him, because this cycle of denial was one he refused to break. He'd always be alone because of it, no matter how many people surrounded him.

"Bye, Brody." She turned and left him, walking out the door. After she closed it behind her, she heard something shatter against it. Mutt started barking, but the tears made it difficult to pay him much attention.

Abby wanted to give Brody space and time, but she had a bad feeling none of that would matter in the end. She couldn't live with an emotionally unavailable man. Not again. Because there was more to life than the carefree fun moments. She needed a give and take. If Brody didn't think he deserved love, how could he ever love her? A chubby, unattractive little woman who wrote the fiction she wanted to live, always looking for love but unable to find it?

She wiped her tears in the car and looked at herself in the rearview mirror. "No." She refused to go down this path again. "I am not unattractive." Men seemed to like her, at least, according to her roommates. Hadn't that bartender and Rick tried to flirt? "I'm strong. I'm loveable. I am not going to repeat old bad habits. I'm a success. I write sexy books, and anyone who doesn't like that can fuck off."

Saying it out loud made her feel powerful. Like a goddess.

She smiled through watery tears, wishing Brody the best, hoping they could have their happily ever after but refusing to spiral into his negativity. Abby had friends and family who loved her. She'd learned to love herself. Wholly. Truly. Finally.

~~~

Brody stared at the shards of an old glass ashtray he'd been meaning to toss for weeks. Then he launched a tacky vase and a bobble-head wooden sailor against the door, adding to the mess on the floor. Across the room, away from his tantrum, Mutt sat trying to look smaller. He kept glancing from Brody to the door, as if to say, "What's the deal, man? You losing your mind?"

Not liking the dog's fear, Brody blinked away tears of shame and fury. Not only had Mutt seen him looking like a loser. So had Abby. *"I love you,"* she'd said. Well, not anymore. Fucking Abby. Had to come see him when he was at his most vulnerable. An embarrassing pussy who cried at his friend's funeral and couldn't handle being lonely.

Strange as it was, with Seth next door, Brody hadn't felt so alone. He'd looked up to the old man, as crotchety as Pop used to be, and apart from the world as Brody often felt.

Bitsy and Pop had showered him with love for years. So had Flynn, Mike, and Cam. Colin loved him unconditionally, like Mutt still looking at him with concern in his big brown eyes. But deep down Brody knew he didn't deserve it.

"I don't, you know," he whispered to Mutt and sat on the floor. He held his head in his hands. "I'm a piece of shit. A no-good fuckhead who doesn't deserve you either."

Mutt walked over to him and put his head in Brody's lap. So trusting. The dog had nowhere to go, no one to love him but Brody. Kind of like Brody had nowhere to go but the McCauleys. A filthy little kid with sticky fingers who'd only managed by the grace of God not to be shoved into a series of foster homes, thanks to the kindness of Bitsy and Pop.

Always making sure he had enough to eat. Throwing him in the van with the rest of the brood on family vacations. Putting his pictures on the fridge to show off his God-awful stick figures and artwork that Cam incessantly made fun of and Flynn defended.

He gave Mutt a half-smile. "Cam was such a pisser. Mike too. Noogies and teasing. Stealing my army men only to put them back after painting them pink." He wiped his cheeks, remembering how Bitsy would rock him to sleep after a nightmare, or how Pop had taught him to throw a baseball, a football, shoot a basket.

And the women through the years, they'd all

demanded so much, growing too clingy and obnoxious until he wanted nothing more than to race from their lives.

But not Abby. She hadn't wanted gifts or lavish attention. She didn't know how gorgeous she truly was, how kind and caring. He found himself stroking Mutt's head as he remembered how he'd come back to his house after her week staying there. How she'd left him a clean place and leftovers in the fridge. She'd taken care of Mutt and made Brody's ugly-ass house feel like a home.

And she loved him.

He wiped his cheeks, not sure when he'd started crying again. Maybe he'd never stopped. He and Mutt sat for a while as he mulled over the fact that she'd loved him, and he'd lost her affection before he'd grasped that he'd had it. Had *her*. Seth, Abby, his life seemed like a never-ending spiral out of control.

The doorbell rang.

"Shit." He didn't think he could face Abby and her stupid claims that he felt unworthy again. Felt unworthy? Hell, he *was* unworthy.

Accompanying the doorbell came banging. "Open the damn door."

Flynn. The bastard would stand there all night if he had to. He'd done it before.

Brody hastily wiped his cheeks and blinked a lot, hoping he didn't look as if he'd been crying. Then he crossed to the front door and unlocked and opened it. "Yeah?"

Flynn gave him a thorough once-over. "Yep. You look like shit." Flynn muscled past him and tiptoed through the shattered glass on the floor. "Had a hissy, eh?"

"Abby was here." He hadn't meant to admit that, but it slipped out. He closed the door and stepped around the mess to stand with Flynn in the living room. Mutt stayed by Brody's side.

Loyalty to a man who had no idea what to do with it. Ironic.

"Yeah? So she threw the shit?" Flynn asked.

"Ah, no. That was me."

"Uh-huh." Flynn cleared his throat. "About that. She stole my key from Maddie, who stole it from me. Thieves." He shook his head. "Sorry if she disturbed you." Then Flynn took a deep breath and let it out in a rush. "But you know? She's right. You need disturbing." Flynn shoved him, and the move surprised him because Flynn felt like he meant business. "What the fuck is wrong with you? Stop hiding and talk to me. I'm your best friend. Your twin. Your brother, man. I get you can't talk to Abby. Chicks don't understand where we're coming from when the emotional crap hits. But I do."

He could see Flynn's frustration, and something in Brody snapped. "No, you don't. You have no fucking clue who I am."

Flynn blinked at him, then narrowed his gaze. "So tell me."

"I'm a thief and a loser. The son of addicts, Flynn. Not your mom-and-pop fairy-tale family. No McCauley genes in me." He thumped his chest. "Alan is a fucking nightmare. Jeremy too. Except now that he's sorry, he wants to apologize for all the shit he put me through."

"What shit?"

Brody didn't want to tell him. Enough that he'd

talked to Abby about it, that Seth had known his shame. Seth…

"What? You mean all those bruises and scratches no one was supposed to know about? Dude, we lived in the same room for years. Did you really think I didn't know your brother used to beat on you?"

Brody paled. "You knew?"

Flynn scowled. "Yeah, I knew. You never talked about it, and Mom and Dad told us to let you be. That you'd tell us when you were ready. But you never did. And anytime they'd come around, force you on those visits, you'd turn into a zombie for days and weeks after. Of course we knew something was up. But you wouldn't tell Mom or Dad, always threatened you'd run away if we forced you to see a shrink or a doctor, so we had to respect your silence. Or so Mom said. I always thought that was for shit."

"You never said anything before."

"Neither did you. Why not?"

He snorted. "It's not something to brag about."

"Don't be an asshole." Flynn seemed angry. Really angry. "If you knew someone had been hurting me, what would you have done?"

"I wouldn't have had to do anything. Between Mike, Cam, Bitsy, and Pop, they'd annihilate the fucker."

"But you didn't deserve the same consideration? I thought we were brothers."

Great. Now Flynn looked hurt. "We're tight, but I'm not a McCauley. *I'm not*," he yelled. "Don't you think I'd give anything to have been born into the family? To know Bitsy was my real mother and Pop my dad? I used to dream that I was really your twin, and we'd always be together." Brody's eyes burned. "But the truth was my brother and father never went away. They always reminded me how easily I could go back with them if I fucked up."

He went silent a moment, then admitted in a sick voice, "I stole cars, booze, drugs. I sold baggies in alleys for Jeremy, to make enough money on shitty drugs so he could buy the good stuff." He felt sick, remembering some of the things he'd done. "Flynn, I was a bad kid."

Flynn seemed surprised. "Are you serious? You really feel guilty because those shitheads abused you and made you do illegal crap as a kid? You're smarter than that." He paused. "Did they touch you? Like, molest you or something? Is that why you're all messed up?"

Brody let out angry laughter. "No. The one thing they never did, believe it or not. But yeah, I am all messed up. Flynn, just leave me alone."

"Abby told Maddie she said she loved you."

Brody froze. "What?"

"Yeah. Cried about it a bit, but she's okay—she'll be okay, I mean." Flynn sighed. "You are so fucking stupid. You're lucky you have me."

Not having expected that, Brody could only stare. "What are you talking about? I'm messed up. A loser. A drug dealer, a car thief, a—"

"Card cheat. Yeah, the list goes on. I know. Deal with it. It's the past. Unless you're selling drugs and stealing cars now? Is that it? Is that why business has been so good lately? You cleaning your drug money through our business?" Flynn looked more intrigued by the idea than disgusted.

"That's a lot of bullshit fiction. You sure you're not reading Abby's books?"

Flynn grinned. "Well, just the dirty parts."

Brody wanted to laugh, but he was so confused. He'd never expected to tell Flynn his ugly truths, or that Flynn would just shrug them away, like they weren't important.

"Brody, I never thought I'd say this, but stop thinking so hard. Man, you're a McCauley any way you look at it. Blood, last names, they don't matter. *You* matter. You're my best friend." Christ, Flynn was tearing up. "I tell you everything. I always have. Hell, we're closer than I am to Mike and Cam. You know me, and no matter what fucked-up nonsense you have going on in what passes for a brain in that head, I know you. The real you. The guy who's so in love with Abby he's running scared. The one who's as freaked out as the rest of us that Mom and Dad are having problems. The guy who taught *our* nephew how to palm a card and make money disappear. Damn kid keeps borrowing quarters to pull out of my ears, then makes them vanish and demands more money."

Brody choked on a laugh. "He's a good one."

"Because he has you in his life."

Brody tried hard, but he started to lose it. He felt a tear trickle down his cheek. "Man, I'm just... I'm nobody, Flynn. A big blond shell of nothing." He started crying like a goddamn girl. "Shit. I hate this. I hate Seth dying. I hate Alan, Jeremy. Those fucking assholes," he snarled and wiped his eyes. "I hate you seeing me like this. Knowing that I'm..."

"What, human?" Flynn wiped his own tears. "And yeah, I cried. I'm as big a pussy as you are. See? Twins."

Brody laughed, and to his horror that laugh turned into a sob he couldn't stop. "I—I—"

Flynn caught him in a bear hug and refused to let go. "Brody, you dumb fuck. I love you. We all love you. Just accept it and deal. Jesus, you're stubborn. Abby was right. You have a hard head. And an even harder heart."

Brody hugged him back, accepting the lifeline for once in his life, and refusing to let it go.

Chapter 20

BRODY STARED AT THE MUG OF SHITTY COFFEE FLYNN had made for him and forced him to drink. Hours later, they sat together in front of the glowing fireplace. Mutt lay sprawled out beside him, lost in doggie dreams.

"Now we agreed. We never speak of what happened here tonight. *Ever.*" Flynn looked serious.

"Like I want to shout out how I cried like a fucking girl and broke down until I could barely stand?" Brody asked in a hoarse voice, still emotionally and physically drained. He linked pinkies with Flynn and shook, the way they'd done as kids.

"True." Flynn let him go and took a long sip of coffee. "Ah, good stuff."

"It's crap."

"Yeah, but with these cookies, it's awesome." Flynn had a plate of peanut butter cookies and snickerdoodles Abby had insisted he take with him, knowing he'd been going to Brody's.

Brody stared at the cookies. "She's really mad at me. I think I blew it." And that made him want to cry all over again. *Jesus Christ, man. Get a grip.*

"Well, she's not pleased, that's for sure. But I think she's really concerned about you. And she's right. We coddled you for too long. I can't believe you'd ever think you aren't good enough to be a McCauley." Flynn snorted. "That's so stupid it isn't funny. I mean, Mike went through that phase where he refused to wash his feet for nearly a year. Remember that? Mom had to constantly force him to change his socks and bathe."

Brody grinned. "Right. When the football team was in their championship season. He was afraid to wash his lucky socks. Thought they'd lose if he did."

"And Cam? All those prissy math and chess club competitions?" Flynn grimaced. "I almost died of boredom until he started track. He's almost half girl, our younger brother."

Brody knew what Flynn was doing, but he didn't call him on it. Emphasizing all those "*our* brother" and "*our* mom and dad" comments. To his bemusement, the inclusion felt…right. Not as if he had to remind himself to be grateful for his role in the family, but that he truly belonged. He deserved it.

An odd feeling of acceptance filled him with calm. He took a snickerdoodle and bit into it, the flavor of cinnamon and Abby bursting in his mouth.

"So you going to be okay now?"

"Yeah. I might need a day or two off."

"No problem. Aunt Linda called Mom and bitched that Theo's driving her nuts and that the kid needs some extra money for the holidays. So I brought him on to help me the next few days. I figure we'll slow down and just take emergency calls then until after Christmas."

"Shit. Christmas."

"Yep. Just two more weeks. Stores are emptying out, and they're calling for snow next week. Joy."

"I haven't done any shopping."

Flynn smiled. "Brody, I don't think anyone will mind if they don't get anything from you this year. You've had a shitty couple of weeks. Well, Colin might sulk, but he's a good kid. He'll get over it and end up convincing you to buy him twice as much for missing Christmas."

They both chuckled.

Brody needed time. "You think I could take off 'til next Wednesday? I know that's putting us in a bind, what with the Janson house, but—"

"It's not a problem, Brody. You never take time off as it is. And I'm planning on vacationing next year with Maddie somewhere, so you'll suck up the work then. Go ahead, call me a pussy. But when I make her happy, she makes me so, so, *sooo* happy." He wiggled his brows.

The comfort and familiarity of being with Flynn eased him deep inside. "Good. You deserve it. And she's hot, so you need to do whatever you can to hold on to her. One day she might wake up and realize how ugly you really are."

Flynn frowned. "Please. This face? I could model with this face."

"Ski masks, maybe." Brody grinned at the finger Flynn gave him, then let out a tired sigh. "A few days and I promise I'll be back to work. I need some time to just be, you know? Not all fucked up like I have been, but time to recoup and just think about things."

"Abby one of those things you'll be thinking about?"

"Maybe. Probably." He groaned. "Totally."

"Good. She fits you, man. I know the women you've dated. Fuck-buddies, some nice girls, but no one like Abby. She'll stick. And I'm not just saying that because she's Maddie's best friend, which would *totally* make couples date night bearable."

"Oh right. Maddie made you go out with Robin and Kim a few weeks ago."

"It was torture. Kim's all hot, and Robin's kind of cute. So I'm sitting with Maddie and trying hard not to think about her friends going down on each other. It's so weird. And I can't tell Maddie that, because she'll think I'm into her friends. Which I'm not."

Brody chuckled. "Be honest. You think of them going at it, and you wonder what Maddie might look like with another chick."

"Well, sure. I'm a guy." Flynn huffed. "But it's one thing to fantasize. I'm a one-woman man, and she's a one-man woman." He paused. "My point, before we got off track, was that I know you."

"As you've said many, many times tonight."

"This thing with Abby for you, it's not casual. You really like her. Even love her, maybe?" Flynn watched him.

Brody slowly nodded. "I think so."

Flynn's white grin blinded him. "I knew it. Oh relax, Nancy. I'm not going to tell anyone. Your place is like Vegas. What happened here stays here. I mean it." He scowled. "Cam finds out I was sharing and crying with you, he'll want to join in. And that kid is not afraid to tear up. It's embarrassing."

"I know." On that they both agreed.

"So we're good then?" Flynn stood and yawned.

Brody did as well, then noticed the time. "It's two in the morning."

"Hence the sleeping dog." Flynn nodded at Mutt, who twitched and growled without opening his eyes.

Brody walked Flynn to the door but stopped him

when Flynn would have left. "One thing. I don't know that I said it before, but—"

"You're welcome."

"I wasn't thanking you." Brody frowned, screwing up his courage. "I just—"

"Don't worry, bro. I know Abby will forgive you if you apologize. I think. Anyway, I'll get Maddie on our side and then—"

"No. Not that. Will you shut the hell up? I love you too, okay? There. I said it." Why was it still so hard to say? Maybe because Flynn knew the ugly ins and outs of him, and Brody half-expected Flynn to reject him? *I'm not that jacked up, am I?*

Flynn winked. "I appreciate the sentiment, but I don't swing that way."

Brody punched him. "Asshole."

"Love you too, bro. Right back at ya." Flynn smacked him in the head, gave him a bone-crushing hug, then left.

Brody stared at the door as he closed it. He walked past the now spotless floor that Flynn had helpfully cleaned up hours ago and joined Mutt in front of the fire again, but not before yanking an afghan off the couch. He lay down next to his dog, pulled his blanket over himself, and stared at the plate on the table that flickered in the firelight. Two uneaten cookies remained.

"I love you, Abby," he whispered, and prayed he wasn't so screwed up that he couldn't untangle the knot of emotion scarring his brain so that he could figure out how to win her back. *If* he could win her back. *One step at a time*, he told himself, and allowed himself the rest, and love, he deserved.

———*w*———

Abby had just six more days until Christmas. At the sight of all the snow outside, she figured it would be a white Christmas—her favorite. Her agent had given her terrific news that her proposal was in a bidding war with three major houses. *Cha-ching*. If the deal went through the way her agent thought it would, Abby could count on being able to eat through next summer. She absolutely loved the ability to pay her bills *and* afford food.

She felt bad about celebrating an electronic Christmas with her family, but she didn't have the time to shop and mail gifts this year. Despite her rift with Meg, she decided to be the bigger person and include Meg's children in holiday well wishes. It wasn't their fault their parents were morons.

Her parents had sent her a Christmas card and money. Abby had talked to her mother once since being back, to reassure her she'd arrived home safely. But they hadn't spoken about the ugly altercation with Meg or made mention of Abby's writing career.

Instead, she'd shared her good news with Vanessa and Maddie, who were thrilled for her. Well, Maddie at least. Vanessa had returned to being a disgruntled accountant and clean freak who rarely smiled. She also wasn't speaking to Cam anymore. Abby had a bad feeling the silence was due to Abby and Brody no longer dating.

Though she'd been honest with her roommates about harboring no ill will toward Brody, Vanessa blamed him all the same. Apparently that animosity extended to anyone who sided with him. Even Flynn had borne the brunt of her aggression. But good-natured Flynn simply ignored her and took Maddie to his place more often than not.

Humming as she finished the last of her Christmas cards, Abby found her thoughts straying to Brody, as they always did. But she'd gotten smart, focusing on what she could control. She had taken to building herself up, not putting herself down. No more *loser*, *fat girl*, or *lonely geek* self-references. The new Abby was smart, successful, voluptuous, and pretty. She had friends, and she no longer hid the fact that she wrote erotic romance.

She spent the rest of the day doing chores and finishing her holiday gift list. Around six, the snow picked up again and the door opened.

"It's just me," Vanessa called as she trudged inside. Vanessa was working overtime to get a week off over the holidays. What the woman planned to do with it was anyone's guess, because if Vanessa wasn't busy, she was miserable. But Abby wanted her friend to get what she worked for, so she said nothing.

Abby leaned back over the couch to look down the hallway. "Hey, welcome home...Mom?"

"Oh. Did I fail to mention I have your mother with me?" Vanessa grinned. "There she is, as promised, Mrs. Dunn."

Margaret smiled. "Oh, call me Margaret. You know you want to."

Vanessa chuckled. "Yes, ma'am. I do." She walked around Abby's mother and slid her feet out of her muck-covered boots. "Margaret?"

"Yes, dear?"

"Please take off your shoes. This is a non-shoe house. Only way to keep it clean." Same old Vanessa.

"Oh, of course."

Abby stared, still not sure what her mother was doing thousands of miles from home so close to Christmas. "Is Dad here with you?"

"No, but Megan is in the car." Her mother waited a moment, then burst out laughing. "I'm kidding. Your sister is a snot. She's still at home nursing emotional wounds from your verbal darts."

"Wow, Abby. She even talks like you." Vanessa waved. "I'm hitting the gym. I'll be back later. Oh, and Maddie told me to tell you she's hanging at Flynn's tonight and tomorrow night. So your mom can use her bed." She darted upstairs.

"Mom?" Abby left the couch to give her mom a big hug. "What are you doing here?"

"I missed you as soon as you left, honey. Thanksgiving was a disaster."

"I should apologize, but in my defense, Meg started it."

Her mother sighed. "You know, I've been hearing that for years."

"I'm sorry, Mom. I didn't mean to ruin Thanksgiving. It's just…Meg took something I've worked hard on for years and turned it into something dirty. And that's not right."

"I know, sweetie. In any case, what's done is done. I wanted to come visit, because I haven't seen your house since you moved. I left your father at home with the others, so I can only stay two days. You know what that man's like when I'm not home."

"Oh yeah. He turns into a mutant Mr. Fix-It. What did you leave him to do to distract him?"

"A faulty dishwasher. I want a new one, so I figure if I let him try to figure it out, I'll get the machine I want next year." She smiled. "Which is in about two weeks. Oh, Jack and Teresa have been by a few times. I really like Jack."

"He's good for Teresa," Abby agreed.

They walked together into the kitchen, where Abby made them both a cup of tea. "Not that I'm not happy to see you, but wow. Big surprise."

"I wanted to tell you face-to-face how proud I am of you."

Abby's heart raced. "Really?"

Her mother smiled. "I was so shocked when you said you wrote books. Part of me was hurt you hadn't confided in me. Then your sister kept talking about porn, and I was admittedly confused."

Abby chuckled. "Teresa or Megan? Because Teresa likes what I write."

"Me too. I read one of your books right after you left. And honey, I thoroughly enjoyed it. I don't know what Megan was thinking to equate it to the adult industry. I went out and told all my friends about you, and now they're all reading you too, the ones who weren't already." Her mother let a tear slip. "I'm so proud of you, and I'm sorry I disappointed you by not telling you so."

"Oh, Mom. It's okay." Abby smiled, amazed at how great her holiday was shaping up to be. Her mother's surprise visit didn't completely mitigate her heartache over Brody, but it sure did help boost her spirits. "I'm sorry I sprung it on you like that. I'd wanted to tell you when I first got published, but I was scared you might not approve."

"Oh bother. I know, there's sex in the books. And as my daughter once said, there aren't any virgin births in our family." She grinned. "Your father read it too. He skimmed over the sex parts, or so he said. But he's as thrilled as I am with your success. Honey, when I mentioned your name, a few of my friends knew who you were! Your alter ego, I mean."

"Wow." She felt ten feet tall.

"Anyway, I'm here for the next two days. I called Maddie and conspired." Her mother winked. "She was busy, so Vanessa offered to pick me up from the airport. You have such wonderful friends."

"Yeah, I do." She lowered her voice. "But don't tell Vanessa I said that. She already has an unhealthy ego the size of her monstrously large feet."

Margaret burst out laughing. "Too funny. But she's just as you described." After Abby handed her mother the tea, her mom fiddled with the tea bag. "Tell me something."

"Sure."

"What's this about you being in love with a man named Brody Singer?"

Vanessa chose that moment to enter the kitchen. She glanced from Abby to Margaret and turned around and left. "Gotta go," she yelled from the hallway, and not two seconds later, the front door opened and slammed shut.

"Big mouth." Abby sighed. "It's complicated."

"I know. Vanessa told me all about it." Margaret smiled. "So in addition to her supposedly large ego, she has a big mouth. To match her big feet. I mean, wow. I didn't know shoes came in that size."

"For women," she and her mother said as one. They laughed together. And then Abby tried to explain how she was doing her best to get over Brody. One day at a time.

———

Brody clenched the card in his hand and waited with Mutt outside a local coffee shop. They were both freezing in the snow, although Mutt liked the coat Brody had bought for him. An early Christmas present.

The past week had been fraught with thinking, feeling, and general pain-in-the-ass, unannounced drop-ins from the rest of his family—the McCauleys. Pop had stopped by to measure his living room for the new built-ins he intended to help out with. Mike had shown up in time to argue with his father about who was building what. Cam found time in his busy schedule to bring Chinese food and bitch about Vanessa, who was driving him crazy. That Brody could see the sparks flashing between the pair was a clear warning they were going to clash, and clash hard.

Flynn brought Colin a few times to play with Mutt and complain about Theo, though he also hoped his cousin would join the business, because he had promise. Even Bitsy made an appearance, wanting to bring Brody some home-cooked meals and talk about Seth, whom she'd met and liked instantly. Flynn innocently denied any involvement in the clan showing up, though Brody knew damn well he'd gabbed about poor old Brody.

All in all, he'd had one hell of a busy "alone time."
It had been difficult at first, because despite his break-
down with Flynn, Brody wasn't used to talking about his
feelings. With the guys, they provided that presence, the
untalked-about support, which he appreciated. Bitsy, on
the other hand, had managed to drag all his insecurities
out of him and gently chastised him for ever doubting
his place in the family. She'd had a good cry about it
too. Fortunately, he'd used up all his tears last week, so
he'd been able to comfort her even as she read him the
riot act for being so stand-offish. Then she'd forced him
to confront his feelings for Alan, Jeremy…and Abby.

Alan he wrote off. He hated the bastard. But
Jeremy… He'd told Bitsy what Jeremy had said and
tried to figure out how it made him feel. In the end, he'd
been able to identify reluctant curiosity, anger, and pity.
With her help, he'd decided to crack the door open. No,
he'd never be best friends with the guy. But he could
offer some forgiveness. Maybe. If Jeremy begged for it
on spikes, on his hands and fucking knees.

So he waited to meet the guy outside on the snow-
covered sidewalk, still wondering if he'd made a mistake in reaching out.

He recognized Jeremy as soon as he turned the
corner. To his bemusement, they really did look alike.

Jeremy lit up with a smile as soon as he spotted
Brody. "Hey."

"Hi."

Mutt barked once but otherwise sat quietly. He and
Brody had made tremendous progress, and ever since
Brody had lost his friggin' mind and poured out years'
worth of grief, the dog had become the most loyal creature.

"So you brought your dog. We going to get the coffee to go?"

"I thought we could walk and talk. It's only snow." Hey, if the guy didn't like the cold, he could—

"That's fine with me. The snow is light enough. Besides, all the Christmas lights are on—it's pretty, actually."

It was surreal, having a conversation with Jeremy that didn't involve fists, drugs, or guns. Brody kept waiting for the guy to ask for money, but Jeremy paid for his own coffee after Brody bought his. They walked down a mostly empty Queen Ann Avenue and talked about Jeremy's life since he'd had a crucial awakening.

To Brody's surprise, it sounded a lot like the turning point Brody himself had gone through, realizing how he kept everyone at arm's length, how he wasn't worthy, how he'd never fit in the way he wanted.

They walked in companionable silence for a while, sipping their coffee while Mutt sniffed at everything within reach, enjoying the walk.

There was something to be said for dogs, who took pleasure in the simplest of things.

"So do you still hate me?" Jeremy asked quietly.

Brody drank his coffee, giving the question some thought. "I don't think so. I still haven't forgotten what you did. I don't think I ever will."

"I don't expect you to." To Brody's bewilderment, his brother seemed to mean it. "I admit, I want your forgiveness, but I came to you and gave you my number because I wanted you to know that back then, the problem was me. Not you. And you shouldn't have to bear that burden."

"I don't. Not anymore." It was true. He'd been feeling better about life lately. Getting over his past had given him a sense of peace he'd been sorely lacking.

"I'm glad. I hated Dad for a long, long time. Some days I still do. I blame him for making me this way." Jeremy paused and looked up at the sky, smiling. "But there's too much good in the world for that. I mean, dwelling on him just takes me down, back where I don't want to be. You know?"

"Yeah."

Jeremy looked at him. "I'm focusing on the good. Trust me, I'm not all Pollyanna and shit. But why worry about crap you can't change? I'm taking control of my life. It's never too late."

"Good for you." Brody looked into Jeremy's clear eyes. "You sound like you're in a good place."

"I am. You?"

"Almost. I'm just about where I need to be. I just have my own atonement to handle. And it's not going to be easy."

Jeremy gave him a rusty laugh. "Trust me, I know. Facing you was the hardest thing I've ever had to do in my life. I know you don't owe me jack shit, but I can't thank you enough for seeing me." They started walking again, no particular destination in mind. Just enjoying the crisp, snowy afternoon.

Brody had thought long and hard about what he wanted to say to Jeremy. All the hurt, the cycle of abuse, the heartache. "Jeremy?"

His brother stopped. "Yeah?"

"I forgive you. I still think you were a total shit for what you did, but I forgive you. Ever try looking at me the wrong way now, though, and I'll kick your ass from here to Canada."

Jeremy's smile grew wide. "Yeah, I get you. You're pretty big now anyway. No way I'd ever make a move on you, and not with that monster by your side."

Mutt stared at the snow, grinning, his tongue hanging out.

After a few more blocks Jeremy said, "Merry Christmas."

"Yeah. You too."

They walked again, not speaking, and saying exactly what the other needed to hear.

Chapter 21

BRODY HAD INTENDED TO GET HIS APOLOGY TO ABBY over and done with so he could focus on making it up to her. But the next day when he knocked on her door, he found Vanessa at home alone.

"Damn. I was looking for Abby."

The cool blond quirked a brow. "Were you now?"

He blew out a breath. He'd known this was coming. After Cam had told him what a pain in the ass the woman had been about Brody's many grievances against her friend, he'd realized he'd have to battle her as well as Abby to earn Abby's forgiveness.

"Look—"

"Save it." She held up a hand. "Do you love Abby or not?"

"I do." He didn't have to think twice.

"Then prove it. That woman thinks the world of you. She's gone out of her way to tell all of us to give you space. I wanted to chop your nuts off, but she insisted I leave you alone."

He forced himself not to cringe. "Uh, thanks?"

"Her mom's in town."

"How's that going? Because last time her mom gave her a lot of shit." He worried. Had Abby been having a hard time, dumped on by him *and* her family?

Vanessa smiled, not her wolf-like, I'm-going-to-suck-the-marrow-from-your-bones grin, but an honest expression of happiness. "Her mom saw the light. She's now Abby's biggest fan."

He relaxed. "Good. She deserves it."

Vanessa's joy faded. "Yeah, she does." She poked him in the chest with a bony finger. "So unless you mean business, go back to being the funny blond doofus and leave her alone."

"Wait. Doofus?"

She crossed her arms over her chest and glared.

"I can't leave her alone. I tried. I miss her too much."

Her tension eased. "Well then. What do you plan to do about it?"

"I think I know how to show her I'm serious, but it's going to take a few favors and some wide leeway on your part."

She narrowed her eyes. "What kind of leeway?"

When he explained, she groaned. "Oh my God. What I do for you people in love."

Saturday morning, after Abby dropped her mother off at the airport, she drove home in a much better mood. But as she plowed through the snow and listened to Christmas music, a familiar melancholy settled over her.

"Oh, Brody. I miss you." Part of her knew she never should have gotten involved with him. Things could only have ended badly. What did she expect? That, like her gorgeous, successful roommate, she'd find love with the perfect man?

No. Stop thinking that way. Reverse. She forced herself to be positive, even though her heart felt like it had gone three rounds with a kangaroo in boxing gloves and lost. "I had a wonderful affair with a sexy man. He gave me orgasms. Many, many orgasms. We had fun. Don't regret it, Abby. You deserved that sexy happiness. You are capable of it." She wondered if she should phone Rick when the holidays ended.

Glumly, she knew she wouldn't. She didn't know if she would ever get over Brody. And there was still that slim chance he might change. She couldn't give up on him just because he'd given up on himself. Then she had to ask herself if she was hanging around only to fight a losing battle.

Abby sang along to Rudolph and Frosty and forced herself to think instead about her new series, excited to put Del—er, her tough mechanic—in tune with her feelings over a stubborn man who refused to open himself to love again. Brody. Or Mike, as she'd started thinking about them. Del and Mike—they made a nice couple. Though her readers would soon be introduced to them as Selena and Chance.

She sang and envisioned her characters having a snow-covered, intimate Christmas together. Abby planned on finishing decorating the house. She, Maddie, and Vanessa had found a tree they liked at a nearby tree farm, and Maddie had coerced Flynn into setting it up for them the other day.

The three of them had appointed Abby head decorator, so as soon as she built her Christmas spirit back up to snuff, she intended to spend her weekend decorating the tree and the house, readying for Christmas in just a few days.

Before she could head home, she realized she had forgotten Vanessa's lengthy grocery list. With a groan, she turned the next corner and made her way toward Whole Foods, because God forbid she didn't buy organic.

An hour later and a hundred dollars poorer, with only two bags to show for it, Abby wrestled the groceries into the car and headed home. Before she arrived, her phone rang.

She pressed a button on her car. *Hurray for hands-free, especially in this snow.* "Make it quick. I'm driving."

"Oh good. I caught you in the car. Say, where are you?"

"Hello, Vanessa. Why yes, I did get your expensive vegetables. You owe me."

"Yeah, yeah. Hey, I'm trying to help Flynn out with Maddie's gift. It's a diamond necklace, or is it earrings? Right, earrings. That jeweler down in Green Lake. Can you run and grab it for me?"

"Me? I have groceries in the car."

"It's cold enough they'll keep. You know that place with the blue banner facing the lake? Mortel's or Mormon's or something like that?"

"Yeah, I know it." She'd once gone in to get some information on jewelry sizing and repair research for a book. The guys there had been most helpful.

"Right. Your research." Vanessa was great at reading minds. "Anyway, go in and pick up the earrings. Or earbobs, as you fancy writers say."

Abby grinned, despite the hassle. "Fine. I'll pick them up. He paid, I take it?"

"Yeah. I called them and let them know you'd be picking it up instead of me. Joaquin remembers you. Thanks!"

Before Abby could think to ask why Vanessa couldn't get the earrings, or Flynn for that matter, Vanessa had disconnected.

Another hour and a half later, after slugging through snow, around an accident, and up the driveway, she returned home, tired. She managed not to drop everything as she made her way awkwardly to the door.

With Maddie going out of town this weekend with Flynn, and Vanessa off to God knew where, she wouldn't get a better chance at downtime than now. A nap seemed in good order. Maybe after a cup of hot peppermint cocoa—her one extravagance at the market.

She unlocked the front door and froze at what sounded like a...bark? After a moment, when nothing materialized in the entryway, she told herself she'd been hearing things. She closed the door behind her and locked it, then dropped everything to strip down to her jeans, sweater, and fuzzy socks. Lugging the bags and Maddie's gorgeous diamond earrings—that Abby had been salivating over forever, since she'd first spotted them while doing her research—she walked down the hallway past the open living room, backtracked, and then froze.

She stared in awe at a gorgeously decorated Christmas tree. Gold ribbons and red and gold balls draped the fir, lending it a majestic air. No kid tree festooned with paper ornaments and cutesy crap. A few gifts had been planted around it, dressed in sparkling bows and ribbons. The entire living room and hallway, now that she took a good hard look, had been tastefully decorated in a red, gold, and green rustic Christmas theme. And there. She cocked her head, bemused to hear the growing hum of Christmas music near a...

"Crackling fire?" She gaped at the fire blazing in a hearth she hadn't realized actually worked.

She wondered if she'd mistakenly interrupted a romantic date between Maddie and Flynn. But she could have sworn the pair had gone out of town. Hurrying to the kitchen, she shoved the cold things in the fridge, put the rest of the groceries away, then took the bright blue foil box of jewelry and set it under the tree.

When she straightened, she turned around...*and shrieked*.

"Well, not exactly the welcome I was expecting." Brody stood near the couch with a fresh haircut, a navy blue sweater that did wonderful things for his coloring, and a pair of black jeans.

God, he was swoon-worthy. She cleared her throat and tried to calm her racing heart. "Oh, hey Brody." Confused, she glanced around. "Are you looking for Flynn?"

He smiled, and the warmth in his expression turned her inside out. "Actually, I was looking for you."

"Huh?"

He closed the distance between them. "I've really been missing you, Abby. I'm so sorry."

Yeah, she'd heard that before. He placed his hands on her shoulders and leaned down to kiss her. She hated herself for doing it, but she put a hand on his chest to stop him. "Hold on. What the heck are you doing here?"

He sighed and pulled back. "Think we could sit and talk?"

She glanced around, and seeing no one else, figured why not. "Sure."

They sat, but before she could speak, he rose and held up a finger. "Hold on. Be right back." He left, headed toward the kitchen, and returned moments later with one of those cocoa makers she'd been wanting. It sat on a tray with two mugs and a small bowl of marsh-mallows. "Would you like some hot chocolate?"

She blinked. "Er, yeah."

He poured her a cup and gave her two marshmal-lows. Just the way she took it. To her astonishment, he'd used her favorite, the peppermint cocoa. Then he poured some for himself.

"This is terrific." She sipped and sighed, in heaven. Snow outside, a toasty fire, cocoa, and a smokin' hot man by her side. Too unreal. "I just bought more of this. I was almost out."

He drank some and licked the excess from his mouth, making her wish she'd thought to kiss the chocolate off first. "You have good taste."

Easy, girl. Down, libido. She drank some more to give herself time to concentrate. "So you had something to say?"

"Yeah. Seth's passing hit me hard. Right on top of dealing with Jeremy, it was too much for me to take."

"So you ran away," she had to say and wished she hadn't.

"You aren't going to make this easy, are you?" he asked wryly.

She flushed. "I'm sorry."

"You're right, though. I don't seem to do well with drama. I can't process it without stressing, so I shut down. I always have."

She remained quiet, letting him talk. She sensed he needed to say it as much as she needed to hear it.

He stared at the mug in his hands. "I had a really hard time growing up. I mean, I loved Bitsy and Pop and the guys, and they've never been anything but good to me.

But I think maybe I felt like I never really belonged."
He glanced at her. "It took me a long time to trust Bitsy,
and an even longer time with Pop. I loved them, but letting them comfort me wasn't easy. I laughed and joked,
was easygoing, to hide... This isn't easy."

She put the mug down, placed her hands over his,
and squeezed. "I know. You can stop anytime you like.
I appreciate you telling me."

"But you're still pissed."

She shrugged, uncomfortable at being honest because he'd bared a part of himself and no doubt felt
raw. "You hurt me, Brody. I put it all on the line for you
and you rejected me."

"I know." He let out a heavy breath. "Wait a minute."
He set his mug down on the coffee table and circled
around behind her. His hands settled on her shoulders,
and she tensed.

"What are you doing?"

"I thought about strangling you, but people saw
me enter the house. And you know, I left prints
everywhere."

"Ha ha." She moaned when he started rubbing her
shoulders, easing her tension. "Oh, that's nice."

"Good. You relax and I'll finish what I came to say."

"Sure. Go ahead."

He chuckled, then cleared his throat. "I'm sorry I
blamed you for anything. I know Seth was at his end. I
just... The guy was a friend. A good one. He acted all
tough, but inside he was alone, like me. He never had
real family, you know. He made that up so I wouldn't
feel sorry for him." He snorted. "Old bastard was just
like me. I used to pretend a lot. That I was happy

being alone all the time, dating and skating. That I had no problem adjusting to being part of the clan. Sometimes it was overwhelming."

His fingers eased up her neck and he started massaging her scalp. Besides soothing her, he was arousing her just by being near. When he shifted, she caught a faint whiff of cologne that went straight to her head. God, could she possibly be dreaming this? Brody not only apologizing, but explaining himself to her?

"I didn't go into too much detail with you before, but my older brother did a real number on me. He hurt me bad growing up. A lot of it was screwing with my head as much as pounding on me. I didn't want anyone to know. I was ashamed, like it was my fault. I know." He squeezed her shoulder in warning, and she stopped her automatic denial. "Stupid to think that, but I was a kid at the time. And as I grew older, the shame and fear grew with me. But Flynn knew anyway, he just never said anything. Asshole."

He rubbed her head again. Small circles that pressed into the base of her skull and relieved pressure she hadn't been aware she was holding. "Oh my God. I'm totally listening to you, but this massage is just... I'm a limp noodle."

"Good. You had a lot going on. You had to handle my drama, then your mom's visit. I heard that went well though, huh?"

She smiled and closed her eyes. "Yeah. She came to apologize and tell me how sorry she was. You two have a lot in common."

He paused on her shoulders. Then he circled around to her front and sat next to her on the couch again.

"You're right. She and I both love her daughter," he said softly.

She blinked at him. "What's that?" No. He hadn't really just said he loved her, had he?

"Scoot back and put your feet in my lap."

She stared.

"Offer expires in three-two-one—"

She nearly gelded him.

"*Oomph.*"

"Well, you started the countdown."

"So I did." He chuckled, pulled off her socks, and started rubbing her feet with large, warm hands. "I also hear you're going to be filthy rich since your books are being fought over in a bidding war. Congrats, baby."

She flushed. "Well, filthy rich is a relative term. For a writer, it's like moving a step beyond welfare. But I'm happy to say my agent expects good numbers, enough to keep me in rent and food money through next year."

"Merry Christmas to you."

"Yeah." She smiled, extraordinarily happy just to be with him. But… "Did you say you loved me?"

"No."

Her hopes dashed.

"I said *love*. As in, present tense. You writers need to pay attention to that shit."

"Nice mouth." Her pulse pounded. "All this decoration, the hot cocoa, the massage. Flynn and Maddie aren't coming home, are they?"

"Nope." He grinned, and the wicked look he shot her had her taking a sharp breath. "They're in Snoqualmie for the weekend. Vanessa's with friends. It's just you and me." He paused. "Well, you and me and Mutt."

"Oh?"

"I'll get to that in a bit. You just relax and enjoy this foot rub."

She was touched he had gone to so much trouble for her. But she didn't trust his turnaround. "Brody, you don't have to tell me what you think I want to hear. I want you to be happy. And I'll miss you, but you need to be—"

"I saw Jeremy the other day. Went for a walk with him and talked."

"You did?"

"Yeah. He's changed a lot. He's not a bad guy. I mean, he was a dickhead for doing what he did to me. But a lot of it was drugs and Alan." He continued to rub her feet but maintained eye contact. "I told him I'd never forget what he did."

Her heart sank.

"But I forgave him. And I felt lighter for it."

She smiled. "I'm proud of you." When he flushed, she fell deeper in love with him.

"Thanks. But you're the one I'm proud of. You didn't take my bullshit excuses. You kept going even when your family dissed you. And you live with Vanessa, which is some scary, scary shit to deal with on a daily basis. I think she might have made Cam cry the other week."

She laughed. "Brody, stop. No, not the foot rub. I mean, you're kidding me."

"Maybe. With Cam, who knows?" He put one foot back and attended to her other one. "So tell me. Are you busy today? What were you planning?"

"I was thinking about a nap and hot chocolate, but

this foot rub is so much better. And the hot chocolate was superb."

"You didn't finish it all." He nudged her cup. "Drink up."

"Why? Is it drugged?"

"For God's sake."

She crossed her eyes at him and drank the cocoa as he moved from the couch and neared the tree.

She glanced at it in appreciation. "The tree is gorgeous."

"It should be. Maddie oversaw the decorations while General Vanessa ordered Flynn, me, and Cam around like monkeys."

"You did all this for me?" She still couldn't believe it.

"Well, mostly. I think Maddie did a lot of it for herself as well, because she made sure only the prettiest, classiest decorations were used. We took the good stuff, like the big blinky lights, to Mike's. Colin's in heaven."

She grinned, so happy she wanted to burst. But she couldn't let him off the hook that easily. "This is so nice. Really special. But—"

"Hold that thought." He dug behind the tree and pulled out Maddie's earrings. "This is for you."

She snorted. "That's really sweet of you, but I don't think Flynn's going to appreciate you giving me Maddie's gift."

"Just open it, smart ass."

"But we haven't talked about you ditching me. Again."

"I'm getting to that. Stop being difficult, woman. Open the damn box," he growled.

She rolled her eyes. "Fine." Smiling at his anxious

face, she unwrapped the package, lifted the lid, and stared down at the glittery diamond studs she'd coveted for some time.

"Put them on."

She bit her lip and looked into his eyes. "But…"

"Abby, please."

Not sure she liked this game anymore, she put the earrings on and felt like a million dollars.

Brody whistled. "They sure do sparkle, don't they?"

"I want to see them."

"First, read the card."

Her heart racing, she reached into the box and pulled out the card, one she hadn't seen when she'd picked up the already wrapped package.

"Read it out loud," he murmured and moved next to her on the couch.

"Dear Abby." Her eyes widened. "I'm sure you could write this much better than me. But I wanted you to have this apology along with the earbobs. (Your word, not mine.) I love you, Abby. I have for a while, but I was too scared to tell you. I still think you're too good for me, but I'm nothing without you. I miss you so damn much, and the thought of not having you in my life makes everything dry as dust. So gray. So blah without you. I see these diamonds, all the color and sparkle, and I think of you. Because you bring this to my life. I may be a cheat, a liar, and a bunch of other things I'm never going to tell you about, but I'll always be true to you. I love you. And I really, really want you to come live with me. If you play your cards right, you could be the lucky Mrs. Brody Singer. Unless, of course, you strike it rich. Then I'm okay to take your last name. Brody Dunn has a nice ring to it too. Love, Brody."

She stared at the note, unable to believe what she'd just read.

"You okay? You look pale."

She glanced at him to see him looking worried.

"What? Was it my grammar? I had Cam help with the wording a little, but he's better with numbers, you want my opinion."

"Do you mean this?" she whispered and clutched the note to her heart, the box forgotten.

He pulled her into his arms and smiled. "Every word. Especially the part about you striking it rich. I want it known I'm marrying you for your money and your body, but not in that order."

He kissed her before she could blink, and she settled into his arms with a long, satisfied sigh.

He broke away, breathing hard, and cleared his throat. "There's just one or two more things we need to clarify."

"Yeah?"

"I come with baggage. It's me and the dog. You take me, you take Mutt. Which leads me to my last gift. It's upstairs."

She followed him up, holding his hand, and saw a trail of rose petals at the top of the stairway.

"Oh Brody." He remembered. All her talk of what she wanted in a romantic gesture. A massage, making her cocoa, the rose petals. She had to blink back tears.

She walked along the trail into her bedroom, where Mutt sat with a bright red bow around his neck. He'd been scrubbed and groomed and looked like a brand-new dog. Almost. He had a sock hanging out of his mouth, which the candles all over the place draped in romantic doggie shadow.

"Damn. Sorry. Thought I'd scrubbed the room for potential disaster. Mutt, drop." The dog spat out the sock but didn't look the slightest bit sorry. His tail thumped so hard on the floor she feared he'd damage himself. "Okay, Abby. It's time. Give him his name."

She smiled at the dog and the man. "Don't you want to know if I'll say yes to everything?"

"I'm not asking. That way you can't say no."

She heard the teasing, as well as the anxiety he tried to hide.

"Hmm. How about if I don't say anything? I'll name the dog, keep him and you, and after our long engagement, to make sure you know what you're getting into, then I'll say yes. On our honeymoon."

He scratched his chin. "That's not how I'd planned this. But you throw in a few orgasms and it's a done deal."

She laughed and threw herself at him. He caught her and twirled her around, and Mutt danced beside them.

"God, Abby. Don't do that to me. You can't say no. I need you like crazy. I'm out of cookies."

"Big baby." She kissed him, but before she got lost in the kiss, she pulled away. "I have his name. I've had it for a while, actually. It suits his personality."

"Terrific. But you'll have to tell me after. Now for the last part of the evening."

She arched a brow in question.

"Go into your bathroom across the hall. There's something waiting for you. Put it on."

She left him and the dog behind, both watching her

with love in their eyes, and found a sheer rose-colored nightie on a hanger over the shower bar. It had spaghetti straps and a plunging neckline. And to her delight, it fit her like a glove. Had to be Maddie's doing.

She undressed and put the nightie on, which barely covered her ass when she moved. In the mirror, she saw her bright eyes, her shiny diamond earrings, and her entire body exposed by the see-through lingerie.

Walking quickly back to the room, she entered to find Brody wearing a thick robe. Mutt was nowhere in sight.

"He's in Vanessa's room. Don't worry, it's okay. I cleared it with Her Highness before today."

"That must have taken some serious bargaining."

"Well, I owe her my firstborn. And there was something about spinning bales of straw into gold later on. But I'll handle that when we get to it."

Abby laughed, so in love she never wanted the feeling to end. "I love you, Brody. With all my heart."

"Me too, Abby. I love you." He came closer and nuzzled her cheek. "I don't know if you noticed, but I'm doing my damndest not to stare at your perfect breasts and pussy in that all-but-invisible gown. I'm trying to be romantic, but I can't help wanting to fuck you until we both pass out."

He drew her hand to the robe and parted it to expose his thick, heavy erection. When she grabbed him, he groaned. "Get on the bed and lie back. It's my turn to play."

Brody hadn't known he could feel like this, so high he wanted to fly. She loved him. She fucking *loved* him. He hadn't blown it after all. He owed Vanessa and Maddie big time. Their help in showing him what Abby liked made all the difference. She'd bought into the whole romantic setup. But more fool he, so had Brody.

"You look exactly the way you did on Halloween at the party." He sighed and disrobed, loving her heavy-lidded gaze as it wandered over his body and centered on his cock. "Like a goddess."

"Your goddess."

"All mine." He covered her, no longer able to wait for a kiss. He met her mouth, exchanged a breath, and found heaven in her embrace. The kiss started out sweet, tender, a promise made and kept. Moving in, marriage, everything. And she hadn't said no.

"God, Brody. I want you so much. Feel." She dragged his hand between her legs, and he loved her assertiveness. Especially when his fingers slid through warm, wet cream.

"I need a taste."

"So do I."

He swiftly turned around, not ready to concede his position on top. He lowered his face and pulled up her dress, in love with the design. Then he kissed her clit, sucking the taut bud and reveling in her gasp and moan as she put her mouth around him.

She sucked and licked his slit, and he fought against embarrassing himself by coming so soon. But Christ, he'd been without her for too long. He gave her less attention than he wanted, but he neared his end too quickly.

Brody pulled away from her and hurried to mount her. "Missionary just this once. Then we get really kinky."

"Anything for you," she breathed, then cried his name when he speared her with one smooth, firm thrust.

She felt tighter to him, and he felt harder than he'd ever been in his life. Their coupling was rough, demanding, and thorough. And over too quickly. He came just as she seized around him. Their bodies milked each other of pleasure, setting the room ablaze with satisfying belonging.

"Oh my God." She panted under him, dwarfed by his size and utterly perfect. "I think you killed me."

"Now, Abby. You know that's only round one." He grinned and nodded to the night stand. "Silk ropes and a blindfold. I figure we'll save the nipple clamps for when we're feeling not so romantic and more lusty."

"Great. I can't wait to see you wearing them," she deadpanned, and they both laughed.

She toyed with his hair and after a moment, when he made no attempt to move or withdraw, she said, "I meant it about being engaged. I love you, Brody. I don't want anyone else but you. Not even Rick."

He took a moment to process, and then he growled, "Words like that can get you punished, dear fiancée." He nipped her lower lip. "God, I love you."

She smiled, beautiful and funny and true.

"How about this deal," he suggested. "You pick out the ring, then I give it to you on a day I choose. Not Christmas, because everyone but Maddie knows Flynn's going to propose."

"Um, she knows too. But don't tell. He really wants it to be a surprise."

Brody chuckled. "Women."

"You have a deal. But only if you agree to a little

more research. I'm particularly interested in how men worship breasts, and how the blindfold comes into play."

"Great questions. And do I have some even better answers…"

Epilogue

CAM THOUGHT THE ENGAGEMENT WENT OFF WITHOUT a hitch. Maddie gushed over the rock Flynn had bought her, and everyone *oohed* and *aahed* over Abby's earrings. That and the fact that Brody was smiling again and refusing to stop hugging, kissing, and holding her.

Apparently Mutt had finally found a name. Abby introduced him as "Hyde," of *Dr. Jekyll and Mr. Hyde*. Because while he'd finally turned into somewhat of a gentleman—her words—the dog continued to eat socks, dishtowels, and anything white. Freaky dog, but everyone seemed to love him. Even Cam approved. Oddly enough, the dog responded to his new name as if it had been his from day one. Weird to think Brody owned an intelligent dog.

Maddie laughed and patted Hyde, acting as if she'd always loved the mutt. Cam stared at the new couples around him with pleasure. He couldn't have imagined a better woman for Flynn. And Abby seemed to have been tailor-made for the blond McCauley. She'd even managed to pull Brody out of his funk. Would wonders never cease?

Colin zipped around wearing his brand-new Spider-Man pajamas and shrieked at Vanessa, who chased him with his brand-new monster dolls. Mike called them action figures, but come on. The things had hair you could braid as well as toy guns, alien pets, and spaceships. Like alien Barbie on crack.

The sexy blond bane of his existence stopped in front of him and raised a perfectly arched brow. "Cameron."

God, he loved it when she called him that. Vanessa never shortened his name the way everyone else did. He liked to think of it as a pet name she only reserved for him.

"Vanessa."

She nodded. "Merry Christmas."

"I do believe we exchanged our perfunctory greeting when you got here." An hour ago. She'd been dodging him ever since.

"Yes, well. Since I have nothing *else* to say to you, Merry Christmas seems to work well enough."

Stubborn little—*big*—witch. She sure knew how to wear her clothing to accent that hot Amazon figure though. Almost as tall as he was, she wore stylish brown boots, camel wool trousers, and a blue sweater that hugged her lean lines and brought out the burning sapphires in her eyes.

"So you're going to hold the fact that I was sticking up for my brother against me," he stated as fact when she gave him that look, the one that said she was fast losing patience with him.

Expecting her to forgive him for what he shouldn't even need forgiveness for, he nodded even as she said, "Yes."

"Wait. What?"

"I said yes. You clearly took the wrong side."

"You have to be kidding me."

"Cameron, just admit you were wrong and all is forgiven."

He scowled. "Sticking up for Brody wasn't wrong.

Abby shouldn't have…" He trailed off as he saw his mother and father walk together down the hall toward Mike's bedroom.

He and Vanessa glanced at each other, then at Mike who stood laughing with Colin and Hyde in the living room, surrounded by the rest of the family.

Together, Cam and Vanessa tiptoed down the hall and lingered by the crack in the door of Mike's bedroom, where they overheard his mother say, "…so we'll tell them after the new year. Not now, James."

"Fine." His father cleared his throat. "I think this is for the best."

"I'm sure you do," she answered in a waspish tone. So unlike his normally pleasant, joyful mother. "We have nothing more to say then. At least pretend you're enjoying the party. For Colin's sake."

"Hell, woman. I'm not an ogre."

They heard movement near the door and panicked. Vanessa pulled him into Colin's room, across from Mike's, and closed the door enough to hide behind it without it clicking shut.

"Did you hear something?" his mother asked, and they heard her step closer.

Vanessa's eyes widened.

They were about to get caught. So Cameron did what any self-respecting McCauley would do. He kissed the beautiful woman in his arms.

When the door opened, Cam was only partially aware of his father's chuckle before the door shut behind him, because the rest of him was focused on the cool blond in his arms, who lit up like an inferno when he touched her.

Cam groaned and pulled her closer, deepening the

angle of his kiss to better devour her. She tasted so incredibly sweet. Like cinnamon and spice. But Vanessa
was anything but nice. And that added edge only height-
ened her appeal.

When his hands neared her ass to tug her closer to
that insistent part of him, she pulled away and tried to
catch her breath.

"Cameron?"

She touched her lips and stared.

As did he. His gaze found the hard nipples straining under her sweater, saw the flush on her cheeks and
the ripe lips parted for him. Practically begging him for
another kiss.

"Wh-what do you think they meant?" she whispered.

"Hmm?" He took a step forward until she stopped
him with a hand to his chest.

"They… You really work out, don't you?" She spread
her fingers across his pectorals, and he wondered if she
could feel his heart racing.

"Yeah." He tried to will away his erection. Focusing
on Ubie, Colin's stuffed bear—so named after the
scoundrel who'd given it to him—seemed to do the
trick. "They said they'd tell us after New Year's. But
I'm betting whatever it is can't be good."

"I know." She swallowed hard. "So, um…"

"I know. You're sorry, and you want another kiss."
Time to get the upper hand on the woman before she
took him under again with that slick, heavenly mouth,
mean temperament, and amazing body. "Sorry, honey.
I know it's Christmas, but until you apologize for being
so wrong about my boy Brody, this body"—he pointed
to himself—"is off limits."

She opened her mouth to retort when Colin burst in the room, Mike on his heels. Mike took a good look at them and tried not to smile.

"Hey, there's my Gooberon," Colin said with a smile and grabbed his alien from the floor. "Thanks for finding him, Vanessa."

"That's Major Campbell to you, recruit," Cameron corrected.

"Try General, you lowly alien scum," she said to Cam. *Figures she'd make herself the highest ranking officer around.*

"Agent Colin," she continued. "We've found a traitor. Take the lackey behind you—"

"Hey," Mike grumbled.

"—and rid our world of this ugly beast." She pointed at Cameron.

"Ugly? I think not. I—*oomph*."

Mike tackled him to the floor. Then Colin jumped on him and started tickling him, which Cam absolutely hated, because he couldn't stop laughing. He cried out for help, but no one but Vanessa was nearby. She watched his helpless agony as his bastard bulldozer of a brother pummeled him unceasingly. Colin's war cries didn't help his dignity either.

"Oh fine. Hold on." Vanessa yelled for backup, and Brody and Flynn entered with Maddie and Abby following. Hyde barked incessantly behind them. "Help the young one! Those two are trying to kill the young earthling!"

Colin, quick on the take, cried for help. Then Brody and Flynn jumped on them and elbows started flying once they'd rescued the boy. But while they played,

Cam noted that neither his mother nor father joined in the fun.

He wondered what to make of that. Then Vanessa gave him her trademark sneer, and he ignored a potential family disaster in favor of getting even. And trying to figure out how to get the woman to be less right about everything and more interested in being wrong about him. Because he had to figure out a way to get another kiss. And maybe a hug. Followed by a date…or three…

Enjoy a sneak peek at book 3 in
the McCauley Brothers series,

Ruining Mr. Perfect

"Hello?" Cam knocked as he opened the door. "Yo,
Mike, you here?" He entered the house and closed the
door behind him. A study in brown, his brother's living
room might not be stylish, but it provided comfort and
the perfect place to indulge in family Friday night poker.

But on this particular Friday afternoon, the house
seemed dead.

A door opened and slammed shut, and a whirlwind
of energy burst through the kitchen into the living room
and stopped.

Cam noticed two things. Colin McCauley looked as
if he'd been playing with Mike's grease gun again, and
he heard the shower running.

"Hey, dude."

Colin didn't smile, didn't blink, and gave him the
snake eye.

Cam sighed. For a six-year-old, his nephew could
hold a mean grudge. "Still mad I told your dad about
your prank on Abby?"

Used to be the place was full of nothing but men.
Mike's wife had died giving birth to Colin, and none
of the McCauleys seemed to be able to hold on to a
woman like their dad had. Then again, Beth McCauley
was special.

Now they had a houseful of hot women living next

door. Flynn and Brody had already claimed two of them, leaving the best for Cam. That's if he could get the stubborn woman to stop arguing long enough to ask her out.

Colin continued to glare at him. The spitting image of Mike with those bright blue eyes and short black hair. They even shared the same dimple.

"Colin," Cam tried again. "You know dumping water on someone in the shower is a no-no. And especially Ubie's new girlfriend." Ubie—short for Uncle Brody. Brody Singer, the blond "adopted" McCauley who had grown up as part of the family.

"But he told me to do it."

Cam blinked. "He did? Well, you should never—"

"Dad thought it was kind of funny after he yelled at me." Colin gave him a sharp nod, then added with a smirk, "Dad said he used to do that to you, and that you cried like a *girrrl*." Considering Colin's anti-girl phase, that was a high insult.

"Is that right?" Cam frowned, remembering being the butt of too many jokes while growing up. "Mike has no idea what he's dealing with. You think your dad's tough? Watch Uncle Cam." Knowing he shouldn't encourage the mischief in his nephew's eyes but unable to stop himself from the unspoken dare, Cam hurried to the kitchen, found a large glass, and filled it with ice-cold water. Considering the freezing January wind outside, Mike would be basking in a hot shower to warm up. Cam grinned, looking forward to his brother's howl of misery.

Colin trailed him like a puppy. "Oh wow, Uncle Cam. Are you going to get Dad?" He clapped.

"Shh."

"Oh, sorry." Colin's big grin showed a missing front tooth.

Cam walked down more ugly brown carpet that looked as if it had been vacuumed to death—Mike and his obsession with cleanliness—and tiptoed into the big guy's room. He made sure he had a clear exit. If his goliath big brother caught him, he'd be toast. Fortunately, he could move like a gazelle.

Gliding into the master bathroom, he readied himself. One, two...*three*. He yanked open the curtain and tossed the cold water at...*Vanessa Campbell*?

He stared in shock at the sexiest woman he'd seen in a long, long time. Naked, her creamy skin glistened with water as she gaped at him in horror. Which quickly turned to anger.

"*Cameron McCauley!*"

"Oh, wow." He couldn't look away. Even as manners dictated he close the shower curtain and give her privacy, he couldn't stop staring at her slender belly, legs toned from years of running, and those beautiful breasts tipped with rosy pink nipples. God, he'd imagined what she might look like, but reality far surpassed his fantasies.

She yelled a string of obscenities as she whipped the curtain closed.

While Cam tried to catch his breath, he heard muffled laughter behind him and turned to see Colin with his hand over his mouth. His nephew's eyes widened and he took off.

Cam caught him easily, though the kid had made it to the kitchen before being snagged. As he took Colin by the collar, Mike strolled into the kitchen from the attached garage.

"Colin, I said get me the paper towels five minutes ago." Mike glowered at Cam holding his son. "What's up, little brother?"

Gritting his teeth, because he hated always being reminded that he was the baby of the family, Cam shook Colin like a rag doll.

Colin, of course, laughed and asked him to do it again.

"Your son played a nasty prank."

"Yeah?" Mike's lips quirked. "What did he do?"

"He convinced me to throw cold water at you. In the shower."

Mike frowned. "But I'm… Shi—oot." Mike looked from Colin to Cam and tried to hide a grin. "So, um, how is Vanessa?"

"Why is she in your shower?" He'd called dibs. Secretly, but still.

"Wouldn't you like to know." Mike's wide grin wasn't helping. "So you froze her thinking it was me, eh? Poor, poor Cam. You never learn. I am the master of the prank."

"And me," Colin added proudly. "Shake me again, Uncle Cam. It's fun."

"Gah." Cam dropped Colin, tickled him soundly, then gave him a light swat on the behind. "You owe Vanessa an apology."

"Oh?" Mike crossed his mammoth arms over his chest. "Seems to me you're the one who threw cold water on my unsuspecting neighbor. Or are you trying to tell me that my six-year-old forced you to mess with her?"

Cam glared. "You're just encouraging him."

"Now, now. Take responsibility for your actions. Act like the twenty-seven-year old you should be."

"I'm twenty-nine, moron. Just because you're older doesn't mean you can boss me around like you *tried to* when we were kids."

Mike just raised a brow. Then Colin did it. The similarity made it hard not to laugh.

"For God's sake. Fine. I'll apologize." He turned.

"Might want to wait until she's dressed. Then again, if what I saw at Christmas is true, maybe not." Mike chuckled at the look Cam shot him and yanked his son with him back into the garage.

"What, Dad? What did you see?" Colin pestered as Mike shut the door.

There hadn't been that much *to* see. After Cam and Vanessa had eavesdropped on Cam's parents, they'd hidden in Colin's room, so as not to be discovered. Then, well, then Cam had kissed her. To keep their cover when his parents found them. Yet honesty compelled him to admit he'd been dying to kiss her for months. Ever since Vanessa had moved next to Mike nearly a year ago, he'd been fascinated by her.

Drawn to her beauty, her brains, and that waspish tongue. But holy hell, when she'd used that tongue during their kiss, she'd hooked him but good.

He waited in the living room, wondering how to take the next step with her. She was going to be livid after getting spied on in the shower. And on a normal day, Vanessa wasn't a typical woman to be wooed with charm and wit. She saw through games. A lot like him. Unfortunately, he had a feeling the truth would freak her the hell out.

I think we'd be good together. Let's date, see where it takes us. Then we'll get married, have kids, double the size of our mutual portfolio...

Fifteen minutes later, Vanessa stalked down the hallway holding her bag. Her blue eyes were lighter than his, bright and full of a cold anger.

How screwed up was he that her rages turned him on? She was so different from other women he'd dated. She didn't try to cozen up to him or flatter him with true but tired compliments.

"So, Cameron. What do you have to say for yourself?"

Acknowledgments

To Matt Emery, of Emery Plumbing, your knowledge was invaluable. Thank you *so much* for your help and patience.

To my beta readers—Charity, Kim, Eniko, Angi, and April—your feedback helped shape this book into what it is. You guys are awesome!

And I have to thank Cat C., my editor, for making this book shine.

About the Author

Caffeine addict, boy referee, and romance aficionado, *USA Today* bestselling author Marie Harte is a confessed bibliophile and devotee of action movies. Whether hiking in Central Oregon, biking around town, or hanging at the local tea shop, she's constantly plotting to give everyone a happily ever after. Visit marieharte.com and fall in love.

Ruining Mr. Perfect

The McCauley Brothers
by Marie Harte

USA Today Bestselling Author

It's tough always being right

Vanessa Campbell is a CPA by day and a perfectionist by night. She's fit, smart, healthy…and decidedly lonely. She can't stop thinking about the youngest McCauley brother, Cameron. He's just like her: smart, beautiful, and usually right—except when dealing with her.

…But someone's got to do it

Cameron McCauley likes the look of Vanessa a little too well. She's a blond goddess and she knows it. She hates to be wrong, just like him. They tend to rub each other the wrong way, which is unfortunate considering how well they could fit. He's dying to shake Vanessa up—get her to let loose. But if he succeeds, can his heart handle it?

Praise for Marie Harte:

"Off the charts scorching hot. Ms. Harte wows with sex scenes that will make your heart pump." —*Long and Short Reviews*

For more Marie Harte, visit:

www.sourcebooks.com

What to Do with a Bad Boy

The McCauley Brothers
by Marie Harte

USA Today Bestselling Author

She can fix anything...

It's great that all his brothers are finding love, but Mike has been there, done that. He had his soul mate for a precious time before she died giving birth to their son. She left him with the best boy a guy could want, so why is everyone playing matchmaker? He's sick of it...until he meets Delilah Webster. For some reason, the foul-mouthed, tattooed mechanic sets his motor running.

But can she fix his heart?

When Del first met Colin, Mike's young son, she fell in love with the little scam artist. But his father's like an overprotective pit bull. Too bad they rub each other the wrong way, because Mike is seriously sexy. But when a simple kiss turns hot and heavy, she can't get him out of her head.

Mike can't forget that kiss either. He sees the loving woman buried under the rough exterior. But the closer they get, the more the pain of past wounds throws a monkey wrench into a future he's not sure he can handle...

Praise for Marie Harte:

"Charismatic characters and sexual tension that is hot enough to scorch your fingers." —*Romance Junkies*

For more Marie Harte, visit:
www.sourcebooks.com

The Day He Kissed Her

by Juliana Stone

Coming home is the only way to heal his heart.

Mac Draper thought he had everything he ever wanted when hired by a hotshot Manhattan architectural firm. But he still needed one last visit back home to Crystal Lake to face the demons of his past. For Lily St. Clare, the charming small town she just moved to was a haven. Big cities only wanted to eat you up and spit you out.

Neither was expecting to stay very long…until the day they found each other, and one amazingly red-hot night followed. But old wounds almost always leave a mark, and Mac's scars run deeper than most. With her flirty charm, Lily could be exactly what he needs—if he's willing to give love one more chance.

Praise for Juliana Stone:

"Stone wastes no time establishing her ability to tell an enthralling story." —*RT Book Reviews*

For more Juliana Stone, visit:

www.sourcebooks.com

Find My Way Home

Harmony Homecomings
by Michele Summers

—⌇—

She's just the kind of drama

Interior designer Bertie Anderson has big dreams for her career, and they don't include being stuck in her hometown of Harmony, North Carolina. After one last client, Bertie is packing up her high heels and heading for her dream job in Atlanta. But her plans are derailed by the gorgeous new owner of that big old Victorian she's always wanted to renovate…

He's vowed to avoid

For retired tennis pro Keith Morgan, Harmony is a far cry from fast-paced Miami—which is exactly the point. Keith is starting a new life for himself and his daughter Maddie, and he's left the bright lights and hot women far behind. Bertie's exactly the kind of curvaceous temptation he doesn't need, and Keith refuses to let their sizzling attraction distract him from his goals. Keith and Bertie both have to learn that there's more than one kind of escape, and it takes more than wallpaper to turn a house into a home.

—⌇—

For more Michele Summers, visit:

www.sourcebooks.com

CHECK OUT MORE CONTEMPORARY ROMANCE FROM SOURCEBOOKS CASABLANCA

he can't get her out of his head

It's lust at first sight when Brody Singer first lays eyes on Abby Dunn. The dark-haired beauty looks a lot like a woman he once knew. At first, Brody fears his attraction is a holdover from that secret crush, but Abby's definitely different. She's a lot shyer, a lot sexier, and despite her attempts to dissuade his interest, absolutely mesmerizing.

she can't get him out of her books

Abby isn't having it. She's still trying to put her last disastrous relationship behind her and overcome the flaws her ex wouldn't let her forget. But somehow Brody isn't getting the hint. It doesn't help that when writing her steamy novels, she keeps casting Brody as the hero.

Brody is more than happy to serve as her muse and eager to help make sure her "research" is authentic. But when their research turns into something real... will she choose her own happily ever after?

MEET THE MCCAULEY BROTHERS